THE BLACK CURSE

Satirical Novel

LIONEL MARTIN

Zeta Publishing, Inc
P.O. Box 953
Silver Springs, FL 34489
www.zetapublishing.com

Ordering Information:
Quantity sales. Special discounts are available on quantity purchases by corporations, associations, and others. For details, contact the publisher at the address above.
Orders by U.S. trade bookstores and wholesalers. Please contact Zeta Publishing: Tel: (352) 694-2553; Fax: (352) 694-1791 or visit www.zetapublishing.com

Rev. Date: 10/3/2018

ISBN: 978-1-7327914-1-1 (sc)
ISBN: 978-1-7327914-2-8 (hc)
ISBN: 978-1-7327914-3-5 (e)

Library of Congress: 2018959574
Printed in the United States of America

To my physicians the best in their fields:

Dr. Mina Bhatt, Internal Medecine,
Lake Placid, Florida

Dr. Daniel Panassa, Cardiologist,
Seabring, Florida

Dr. Alessandro Golino, Thoracic & Cardiac Surgeon,
Brandeton, Florida

Dr. Sidney Peykar, Cardiologist,
Port Charlotte, Florida

Cover Design by: Anthony Ortiz

To My lovely Wife: Ginette Rameau Martin

To My Son: Joseph Lionel Martin whom make this project possible

A special thanks to Mrs. Mary Thompson whom edited the manuscript.

CHAPTER I

There was a carnival atmosphere on the city square of Montjolly, when Dr. Carl Sommers, after a long trip in his old, yellow, convertible Cadillac, arrived on the vast esplanade in front of the parish church. Montjolly celebrated the opening of the brand new hospital the city had built with the generous assistance of the new elected Governor of Mississippi.

Dr. Sommers, graduated for some time, was finally hired as a surgeon at the Saint Cécile Hospital in Montjolly. Despite himself, he followed the noisy and picturesque parade that blithely ascended a flowered hill leading to the ultra-modern building, glass and steel, three stories high. The building shone in the sun like a jewel set in lush greenery.

The city band played a catchy tune. Majorettes dressed in gleaming parade uniforms, danced, twisting and turning in synchronized spins that earned the frantic applause of the delirious crowd. The mayor, flanked by his eager assessors and the personal representative of the Governor Pete Rogers, the sheriff and the director of the hospital, walked, proud as Artaban, at the head of the procession. Students from different schools in the city, dressed for the occasion, were in disarray, ignoring the useless efforts of teachers who were trying to restore the order broken by the contagious euphoria of the excited crowd.

Cars honked intermittently and produced a deafening uproar that scared the old, pretty ladies dressed in the latest fashionable outfit. They watched the parade, riveted, by their windows or they sat in their rustic balconies decorated with plants and flowers.

Dr. Sommers was the last person to enter the courtyard of the hospital. He parked his car behind the building. He put on his jacket to join the crowd who was listening to the pompous speech given by Mayor Simon Morgan, when a police officer approached him.

"Stay where you are!"

"I have an appointment with the director," responded Sommers. "Get back in the car and wait until I come back for you."

"What's wrong?" insisted Sommers, who didn't understand the police officer's nasty attitude.

"It's an order," the retorted the officer sharply, "I don't owe you any explanation."

Dr. Carl Sommers returned to his car and sat down, not willing to confront the inexplicably hostile behavior of the officer. He was miles away from assuming that he wasn't welcome in this beautiful little town, whose bucolic charms and flowering beauty, he fell in love with at the first sight.

After a few moments of wondering, he was perplexed. Why was he being singled out? He shrugged and put a CD into the CD player. The haunting music of Max Bruch's Scottish Fantasy invaded the car. He closed his eyes. He saw or heard nothing around him. The enchanted melody plunged him into a delicious torpor. He was swimming in the troubling euphoria of his dreamlike meditations.

Time suddenly darkened. There was a blinding flash of light across the sky. The crowd amassed in front of the hospital to listen to the speeches dispersed in the blink of an eye. Rain fell for more than two hours straight.

Dr. Sommers waited, engine running, to be picked up for his appointment with Dr. Joe Merville, the Hospital Director. He intended to submit his letter of nomination, signed by Governor Pete Rogers himself.

Dr. Sommers wondered again puzzled, why had the policeman prevented him from joining the crowd?

A worrying silence had replaced the happy animation of the celebration. There were almost no cars in the parking lot. The rain had significantly shortened the opening ceremony.

At around seven o'clock in the evening, after a long and boring wait, a chubby, paunchy policeman sporting a scowl came to greet Dr. Sommers. "Follow me," said the laconic policeman.

Dr. Sommers picked up the briefcase that was lying on the floor of the Cadillac, locked the doors of the vehicle and moved into step beside the big policeman, who headed for the back of the building.

They took the service lift a glass cage, flooded with a raw

And blinding light that darted like a rocket and stopped almost immediately on the second floor. They walked through a long corridor of rectangular, white flagstone mosaics. The corridor led to an unoccupied wing of the building. To avoid any distractions, the director had chosen this place to receive this unwanted visitor discreetly.

The room where the man introduced Dr. Sommers was very spacious. It was partially furnished. There were a few upholstered chairs and a small round table with some magazines piled on it. The officer knocked on a huge door, encrusted with gilded bronze roses. He opened it without waiting for a response and announced in a husky and unpleasant voice, "Dr. Merville, the individual in question is in the waiting room. Should I introduce him?"

"Of course, Luke," he replied in an irritated and upset voice. The named Luke motioned to Dr. Sommers a little taken aback by this unusual trip and all of the mystery surrounding this simple business appointment.

Dr. Merville sat on a wide leather high back chair and did not appear to have noticed the presence of his visitor. He seemed to be reading a document spread out on his desk.

Obviously, Dr. Merville, wanting to avoid the rage of the hospital staff and hostile curiosity of the people, could not receive Sommers in his own office. He thought of how to get rid of the bulky intruder, before his presence was known and became the subject of scandal in this quiet community.

"Excuse me for making you wait", said Merville, "but you arrived unexpectedly in the middle of a popular celebration. I was very busy all day. I wasn't able to get away earlier. I also had to meet with the management committee to make it aware of your presence at Montjolly. I submitted the content of the proposals that I am going to offer you to the committee. I got its approval and carte blanche to negotiate with you."

Sommers kept an obstinate silence. He expected that his interlocutor would tell him the real reasons for this abusive reception. In addition, the superior and condescending attitude displayed by this arrogant doctor irritated him somewhat. Having no seat to sit in, he remained standing. He had his briefcase under his arm and a scowl on his face. His mind was dreary and his pupils were enlarged in the diffuse, sad, half lighted room. His eyes may have indicated his fear, but his phlegmatic composure betrayed anyway his concern and his legitimate apprehensions for the outcome of his interview.

"Dr. Sommers," continued Merville a bit embarrassed, "I regret to inform you that Saint Cecile Hospital will not be able to honor your contract. Circumstances beyond our control require us to renegotiate its terms. However, in the interest of fairness, we will offer you a substantial compensation package to alleviate your disappointment and for your troubles."

"Why do you want to cancel my contract?" asked Dr. Sommers coldly.

"We offered you a job, but this position is no longer available. What do you want us to do?" stated Dr. Merville, his voice laced with thinly veiled irritation.

"I don't understand you, not at all Dr. Merville! You look like a smart man! So, think again. Is it possible to discuss the amount of my compensation without previously having been fired? Do have doubts about my qualifications? Am I a terrorist? A renegade to the homeland? A dangerous murderer? A pariah? Rest assured, Sir, that I will not let you destroy my reputation and ruin my career without knowing the charges against me, unless I can defend myself. I am not going to passively accept your absurd proposals. Far from it, Sir! Don't expect to see me resign or be fired."

"Oh no," said Dr. Merville, a bit embarrassed, "we do not question your skills, or your impeccable reputation, but here … we cannot accept a black doctor in the hospital."

"What! Did I hear you correctly? Of course! You deny me the job because I am a nigger? In what era are we living here? Are we back to the blessed time of segregation? Why did you hired me to begin with?

"Rightly, we didn't!"

"Who or what could possibly prevent you from employing a person of color in this establishment open to the public, white and black?"

"There is no black in the city, Mr. Sommers."

"There is no black in the city? Are you serious? How is that possible?"

"It's a long story," replied doctor Merville hesitantly.

"Okay, but you must have the courtesy to offer me a seat. I'm very curious to know the habits and customs of this charming and welcoming town," said Dr. Sommers with a bitter irony in his voice, imperceptibly shaky and irritated.

"Luke," said Merville, speaking to the police officer leaning against the front door, who was loosely following the conversation between the two men, "bring a chair for Dr. Sommers."

Luke, without answering, took a chair from the corner of the room and brought it to Dr. Sommers. He sat down as best he could and waited patiently to hear his host telling him the story of Montjolly. Sommers gaze was piercing. Dr. Merville sported an upset mind behind the large tortoiseshell glasses that housed his small grey eyes. He hid under a tuft of graying hair, folded on his balding forehead, a severe baldness. His pinched nose and thin lips gave his hairless face a serious look of patronizing importance.

"You see," began doctor Merville, after a few moments, "this community has lived for more than fifty years away from the infighting that had plagued the country during the tumultuous and bloody period where the black population was claiming its civil rights, waving the clauses of the constitutional amendments as spears and shields.

"Exasperated by the violence of the conflict, the deadly fighting that indulged the rabid protagonists of the two opposing sides, a few families in the suburbs of Jackson (the capital of the State of Mississippi) came to settle in this peaceful and welcoming region. They took refuge in this quiet area, away from the noise of the revolts and the riots. They wandered from the febrile bustle of big cities to avoid this existential crisis that would disrupt the social order they knew and plunge this frightened, distraught nation, uncertain of its future, into a deep dismay.

"The number of families which came to refuge in this haven of peace, increased rapidly. The community, with the forest's resources and a striving fishing industry, became very successful and attracted more people. All shared the same ideology, the same philosophy as the pioneers.

"The clan is sufficient to itself. We have workshops, factories, and we receive support from the major companies that share our way of life. The population supported a formal opposition to the Government, and didn't accept public aid to avoid interference by the authorities in our private affairs."

"Doctor Merville," interrupted Sommers, "it does not really interest me to know the genesis of your community. After four hours on the road and five hours waiting in the rain, I'm not in the mood to listen to these details. What I need now is the apartment I will occupy in that hospital, according to the terms of my contract, so I can relax and rest after a tiresome and hectic day."

"I'm sorry Dr. Sommers, but I can't keep you here."

"This is shocking, Sir! Please, tell me where I can find a hotel to spend the night?"

"No hotel will receive you."

"This is outrageous. You know what, Mr. Director? You are not going to get away with this. If you refuse to host me, the entire world will know the anachronistic existence of this bastion of apartheid in America by tomorrow. Well known activists will invade the place and you will no longer hear the melodious singing of birds, but the din of protesters. The press will not fail, I am sure to snoop in your sordid little secrets."

"You wouldn't dare!" exclaimed Dr. Merville, whose apoplectic looks alarmed Dr. Sommers. Merville had faltered under the threats of his interlocutor. Had he seriously thought that Sommers was ready to yield to his outright refusal and compelling arguments?

"Can I use the toilet?" asked Sommers, looking right and then left as if to emphasize the urgency of his need.

After a long moment of hesitation Dr. Merville answered, "The toilets are down the hall near the service elevator."

Dr. Sommers rushed down the hallway and entered elevator which was waiting on the second floor. As soon as he reached the first floor, he ran to his car and drove out of the courtyard of the hospital without turning on the lights.

He drove down Rose Avenue, turned right onto Lilac Street and took a forest road in the direction of Highway 49 the main artery crossing the southeast region of the Mississippi. He drove full speed for about half an hour, wanting to put some distance between himself and any possible pursuers.

Some fifty miles from the town of Montjolly, he stopped in a bustling rest area to refuel and to eat something. He was literally starving because he hadn't eaten anything since arriving in this enchanted mousetrap.

Sommers called his good friend Dr. Ricardo Ponce, to make him aware of the situation. He didn't really know what to do. Should he alert the authorities? Denounce this den of federalist racists? Try to find a modus vivendi with the Montjollians?

Ricardo recommended a lawyer and advised him, before any hasty approach to evaluate the proposals of Dr. Merville. He couldn't fathom that in the 21st century, such a place could exist in the United States.

"Be careful my old friend. I know you well, Carl!" Ricardo told him. "Don't think you can redeem these people and force them to accept your presence among them. If you can get fair compensation, fold your tent and go seek your fortune elsewhere. Don't embark on an abstruse adventure where you risk compromising your career and your good reputation."

Carl Sommers reassured him the best he could and promised not to engage in any risky adventure. He wanted simply to exploit the situation to gain a pecuniary benefit from this bizarre imbroglio. Dr. Sommers telephoned the hospital.

"Hospital Saint Cécile! May I help you?" said the eager receptionist.

"Can I speak to Dr. Merville?" "Who should I say is calling?"

"Dr. Carl Sommers!"

"Wait a moment, doctor. I don't believe he is still at the hospital ... he is not in his office."

"Try to locate him... This is very important."

A few minutes went by, during which Dr. Sommers heard the sound of precipitated steps of the receptionist on the polished slabs on the deserted corridors. It was the young lady looking for the Director, the phone in hand. "Hello! Dr. Sommers?"

"In the flesh", he answered ironically.

"Why did you leave without warning? Were you afraid of us?"

"I needed to think and consult my lawyer. I have my interests to safeguard, I don't want to be duped in this matter."

"Rightly so! We have a new proposal, much more advantageous for you. Where are you?"

"I could return to Montjolly, but only if you provide assurance for my safety and accept my requests; otherwise, I will hand over the case to my lawyer and I will call the well-known civil rights activists, Al Sharpton, Jesse Jackson, and Cynthia McKinney, who are all dedicated defenders of minorities, in fighting abuses and the injustices done to people of color with courage and determination. I don't know if I'll succeed, but I am convinced that you have much more to lose than me."

"First listen to my proposal," replied Dr. Merville with a conciliatory tone. "We are offering you fifty thousand dollars to compensate you."

"But," protested Dr. Sommers, "I already refused this proposal!"

"Wait," cried impatiently Merville, "We accept the terms of the original contract with, of course, some minor corrective changes. In addition to the fifty thousand dollars, we will pay you the full amount of your annual salary for the duration of your employment, as stipulated in the contract. In addition, you will be provided an apartment in the city, not at the hospital as agreed, for reasons of logistics and security. Your supplies will be provided by the administration on a weekly basis to be determined later."

"In return, we ask you to make your presence as discreet as possible, an invisible presence. We exonerate you from hospital duty and the obligations inherent to your job. We ask you this is very important to avoid public places: the market, cinema, bank, post office, sports and religious institutions; in a word, to keep away from inappropriate contact with the population. Please, please, do not respond to the inevitable provocation from people on the street, rooted in their convictions and taboos.

"You are free to come and go as you please, not during the day, but in the evening. These are our conditions. If you agree, we will expect you tomorrow morning at Briar Rose, it's a blind alley off of

Rose Avenue, house number seven."

"I will consult my lawyer so that he can evaluate the offer. He will weigh the pros and cons of this strange proposal, examine the risks. It is he who will have the last word."

Carl Sommers called his friend Ricardo again to share the new development in the situation. He spared him the details that would upset him. Ricardo, knowing the unorthodox nature of his friend, tried to dissuade him.

"Carl, how are you going to be able to live in the middle of hostility and harassment? Don't cram yourself into this Bee-eater, my old friend, I implore you! You'll regret it all your life. You are going to waste your time and energy trying to change the behavior of these ridiculous racists."

"Ricardo, my dear colleague," joked Carl Sommers, "the segregationist offer is very tempting, I am really tempted … I have nothing to fear from the depravity and the wickedness of these bigots. Besides, if things became untenable, if this poisoned and treacherous city prevents me from breathing, I will fold my tent and go seek my fortune elsewhere, as you suggested.

"I am not worried, dear friend. You know that I'm not a man to capitulate to difficulties or to flee from a battle, no matter how violent or dangerous it may be."

"Wish me luck," said Sommers, "because my decision is made. I will keep the contact and, God willing, you will not need to come to the rescue."

Dr. Carl Sommers cracked open the windows of the car, stretching his legs as best he could in the back seat, and fell asleep almost immediately, broken, tired and fearful of the future.

Dr. Sommers woke up the next morning, a little sore and bruised by this night curled up in the back seat of his car. He made a few summary ablutions in the public toilets of the rest area and had breakfast: a croissant and a cup of black coffee. He filled up his tank and set sail for the blind alley of Briar Rose.

He arrived at Montjolly, took Lilac Street, and then turned left onto Rose Avenue, in the direction of a beautiful square. A few old ladies sat on granite benches, warming up in the sun. A few old gentlemen were strolling on the wet sidewalk, which was paved with red bricks. They were all outraged by the presence of this intruder. They feared that this undesirable individual could disturb the peaceful atmosphere of the city.

Sommers ignored the effect provoked by his presence in the town. He drove up the oblique slope leading to the hospital and turned sharply onto a secondary road that was on the edge of the forest of pines and oaks. The forest was a natural and impenetrable bulwark around Montjolly. A mailbox posted on the path indicated the entrance to the blind alley of Briar Rose.

He continued into the cul-de-sacs, bordered on both sides by a bushy hedge of wild roses in bloom. Number seven was located at the rear end of the blind alley. It was a yellow brick, two story building, constructed in a severe and naked architecture, without frills or elegance. The villa was surrounded by a high wall of rough stones with a decorated top of three rows of bottle shards. It prohibited access to malicious intruders. When he approached the house, a massive wrought iron fence slipped on its rails and opened wide. Luke, the chubby and paunchy policeman who was guarding the house had activated the remote control. Dr. Sommers entered the courtyard of large stone slabs, squared, veined as polished marble. A thicket of wild roses adorned the middle of the courtyard and broke the monotonous coldness of the pale façade of the house.

Dr. Merville, the Mayor, Simon Morgan, and the Sheriff, Al Linden, arrived almost at the same time as Dr. Sommers. The municipal delegation invited him to enter the house, where he would obviously stay as an undesirable and embarrassing guest.

Luke, the police officer, slammed his heels to greet his hierarchical superior. He hastened, to open the entry oak door as massive and solid as a prison gate. It was decorated with sibylline patterns or cabalistic signs, similar to the Indian amulets on the family totem pole, intended to drive away evil spirits and attract blessings and favors from the gods on the house.

Dr. Merville offered a seat to Sommers and sat himself on one of the sofas. His two acolytes remained standing. For the occasion, they each wore a dark and sullen face.

"Here's the new contract," said Dr. Merville presenting to Sommers a rather large document. "Everything is there; you just have to sign."

"No way. It's out of question! My lawyer specifically told me not to sign anything. If I sign this, the original contract would be invalidated and I will not have any legal recourse."

"But then," retorted doctor Merville with impatience, "do you agree or not to our proposals?"

"Yes I do! Why do you think I am here?"

"You know, sir, we already made too many concessions," intervened Simon Morgan in a husky, dismissive voice.

"You're making a big mistake, Sir. On the contrary, it's me who is doing you a favor in bending myself to your absurd requirements, making me an accomplice in this small, nasty histrionic of your racist stupidities.

"I am doing you a huge favor. I could have reported you to the judicial authorities for violating my civil rights. I could file a lawsuit because of your refusal to hire a black doctor in a public institution, even though it is private. I could rouse the press and cause a scandal, a tremendous scandal ... don't push so hard gentlemen! You have my word; this must suffice you!"

The two men standing in front of Sommers, the Mayor and the Sheriff, looked at him, puzzled, amazed by his sharp tone and hard words.

After a moment of silence, Dr. Merville drew from his pocket a check and handed it to Dr. Sommers saying, "I can't understand your reasons, but in your place me I'd choose to go. You may not know what a mess you getting yourself into? I don't think you will be able to live in complete isolation in a town where the entire population sees you as a pariah."

"Dr. Merville," replied Dr. Sommers, "you don't know, I am sure, what I am capable of doing. My ancestors endured worse on plantations like this one. I will survive, don't worry about me."

"I am watching you," said Sheriff Al Linden, speaking for the first time in the conversation. "I know you, you're a troublemaker, come to interfere in the affairs of the people, to sow mayhem and cause damage. Don't think you can cause us hassle without serious repercussions. I won't tolerate even a hitch, the slightest deviation of conduct, no mayhem, no disruption in my jurisdiction, under any circumstance."

Dr. Sommers answered nothing, he merely shrugged. He got up from his chair and met the Sheriff's gaze, who thought he had frightened the pariah.

Dr. Merville explained, then, the decisions taken by the committee to make his stay, perhaps not nice, but acceptable. "Luke, now," he added, "will serve as a liaison between the Villa Vaudreuil (name of the house) and Saint Cécile Hospital."

The eccentric Cédric Vaudreuil, had built this villa, as a refuge and a welcoming Ali Baba cave, to house the treasures, gleaned from the four corners of the world, during long trips on his yacht: Aventura.

On the ground floor of the large living room equipped with diverse and disparate furnishings, were: empire chairs, English sofas, Chinese coffee tables where we found uncool antique porcelain vases. There were Venetian lamps, precious carpets from Turkey, an array of Dali's work, a drawing by Picasso, and several other paintings by lesser known painters. There was a gaggle of strange objects hung here and there on the walls, which gave this extensive room the feel of an antique dealer's lair.

The library occupied the left wing of the exhibition, a space extended up to the dining room. It was bursting at the seams. Spread over all of the shelves and tables was an indescribable mess of books. Books in French, English, Spanish, Italian, books stacked in unstable columns, encyclopedias, books bound in leather with gold accents. Piles of manuscripts closely tied, covered with dust littered the ground. An assortment of cheap novels and journals made this place a true Capernaum.

A long desk made of walnut was placed between two large windows that lit this vast room well. It looked like a boat loaded with cargo, as it cruised to a hospitable port. The library was crowded with stacked boxes. Finally, here and there, African music instruments and a conical drum, made it very difficult to maneuver in the room.

The walls of the library were covered with reproductions of old maps, sketches of Ferdinand Magellan, sketches of Amerigo Vespucci, yellowed copies of Martin Waldseemüller, Gerardus Mercator, and unreleased Abraham Ortélius tests.

A mahogany table with eight chairs occupied the center of the spacious dining room. The chairs were carved in a baroque style with high backs and didn't match overall style in the room. A large sideboard was stuffed with dinnerware, earthenware and porcelain. There were also rare crystals, Chinese miniatures, and knickknacks that had been artistically decorated. That completed the home furnishings in the room.

The kitchen seemed to have never been used. The utensils that hung on the walls or were placed on shelves seemed new. A microwave oven sat as a trophy in the middle of the other electrical gadgets: a toaster, a mixer, an electric coffee maker, and a food processor.

A very airy veranda was summarily furnished with a few disparate sofas and a few plastic chairs. This completed the inventory of the ground floor of the villa.

The notable presence of a toilet located at the bottom of the stairs, with the wrought iron banister represent a yacht sailing on stormy waves, all sails deployed.

Luke, the chubby officer, despite himself, served as host. He would answer only in monosyllables, laconically, any questions ask by Dr. Sommers. There were three bedrooms upstairs and a huge gallery at the rear of the villa. The master bedroom was furnished with a four poster bed, a cupboard with two wings, a nostalgic remnant of a time past. Another bedroom was filled with an impressive cargo of debris, wrapped and tied with string. It was crowded with an array of exotic objects. It was also occupied by a bunch of valuable stuff, loaded from floor to ceiling by odd items. There was a small bed in the third room, a chair and a crowded jumble of toiletries, a radio, a kepi, and two or three pieces of loose clothing on the floor. Another room, somewhat smaller, was built above the garage as a laboratory, and was equipped with a sophisticated apparatus with a complete and modern assortment of instruments and containers, such as a still glass including a fractionation column, a strong condenser, and a large receiver. In a glass cabinet there were vases and labeled bottles, and an array of acids, sulfites, and metalloids, alcohols, and salts. The workbench on which an alembic rested, also supported other essential accessories; an oil stove, a wooden pestle which still contained a few residues of a crushed substance, a precision balance, a big thermometer, a mixer, and a small vise adjusted on a corner of the table. At one side of the room was a fridge, at the other end, on the side of the entrance door, there was a wide sink flanked by two small metal cabinets.

One of the lab doors give access to the gallery. Thence, it dominated the back paved court, in the middle of which stood a huge chestnut. The prominent roots of the tree raised a few ill-fitting slabs. A large clearing, cut in the large forest of pine and oak stretched out of sight, to the top of the mountain. This clearing was planted with trees and shrubs with healing virtues from tropical regions. These exotic plants, constituted an embryo of a Botanical Garden, a successful attempt of acclimatization of rare, foreign vegetation to the area.

Luke was the police officer who kept an eye on the villa in the absence of the owner, Cédric Vaudreuil, who was one of the pioneers and the main architect of the city. Cédric Vaudreuil gave each of the streets the name of a flower. It was he who had discovered this beautiful place during an expedition, isolated and protected on one side by a forest on the side of a mountain, and on the other by the unbridled waves of a stormy sea that plunged deep into the estuary of the Oval River, dangerously unreachable, at high tide.

Sailing out two years ago for an expedition to South America, Cédric Vaudreuil did not return. The Colombian Government, after research, identified the skeleton of the yacht, the Aventura, stranded on a beach in the city of Cartagena, and informed the concerned authorities. This was a regrettable tragedy. No one knew yet what had happened to the eccentric adventurer, having disappeared at sea without a trace.

The visit ended. Luke handed a set of keys and a remote control to Dr. Sommers, jumped on his motorcycle and left the villa in a swirl of deafening noise.

Dr. Sommers brought up his bags, his computer, his clothes, and his CD from the trunk of the car. He carefully put them in the cupboard of the room that the man had evacuated. Dr. Sommers then left Villa Vaudreuil. He turned right onto Briar Rose Street, and then took Rose Lauriers Avenue, a freeway recently constructed to facilitate the flow of traffic in this new district. It was built on the flank of the mountain, to host the five hundred refugee families from South Africa after the collapse of apartheid. He went to Biloxi, the nearest city to Montjolly, just a few miles away.

The rapid expansion of the city was due in large part to the sudden increase of the aboriginal population. These political immigrants had vast economic resources and a lot of individual talents. However, their integration in Montjollian society forced the municipality to enlist the help of the provincial government in order to achieve the necessary infrastructural works: a hospital, high school, two primary schools, the construction of the Town Hall, the new neighborhood planning, the supply of drinking water, and much more!

When he arrived in Biloxi, Dr. Sommers went first to the Union Bank to open an account and deposit the check drawn on the funds of the municipality of Montjolly. He then went to Biloxi General Hospital to offer his benevolent services twice a week. The administration welcomed his generous offer with enthusiasm. They gave him a tour, made him feel at home, and most importantly, showed him the operating room where he would be working.

Dr. Sommers ate at the Tivoli restaurant, renowned for its delicious Italian dishes. Then, he went to buy what he needed for the house: bed linen, blankets, two pillows, and cleaning products. He then went to the XTRA, the busiest supermarket in the area. Then he lingered at a record store. As a passionate music lover, he was looking for an old edition of the opera Madame Butterfly with Maria Callas in the role of CioCioSan. His search proved unsuccessful, so he bought the live concert version, by a famous Greek diva in Munich in 1958. As it began to rain, he went back to his Cadillac and headed back to the villa.

Dr. Sommers unloaded his provisions and put them in the cupboards or in the refrigerator. After that, he went back to get his computer from the back seat of the car. To his surprise, upon opening the car door, he saw a big cat, white as snow, sitting majestically on his computer. The cat looked at him with somewhat faded green eyes, slanted eyes which glistened in the dim light like two candles. The cat, ignoring the stupor of the doctor, got out of the car slowly and he rubbed two or three times against Sommers' leg as a token of friendship. Then, he walked, head and tail up, and entered the villa as an old frequenter of the house. Carl followed the animal who went directly to the refrigerator, desperately meowing. Sommers poured some milk into a bowl. The cat greedily drinks the liquid, licked his chops, and returned to the fridge mewing like a madman. Dr. Sommers put more milk in the bowl and the Tomcat drank with avidity and copiously licked the container. Finally sated, the cat sought refuge on one of the sofas on the veranda, satisfied and happy.

Dr. Sommers didn't know where he had picked up this new companion. It wouldn't be so difficult to find the owner of the cat. He decided to keep it on an interim basis, then post an ad in the newspapers in Biloxi later.

Dr. Sommers then went into the room where he had stored his belongings, and made the bed with the new linens he had purchased. He covered the new pillows with the new pillowcases and proceeded to do a systematic cleaning of the premises. He cleaned the bathroom and went down stairs to drink a glass of water. He took the opportunity to fill the cat's bowl with and leave him a slice of ham, in case he was hungry. Dying of fatigue, Sommers slept all night like a baby.

An unusual noise awoke Dr. Sommers the next morning. It was an aggressive scratching under the door of the room, accompanied by a tearful complaint, almost human. He stood up. Sunlight flooded the room with a bright and warm luster. He put on his robe and opened the door. The cat came to rub shoulders with him, and walked on the side of the staircase. The cat ran down and stopped at the veranda door overlooking the courtyard. The cat went out nimbly as soon as the door was opened, to take care of his business.

In the middle of the kitchen Sommers saw a pile of a dozen dead mice. These critters, attracted by the tempting smell of ham had come, literally, into the lion's mouth. The cat didn't spare anybody. He made a slaughter, a real massacre. Dr. Sommers put the result of the nightly hunting of his companion in a plastic bag and went to throw it in the trash can, which stood in a corner of the large courtyard of the chestnut tree. At the approach of the cat, plump lizards that were sprawling in the sun, ran abruptly. Taken to panic and fear, they climbed the fortified wall and rushed without care to the other side. The cat didn't even notice the frenzied flight of these crazed reptiles.

When he had finished a summary inspection of the paved courtyard, the cat returned and Sommers, who was watching, closed the door and went to take a shower.

Sommers spent the day putting his affairs in order. He moved his computer to a small table he found, borrowed a chair and a lamp with shade, as well as a small shelf to complete the furnishings of his bedroom. He replaced the door lock because he did not want someone to come rummaging in his business when was absent. He took precautions. He didn't trust these people.

The cat followed him everywhere and seemed, by its cheery attitude, to approve the changes he made in the room and the additional measures of security, guaranteeing its comfort and its intimacy.

Dr. Sommers prepared an omelet with ham for his lunch. Toasted a few slices of bread and laid them on the table. The cat which followed those activities with increased interest, climbed on a chair, seized two pieces of bread and went dip them in his milk. After having enjoyed his delicious meal, sated and disinterested, the cat lay down on the sofa and fell asleep.

CHAPTER II

The next day was Friday, the day when he would begin his volunteer work at Biloxi General Hospital. He got up very early, put the cat out and filled the bowl with milk and bread. The cat watched him with an oblique eye and pretended not to understand what was happening. When the doctor was ready, he entered the garage from the dining room and opened the car door. The cat who had followed him without him noticing, jumped in the car and moved on the front seat, as comfortable as possible. The cat's eyes sparkled of boldness and challenge. Sommers shook his head, incredulous. The doctor couldn't explain the bizarre behavior of the cat and its cavalier way. Sommers thought he could get rid of this funny gun at Biloxi. Who knows, maybe he could find his owner there.

Sommers entered the reception area of the hospital, the cat on his heels. Dr. Sommers stood in front of the receptionist asking her to let Dr. Morton know that he would be waiting for him in the operating room. She didn't even hear him, instead exclaiming, "Here's Mikado! Linda! Linda! Mikado is back!"

Linda came immediately, took the cat in her arms and said in a honeyed tone, "You gave me a nice scare, you know? EH! Where were you? You were just up and gone without warning! Wicked cat! You left your raisins, your apple, your sweet milk … no jam for you today."

Dr. Sommers listened this interesting conversation with patience, welcoming the idea of getting rid of the so called Mikado for good. He cleared his throat to get the receptionist's attention and repeated his request. The receptionist, absorbed and distracted, was a little embarrassed at not having heard him before.

"Sorry sir! May I help you?" she said.

"I am Dr. Sommers. Let Dr. Morton know I am here. He is expecting me."

"Take the second elevator at the end of this corridor," said the receptionist, indicating the way, a confused, wry smile on her lips. "Third floor, room 313."

Dr. Sommers completed his obligations. He completed two successful surgeries back-to-back a very complicated appendectomy and the removal of a gallbladder. The patient was afraid of surgery. The doctors had first used Ursodeoxycholic acid to try to dissolve a gall stone, which was as big as a marble. But there were unforeseen complications, which necessitated Dr. Sommers' surgical intervention. He had two other surgeries planned for the afternoon. Dr. Morton took him to dinner at the finest restaurant in the city.

They talked about everything and nothing. They exchanged views on the new methods used in surgery to eliminate unnecessary risks inherent to using a scalpel. They praised the laser and its amazing precision, which replaced, very advantageously, heaps of outdated instruments rendered obsolete by this revolutionary technology.

His day completed, Dr. Sommers returned to his home, tired, but happy to have found this excellent distraction to his forced idleness. He stood up very early the next morning, equipped for a long hike in the forest. He went bag in hand, exploring the surrounding area. Excursions in the mountains or hiking in the woods were his favorite pastime when he was at university. He hiked each month, with a few comrades, hooked like him to the great outdoors. He liked camping in the woods, in summer as well as in winter. He ascended the inaccessible peaks of the mountains in the region. He loved exploring the caves and caverns, as an amateur speleologist. It was a way for the future surgeon to free himself from nervous tension accumulated during long evening of studying and it enhanced his introverted character. It was, for him, the most effective way to get rid of the trauma experienced in the operating room.

Dr. Sommers went first in the tropical garden and was amused to identify shrubs and plants, using sketches, definitions, found in one of Monsieur Cédric Vaudreuil's books. Sommers even tasted wild black and tart blackberries with an intoxicating exotic smell and a tasty fruit scented like pink berries from India and Brazil. He also enjoyed the sapodilla fruit which has a velvety and yellow flesh, a full-bodied flavor, similar to licorice.

A vague path allowed him to break a dirt trail through the dense forest, up to the mountain top. From the Monteverdi top there was a spectacular view of the sea. Dark green patches overwhelmed by interval, the atolls tossed by deep waves. Rows of steel platforms belonging to the oil companies disappeared from time to time, concealed by a flock of clouds floating awash by rough sea.

Dr. Sommers stepped to the edge of the trees, near the steep and bare escarpment, swept by winds from the Gulf. This natural feature made it very difficult to access the forest. In the distance, to the right, stretched the beach of snow white sand. It seemed that the entire population of Montjolly was on this beach. They were people everywhere. The ladies gilded in the sun, children were playing in the sand, others bathed under the close supervision of concerned mothers. A group of intrepid teenagers were riding water scooters, wandering without stopping, gesticulating and uttering wild cries. Inexperienced surfers were trying to catch breaking waves. They were trying to reach the shore where fanatical fans were cheering their exploits.

Dr. Sommers wondered where this unpaved road might lead, but as soon as he began his descent, he saw, hidden by a grove of oak trees, the source that fed the waterfall was also filling, with a low musical sound, the Montjolly city water cistern. A sort of aqueduct, whose iron pipes had been placed on arches over the side of the mountain, carried the precious liquid to the purification and distribution center.

Dr. Sommers awoke very early the next morning. He proposed to go to mass, to probe the stubborn intransigence of the authorities and open a dialog, however small it may be, about their fierce determination to deny him mingling with the activities of the population.

The square bell tower of the parish church, Our Lady of the Assumption, whose melodious chime, unmuted by the distance, sounded with fervor, as far as the villa Vaudreuil. Dr. Sommers waited until everyone had entered and the mass had begun, to surreptitiously slip inside the church. He stood near the front door, arms crossed, listening to the priest's homily. The gospel of that Sunday was the Good Samaritan. Dr. Sommers thought, despite formal threats by Mayor Simon Morgan, that they wouldn't dare expel him from the temple, as Christ had chased vendors who defiled his father's house. The Christian doctrine of brotherly love, prohibited them to do such a thing. He was greatly mistaken!

Sommers had lowered his head, plunged into a deep meditation. Nobody, except the two Knights of Columbus who were standing on the threshold of the Church, had noticed his presence. A mere three minutes went by before two police officers, as discreetly as possible, came to escort him towards the exit. He didn't show any resistance, already knowing that it would be useless. He didn't want to aggravate his precarious situation by causing a scandal. Especially now.

Arrived on the square in front of the church, the policemen pushed him with all their strength saying, "Get out of here! Dirty nigger! We better not see your face around here again! Git! Better be faster than that, stupid troublemaker!"

Dr. Sommers, stumbling, clinched at a column to avoid a brutal fall on the square slabs. He walked, limping, shaken by the nasty police brutality, until he reached his car, which was parked some distance away. He returned to the villa, convinced, once for all, of the firm resolve of the authorities to thwart any attempt on his part to impose himself onto the social fabric of Montjollian life.

He spent the rest of the day, sullen, bored, and rather sad, having attempted and failed with his clever maneuver, to penetrate the taboo circle of this xenophobic society through religious precepts. He made a thorough search in the library of Sir Cédric Vaudreuil, not exactly sure what he was looking for in the collection of rare and esoteric works, gleaned by the eccentric Cedric Vaudreuil, during his many expeditions around the world. There was a manuscript of the "Summa Perfectionism" (the Summit of Perfection) in Latin, written in 750 A.D. by the great Alchemist and Arab scholar, Abu Musa Jabir Ibn Rakesh, (Geber); a copy of the New Testament in Euskara (Basque language), a book printed in 1545, rescued from the autodafé ordered by the Spanish dictator Francisco Franco, who wanted to eradicate the influence of Basque language and culture in his country. Sommers, out of simple curiosity, pulled out a book of spagyric scribble in Russian; A Treatise of Toxicology by the Italian Francesco Redi; and many others. He put aside, for a more indepth consultation, a rare edition of renaissance authors such as: Pico Della Mirandola, Jean Bodin, Nicolas Copernicus, Tycho Brahe. Persian literature was represented by a very old copy of the collection of epic poems Chahname. This incomparable work of the poet Firdoussa was completed in the year 1010 A.D.

The library of Mr. Cédric Vaudreuil revealed itself, after this summary search by Dr. Sommers, to be a true Ali Baba cave, fully stuffed with precious objects, priceless archaeological treasures, unpublished manuscripts, capable alone of furnishing a respectable museum.

The expulsion of Dr. Sommers from the church, although discreet, didn't pass unnoticed. Those who attended the scene were surprised, they were in a huff, by the presence of this nigger within their congregation. The old bigots commented with emphasis and indignation, the sacrilege of the holy sanctuary, caused by this despicable individual. Several angry ladies accosted Mayor Simon Morgan, and pressured him to provide, immediately, an explanation for the sudden appearance of this dirty nigger in the heart of their community in prayer on the steps of the Lord's altar.

They found it unacceptable! They said that the administration had failed in its mission of protecting the population against this sudden intrusion of this disruptive individual spreading panic across the city. They didn't know, fortunately for Morgan, that he was the one who introduced the black danger in the heart of the city. Few people, indeed, were aware of this sensitive and compromising situation. The illegal presence of the tenant of the villa Vaudreuil had plunged Montjolly's entire administration into big trouble. The authorities didn't know how to explain and justify this major derogation from the rules established since the early days of the Montjollian community.

Simon Morgan had found it very difficult to get rid of those old ladies who had confronted him after mass. He promised them, while regretting this damaging hitch made to public order, to investigate thoroughly this unfortunate incident. Morgan promised them, in addition, specific and severe guidelines so this does not happen ever again.

The Mayor was reluctant to reveal to these ladies, the whole truth about this imbroglio. He could already imagine the outrage and indignant reaction of these passionate voters. They would be reluctant forgive this mortal sin, the inability to protect their exclusive and magnificent domain, against sporadic incursions of undesirable visitors. The next municipal election, which would be very contested, would be between the current Mayor, Simon Morgan, and the young and dynamic, Matt Potter. It might be decided in favor of the latter, if the scandal of hosting Dr. Sommers in the villa Vaudreuil, broke out now. Morgan also decided that he would present his grievances to the intruder. He accused him of having not honored the terms of the oral contract.

The meeting was stormy. Simon Morgan, angry, threatened to kick Dr. Sommers out of town. He figured out, that Sommers had, despite express recommendations by Dr. Merville, deliberately went to church to be provocative. "This is unforgivable!" Morgan told him. To stand in the middle of the Sunday service, the time at which all bigots were present in the church. He asked him to leave the villa, at least for two or three days to give him time to appease the vengeful anger of the alarmed parishioners, to calm the growing concern of a nigger invasion that this incident had caused.

Morgan recommended Sommers leave at night to avoid attracting the attention of Sunday's retarded passersby, or arouse the curiosity of an amateur Sherlock Holmes on the trail of the intruder. Without recriminating, because he knew he was at fault, Sommers didn't discuss the injunction of the Mayor.

In Biloxi, Sommers rented a room at the Heliopolis Hotel, the most luxurious in the city. Biloxi held an annual sailing regatta which drew fans from all fifty states. This sailing regatta was the national championship of this sport. It was held at the spectacular mouth of the Mississippi River.

From his window, Sommers attended the preparations for the race. There were fifty-five sailboats, each wearing the colors of the state it represented. Competitors from Guam, Puerto Rico, St. Croix, and the Virgin Islands, had hoisted their flags at the top of the main mast of their sailboat, which, all sails deployed, were lined up along the pier ready for the start of the race. A band of merry men, perched high in the stands, playing outdated tunes, entertained the excited crowd.

A buoy anchored at a dozen cables from the coast, indicated to the competitors where they had to turn back, in order not to venture beyond the agreed route. Sailboats spun at a good pace, pushed by the wind from the south, which was very strong this season.

Fans followed the dramatic evolution of the race, using powerful binoculars, admiring the skilled maneuvers of crews to maintain or increase the speed of their boats, willing to stay competitive until the end. The crowd watched with wonder, boats shone like points of light on the horizon, fluttering from wave to wave, like a wisp of fireflies.

The entire fleet reached the buoy and turned swiftly to initiate the final stage. A few boats had taken the lead, and already, people were encouraging their favorite by frenzied cheers and whistles so shrill they might burst eardrums.

The hotel, located on the beach, offered a panoramic view of the river's mouth and was an ideal observatory from which to monitor the activities of the regatta. Spectators wandered on the esplanade of the dock, in compact and lively groups. Loads of people had invaded the beach. A huge crowd was gathered at the gates of the port. Everyone followed with growing interest the rapid approach of the leading boats. They spun in front, the wind in their sails, their sails billowing, and straining to get ahead. The leading boats were closely followed by the rest of the fleet, launched at full speed, tossed about by the stormy waves of high tide.

The Biloxi team, representing the State of Mississippi, the Boston team representing Massachusetts, the city of Los Angeles representing California, and Tampa Bay representing Florida, had far outdistanced the other competitors. The Biloxi crew wrestled with a tireless determination to remain at the level of craft whose sophisticated aerodynamic profile, allowed them to ride the crest of the waves, maintain their stability, and gradually increase their cruising speed.

The seven members of the Biloxi crew, led by Captain Matt Ross, attempted a bold, risky, maneuver which enabled them to compete with much more experienced competitors who were much better equipped than themselves. The intrepid teammates of Matt Ross, firmly clung to the sailboat ropes, leaning into the vacuum on each side of the boat, to ensure a proper balance, for the daring and risky manoeuver they attempted; it was essential to the success of the strategy.

Meanwhile, Matt Ross at the helm, with amazing dexterity, presented the side of the lifeboat to the rising tide and straightened the boat almost immediately so that it could take advantage of the shot of battering and sail for Crete to Crete without going down with the tough wave.

The sailboat leaped like a fiery horse stirred up by the sting of spurs. Its sails like light wings deployed in the wind, gave the impression of clinging to an invisible cloud. This dangerous ride executed with control, allowed the crew of Biloxi to pick up speed and dig a visible gap between itself and its competitors.

The crowd was raging. Delirious enthusiasm manifested by frenzied cheers was shouted in unison by thousands of fanatics from all regions of Mississippi.

The opportunity to win the race for the first time had increased the strength of the Biloxi sailors tenfold, their muscles tense, panting painfully under the strain.

The superhuman will and the fierce determination of the California team were not enough to win the trophy. Despite a desperate attempt by Massachusetts, the Biloxi guys crossed first the finish line. It was delirium! A terrible uproar rose and made the whole city tremble. People were out of control. The crew from Biloxi was hoisted on a bulwark and brought in triumphantly, by an excited public, even before the organizers gave them the trophy and check for one hundred thousand dollars for the winner.

The festivities celebrating the unexpected victory of the home team soon degenerated into a carnival frenzy that toured the city in a frantic gallop. The festival continued on the Place of the Rotunda where the municipal band played for the dancing crowd until the early morning.

Dr. Sommers had followed the race with great interest. He himself had a passion for sailing. The tight struggle between the crews of the first three winners and the heroic effort of the companions of Matt Ross, had aroused Sommers' admiration for the Biloxi team. He remained awake most of the night listening to the echo, attenuated the catchy music and the muted rumor of the crowd in trance.

Despite this unseemly incident of his brutal expulsion from the parish church, which required him to be exiled for a week, Sommers had, nevertheless, decided to stay at Montjolly. Something, he wasn't sure what, just drew him irresistibly towards this inhospitable, hostile city, where he endured ostracism and the derogatory attitudes of a lot of old, racist bigots living in the balsamic comfort of an absurd anachronism.

It became a real challenge for him, a matter of pride, to show these retrograde bastards, that he can live in these absolute precarious conditions, without losing his dignity; without sinking into the gloom that this ridiculous and humiliating situation created.

He spent the week in exile at the hotel, reflecting on the consequences of his whim. The doctor weighed in his mind, the negative and the positive aspects of this absurd challenge he was imposing on himself and concluded, arrogantly and offhandedly, that nothing else could darken his crazy adventure in this city.

On Tuesday and Thursday, Dr. Sommers went on foot to Biloxi General Hospital located some three hundred meters from the Heliopolis where he was staying. Mikado, at each visit came to greet him, rubbing his body against Sommers' legs, purring and looking at up him with big sorrowful eyes. After a day of work, Dr. Morton accompanied Dr. Sommers to the Tivoli Restaurant, where they ate dinner. Dr. Morton appreciated the precious help that Dr. Sommers provided him in the operating room. The situation in Iraq had dangerously deteriorated, increasing the number of wounded that had to be repatriated to receive urgent care exponentially.

Dr. Morton relished the idea of adding Dr. Sommers to his team of skilled surgeons. The economic restrictions imposed by the administration of the hospital as a result of a serious budget deficit prevented Dr. Morton from offering employment to his friend. He took solace in thinking that an improvement of the financial situation of the institution could soon allow him to realize his wish.

Upon returning to the villa Vaudreuil, Dr. Sommers retreated to the library to discover the treasures accumulated by the missing owner. The glass cabinet which housed an impressive number of sports trophies had attracted his attention and aroused his curiosity his first day there.

He carefully examined each of them. Mr. Cédric Vaudreuil excelled at all sports: football, tennis, basketball, baseball, swimming, you name it. Under the plaster of the pugilistic trophy base, Sommers found a small key. He proceeded to do a thorough investigation of the cabinet, and eventually discovered a secret drawer filled with documents and manuscripts, hidden under a sliding metal plate. Dr. Sommers immediately began to read these papers Mr. Cédric. He found two old expired passports, some property securities, insurance contracts and two notebooks filled with notes and sketches, like those of Leonardo da Vinci, with seemingly indescribable cryptic formulas.

A particular book attracted his attention. It contained an abundant amount of information on how to extract the essence of flowers, leaves and roots of certain medicinal and odoriferous plants. These delicate extractions were used, according to the author, to manufacture perfumes, ointments and lotions of all kinds. Also meticulously detailed, was the manufacturing process of high quality spirits and ordinary vintage wine flavored with flowers or fruit essence.

Dr. Sommers thought seriously about adopting this new hobby distillation of essence and liquor to occupy his leisure time at the villa. Finally, someone would find an appropriate use for the sophisticated laboratory of Mr. Cedric Vaudreuil.

Dr. Sommers carefully put the documents back in the drawer, however, he kept the book containing the methods and formulas necessary for achieving his ambitions as a distiller.

The next day, Saturday, Dr. Sommers went to the laboratory to become acquainted with the devices gathered in the still lab before beginning his own experiment with the hermetic science of the cult of Bacchus.

He made a complete inventory of the supplies. He put aside chemicals and accessories he needed to learn the art of wine making and initiate himself in the captivating mysteries of perfumery.

On Sunday morning, Dr. Sommers, backpack in hand, put on his hiking shoes. He headed to the oak forest, climbing the steep slopes of a badly traced trail, which was difficult to access. Arrived at the top of the escarpment, he was astonished to see the beach completely empty. Nobody was in the sea; no one was on the beach. He scanned the horizon with his binoculars, not a sailboat on the water, not a worker on the artificial atolls, abandoned in stormy waves.

It was a very interesting discovery for Sommers. He decided now that he would spend his Sundays on the beach, as it was deserted by Montjolly's bigots.

Dr. Sommers wondered, about the occult motivation that seemed to guide Montjolly's actions. It was absurd. He resigned himself to voluntarily adopting these shameful restrictions to his freedom and this humiliating role of pariah. He was living on the margins of a society, even more marginalized. The majority of the people in Montjolly was unaware of his presence among them and the rest had a hateful hostility towards him. What on earth he was doing here? Why was he alienating himself in this dark hole and wasting his youth?

In truth, nothing could keep his mind in this picturesque and troublesome harbor. It was certainly breathtakingly beautiful, but obviously not enough to entice his him. It was a diffuse, but insidious, persistent feeling, that his fortune, as Orestes, would begin a new phase in this boring town.

Sommers had these thoughts on his way back to the villa. He returned in the afternoon, weary, puzzled, his brain on fire. Dr. Sommers trusted his instincts. He had nothing to lose, he could wait a little longer to realize his dreams of a more exhilarating, more meaningful and happier life.

However, Dr. Sommers resumed its usual routine. He shared his time between Biloxi General Hospital, his work as amateur chemist in the laboratory of Mr. Vaudreuil, and hiking in the surrounding forest, and reading specialized medical journals to keep abreast of new medical products.

One Saturday evening, Sommers received a phone call from Dr. Morton asking him to replace one of his doctors, who had suddenly fallen ill. He immediately went to Biloxi.

He worked all night in the operating room to take care of the many victims of a train derailment in the vicinity of Biloxi. In the morning, exhausted, he lay down on a chaise longue in an empty room next to the operating room and fell asleep immediately.

At ten o'clock, he left Dr. Morton, who thanked him warmly. Reaching the forest road that lead to Montjolly, he suddenly decided to visit the beach, he knew it was deserted on Sundays. He had never ventured on this side of the city before. The narrow road down towards the shore was sloping, soft and sinuous. Majestic oak trees and flowered shrubs lined the shady lane, bathed in a picturesque serenity. The breeze was stroking his face. The moist forest smell, mixed with the butterball scent of the sea, intoxicated his senses and plunged him into a kind of wistful and blissful euphoria. Arriving suddenly at a sunny clearing, Dr. Sommers stopped for a moment at the top of this rocky headland, to admire the deep blue sea and how the frothy waves were continuously, layer upon layer, dying on the sand.

He remained a minute, pensive, absorbed in his gloomy thoughts, before continuing his descent. He parked his car in a dense underbrush behind a bushy brush, away from prying eyes. He donned his bathing suit, put on a gaudy shirt, dropped his keys and his mobile phone in his pocket, and barefoot, went on the beach.

The water was very cold since it was the end of winter, but the sand was hot. He walked head down, soaking his feet from time to time in the foam of the waves coming to die on the fine sand with a melodious sound.

Turning his head to track the majestic flight of a seagull, he was blinded by a dazzling reflection like lightning from a green bush. His natural curiosity aroused, he headed under the cover of a giant palm and a blooming almond tree to the shaded bush. In the middle of thorny shrubs, hidden from passerby's' eyes, was a brand new convertible Mercedes. About ten meters away, sitting on a log reading, he saw the most wonderful creature he had ever seen in his life. His heart skipped two or three beats momentarily. He remained frozen for a long time, seized by strong emotion. He was shocked by this angelic appearance.

He finally begun to walk toward her. The sound of his footsteps in the dry leaves littering the ground startled the girl. She got up nimbly. She was frightened, on the verge of panic.

"Who are you? What are you doing here?"

"I am Dr. Carl Sommers. Excuse me if I scared you, miss!" "Ah! It is you," she replied spontaneously.

"Yes! It's me!" repeated Dr. Sommers a bit maliciously. "I guess I was mistaken in thinking that nobody knew me in Montjolly."

He stared at the girl, fascinated by her extraordinary beauty. Eyes, blue like the sky, were ensconced with long golden eyelashes. Her long, blond hair framed her face, which shone with serene innocence. The exquisite purity of her shy gaze showed an innate nobility and sophisticated refinement of this wonderful creature.

With a medium build, she was svelte. Standing motionless and frightened, she was wearing a figure hugging yellow bathing suit, which complemented her slender figure. The girl looked like the woman in the Birth of Venus by Sandro Botticelli, the Italian renaissance painter.

"You're beautiful!" he told her.

The young girl blinked rapidly, her long eyelashes as to wake up from a paralyzing spell and blushes from ear to ear. She ran to her car and donned a yellow robe which was on the hood of the vehicle. In her haste to cover herself, she dropped the book she was reading. Sommers approaching picked it up.

"Don't run away like that! You don't need to be afraid of me.
What's your name?" She didn't answer.

"I found you today. You are my soul mate. I do not want to lose
you!" Dr. Sommers spoke in a distraught voice, unable to contain his
excitement.

The young girl who was sitting in her car now, said with a shaky
tone, "I'm Isabella! Isabella Morgan!"

"Isabella! Isabella!" repeated Dr. Sommers, really moved. "Please.
I would like to stay in touch with you, even though I know its taboo
in Montjolly. May I ask you for your phone number?" She shook her
head no.

"Then, I'm giving you mine."

She smiled. "I thought they had no phone at the villa?" replied
Isabella a bit more relaxed.

"You're right, miss! This is my mobile phone number. I note with
great pleasure that you know my address. I'm not the pariah I thought
it was."

The young lady knew she made a mistake. She kept silent and
smiled maliciously.

"Do you have a pen?"

Isabella handed him a pencil. He wrote his number carefully on the
last page of the book that he still held and handed it to the young lady.

"I must go," said Isabella.

"Please promise me you will keep in touch!"

"I don't promise anything," replied the young lady, smiling shyly.

She started the engine and was preparing to leave when Dr.
Sommers interrupted again. "Allow me, please!" "What?" asked
Isabella anxiously?

"I would like to keep a souvenir of this wonderful meeting.
Otherwise, I will think it was a dream." He took his phone from his
pocket and said, "Smile, please!"

A dazzling smile lit up the face of the girl. She looked like La Belle
Jardinière of Raphaël Sanzio. Sommers was upset. With tearful eyes,
he followed the girl until the car vanished from his view.

Sommers remained idle for a moment. Sadness preyed upon his
heart. An unknown and unsettling feeling clung to his wounded soul.
He had lost his composure and confidence. He felt invaded by a feeling
of emptiness, of profound melancholy. He was sad and happy at the

same time, in a word he had fallen … in love.

He returned home very excited. He uploaded the two photos of Isabella that he had taken with his phone camera to his computer. He spent hours admiring the enlarged, smiling image of this beautiful stranger who has just stolen his heart.

He didn't sleep all night. He only tossed and turned in his bed, imaging scenarios, each more absurd than the others, where he and Isabella were living in bliss and happiness, their love endless. He imagined taking Isabella away from the harmful influence of this archaic city. Nothing could stand in his way. He felt alive with an irresistible force like the legendary courage of knights, ready to journey to cursed tower where his sweetheart was held prisoner.

His brain was on fire. He was rehashing the most extravagant ranting of his soaring imagination, blaming the dismal failure of his chimerical efforts and the pathetic futility of his dreamlike endeavor.

At dawn he fell into a restless sleep. He awoke about ten o'clock, tired, dazed, disoriented, with an empty head and a heavy heart. Fortunately, he did not have to go to Biloxi today. He wandered around the house, not having the strength to do anything. He called his friend Ricardo Ponce (Colon) to catch up, but above all, to talk about Isabella. Dr. Sommers painted a wonderful portrait of the young girl, boasting of the incomparable beauty of his Venus.

"I thought," said his friend Ricardo, "that you had no contact with the people of this bizarre little town? Is she not from Monjolly?" "I met her on the beach and we got acquainted."

"Don't complicate your situation, which is already quite precarious, by falling in love with one of these racist bigots. This is not a good omen. Who could have thought, my dear friend, that the young, talented and ambitious surgeon I knew and admired, celebrated by his peers and his teachers, could give it all up to fight, without lance and armor, against windmills like Don Quixote? Carl, my old friend, I am telling you straight. Stop this foolishness. I don't understand you anymore. You don't realize it yet, but you're on your way to ruining your life. I really don't know why you insist on continuing this nonsense? Come back to reality and common sense, I beg you!"

Sommers reassured Ricardo the best he could, because he shared the same concerns and doubts as his friend, but he wasn't about to admit them openly.

He spent the week in a feverish expectation, powerless to influence the course of events. Sommers mechanically fulfilled his task at the hospital. He monitored his work closely to avoid making irreparable mistakes.

At the villa, Dr. Sommers locked himself in the laboratory, trying to tame his boredom by engaging himself, body and soul, in trivial pursuits which required his full attention.

Two long and agonizing weeks went by without receiving a word from the young girl. This silence was overwhelmingly torturous. He lost his energy and was living in a debilitating state of anxiety. Discouraged and sad, he was seeking refuge from his grief. He was beginning to give up his dreams after one month spent languishing, day and night, and complaining unnecessarily. He finally admitted the painful truth that Isabella had forgotten about him. She never had the intention to maintain any friendship with this troublemaker who threatened her way of life, it was that simple.

On a Friday afternoon, as he was preparing to leave, his work done, he heard the receptionist on the intercom, "Dr. Sommers! A phone call for you, sir. Dr. Sommers, line two please."

He picked up the phone, selected the second line and said,

"Hello!"

"Dr. Sommers, this is Isabella. Do you remember me?"

He had recognized the voice of the young girl immediately, but his heart had stopped beating for a whole minute and the emotion paralyzed him.

"Dr. Sommers, listen to me!"

"I'm listening," he said, when he could finally articulate, albeit weakly.

"I must go to New York with my mom, who is very sick. She has a heart problem. I am being monitored very closely. I will be at the Marriott Hotel in Manhattan for a week. My brother, Harry, and my father went out. I took this opportunity to tell you that I haven't forgotten you."

"Where are you now?" asked Sommers.

"I am in Jackson, Sorry… my folks are coming back, I have to go."

Dr. Sommers hung up and sat down on a chair, he felt faint. His legs were shaken by a sudden vertigo. He hadn't ever expected this phone call from Isabella. He stood up abruptly as if propelled by an invisible spring. He was not going to stay at the villa, crestfallen, hoping to hear from Isabella. He was going to New York right away, to see her, talk to her, and confess his love.

First, he called the airport in Biloxi, to book a seat on the next flight bound for the Big Apple. The first class ticket, since he bought it at the last minute, was very expensive. The Continental aircraft would leave for New York at six o'clock, announced the employee of the company. He cast a quick glance at his watch: it was three o'clock, so he must hurry to catch the flight in time.

He telephoned the Marriott Hotel in Manhattan to reserve a room. Then, he went to the bank where he withdrew two thousand dollars from his account. At the Chic Man store he bought two suits, one gray, one blue, black shoes, six shirts with matching ties, socks, and underwear. Everything he needed to be suitably dressed for the woman of his dreams.

His suitcase packed, he returned to the hospital to notify Dr. Morton of his unexpected, but necessary absence that would last one week.

"Do you have an emergency?" questioned Morton.

"I must go to New York for an urgent business matter," said Sommers, without compromising his privacy.

"Is it serious?" inquired the worried Dr. Morton.

"I don't know yet, I hope it isn't."

"Good luck, Dr. Sommers. Come back to us quickly," said Dr. Morton, shaking Sommers' hand

CHAPTER III

It was raining. The downpour had flooded the runway of John F. Kennedy airport where Dr. Sommers landed at nine o'clock.

He hailed a taxi, which got on the highway at full speed, splashing water from many puddles spread over the pavement. The wet streets of Manhattan were reverberated with colorful reflections of illuminated storefronts and dazzling lights of an intersecting, infinity of cars.

The taxi dropped Dr. Sommers off at the Marriott in Manhattan, located at the corner of 85th Street and Albany. The receptionist gave him the key to his room and a sealed envelope. The bellboy led him to his room and received a twenty-dollar tip.

Dr. Sommers was really surprised and intrigued to receive this envelope. Only Dr. Morton was aware of his impromptu trip. Who could have known his whereabouts and about his reservation at the Marriott?

His name had been written on the envelope, and what appeared to be a hesitant hand, in capital letters which he opened. On a large sheet of paper were these few words: *Upon your arrival, please come immediately to St. Thomas Hospital, room # 212. Times Square.*

He quit got himself ready. He wears his gray suit, a blue shirt, a blue tie with grey circles. He returned his key to the reception desk, and was ready to venture out. The girl sitting behind the counter reminded him

33

that he could not venture outside dressed so light. It was very cold, and the weatherman had announced a snow storm for later in the evening.

"I would advise you doctor, to bundle yourself better than that. A coat, hat, and gloves perhaps? Otherwise you risk catching a bad cold."

"I didn't bring any warm clothing. I didn't know it would be necessary. Where can I purchase those items?"

"Wait here Dr. Sommers," the girl told him, "I will take care of that."

The receptionist returned a few moments later with a wide variety of coats on the arm. Sommers chose a blue one, not too dark, and a matching hat and gloves to complete his elegant outfit. He handed his credit card to the girl and discreetly slipped her a tip.

"You are really chic! Said the young receptionist, when he finished signing the receipt. He donned his coat and his gloves.

"Thank you," answered Dr. Sommers.

The doorman opened the door of the taxi that was waiting to take him to St. Thomas Hospital, Times Square. The driver drove off with a bang and eased into slightly chaotic traffic on the snow covered road.

The reception of St. Thomas Hospital was vast and decorated with exceptional luxury objects. A dozen crystal Baccarat chandeliers were suspended from the ceiling by gilded bronze chains, lighting up the room with a soft, tinged blue light which made the decor seem much more sophisticated than it really was.

Solid mahogany armchairs, upholstered leather or velvet furnished the entry. Here and there porcelain vases were perched on pedestal tables and filled with red roses and white carnations. Tintinnabulary crystal chandeliers, flooded the vestibule in a stunning halo of refined elegance.

Hesitant, feeling a little strange in this unusual setting, Dr. Sommers sought eye contact, while peering among the crowd of visitors.

"Dr. Sommers!" whispered a tender, crystalline voice behind him.

He turned abruptly. His astonishment was obvious. An influx of repressed passions forced him to close his eyes momentarily. Isabella was smiling, her radiant smile expressing her joy in meeting him again. Dr. Sommers was paralyzed.

The girl took his arm. "Let's go, doctor! I want to introduce you to my mother."

"Your mother?"

"Don't worry! She has been warned, she is expecting your visit."

He hadn't seen Isabella since the day on the beach. She led him to the elevator. Isabella was wearing a blue suit. Her blond hair was graciously rolled into a bun on her head. Light makeup brightened her face and highlighted the incomparable beauty of her lovely blue eyes.

"You are so beautiful, Isabella!"

"Please don't say that! Carl Sommers, you make me blush!"

Indeed, blood had flocked to her face and her eyes sparkled with excitement and happiness. They entered the room, tiptoeing to avoid waking up the patient who was dozing peacefully. Isabella took Dr. Sommers' coat and hat and deposited them on a chair. At that time, the patient opened her eyes and said, "Are you back, Isabella?"

"Yes, mother," replied Isabella very excited. "I present to you, Dr. Carl Sommers."

"Isabella my darling, please turn on the light so I can get a good look at the intruder."

"Mother!" exclaimed Isabella with a tone of reproach.

"Don't be upset my darling! Sooner or later Dr. Sommers will know the name people in Montjolly call him."

"Come near me doctor! Don't pay attention to my words. Most of the time people use them to hide, rather than express feelings; mine are pure and sincere. As Talleyrand Périgord once said, 'speech was given to man in order to alter his thought.' I am Elsa Morgan. For more than a month, Sir, this young lady here, had only one topic of conversation. Dr. Sommers this, Dr. Sommers that, mother you must meet Dr. Sommers. I am really pleased, despite my miserable condition to make your acquaintance," she said, reaching out her hand to him.

"My pleasure, Mrs. Morgan!" replied Dr. Sommers, shaking her hand.

"Oh!" He said, as he touched Mrs. Morgan hand.

"What's wrong Dr. Sommers?" asked Isabella.

"Your mother has a scorching hot fever. Isabella, can you please buzz the nurse?"

The nurse appeared immediately.

"Will you take Mrs. Morgan's temperature, please?"

The nurse looked at him with a surprised look, but complied with the request anyway. She carefully placed the thermometer under Mrs. Morgan right armpit and waited for the beep.

"I'm going to call Dr. Schulz. She has a 103° fever." The nurse rushed out the room.

Dr. Sommers approached Mrs. Morgan to take her pulse and examine her dilated pupils. He asked Isabella to bring him some ice water compresses, which he pressed to the chest and abdomen of the patient who had nearly fainted.

Then, he noticed blackish spots on Elsa Morgan's temples, under faded traces of heavy makeup, a symptom of a thyroid infection. To be sure, he checked the soles of her feet, which were covered by the same black spots. He left the room, asking Isabella to come join him in the hallway when Doctor Schulz arrived.

"It's important."

"I'll be there," replied the girl a little distraught.

"I'm afraid your mother can't have surgery tomorrow morning."

"Carl Sommers," said Isabella, "when are you going to stop addressing me so formally?" She looks at him with watery sad eyes.

"I am dying to."

"Why don't you?"

"Frankly, you intimidate me. I feel like I am living in a dream, like I am a little dazed. I couldn't even recognize myself ... I even can't tell you how happy I am now, to see you, to talk to you. But, do you know what kind of surgery your mother is having tomorrow?"

"I think it's a surgery to correct a congenital heart defect. If I can remember, it's her ductus arteriosus."

"I understand, now, why the experts have misdiagnosed the bluing of the skin. It's due to a thyroid infection, not a cyanotic state."

"What is a cyanotic state?" questioned Isabella.

"It is also a skin discoloration, but it caused by a lack of oxygen in the blood. Anyway, I took the liberty of calling an expert, my former professor Dr. Peter Grant. He will give you a definitive diagnosis. Then you will know where your mother stands. Go to your mother now. I will wait here in the hallway for Professor Grant.

Professor Peter Grant confirmed Dr. Sommers' spontaneous diagnosis. He called the attending physician Mrs. Morgan and obtained permission to consult the patient's complete record. He ordered immediate treatment to regulate her heartbeat, which had been accelerated by the thyroid infection. Professor Grant ordered a nuclear medicine treatment, to cure once for all, her serious illness, *Exophthalmic goiter.*

Dr. Sommers and Isabella watched the patient all night. The private nurse hired by Harry Morgan was starting the next morning at six o'clock.

They didn't talk, not wanting to wake up Mrs. Morgan, who was sleeping peacefully. They were staring into each other's eyes. Isabella smiled under his insistent loving gaze. She dropped her head blushing. She marveled at these new and scary sensations that enfolded in the innermost regions of her being, providing visceral and delicious enjoyment to her senses. She lost awareness of reality, her soul swimming in a frantic happiness, diving in an ineffable bliss. Around four o'clock in the morning Mrs. Morgan opened her eyes.

"You're still there, sweetie?"

"Yes, mother! How do you feel?"

"My poor heart is not pounding I'm feeling much better."

"You can thank Dr. Sommers. He saved your life."

"I know now, why you have insisted on introducing this 'intruder' into our lives. It was to avoid prematurely losing your best friend, isn't it? Dr. Sommers, I thank you from the bottom of my heart."

"If everything goes well, and I hope it does, you'll be completely healed by the end of the week. I am pleased that Professor Grant has been able to persuade the other doctors to follow a new health plan. Those people, I know them ... they are sometimes more stubborn than mules."

"When you say 'those people', are you not including yourself in the count?" asked Mrs. Morgan.

"Who? Me! I'm not like that," said Doctor Sommers, laughing out loud, which sparked a hysterical giggle.

At about five o'clock, Dr. Sommers left the hospital. He didn't want to meet the agency nurse, hired by Harry Morgan, Isabella's brother. He didn't want to jeopardize the precious moments of pure bliss he hoped to share with Isabella. She was radiant with grace and beauty. He did not want to go away, to leave her for one second. The presence of Isabella exalted his delicate feelings. The stakes were high, especially when love and happiness were on the line. He made the sacrifice to increase his chances of seeing her again.

Although he hadn't eaten anything since his arrival in New York, he was not hungry, this unexpected happiness had ruined his appetite. He got back to the hotel and slept like a baby. The phone rang, waking him around three o'clock in the afternoon.

"Dr. Sommers, this is the front desk. You have a phone call. Wait a minute, I'll connect you."

"Hello! Carl, have I awakened you?"

"I am glad you did. How are you Isabella?"

"Very well. Listen, Carl! I'm going to see my mother. Her condition has improved immensely. The agency nurse leaves at four, so I'm expecting you at the hospital at five o'clock. We will spend time with mother, and then we will go to dinner and catch a

Broadway show, *The Chorus Line*. Sound good?"

"It would be my pleasure, Isabella."

"Okay, so five o'clock, Carl."

He dressed in his blue suit, a white shirt, and a red tie. Carl Sommers, who had never cared about his appearance before, suddenly became particularly aware of his look. The news weather had announced a terrible snow storm. It was even colder than the day before. It was very windy, gusts of snowflakes splashed the faces of the passersby who vainly tried to protect themselves. To avoid ruining his outfit, Dr. Sommers slipped the doorman a twenty, telling him, "The weather is awful! Can you get me a cab?" "Right away, doctor," replied the doorman.

At exactly five o'clock, Dr. Sommers knocked on the door of room 212. Isabella opened the door, smiling and said in a slightly mocking tone, "You look very elegant! Are you always this punctual, Dr. Sommers? Please, give me your coat and your hat."

"I try sometimes. By the way, you are absolutely stunning, ravishingly beautiful."

"My, aren't you a flatterer!" she replied, smiling.

Sommers crossed the large, luxuriously furnished bedroom to the bed where Mrs. Morgan was sitting, supported by some velvet cushions. She was dressed with care, wore discreet makeup, red on her lips and a slight blush on her pale cheeks.

"Our patient has made tremendous strides!" said Dr. Sommers.

Mrs. Morgan, without responding, held out her hand. Sommers kissed her hand with respect and devotion.

"How do you feel, Mrs. Morgan?"

"Since we already are at hand kissing, please, call me Elsa. I'll call you Carl. Agreed?"

"And me, I'm getting jealous," said Isabella, with a mischievous sparkle in her big blue eyes.

"I'm truly embarrassed of my poor manners, but be assured that your warm welcome went straight to my heart. I appreciate very much your kindness. I will be eternally grateful."

"That's strange how people can change overnight! Yesterday, I was unable to articulate a word; today, I have metamorphosed into a skilled orator," said Elsa Morgan, chuckling with laughter.

"Carl," said Isabella, also laughing out loud, "do not pay attention to mother, she is incorrigible, so tongue-in-cheek. She mocks everything and everybody she loves."

"Jokes aside, I haven't felt this healthy in a long time. Thank you, Carl."

"You are embarrassing me even more, let's talk about something else, okay?"

At that moment, the night nurse Isabella had hired entered the room. She greeted them and read the instructions left by the previous nurse.

"Mother," said Isabella, kissing her forehead, "we must go, we will return to spend some time with you after the show." Sommers kissed Mrs. Morgan's hand and left the room, asking the young nurse to take good care of the patient.

Isabella was wearing a pale yellow organdy dress, which showed off her lovely shoulders. The dress was tight at the waist, hugging her svelte figure in a silk mousseline sheath. To protect herself from the cold, she had a red wool coat, a red fur hat, and matching shoes. Her golden, blond hair framed her face like a Madonna.

"You are especially beautiful tonight," said Sommers who couldn't stop staring at her.

"Carl, this is getting ridiculous. How many times do you have to tell me, I am beautiful?"

"All my life," said Sommers, "through time and beyond time." "You are impossible," she responded with a smile.

They crossed the lobby of the hospital, hand in hand, like two lovers. People turned to stare at them. To tell the truth, they were a very nice couple.

The snow fell profusely. The cars were covered under thick blankets of white powder which made them unrecognizable. They went up to the first taxi waiting at the front door.

"John's Restaurant on 12th Street, please," said Isabella speaking to the driver.

"Yes, ma'am," replied the taxi driver.

They remained silent during this brief trip. The car stopped under the awning in front of the restaurant. Sommers helped Isabella get out of the car. Her hand, covered in a red velvet glove, trembled slightly when it leaned on Sommers's arm.

"Are you cold, Isabella?" asked Carl.

"Oh, no! I'm fine, thank you."

Their reservation was confirmed, the maître wearing white smoking gloves, led them straight to their table. He presented them with wine menu and told them that the waitress would be at their service momentarily. The decor was beautiful. Blue Venetian lanterns flooded the room with a bright blue stream of filtered light which reflected off of the crystal glasses, creating a wonderful kaleidoscope effect.

"What would you like to drink?' asked Sommers who glanced at the wine menu vaguely.

"We are going to celebrate this miraculous meeting and the birth of our wonderful friendship with champagne," replied Isabella, pulling back a bit of golden hair that obstructed her view.

"A bottle of your best Lanson and some hors d'oeuvres please," said Sommers to the waitress Maria, who was at the table to take of their order.

"I'm starving," said Isabella suddenly.

"That makes two of us. I haven't eaten since I arrived in New York."

"My mother would have said without hesitation, that you 'Dr. Sommers lives of love and fresh water!'"

"You're more of a prankster than your mother."

"You don't know Elsa Morgan. She is an extraordinary woman, full of humor and vivacity. My mother is an excellent psychologist. She is passionate and romantic. She has been blessed with the gift of intuition. She gauged people the moment she met them."

"You look like your mother, Isabella. I believe that you could possess all her qualities and maybe much more."

"You have greatly disappointed me, Carl Sommers!" she said, pouting. "You are not sure I have the wits and the good nature of my mother?"

"Forgive my poor choice of words, my darling. I don't doubt your intellectual skills. I am absolutely confident in your incomparable beauty of heart and spirit."

Isabella heard only the words *my* darling. These two words went straight to her heart. She blushed and closed her eyes, feeling a little dizzy. She didn't respond, her emotions were overwhelming.

The maître placed a silver champagne bucket on the edge of the table and opened an old bottle of Lanson. He filled the glasses and put the bottle back in the bucket. The waitress then brought a dish of appetizers *bouchée à la reine* and placed it in the middle of the table. "*Bon appetit, ma'am, bon appétit monsieur.* I'll be back to take your order in a moment."

Dr. Sommers stood up and said, "I propose a toast. I raise my glass to Isabella's beauty and the incredible honor she has bestowed upon me by accepting my humble friendship. Blessed is the day I met her on the beach in Montjolly. Toast to beauty and luck!"

They drank a few sips of sparkling champagne and ate the delicious *bouchée à la reine.* Isabella stood up, it was her turn. "I propose a toast. I raise my glass to the friendship and the joy you bring to me, Carl. Since I met you, I have been living in a mild euphoria. I am so happy it makes me cry. Let's drink to friendship, joy and happiness!"

The waitress returned. She waited, notebook in hand, for the couple order. She filled their glasses once again and asked Isabella, "Have you completed consulting the menu? Is ma'am ready to order?"

"Just a minute, Mademoiselle." Then speaking to Carl, "Shall I also order for you, Carl?"

"Of course," he answered without hesitation.

And addressing the waitress, she said, "We will take two lobster tails *à l'italienne* and one dish of mushrooms rice. We can share, right,

Carl?"

"*Ma'am* wants something else? Dessert, perhaps …?" "After dinner, perhaps!" answered Isabella.

"I'm proposing another toast," said Sommers. "As the poet Alfred de Musset said, 'I was wearing my heart in a Sling. Fate one day, put on my route: the most beautiful, the most intelligent, and the most loving girl in the world. With a single glance, she healed my incurable wounds and quieted my unspeakable suffering. I fell in love, crazy in love with her.' Toast to love and happiness!"

Tears welled in the corners of Isabella's big blue eyes. They streamed down upon her cheeks like a rain of pearls. Dr. Sommers wiped out the pearls which flowed along her blushing cheeks.

"Thank you," she said simply.

"At your service, always."

"*Madam* is served, said Maria, the waitress who witnessed this charming love scene. "*Bon appétit*!"

They ate in silence, a little hampered by the presence of the waitress who was attending on them.

"It's delicious! Isn't Carl?"

"Quite."

Isabella, although she said, was starving, ate very little. She just couldn't swallow the food. There was a knot in her throat and her stomach was very tight. She was content to watch Carl enjoying his lobster tail with so much pleasure.

The waitress carried away dishes and glasses, dusted the tablecloth, and presented to Isabella the dessert menu.

"No, thank you!" said Isabella.

"If that's the case," asked Dr. Sommers, "please, bring me the bill."

"Carl! You can't do that," said Isabella when the waitress went away. "You are my guest. This is my treat, don't spoil it please! Guest or not, my darling, I am paying the bill."

The waitress came back with the bill, which he didn't bother to glance at. He handed her his credit card, then he pulled a hundred-dollar bill from his pocket and placed under an empty glass.

They arrived at the theater just in time. The show was about to begin. The dancers were amazing. They were perfectly synchronized. The line formed, moved and changed with amazing symmetry to the rhythm of the frenzied music. Women in short dresses, swiveling breathlessly, were dancing a very daring version of the French *cancan*.

Dr. Sommers had suggested to his companion, that they leave five minutes before the end of the show, to avoid be jostled by the crowd.

Elsa Morgan was asleep when Isabella and Carl entered the room. The evening nurse was leaving.

"How did she spend the evening?" asked Isabella.

"She slept must of the time, but she is doing much, much better. Professor Grant came to see her. He said he is going to try the nuclear medicine treatment tomorrow. It is a very good sign. I wish you a very good night."

The strong voice of the nurse woke up Mrs. Morgan. "You're back, children? I received quite a few phone calls today. Your brother was surprised you weren't at the hospital. Your father blames me because I fired Dr. Murphy, a dear family friend. Dr. Merville, the moron, explained to me, to give me the jitters, that the diagnosis of Dr. Murphy, corroborated by eminent specialists, was my only chance of salvation. That the treatment proposed by Dr. Murphy, based on a rigorously scientific curriculum, offered me the unique opportunity to get cured. In addition, he knew, as one and one make two, that this nag of Isabella had worked this plot to discredit his friends. I also received the visit of Professor Grant, he told me we were going to try the treatment tomorrow. Good! Let's talk about something else. How was your evening, my darling?" "Mother, Carl and I spent a great evening together." "Oh, tell me all about it," said Elsa.

"First, we ate dinner at John's. Carl ordered a bottle of champagne, an old Lanson. We took turns toasting. Then we ordered lobster tail *à l'italienne*. After dinner, we went to see *The Chorus Line* on Broadway."

"Elsa," interrupted Dr. Sommers, "I must make a small, factual correction to your daughter's story. She didn't eat anything, except for a few crumbs."

"Oh, Carl!" said Isabella, in a griping tone, "Have you forgotten all the *bouchées à la reine* I ate?"

"Am I, my dear children, witnessing your first 'lovers quarrel?" laughed Elsa.

"The second mother," retorted Isabella.

"The gentleman has already offended you, darling?"

"I invited Carl out to dinner, but he insisted on paying the bill."

"Ah, yes!" exclaimed Elsa Morgan, laughing. "That's actually a very serious offense. My dear Carl, you must apologize immediately."

Dr. Sommers stood up from his chair, took Isabella's hand and kissed it saying, "I am asking for your gracious forgiveness, Isabella. This pariah has forgotten his good manners. Please accept my humble apologies. But, paraphrasing my colleague, Pierre Corneille, 'I'd do it again, if I had to do it.'"

"You see my dear," said Elsa Morgan, "Dr. Sommers will not let you stand in the way of his gentlemanly duties, not even for your beautiful blue eyes. He is a man of principles. I fully agree with him. But let's change the subject. How do you live in the ruins they call villa Vaudreuil?"

"I have lived alone since my parents' tragic death. I am used to the life of a recluse. When I am tired of reading, writing or studying, I explore the local area, climbing the abrupt cliffs and hiking through the forest. In addition, I found a book of recipes belonging to Mr. Cédric Vaudreuil. I have enjoyed trying to make spirits in the laboratory."

The two women busted into laughter. A hilarious joy shone in their eyes. They laughed out loud uncontrollably.

"As Demosthenes, the great Athenian orator, said, "Did I say some nonsense?"

"My dear Carl," said Elsa Morgan, in a conciliatory tone, "I haven't laughed like that a very long time. I haven't had such a great laugh since Isabella's forced return from Switzerland. She stopped laughing completely and I have missed her infectious laugh enormously. I have a secret to share with you. This Cédric

Vaudreuil whose wine hobby you have inherited, was my father."
"So, the villa is yours," exclaimed Dr. Sommers.

"And everything in there," emphasized Elsa Morgan.

Dr. Sommers was perplexed, looking from Isabella to her mother for a moment. Isabella broke the awkward silence that followed this unexpected revelation of Elsa Morgan. She was radiant of joy and happiness.

"Mother, we must go. Try to rest. Sleep well, tomorrow is the big day." Dr. Sommers kissed Elsa Morgan's hand and wished her a good night. Isabella kissed her mother and left the room accompanied by her friend.

"Carl," said Isabella, "it's late, go rest. We have a very busy schedule for tomorrow. We must be at the hospital as early as nine o'clock."

"Oh, no, darling, I will take you to your hotel. Do you really think I'd leave you alone, in the streets of New York? You're not in Montjolly. Besides, I am a doctor. I am accustomed to waking up at awkward hours."

The taxi dropped them off in front of the illuminated entrance of the Sheraton hotel. Sommers stepped inside the luxury hotel for the first time. He took the elevator with Isabella and led her to her doorstep.

"Good night, my darling," he said, "see you tomorrow." Dr. Sommers waited until she closed the door to leave.

He was already leaving when he heard Isabella's voice in the hallway, "Carl! Are you really going to leave without kissing me good night?"

He joined her nimbly. Taking her in his arms, he muttered softly, "My God! What have I done to deserve so much happiness? I love you, Isabella. I love you so much." He grazed a shy kiss on her soft lips, and she shivered under his light caress. She suddenly pulled away and ran to her room. She double locked her door.

Sommers remained standing in the deserted hallway for two long minutes before leaving. He wasn't going to be able to sleep tonight. He wondered, *why had Elsa Morgan, without knowing him, welcomed him so confidently?* There seemed to be a subtle complicity between Elsa and Isabella which aimed to integrate him very quickly into their sophisticated and exclusive life.

Isabella, an ingénue, timid and sentimental, is trying to stifle her natural modesty, to make me understand, with my intimidated and awkward manner, that she loves me without reservation, despite the taboos and prejudices of her social standing in Montjolly. Me, I don't want to rush things. Elsa, perhaps sensing an irreparable misfortune, had to know me before she could approve of her beloved daughter, the apple of her eye, being in love with me. She fell in love with me, madly, at first glance.

He left his room in the early morning. Since the front desk receptionist at the hotel who had helped him his first day was absent, he spoke to the doorman who directed him, where he could find a men's clothing shop.

"Go down to the corner and take a right, doctor. It's called Schuster and Son. It's renowned for its sophistication!"

"Thank you," said Sommers, sliding a ten in the doorman's pocket.

He bought himself two new suits, a beige, and a brown. He also acquired a brown coat, hat, shoes and matching gloves.

Elsa Morgan was still in the recovery room when Dr. Sommers entered the room the next morning. Dr. Murphy, Elsa's doctor, was conversing with Dr. Schultz in the doorsteps. Professor Grant and Isabella were sitting on the leather couch, eagerly awaiting Elsa's return.

Sommers greeted Dr. Murphy who stood aside to let him pass. The professor stood up to give him a friendly hug. Isabella held out her hand which he kissed tenderly.

"Well, Professor Grant," said Sommers, "was the operation successful?"

"It went perfectly, beautifully! The disturbing symptoms of a cardiac pathology have completely disappeared. The thyroid biopsy has revealed no cancer. My dear Carl, I expected no less of you. Congratulations! Your diagnosis saved Mrs. Morgan's life. My assistant has left me, by the way. Why don't you come to work with me? Your friend Ricardo Ponce mentioned that you were in a precarious situation, a sort of mouse trap, and that he feared for your physical and mental health."

"As you can see for yourself, Professor Grant, the prognosis of my friend Ricardo, does not reflect the actual state of my health. I would not leave this mouse trap for all the gold of Peru."

Elsa Morgan made a very notable entry into the room. She was radiant. She thanked Professor Grant, who reiterated the assurance of a speedy recovery. "Mrs. Morgan," said the Professor, "you will remain under observation for an additional twenty-four hours. I will return tomorrow to release you. These conditions have already been approved by Dr. Murphy."

"Dear Mother," said Isabella when Professor Peter Grant was gone, "It is nearly ten o'clock, and we must go to mass. Dr. Sommers is a good catholic, even in Montjolly he tries to go to mass on Sunday."

"Ah! Now, I understand why Carl has donned his finery today.

You are really chic. How elegant!"

"You flatter me, Elsa."

"My mother speaks the truth, Carl!" interjected Isabella. "Your beige suit contrasts nicely with your brown coat to highlight the radiance of your complexion."

"I am trying, quite simply," responded Sommers, "to dress as suitably as possible, in order to complement the refined elegance of your daughter. In fact, I didn't want to look out of place next to this wonderfully perfect beauty."

Isabella was wearing a pink dress with the silk sequin embroidery of orchid and white carnations. Her white shoes, decorated with small pink flap, flashing light with each step. Isabella took her white coat with fur collar and said to her mother, "See you later mother."

Elsa looked at her with genuine admiration and pride. They were a beautiful couple. A worried smile floated, however, on her thin red lips. Despite her deep apprehension, she was happy to share in the happiness of her daughter. Since returning unexpectedly and forcefully from Switzerland (where she had earned a degree in education), Isabella cloistered herself in a rebellious frustration. She refused to meddle in social life. She lived in isolation and didn't participate in any worldly activity organized in Montjolly. She was languishing in a dark solitude where slowly, but surely her youth and beauty were declining.

Elsa knew that these moments of pure bliss that Isabella was enjoying now would be followed by a bitter period of despair; when she returned to Montjolly, she would no longer freely express her passion and live her love.

The two unequal spires of St. Patrick's cathedral were projecting their two disproportionate shadows on the snow covered pavement. This imposing neo Gothic style building somehow didn't look out of place in the middle of the spectacular skyscrapers of Manhattan.

Isabella and Carl arrived at the Church on time. Cardinal Mahoney, was escorted by two of his acolytes as he walked down the central aisle of the nave, spraying the faithful with holy water. This traditional rite of the Catholic Church, was derived from the Jewish Mosaic law, which ordered sinners to wash their hands and face, before entering the temple of the Lord.

The mass was said in Latin. Isabella prayed fervently and seemed to forget the presence of Carl beside her. They both took communion. When they left the church when mass ended, they saw a group of homosexuals displaying handmade placards, protesting the intolerance of the Catholic Church towards them. The Sunday protests had begun under the now deceased Cardinal O' Connor, when he had kicked out a few members of the gay brotherhood from the Cathedral. They had wanted to display conspicuous manners and indecent behavior to the community in prayer.

Carl and Isabella walked hand in hand down Fifth Avenue. It was still cold, but the wind gusts had ceased. Isabella stopped at few storefronts to admire the new outfits and pieces of the couturiers in fashion. At several places they were invited in to take a closer look at the fine commodities.

Isabella didn't stop at the Tiffany and Co. storefront, a world famous antique jewelry. A bunch of jewelry, arranged artistically in the illuminated window twinkled brightly to attract the gaze of passersby.

"Look, my darling," said Dr. Sommers, holding Isabella's hand.

"What?" asked Isabella, a bit suspiciously?

"You see this beautiful topaz?"

"Where is it?" inquired the young girl vaguely.

"Come here. Look! It is the color of your golden hair. Let's go take a look inside."

"Carl, we can't dillydally. Mother is waiting for us." "It'll only be a minute, sweetheart".

She followed her friend, despite herself. One eager employee came up to them immediately, "Can I help you?"

"I'd like to see this topaz and diamond ring," replied Dr. Sommers indicating the ring with his finger. He took the red setting case from the seller's hands and examined it for a moment. It was a beautiful design by Louis Comfort Tiffany, one of the greatest modern jewelers. He picked it up and placed it on Isabella's finger.

Ignoring the protests of the young girl, Dr. Sommers handed his credit card to the saleswoman who immediately headed for the cash register. She returned a few moments after, handed the card and an envelope to the doctor saying, "We offer our customers two years' insurance on all jewelry purchased with a credit card. In addition, we guarantee for life, the purchase of any exclusive creation of Tiffany.

Your receipt and other paper works are in the envelope. Madam has made an excellent choice!" said the saleswoman smiling.

"Carl," reproached Isabella, when they left the jewelry store,

"You shouldn't have done this."

"Why not, sweetheart? You don't like the ring? It is very pretty."
"You know very well what I mean. It was not necessary. It's too much."

"I saw that you don't wear any jewels, my darling, so I am offering this ring as a symbol of my deep and eternal love. Please accept it, as a symbol of my cherished love. My heart has been in pain for too long, and this will help heal it and make it pain free."

During their trip back to the hospital, Isabella didn't open her mouth. She was visibly upset. She felt she had encouraged Dr. Sommers to make this costly purchase because of her frivolous curiosity.

Isabella kissed her mother, who was sitting on the bed reading a newspaper, while waiting for their return.

"You look upset, my darling. What wrong? You didn't argue with Carl again, did you?"

"See, Mother," exclaimed Isabella, holding out her hand to Elsa. "I tried to dissuade Carl from buying this extravagant ring, but he didn't listen. He never listens to me."

"Oh! What a pretty yellow topaz, honey!" Elsa exclaimed, grabbing her daughter's hand. It is a beautiful jewel, a work of art. The topaz was set in an oval golden basket, surrounded by six cut diamonds that enhanced the incomparable beauty of this goldsmith masterpiece.

"Darling," said Elsa to her daughter, in a serious tone. "Darling don't be upset by these trifles. You have to enjoy these happy moments. I want you be cheerful and carefree. I want you to enjoy this time of bliss. It's exhilarating miracle of a new growing love. Enjoy it!"

The nurse brought dinner to Elsa and placed it in on a rolling tray table next to the bed. The food gave an appetizing aroma to the room. She then pointed out to Mrs. Morgan that the hospital, on Sundays, offered a snack to visitors.

"We haven't eaten a thing, Carl and I." "Are
you interested, children?" asked Elsa.

"What are they offering today?" asked Isabella.

"A fatty liver patty, anchovy fillets sautéed in olive oil with a heart of artichoke with dressing."

"It sounds good to me. We will take it," said Isabella to the nurse. "For two?"

"For two," replied the girl.

The atmosphere was relaxed. From time to time, Isabella threw a furtive glance at Carl and smiled shyly. She blamed herself for not having accepted, in a burst of affection, Carl's generosity, the invaluable symbol which now sealed their love forever. She promised herself she would apologize to him when they were alone. Isabella had acted like a spoiled brat. She had had a stupid reaction that she bitterly regretted now.

Isabella Morgan, of sensitive and noble lineage, with a refined education, had committed this insulting error twice by refusing the generosity of her friend because she thought he was broke. Isabella was convinced that Sommers was not able to afford this costly expenses without going into debt. Simon Morgan her father, had told his wife this baloney to justify the presence of the intruder in the villa Vaudreuil. Isabella was afraid Carl could run out of money again. That was the reason Sommers had accepted, for a meagre compensation and accommodation at the villa, to give up his contract with the hospital. That was the false version Simon Morgan gave to his wife, mocking and denigrating the poor intruder.

When dinner arrived, they ate a little. Elsa, who was feeling much better, deployed her eloquent verve to tease and brighten the lovers' mood, but especially Isabella whose watery eyes reflected a deep sadness. Elsa was trying to erase the dark veil which misted the eyes of her beloved daughter.

Dr. Sommers suddenly said, "I asked myself and I still wonder, why you both have given me this warm welcome and expressed so much affection and kindness, not as a friend, but as an important member of your family? I am still baffled. I know now, and I have learned to appreciate during these past two days, your heartfelt generosity, but I am still intrigued. I would like to know why."

The two women stared at each other a moment in silence. They had the same big, blue eyes shaded by long lashes. Elsa had light brown hair, Isabella was blonde. Isabella's face was a little more elongated than her mother, and yet they looked surprisingly alike.

"Sweetheart," said Elsa Morgan to her daughter. "Go ahead."

"When I met you on the beach that Sunday, I was stepping out of the house for the first time in about three years. I had borrowed my mother's car. I wanted her to come with me, but she pretended to be under the weather so that I could get acquainted anew, to myself, with nature and the world.

"Observing this archaic tradition bequeathed by the old pioneers, nobody frequents the beach on Sunday, the day of rest and prayer. Since my return from Switzerland I never went anywhere, not even at church. It was a beautiful morning. I felt like I was breathing for the first time in my life, the heady, composite, intoxicating smell of the city. I went around the new neighborhoods and then headed to the beach.

"I was coming back from a long walk on the burning sand, when I saw you, looking more frightened than me. Your big, brown eyes, they fascinated me. I was entranced and I was about to faint. With great difficulty I broke the spell and ran to my car.

"Everything then, became muddle in my head. I know that you took a picture of me, I remember you writing your phone number in my book … and your words were engraved in my memory, *I've finally found you! I will never lose you again.* These words tormented my thoughts on my way back home. *How come? How this person that I met for a brief moment can become the only thing I am think about?* I was confused. I was afraid, distraught, my heart experiencing feelings and sensations I have never known before.

You came back quickly, my darling! Mother told me when I walked into her room to greet her. *Have you seen a ghost?* She said.

You don't look well. Are you okay?

It's nothing, Mother, I replied in an effort to smile.

Your vision haunted me at night. For the first time in my life, I was afraid to sleep alone in my room, so I decided to just tell my mother everything.

Don't panic, my darling, said my mother. *This man has made an impression on you, certainly, but you don't know him.*

You're right. I do not know him, but I know who he is.

What do you know? Who is he? Elsa asked me.

He is the intruder, Dr. Carl Sommers.

Ah! Things get complicated. Do you know how dangerous this can be for you, sweetheart? It's not worth it. It's just an infatuation, it will fade away in a few days. I am sure of it. You will forget this man and all of problems and hassles this will cause for you and for me. You see, she said taking me on her lap, *I shouldn't have let you locked yourself in this golden prison. You had a crush on the first man you met, a complete stranger, someone who is an outcast in our society and hostile to our way of life.*

I was obsessed with your image. I saw you everywhere during the day and every night I dreamed of you. Without saying anything to mother, I started to do research. Thanks to my friend Lisa, who works at the Hospital St Cécile, I got a copy of your job application. There, I found essential information that allowed me to continue my investigation. After fifteen days of careful investigation, I handed my mother a report.

The Intruder

Name: Carl Roger Sommers
Born August 15, 1981
City: Jackson (Mississippi)
Father: Paul Erik Sommers (writer, journalist)
Mother: Monique de Foix (French journalist)

Primary education: The Franciscan Fathers (86 - 92).
High school: Idem. (92 - 96).
University of Notre Dame (96-2000)
Harvard University (2000-2004)
Boston Hospital, Massachusetts: Residency, Neurology (05-06)
Patrick Henry Clinic, Virginia: Residency, Surgery (06-07) Character traits: Very reserved, studious, passionate reader, no friends, no social life, and rarely seen in public, movies rarely.
Hobbies: Mountaineering and walking. A loner according to his fellow surgeons.
For unknown reasons the death of his mother and father from their burning house was never classified as a murder nor an accident, Carl was ten years old when it happened. This tragedy wounded his soul for life.

Rescued by aunt Hélène (aunt of his father). She works hard and even sold her house to pay for Carl's expensive school fees and placed him in very exclusive institutions. But unfortunately Aunt Hélène died a few days after his graduation as surgeon and his degree in neurology.

On the paternal side, there are no other relatives known.

Maternal side, the French branch

Monique Thérèse de Foix, born into an old French Traditional family whose nobility dates back to the time of the Crusades. She cuts ties completely with her parents after marrying Paul Erik Sommers.

Gaston de Foix, her grandfather, deceased. The mother of Monique (grandmother of Carl, the widow Simone de Foix) still lives in Brittany, the region of Côtes d'Armor, in Saint-Brieux.
His uncle Gérôme is an old bachelor, he is the one who manages the family estate. His aunt Joelle, married Hugues Simonet and has two children: Hubert and Mireille.

You are terrible, Mother told me when I handed her the folder. She read attentively and asked me what I wanted to do. *I want to meet him mother,* I replied. She wiped the tears that flowed down my cheeks and told me simply, *be happy because you are not afraid to live and suffer.*

"And that is why, Mother and I welcomed you with open arms, without reservations. I will not regret whatever happens in our relationship. You are and will always be my only love."

Isabella's story had plunged Dr. Sommers into deep, dark thought. The memory of the tragedy that had taken away Papy Polo and Mama Mo, as he called them, had been awakened. His heart twisted. Sommers had buried at the bottom of his memory, any reminder of this tragedy, which had taken away his happy childhood and his most valuable treasure in the world, the irresistible smile of his mother Monique.

He tried to maintain his composure, but his eyes filled with tears. This wasn't how he wanted to reveal how much that his past affected him. It didn't occur to him that his open vulnerability made him more human, and cemented the feelings Isabella already had for him.

Elsa broke the melancholy sadness that had invaded the room, saying, "Children, you will need to include me in tomorrow's schedule. I am leaving the hospital. I am glad to share the happiness of my darling daughter, since in making it happen, I found health and joy. Carl, I thank you from the bottom of my heart. You are a friend, no a son and you are a lucky man. You have found another mother who will love you and watch over you."

Dr. Sommers stood up and kissed Elsa on the forehead saying simply, "Thank you!"

Elsa had encouraged Isabella to tell the moving tale of her first encounter with Carl, to mitigate the false impression of her reluctant refusal to accept any gift from her impoverished friend.

"I am going to freshen up," said suddenly Isabella, walking toward the toilet.

"You don't need to," said Sommers, "You are beautiful just the way you are."

"Flattery! 'I want to be the most beautiful girl to go dancing' just like in the song of Sylvie Vartan. Carl, tonight I want to dance."

"I haven't danced since my mother's death. "Said Dr. Sommers

"Then you must. You have a new partner and I am an amazing dancer. I will help you. You won't make a fool of yourself in the ballroom."

"Goodbye, Mother," said Isabella, kissing her tenderly. "We will come back to see you after the ball."

"Goodbye, Elsa," said Sommers kissing her hand. "Thank you again. Your words soothe my heart. I don't deserve this outpouring of love and kindness that you have bestowed upon me, Elsa, but I'll make myself worthy of your confidence, and make you proud of your new son."

The "FIESTA LATINA" nightclub was the place to be in New York. Famous actors, Manhattan's elite, and anyone who could afford to spend thousands of dollars in an evening, came out there.

Four orchestras were playing that night. *Los Meringuitos* from the Dominican Republic, *Salsa Nueva* from Puerto Rico, *El Caballo Negro* from Acapulco and *La Sonora Mágnifica* of Cuba. Isabella had reserved a table close to the dance floor. She had bought the tickets in advance to avoid spending more of Carl's savings. The ticket included food and drink.

They chose a creole dish: grilled pig with a very spicy sauce, fried plantain, cornbread, rice with mushrooms. They drank piña coladas and Barbancourt rum with Coke.

Isabella danced divinely. Elsa had taught her to dance and regularly hosted balls at the "Petit Palais" the residence of the Morgans, a wedding gift from Cédric Vaudreuil to his daughter, Elsa. Isabella studied piano, choreography and dance at the Ursuline Boarding School in Zurich, Switzerland.

Isabella was alive. She did not leave the circular dance floor where over five hundred couples could dance at the same time. She was tireless, despite the obvious lack of training of Carl Sommers; he demonstrated, however, an innate aptitude for the art of Terpsichore. *Los Meringuitos* had a smash hit with their frenzied terse pace *ritornellos*, repeated by the mob that literally shook the entire room.

A little tipsy and stunned by the infernal noise of excited dancers, Isabella finally became very tired. They left the ballroom around ten o'clock.

As soon as she sat in the taxi, she leaned toward Dr. Sommers and kissed him on the mouth by saying, "This kiss is to ask you to forgive the fuss I made this morning. This token of your love, I'll wear it always. Have I told you, Carl that I am madly in love with you?"

"I cherish your love, Isabella. I love you infinitely," answered Carl kissing her back.

She leaned her head over Carl's shoulder briefly, and then she grazed a stealth kiss on the corner of his lips saying, "This kiss is for the love of life that you revived in me with a single glance."

"Hola, lovebirds," shouted the taxi driver, who had witnessed a touching moment of love in the rearview mirror, "you must abandon the nest. We arrived destination."

Dr. Sommers helped Isabella out of the car and handed the driver $20 bill, by telling him to keep the change.

As they entered Elsa's hospital room, Isabella saw her sitting, anxious and pensive, and realized instantly that something was wrong. "What's wrong, Mother? You look upset," she said while kissing her mother's cheek tenderly. "Are you sick?"

"No, sweetie, I'm not sick ... just kinda bored."

"What happened? What has put you down? Did you get bad news from Dr. Grant?" asked Isabella.

"Your father called. He'll be here tomorrow. He is coming to pick me up. He said it would be, more convenient, to spend my convalescence at the Petit Palais. He told me that the businessmen have signed the contract with the factory, and left Montjolly. So now your brother is free to come to New York. But what makes me so angry is the fact that they both lied to me.

"After I spoke to them, I called Amelie (the housekeeper) who confirmed their arrival in New York tonight at eleven o'clock. They were already on their way.

"They want to surprise us. They are suspicious because of Isabella's abrupt decision to accompany me. My dear Carl, you must shorten your stay. They should absolutely not know you were here. Come, give me a kiss. Whatever happens, I want you to know that I am ready to do everything possible to ensure the happiness of my daughter."

Isabella followed Carl out of the room. As soon as she was in the elevator, she threw herself at him and wrapped her arms around the neck of her lover weeping. He tried unsuccessfully to comfort her. "I don't want to lose you, Carl!" said Isabella sobbing bitterly. I can't live without you now. What will become of me?"

This outpouring of love, this irresistible passion, this profusion of boundless affection expressed without restraint by this woman threw him in an indescribable distraught. "Listen, sweetheart, I'll move heaven and earth so we can be together forever. I promise you that here and now. Go to your mother's room and call me at the hotel in twenty minutes. Try to be calm honey love, don't cry, it breaks my heart." He hugged her tightly in his arms, kissed her passionately, and left the elevator, walking to the exit without looking back.

Isabella, with her red watery eyes, sat down near Elsa, buried her face in her mother's shoulder, and continued sobbing. Elsa, restless and silent, tenderly caressed her daughter's hair.

CHAPTER IV

The Petit Palais had been put under wraps since the languishing illness of Elsa Morgan. It had jettisoned into a veil of sadness and melancholy, its darkened façade welcomed the soul of the home, coming from the shores of a deep lethargy.

The unexpected and forced return of Isabella from Switzerland, where she was studying had significantly compounded things and plunged the whole house into silence and darkness.

Isabella invited some personalities of the city, guests, long standing friends, and their parents to a welcome home party; a gala evening, to celebrate the miraculous healing of her mother.

The Petit Palais was a miniaturized replica of the Palace Sans-souci in Potsdam. Cédric Vaudreuil had built it for his daughter, Elsa.

The residence had twenty rooms, including: a theater, a reception room, and a gallery of Venetian mirrors, where masterpiece paintings and works by renowned artists were displayed. The antique furniture was of the Regency style, but the capricious chinoiserie of Thomas Chippendale dominated the décor of the home.

A French garden surrounded the building, flanked by two pagoda shaped turrets. The garden was decorated with clumps of orchids and daffodils. It was adorned with marble fountains where topless naiads soaked their toes in the crystal clear water of the circular pool. Statues of the nine muses ran along the main facade, giving this princely mansion the look of a Greek temple.

Elsa, looking radiant in a water green silk gown and emeralds, received her guests under the porch, accompanied by her husband, Simon, in a smoking suit, proud as Artaban.

The contractor, Max Hollemberg, and his wife Joyce, were the first to present their greetings to Elsa. They congratulated her on her beauty, and handed her a string of fine pearls, as a token of their friendship, and their eternal gratitude.

Indeed, it took the intervention of Elsa to compel the Montjollian municipality to accept the eight hundred South African families fleeing their country after the fall of the apartheid regime. Max Hollemberg was the leader of the African clan.

A continuous parade of guests followed: the retired Admiral

John Dexter and his two daughters, Paula and Amy; the sheriff Al Linden and his wife, Lucy. Cathy and Joan Morgan, her sisters-in-law; the high school principal, Nancy Morice; Lisa Troy, Isabella's friend who had given her Dr. Sommer's information from the archives of the Sainte Cécile Hospital; the assessors of the Town Hall; Joe Crampfort; a lot young people, friends of Harry Morgan and many others.

Valets in livery led the guests to their seats and bustled around the tables, arranged in a horseshoe, leaving an empty space in the middle of the vast reception room.

The musical ensemble, Roma, animated the evening, and was already playing songs from Bohemian folklore to brighten the mood of the eager guests.

A round of applause greeted the entry of Elsa Morgan in the reception room. Everyone stood to greet her. She sat down at the table of honor where, Admiral John Dexter, Max Hollenberg and his wife, Joyce, Joe Crampfort, and the two Simon sisters, Joan and Cathy Morgan were already sitting.

Champagne was served and Simon Morgan offered a toast to his wife. "A fairy godmother has used her magic wand and has brought happiness and joy back to the Petit Palais. Thank God for

his incredible grace. Let us drink to Elsa's health."

The entire party repeated the toast, "To Elsa's health."

They ate with gusto. Cathy Morgan was astonished by Isabella's absence and made an enquiry to her brother, who replied vaguely, because he didn't know what to say. Elsa kept a prudent silence. Matt Potter, unlucky rival of the Mayor in the last municipal elections, personal friend of Harry Morgan, insisted relentlessly, and wanted to know, yes or no, if Isabella would be joining them?

"I have no idea, dude," said Harry, a little pissed off by the bizarre behavior of his sister. "I'll tell you a secret, my dear Matt. For more than three years, Isabella wouldn't talk to me."

"You're kidding! Impossible!" said Matt Porter incredulously. "Three whole years, no way. What did you do to Isabella?"

"Father and I went to bring her back from Switzerland, after her Bachelor degree in education. She wanted to continue her studies and earn a Ph.D. But we had found out that there were some undesirable elements at the boarding school in Ursuline. We didn't want her to follow the bad example of her cousin, Michelle Morgan, who abandoned the community as soon as she completed her education."

The Roms, the band who was playing softly during the meal, took a break and left the room.

During their absence, the murmur of conversations intensified and filled the reception room with confused hums. The beautiful Lisa Troy, Isabella's girlfriend, taking advantage of this interlude, came over to Elsa.

"Where is Isabella?" she asked.

"She will be here, Lisa, don't worry!" Elsa replied.

The musicians took their place on the podium. Renalto, the conductor, adjusted his microphone and announced with emphasis, an invitation to the dance floor. "We dedicate this first waltz to Mrs. Elsa Morgan, wishing her a full recovery."

Simon and Elsa opened the ball, greeted by the enthusiastic applause of the guests. Soon the dance floor was crowded. Young people, a little tipsy from the wine that was flowing in abundance, were enjoying themselves madly.

About ten o'clock, the music stopped abruptly, to the great disappointment of the dancers who protested loudly. The conductor, Renalto, approached the microphone. "Ladies and gentlemen, I have the honor and the pleasure to present to you Miss Isabella Morgan who will interpret, the Sonata No. 14 in c sharp minor, Clair de Lune of Beethoven, the piano trio No. 1 in c by Brahms, with Jean-Luc at the cello and Manolo playing the violin (two musicians of the Roms).

A shining smile on her lips, the dazzling beauty, Isabella, made her entrance in the reception room wearing a pale yellow and silver sequined dress that molded to her wisp waist. Her only jewelry was the topaz and diamond ring given to her by Carl Sommers.

She received a standing ovation, fit for a queen. She greeted the audience with an elegant curtsey and sat at the piano.

The audience was in awe, stunned by the first chords. Her nimble fingers slipped on the ivory with grace. She filled the silent room, with a wonderful and rhythmic stream of music.

Since her return from Switzerland, and to avoid sinking into the bitterness of despair and boredom, she devoted herself to the study of piano. Every morning, after her father and her brother departed, one for the plant, the other for Town Hall, she locked herself in the small theater of the Petit Palais, where she spent hours and hours practicing.

Matt Potter was mad at his friend, Harry Morgan. "How come you never told me that your sister was such a fine musician? She can compete with the greatest pianists in the world. Her performance is polished, flawless, and extraordinary."

"It is one of the reasons why father didn't want her to pursue her studies in Switzerland. She had already received offer, a contract to play with the Philharmonic Orchestra of Bern."

"How could you?! How could you stop her from pursuing her dreams, a career? That's unforgiveable. Plain and simple," continued Matt Potter, offended. "That's why she didn't to talk to you! If I was her, I would have done worse."

Brahms first piano trio, in C, is an incomparable masterpiece, full of nostalgic reminiscences and dreamlike premonitions. The sumptuous and sad melody backed by plaintive violin accents and the languorous leitmotiv of the cello wasn't lost on the amazed public. It was a poignant exaltation of the passionate soul of the artist.

Elsa, alone, among all that were there, could appreciate its value. The gradual evolution of Isabella's talent had been revealed this evening in a dramatic explosion of intuitive feelings.

The chrysalis, once enclosed in a cocoon of absurd frustrations, prejudices, and taboos, transformed under the deep desire of a requited love, a passionate and sensual creature. Her artistry, once suffocated by the constraints of a monotonous life, had suddenly been released in a sublime apotheosis. Isabella was evolving in the sphere of the divine, transported on the mysterious wings of a passionate love.

Enthusiastic applause was everywhere. People came to compliment and kiss her hand. The ball started again with even more liveliness and excitement than before. Isabella danced with everybody. Her brother wondered, puzzled, about what had happened to his sister. He had never seen Isabella so petulant, so joyful, so passionately dazzling of beauty, so lovely and high-spirited.

Matt Potter, timidly, tried to revive his courtship with the young woman, but Isabella, smiling, told him, "Don't insist. I can only offer you friendship," she said, "nothing has changed, I can assure you."

About three o'clock in the morning, Elsa took leave of her guests and retired to her room. This wasn't, however, the end of the party. Some young people, still a bit tipsy, lingered a bit, until daybreak. So did Isabella's good mood.

Simon Morgan was surprised to find his wife and daughter dressed and gloved, waiting for him to go to mass. Those ladies, for more than three years, didn't set foot outside the residence. They had remained cloistered all that time; partly due Elsa's illness, but mainly to protest Isabella's forced return home from Switzerland.

Simon Morgan made a very spectacular entry at the Church that Sunday. Ostensibly supporting his wife, he went to sit in the first row, proud as a peacock. The parish priest, Father Ted Vogel, greeted the lost sheep and promised to sacrifice the fatted calf to celebrate the return of his prodigal children.

When the religious service ended, everyone came congratulate Elsa how well she looked, and to wish her a speedy recovery. Nancy Morice, the high school principal, took advantage of the occasion, to repeat the offer she had made to Isabella, to help as a music teacher. She insisted so much and so well, that the other ladies present, speaking on Nancy's behalf, convinced the young woman to accept this position as a volunteer. Isabella now had a credible excuse to leave the house every day, without the paranoid suspicion of her brother.

Elsa and Isabella went down to dinner. Simon who suffered, without being able to complain, the categorical refusal of his wife and daughter, to participate in the daily activities of the family life. He thanked them warmly for finally burying the hatchet. Harry, sitting in front of Isabella, noticed the topaz ring on his sister's finger. He did not know she wore this piece of jewelry exclusively since her return from New York. He knew that his sister loved beautiful adornments and he was surprised by her sudden sobriety in this matter.

He couldn't figure out why Isabella had had a change of heart. He noticed that she was glowing. He saw a romantic wistful tenderness in her blue eyes and became suspicious.

Simon, speaking to his daughter, said to her, "I think you're going to need your car to go to the high school. I'll ask Jules to fix and clean your car."

"I will not use that car. I never did," said Isabella.

"But, in the meantime, until I can buy you another ..."

"I'll walk to school or borrow mother's."

Harry, who thought that his sister had glossed over her misdeeds, concluded now, at her refusal to use the car their father had given her (a Porsche Cayenne) on her return from Switzerland, that Isabella would never forgive him. She had made peace with her father, for Elsa's sake. She had a sense now of how painful it must have been for her mother, who had done everything to support her, even pushing away the man of her life.

Usually, Isabella ate little. Since meeting Carl Sommers, she hardly ate at all. Her father noticed and commented, "You don't feed yourself enough, you'll ruin your health."

She replied dryly, "I am old enough to take care of myself."

Simon didn't insist. Harry, however, was left perplexed, He couldn't explain the sudden metamorphosis of Isabella. He remained convinced, absolutely convinced, that something drastic had happened in New York. Isabella had morphed from hostile, shy, naïve, and respectful, into a sneaky, contemptuous, unforgiving woman who exuded confidence from every single one of her pores. Nothing escaped the innate insight of Harry Morgan.

The unexpected arrival of Simon and Harry Morgan in New York had prematurely interrupted the romance of the new lovers and put an abrupt and painful end to their magical enchantment. Isabella and Carl were immersed into a delightful and divine rapture.

They had agreed to a secret location where they could safely communicate on a regular basis. Nevertheless, they recognized the risks posed by this plan in a town as Montjolly.

In the early days of her convalescence, Elsa had to go to the city of Jackson every 15 days for lab work. Isabella had suggested rest area 23 on highway 49 as a dropping spot to Dr. Sommers. After this period, they knew that the situation would become exponentially more complicated, but they relied on love's proverbial ingenuity and the inexhaustible resources of a woman in love, to overcome the difficulties and barriers they would encounter on their way.

For three years, Elsa and Simon slept in separate rooms. Elsa had closed her door to her husband since the night of their daughter's return from Switzerland. Isabella was desperate, disconsolate, even attempting suicide.

Elsa had threatened to leave Montjolly, the xenophobic and racist bastion, which wallowed in a stupid and foolish pride. Cédric Vaudreuil, travelling at that time, intervened to ensure that his daughter remained until his return.

Cédric never came back. The commotion caused by the disappearance of the Aventura, the yacht of the ship-owner, and the feverish efforts to find him, had caused Elsa to put her plan on the backburner. Elsa had wanted to leave Montjolly and go live elsewhere with her daughter.

Waiting for a happy ending, Elsa's anguish and grief never rose to the level of Isabella's disappointment. The crisis, though a little healed, remained latent, despite this tragedy which struck the mourning family.

Things had ended in a status quo. Elsa's disease had worsened the situation. The gap between them grew more each day and had endangered their love and their privacy. Elsa's spectacular recovery was credited to having brought the reconciliation of the couple. Having fallen in love herself, Isabella understood, finally, the magnitude of the sacrifice she had imposed upon her mother, keeping her away from the man she loved. She had, therefore, taken the first step to help her parents reconcile and contribute, so slightly, to repair the wrongs her own choices and vindictive character had caused to her parents.

As soon as her father returned home from the office or the factory, she left her mother's room to leave the field open for him, so that he could court Elsa assiduously. Isabella then locked herself in her room to read. Sometimes she went to the garden to take care of the orchids.

She had not seen Dr. Sommers since his return from New York. She counted the days and already anticipated their date at rest area 23, planned in advance in meticulous detail. To prepare for all eventualities, she had announced to Nancy Morice that she could no longer work at the school on Friday.

It was raining. Isabella drove cautiously. Spring was blooming, the trees donned their greenery. The bare shrubs overlapping timid buds were flowering alongside the road. Some black clouds obstructing the horizon, had been dispersed, little by little, swept by the north wind, which was very strong this season.

Isabella stopped the car in front of the main building of rest area 23 and nimbly entered the main hall which served as a restaurant, souvenir shop, postal office and more.

As soon as she entered the room, Dr. Sommers, who was waiting at the lookout, grabbed her arm and guided her towards the small vending machine room.

He hugged her tenderly, pressing her on his heart and kissed her lightly on her lips. They stayed silent, entwined in a long affectionate embrace. Then, Dr. Sommers broke the loving embrace saying, "Here's the key to the 23 postal box where you will find my messages. When and where it will be possible to meet you Isabella, my love? Here is the manuscript of the first sending. Be indulgent, don't criticize my writing too harshly."

"I love you, Carl," she replied simply, "but what can I do, my love? Do you think I can spend days and days without you, without seeing you, without talking to you? The torment of Tantalus, the punishment of the Danaids were less harsh in comparison."

"What do you want me to do. my darling?" asked Sommers. "Do you want us to run off together? What will your mother say? I know she wouldn't support this."

"Dear Carl! Come with me to Jackson. We will spend the day together. I know it would be a meager compensation for the happy time we had hoped to spend in New York."

"I can't, darling, my love! I have two surgeries which can't wait."

"I must go," said Isabella, unable to contain her frustration. "Elsa is waiting for me. I'll think about it, we will talk later, my love." She kissed Carl and ran away. She didn't have the courage to stay longer without crumbling.

"See you soon, my love," shouted Carl Sommers, confused and wondering about Isabella's strange behavior.

"I thought you were going to stay a little longer with Carl?" Elsa told her, seeing her returning running.

"If I didn't rush out, I wouldn't have had the courage to leave. What does that mean, mother? Can you explain what's happening to me? I don't understand, I am troubled and confused."

Elsa burst into laughter. She laughed breathlessly. "Mother, how ...," said Isabella," Are you mocking me?"

"Oh, no, my dear," replied Elsa, still laughing. "Are you asking me to explain your feelings to you? I know and you know, my darling. You have simply fallen in love and you have lost your mind, naturally."

"Watch out! Isabella, you are driving too fast!" cried Elsa. "The Vaudreuil family women are excessive, demanding and passionate in love, but faithful unto death. I am pleased you have inherited the blood and the temperament of a Vaudreuil; it makes you suffer, but it makes you happy. I was as impulsive and impatient as you, sweetie, but you, you have to be much more levelheaded than me, because the circumstances are not the same. Promise me, sweetheart!"

Dr. Carl Sommers would have liked to go to Jackson, but he had two urgent surgeries in Biloxi. He was, despite his desire to spend the day with Isabella, taking the route in the opposite direction. Not willing to attract the attention of Harry Morgan's spies, he rented a small car, less showy than his yellow Cadillac, known as the white Wolf, in the vicinity.

Isabella was now moving at a moderate speed. She had not answered her mother nor promised anything. She was tense. She was on edge. Her gloved hands gripped the wheel, shaking slightly.

"Why did you put yourself in such a bad mood, my darling? Everything will work out fine, I promise. Besides, if you don't calm down, I won't go to Jackson with you anymore!"

"You can't do that to me, mother! I should have insisted and compelled Carl to go with us to Jackson."

"See, Isabella," said Elsa, "that was an emergency. Two people's lives were in danger."

"Look in the rearview mirror, mother!" said Isabella suddenly.

"Don't look back, use the mirror."

"What? What is going on? I don't see anything," said Elsa.

"Your husband and your son are following us."

"Why didn't you say *my father and my brother*?" retorted Elsa in the same mocking tone.

"You see, my dear, in retrospect, aren't you glad Carl's refusal spared us this mess? If Carl had followed you to please your watery blue eyes and your provocative smile, he would be in big trouble. Carl is wise and thoughtful; you must trust his judgment." "I thought, said Isabella, "that they had to be at the factory? Didn't they have to run payroll. Isn't that what they said, mother?"

"I am going to have a serious talk with Simon about this constant surveillance. This is not the first time that I have caught them spying on us. Are we prisoners? Why aren't we able to move freely? He has some serious explaining to do."

"Mother, I don't want to be the cause of any trouble between you and your husband. You have already suffered enough."

"But Simon knows, mother! He took your threats seriously. My father is well aware that you are capable of anything. What are they afraid of?"

"Don't worry, sweetheart, I'm going to hold my rifle on the other shoulder from now on; I'll carry my wand."

Harry who was driving his father's car, kept a respectable distance, thinking that the ladies didn't see them. One hour after Elsa's arrival, the gentlemen came into the clinic. Elsa was ready to leave, having finished with the laboratory technicians.

"What wind brings you here gentlemen? I thought you were retained at the factory, said Elsa.

"We arranged otherwise, I didn't like the idea of Isabella driving six consecutive hours with this ugly weather." After the storm, the road became slippery and very dangerous.

"I'm not a wimp, father," answered Isabella, a little irritated. Don't be condescending, father, don't patronize me. I am old enough now to fend for myself. I can get home all by myself."

Simon did not want to engage in any dispute with Isabella, knowing that his wife would lean on the side of her daughter, and no matter what he said or did, he would lose. "I am taking you out to eat," said Simon, to get rid of his embarrassment.

Elsa ate well. Isabella ate nothing. She was too upset. She had cherished the hope of having a good time in the company of Carl. That dream was extinguished by the professional obligations of her lover, and now the hated presence of Harry Morgan. Her happy day was lost.

Simon had taken the wheel of his wife's car. Isabella curled up in the back seat and remained sullen and silent during the journey back. Harry traveled alone.

Isabella was dying to read what Carl had written, but she had to curb her impatience to avoid arousing the suspicions of her father, who watched her in the rearview mirror.

She feared, not without reason, that a fight with her father could jeopardize the effort to overcome all the difficulties inherent to her particular circumstances; he could prevent the maturation and realization of her love.

Isabella had conjured some complicated scenarios and devised some absurd plans, whose execution required too much sacrifice for Elsa and too much hassle for her. She could go to South America with Carl, living in hiding and anonymity. But how could she leave her mother? She couldn't ask her to run away with them. Harry had threatened to kill her if she fled Montjolly. He would not tolerate that his own mother stigmatized the Morgan family and imposed such a shame on him in particular. She knew him capable of anything. Isabella was afraid of her brother and would avoid, as long as she could, any confrontation with him.

"Are you comfortable, my darling?" asked Elsa suddenly, interrupting Isabella's evocative daydream.

"Yes, mother!" she replied. "I'm fine." Isabella sprung up, moved into a more comfortable position on the seat and resumed her idle reverie, which was only momentarily interrupted.

She was picturing herself in Carl's arms at the Fiesta Latina club in New York, dancing a stunning meringue. She had never felt so happy, so exuberant, so full of life and so profoundly joyful. The souvenirs of her wonderful time in New York overwhelmed her senses. She remembered Carl scent, Barbancourt rum, communion together at St. Patrick's Cathedral. She remembered their wandering, hand in hand, on Fifth avenue, where Carl had bought her this beautiful jewel, her magnificent topaz ring. These cherished memories and sensations brought back a stream of emotions and a flood of happiness.

Upon arriving at the Petit Palais, Isabella left her mother and retreated to her room. As soon as she arrived, she double locked her door, even though she knew that nobody would bother her, Isabella took the large envelope Carl had given her, sat comfortably on her bed with two pillows behind her back, lit the lamp on the nightstand and immersed herself in reading the first love letter.

March 7

My Love,

The flowers didn't wait for the spring sunshine to bloom this season. They needed only the warmth of your love and the incomparable brilliance of your blue eyes. Nature is jealous of your beauty. Everything seems dull and sad without you here. The memories of our short stay in New York are my only refuge, my only consolation. I am living more than for you, I am living more than by you, I am living in you. I can't concentrate on my work, your beloved image haunts me day and night. The softness of your lips transports me into a sphere of prohibited happiness, reserved for the gods.

Did I ever tell you that I am madly in love with you? That my life, like that of Orestes 'has taken a new phase.' I was born the day I met you on the beach, more beautiful than Aphrodite. My eyes were opened to the beauty of the world. My heart, with your love, morphed into a burning bush whose sacred and unquenchable fire will burn for you all eternity and beyond. I love you, Isabella. Should I say it again and again, a thousand times? I love you, Isabella...

Under the headings of premonitory secrets, in the mysterious codex of fate, well before you were born, love, growing in the glow of fertile promises, had inducted your soul, sovereign of beauty and virtue. You are the living reincarnation of the goddess Aphrodite. But this sublime metempsychosis in an ineffable astral sphere, beyond the random beliefs of pagan mythology, has produced this outstanding, beautiful human being as the dawn, to quote the psalmist, passionate and righteous, who bought me life with her love.

Praxiteles died in grief comparing you to his mistress, the courtesan Phryne, who served as the model for his Aphrodite of Cnidus. Pygmalion would have not embraced the cold lips of his marble statue, he would not have needed to seek the intervention of Venus for her metamorphosis from sculpture into the beautiful Galatea. He would simply love the authentic goddess, in this case, the divine Isabella, who exceeds all in grace and beauty.

And Phidias! The poor Phidias, whose fame died with the complete disappearance of his classical masterpieces, would not have permitted that his Aphrodite was transformed into a Venus de Milo, if he had known you.

I thought that luck had led me to Monjolly, I was wrong. An irresistible force brought me here, holding me, despite the difficulties. As soon as I saw you on the beach, I realized that my destiny was going to be here, that all my life would now be devolved to make you happy.

I came to Montjolly, for the first time, the day of the inauguration of the Sainte Cécile Hospital. Then, I saw a jubilant city that seemed welcoming, a picturesque, flowering town that seduced me immediately.

I now know why I stubbornly refused to leave, despite my disappointment, the flagrant hostility of Dr. Merville and the humiliating contempt of the mayor.

I dare at night time to walk through the deserted streets filled with intoxicating scents. The town grew around a very original architectural design. With the risk of being mistaken, I believe it was designed on the model of the labyrinth of Knossos. The mazes of truncated streets, oblique impasses on each side of a wider and deeper deadlock, hermetic arteries, and seemingly dead-end streets make traffic very risky.

My night hikes helped me to appreciate the conceptual idea of this fun topography and eccentric architectural aesthetic of private and public buildings. Some buildings attracted my attention: the small castle of baroque style in the deadlock of orchids, surrounded by a magnificent garden à la française; the villa of the impasse of chrysanthemums, with colored glass windows like a Venetian lantern; and the manor house at the top of Daisies Street, that amazingly resembles a typical residence of the ancient barons of Britain.

Those three days in New York completely changed my life. The tragic disappearance of my mother, had weaned me from any true affection, despite the efforts of my old aunt Hélène, who impoverished herself literally, to provide me an excellent education in the country's most exclusive institutions.

I had become a misanthrope. I lived in people's company, without seeing them, isolating myself in a terrible resentment against mankind. I didn't belong to that crowd, which had nourished the murderers of my parents. They were cruel and unworthy of my care.

I spent more than two months, lying on the floor, prostrated, desperate, not wanting to eat anything. It took Aunt Helene's tenderness, her maternal affection, to pull me from this morbid state of resigned despair.

At the University Notre Dame, they called me the cantankerous misogynist. I systematically refused to participate in any activities beyond those imposed by the curriculum. I never talked to the girls and I rejected, with contempt, any brand of friendship, wherever it came from.

I rendered everyone responsible for the death of my parents, especially white people. I studied, only, because my aunt had persuaded me that it was the only way of booting a defeat to these racist criminals, these loose and fiendish Klux Klux Klan, who had killed my parents by burning their house, disapproving of their interracial marriage.

Isabella, my dearest love, you have given me a second lease on life. My happy childhood, memories repressed for twenty years, hidden at the bottom of my heart, have come alive again. Sometimes, plunged into an excessive state of dreamlike meditation, I confuse your beloved image and that of Monique, my mother. Your tenderness has awakened in me the feelings and sensations that I thought was forever lost. Your affection and your sweetness erased an eternity of bitter sorrows that weighed heavy on my bruised heart.

Your love takes an incredible miracle or a liberality of fate. Could this be a hereditary atavism in the Sommers? My grandfather Erik Sommers married the most beautiful girl in the town and was forced to flee to avoid been lynched. My father married a Breton Princess, despite formal opposition from the family, Foix, but paid with his life and that of his beloved, this bold recklessness.

Our love, our wonderful love, will have a much better fate, I'm making you an oath. I'll move heaven and earth to fight the ridiculous prejudices that prevent us from living our love on the open.

My love, my cherished love, embrace Elsa on my behalf. She showered me with maternal affection, and her contagious good humor has thawed my icy, dark heart. My gratitude and my affection grow day by day. I will never forget the warm welcome you gave me, me this stranger, this intruder. Tell her that as long as I live, even beyond that, I will feel eternal gratitude toward her. My life will now be devoted entirely to make her daughter happy.

The next morning, Amélie, the housekeeper, came to wake Isabella up. She found her still sleeping, dressed, surrounded by a dozen sheets of paper scattered on the bed. She opened the curtains and the morning sun flooded the room. "Mademoiselle is not going to mass today?" she asked Isabella, who was dazzled by the profusion of light.

"What time is it, Amélie?"

"Madame is already ready and waiting for you downstairs in the garden."

"Tell her that I will be ready in ten minutes." Isabella put the yellow dress with sequins she had premiered in New York to go to Church and to the ball at Fiesta Latina, and put on her brown shoes with high heels.

Her mother was surprised to see her daughter being ready so soon. Amélie had told her that she had just woken up. "Sweetheart," Elsa told her, "why don't you put on some jewelry?"

"Of course, I have," hastened Isabella, by showing her mother the topaz ring.

"You know very well what I mean?"

"For now, mother," responded the young woman, "that's the only jewelry I am going to wear. This ring is the pledge of love that I have always dreamed of."

At the end of the mass, and as he had used to do previously, Simon Morgan went to his sisters, Joan and Cathy, who lived at the Villa Morgan on White Lilies Avenue. These ladies were offering, according to an old tradition bequeathed by the pioneers, a light snack to a few friends, a few parents, who came to learn about the activities of the city and feed on derogatory anecdotes, slanderous gossip, which the African colony, (i.e. the South Africans) little accustomed to the puritanical and rigid orthodoxy in use, was, for the most part, paying the costs.

People got the news of the imminent arrival of the daughter of entrepreneur Max Hollemberg, the alluring Mona Lisa, fresh and fully fledged from the music conservatory of Paris. She proposed to open a music school in Montjolly.

"That Matt Potter, once again, broke his engagement for lusting," said a nasty tongue. "The Hollemberg's millions is a valuable lure."

The Morgan sisters published the local weekly newspaper: The Montjolly Gazette. It was the only source of public information, as there was no television or radio. Some public buildings were equipped with phone, such as the hospital, police station, fire station, school, town hall, the Gazette office, the presbytery and many factories receiving orders from the outside. The settlers' council had rejected two or three times, the request of young people to introduce the use of computers in schools and in public institutions.

The Montjollian society lived inward-looking much like the colonial plantations of the old south. Modern civilization only penetrated with parsimony and unwillingness. The community readily adapted to this kind of life, simple and sophisticated at the same time. Young people, especially those who had experienced a different culture, either at the University or in a school of technical education, sometimes rebelled against these absurd restrictions, or often left to seek fortune elsewhere.

The council of elders, long before the construction of the new hospital, had sent six young men studying medicine to three great universities renowned for the excellence of their education: Oxford, Harvard, and Princeton. Their studies completed, they declined the tempting offer to come back to work at the Saint Cecile Hospital.

The elders didn't want to change their archaic lifestyle, despite the drawbacks that this presented to the community. Even with the growing and alarming number of talented defectors recorded, the settlers' council categorically refused to make any concessions. The council was opposed to any change.

Elsa gave Simon the signal that they should head home. She hugged her sisters-in-law and promised to visit them more often.

When they arrived home, Harry was waiting for them to eat. Elsa went in her room to remove her hat and get rid of her lace gloves. The cook had prepared an entrée of Baked Eggplant and Gruyère. Harry waited until the maid had left after pouring the wine into the glasses, to start the conversation.

"Father," he said, in a surly tone, "I have received a note from Dr. Murphy."

"Everything has been taken care of, hasn't it?"Yes, of course. But something intrigues me, father. Professor Peter Grant, according to Dr. Murphy, will not accept payment from us. He said that his was obliging a colleague who solicited his help."

"Mother, do you know Professor Grant?"

Elsa did not respond to her son's question and took a drink from her glass of wine.

"What's the problem, Harry?" asked his father. "If Professor

Grant seeks no payment, it suits us, doesn't it?"

"On the contrary, it complicates things."

"But how?" Simon insisted with a short and impatient tone.

"First your wife should answer the question I asked her."

Elsa kept her silence and watched, from the corner her eye, the reactions of her daughter on her guard, tense, ready to pounce or explode.

"Professor Grant's assistant is none other than the intruder, the so-called Dr. Carl Sommers, with whom your daughter went to dinner at John's Restaurant, the most expensive in Manhattan, and out to dance at Fiesta Latina, a popular night club in New York."

"No, that can't be true!" exclaimed Simon Morgan in a wrathful voice.

"This scatterbrained, Isabella, wants to debase us, shame us, make us the laughing stock of Montjolly, outcasts."

Elsa and Isabella maintained a stubborn silence. Isabella had blemished under the insults of her brother. A cold anger narrowed her sad, blue eyes and her breathing became laborious. But she retained her phlegm, sitting calmly in front of Harry who was vituperating his mother and sister relentlessly.

"Mother! How could you tolerate Isabella in her depravity? It is a humiliation for the family." Saying those words, Harry banged the table with his fists, with all his strength, moving glasses, splashing everyone with wine and water.

"Simon, said Elsa in rising, "ask this idiot to leave my table immediately. I've had enough of his boorish behavior."

Harry Morgan still wanted to protest, but his father took him by the arm and led him into the adjacent room.

"Yes, sweetheart," said Elsa to her daughter. Your brother's idiotic behavior has ruined my appetite. Let's go change."

"Have you lost your mind or what, Harry?" his furious father asked him. "Have you no respect for your mother? You're impulsive and stupid. Is there anything in that hollow head of yours? Do you think you can fix everything by force? You won't put me at odds again, with my wife, like the last time. Your mother, may escalate the conflict and create for us a lot more hassle. You'll apologize to you mother immediately, on your knees, please. Then just join me at the library."

Elsa was sitting on a stool in front of her dressing table, walnut wood supporting three beveled mirrors, brushing her auburn hair, when Harry knocked on the door of her room. She told him to enter. He rushed to his knees begging his mother to forgive him. He promised, taking God for his witness that this will never happen again.

Elsa knew that her son, so proud, so pretentious, would have never came by himself to apologize. "Get up, Harry!" She told him, "I am not mad at you, but don't be as uncompromising and harsh with people who love you. You might find yourself all alone in life and very miserable, despite your fortune."

Then, he saw in the mirror, Isabella lying on the bed, looking at him with contempt, a wry smile at the corner of her lips. She was witness to his humiliation, his disappointment. His pride had taken a blow. He vowed to get revenge, to make Isabella pay for her arrogance. He stood up, crestfallen, promising his mother to better behave now.

Harry Morgan was in a very bad mood. He went to the library to meet his father. He alleged that his father doesn't want to support him in its fight against the ladies, who want to undermine the tested Foundation of the community. They want to establish, (with a few dissenting elements, ready for anything), egalitarian and democratic heresy advocated by liberals and fools.

Harry tried to convince his father of the seriousness of the situation. "Mother and Isabella have deliberately provoked this meeting with the intruder with a spirit of antagonism, as if officially accounting, the opening of hostilities. My investigators have told me that mother was aware of everything and she seemed to be the instigator of the plot.

"They want us to pay for the interruption of Isabella's studies in Switzerland. They have introduced the wolf into the sheepfold."

"I don't believe it," retorted Simon Morgan, who had listened thoughtfully to his son's rant. "I don't believe that they have deliberately developed this Machiavellian plot. No! They took advantage of the presence of this individual inside our walls to engage this litigation process, but above all, to instigate the Foundation of a new social contract, one of demographic diversification, (contrary to the standards established by the pioneers), to adopting the revolutionary behaviorist concept of equality.

"Father," said Harry, taking a conscious and thoughtful air, "It is necessary to eliminate this threat at all costs."

"What do you mean? Come on, what are you saying?"

"I say it and I mean it. Carl Sommers must disappear. This is like the sword of Damocles suspended above Montjolly's head; it is a bomb ready to explode and destroy everything."

"Are you crazy or what?" said Simon Morgan, rising from his seat. You're completely insane. This doctor Carl Sommers has taken his precautions, his lawyer is at the top of the situation and now, the intruder has intelligence inside our territory: Isabella. If you touch one hair of the intruder it will certainly end of our privileged lifestyle.

"So what can we do? Said Harry with a voice that trembled with anger and rage... Are we becoming incapacitated? Unable to put a brake on these Mephistophelian machinations?

"Do not forget that, we have the hands and feet bound. This idiot: Craig Harris (former Mayor) by soliciting funds from the Federal Government to finance the infrastructure works required by the exponential development of the city; put us literally, under the control of the provincial authorities.

"In any case, it is necessary that Sommers receives a severe correction for having touch my sister with his dirty hands... This dirty nigger... I hate him... He must pay very profoundly for his bold, weird audacity.

"Beware Harry! Don't make any foolishness, any crazy nonsense. This will not be like the last time... Do you hear, do you understand what I mean?

"Don't worry, father, I'll be careful.

In addition, said Simon, have you met Max Hollemberg daughter? Mona Lisa a beautiful girl... She is a very nice suitor... By the way, it is time you think seriously to settle down, you're not getting any younger.

Harry left the library, pretending to haven't understood the veiled allusion his father made in reference to a matrimonial project he envisaged for him.

CHAPTER V

Living the rest area 23 where he had this brief interview with Isabella, Dr. Sommers was driving along on his way to Biloxi, at the wheel of the small rental car. At midway, he crossed Simon Morgan and his son who were driving full speed in the pouring rain, in the direction of Jackson. They appeared to be eager to catch the ladies who had taken a substantial lead.

Dr. Sommers welcomed his wise decision, having resisted the tearful pleas of Isabella. She wanted him, at any price, to accompany her up to Jackson, where they could spend the day in tête-à-tête. Isabella had fled rest area 23, running and very upset. The categorical refusal of her friend to comply with her urgent injunction; unpleasantly surprised the girl who believed owning an irresistible ascendancy over her bashful lover.

Sommers was not ready, yet, to confront his opponents: The Morgan, the city authorities and the racist population of Montjolly. Also, he took some precautions to avoid unnecessarily provoke these people, before finding a weapon able to neutralize them. Quite simply, he wanted to fight his battle with the people, without alienating the affection of his beloved.

He went, immediately arrived at Biloxi, to the rental agency. The formalities once completed, a driver of the agency drove him to the Hospital where he recovered his yellow Cadillac. He went on, when he remembered having left his Kit in the surgeon's room. He parked the car outside the front door of the hospital and hastened to go retrieve his Kit. Mikado on the lookout for one such occasion, crept nimbly under the ajar door and spring on the floor, at the rear seat.

Anxious and pensive during the trip back, Sommers didn't noticed the presence of the cat only when he get in the villa Vaudreuil's courtyard. Mikado feeling a climate of security, came to sit in the front seat mewing of satisfaction. You came back? Said Sommers, definitely you don't like the atmosphere of the hospital... you prefer, like me, the quiet life of the countryside...

Are we going to eat something? My dear Mikado, I am starving.

Sommers opened a box of sweet condensed milk, added a cup of water before heating it in the microwave. He poured into a Bowl at the bottom of which were two slices of bread. He put the jam in a saucer and placed the food on the small carpet in plastic, in front of Mikado's favorite sofa. Good appetite, he said, I'm going to cook something for myself.

Mikado took possession of the premises again, having not forgotten his habits, he settled on the couch and fell asleep, almost immediately, the sleep of the just. At the first opportunity, Sommers bought a bucket of sand for the cat, so he could sleep in the morning.

During the week, he visited twice the rest area 23, but he found nothing in the letter's box. He did not know that Harry Morgan had discovered their secret, and exercised a strict surveillance on all the comings and goings of Isabella.

On Sunday night, about nine o'clock, Dr. Sommers donned his sport sweatshirt and went exploring the new areas, inhabited by the South African colony. The streets were a bit broader than those of the old city, but possessed the same outdated characteristics. Cottages, as found in the English countryside, along the streets of floral appellations, which exuded an obstinately intoxicating scent.

Other streets lined with welded constructions joined at the ground floor, but, ended in oblique and separate on the top floor, as in the old districts of Bruges, destroyed by German bombing during World War II.

Sommers sailed along the avenue of Gladiolus where a lane of yellow and white lances, led to each house located at the end of a rustic garden.

Tired, Sommers turned left on Tulip Street to begin his descent to the highly inclined slope that leads to the avenue of Daisies.

Arriving at the intersection of the avenue of Daisies and Tulip street, Sommers turned left again to go back home. He was immediately surrounded by five solid guys. One of them, he recognized, at once, by his likeness with Elsa Morgan. He apostrophized him on a crusty and nasty tone:

"What are you doing on our streets? Dirty nigger! Were you not ordered to stay in your den? You will pay dearly, nigger, your cockiness... How! You have dared touch my sister with your dirty hands? You have dishonored my family...You're going to die, dirty nigger, disgusting, loathsome scum.

Dr. Sommers kept silence, nerves tense, the senses on alert, he was trying to find a way to escape. He pushed suddenly one of the men who blocked the passage and bolted at full speed in the direction of the villa.

The five men rushed in pursuit. Sommers used to race, was gaining ground on his pursuers. Harry stopped and motioned to one of his men to go and take the car parked not too far away.

Sommers was thinking while running. He realized that he could not support this pace until he reaches the villa Vaudreuil. Therefore, he moved towards Rose Avenue, thinking to protect himself from the threats of these bandits, hiding in the hospital.

Harry Morgan guessed the bold maneuver of the intruder who demonstrated agility and exceptional courage. Harry Morgan, seeing his prey almost escaping; alleged to have underestimated the possibilities of Sommers. Harry Morgan accelerated desperately, turned abruptly on Rosehips avenue and lunged right on the closed hospital Sainte Cécile barrier. Sommers was already trying to climb the fence, when one of the bandits who accompanied Morgan in the car, went down quickly, jumped on the hood and captures Sommers leg. Dr. Sommers swung a terrible kick to the face of his assailant who dropped laying at full length on the floor. Harry Morgan jumped in turn on the hood of the car and grabbed with all his strength, Dr. Sommers legs. The other three pursuers out of breath, climbed on the gate. Dr. Sommers tried, anyway to grab the top of the fence, but the beatings he was receiving on his body, finally made him give up his stubborn resistance.

"Help! Help! Cried Sommers being really afraid... The streets were deserted and

Silent. Nobody came to the rescue.

They kicked him badly, before tying him tightly, like a crab, to a tree bordering the sidewalk. Two of Harry Morgan's henchmen, pulled their three strips of leather whip, armed with lead beads attached to the tip.

The two executioners struck in turns. Blood spraying at every shot they took at Dr. Sommers body. Long bloody furrows dug into his back. His flesh torn, gathered in fine shreds at the lips of the deep wounds. Dr. Sommers faints at the fifth shot, he could not endure this excruciating pain.

The headlights of a car suddenly resulted in halting this horrible scene. The executioners, surprised, hesitant, suspended their cruel job and seemed to be panicking by the approach of this inconvenient witness.

Dr. Joe Merville, called at the hospital for an emergency, got out of his car:

"What's going on here? He cried loudly. Damn it! It's you again Harry Morgan? Clear off now!

"Keep whipping! Said Harry Morgan with a loud and authoritarian voice.

Dr. Merville pulled his revolver from his pocket and waving it at the nose of the factotums of Harry Morgan, said to them: one move, you're dead. The cowards didn't hesitate one second, and ran without warning. Go away you also, Morgan or I'll kill you like a mad dog.

"You can't, uttered angrily Harry Morgan.

"You are, a murderer… I hoped that you did not killed this one, as the individual of the last time... evacuate immediately or I'll not give a damn of your life. Said Merville aiming his gun in his direction.

Harry Morgan, didn't insist, reverse and fled at full speed. Dr. Merville remained a moment bewildered by recognizing Dr. Sommers. He ordered his driver to pick up an ambulance in the courtyard of the hospital. They laid carefully, Dr. Sommers on a stretcher and carried him in the ambulance.

Follow me he says to the driver to whom he handed his car key. Dr. Merville headed, to the villa Vaudreuil where he entered, using the key he found in sommers pocket. They carried the wounded man to the ground, in the middle of the living room.

Dr. Sommers was still passed out. Dr. Merville undressed him and found, with anger, the devastation inflicted by the lead beads. He repaired the damage to the best he could; closing the vivid gaping sore lips, with stitches or staples and covered them all with a dressing. He gave him an antibiotic shot.

Dr. Sommers, then woke up He felt a stabbing pain in the back and shoulders. He bit his lip to contain the shout in his throat. Do not turn on your back, said Dr. Merville. I did what was needed. A few scars will remain, but, they will fade away progressively.

"Thank you said Sommers in a slurred voice. Thanks a lot.

I'm thirsty, can you please, give me a glass of water?

Dr. Merville sent his driver Julien, fetch Simon Morgan. He apologized to his wife who reproached him the fact that he was never home. Day or night you will find a pretext to desert the penates and leave me alone!

What do you want to insinuate, beloved Elsa?

I am not suggesting anything. I just noting that you are away too often. A true statement that's all.

I promise you, my dear, replied Simon, your devoted husband, now on, will spend much more time with his love.

You better keep your promise!...

Come and see, said Merville, when Simon entered the villa; the wonders of your son. If I didn't get there, by miracle, we would have a corpse on our arms now.

"You say that Harry is the assailant?...

"How! Simon! You still doubt my words?

You should get used to the idea that your son is a killer... Yes, a killer who has already slain, three people that I know of... We cannot exonerate him each time... It is necessary that you take severe measures against this man; otherwise, you risk, you also go rot in prison. It is the advice of a friend...

The three men hauled Dr. Sommers in his room. Dr. Merville administered him a strong dose of painkiller to reduce his suffering and allow him to sleep. Merville promised to come to see him the following day.

When they were gone, Mikado who had taken refuge under his

couch, reemerged and took the guard at the bedside.

The next morning, as promised, Simon Morgan and Dr. Merville came to visit the wounded. They found him sitting on his bed upside down. Dr. Merville renewed the dressings and gave his diagnosis: a speedy recovery. He recommended to Sommers some exercises to avoid any permanent stiffness of the skin and help the bruised muscles retain their elasticity.

Simon Morgan came to question Dr. Sommers about his intentions, more specifically, on his decisions, maybe already taken to seek revenge against his son.

Because denouncing Harry to the federal authorities would be, ipso facto, an unequivocal denunciation of the whole Montjolian community and his unorthodox lifestyle.

These legitimate approaches would lead to the cancellation of the oral contract. This would put us in an untenable position with the local population, which is at a thousand miles away to suspect the extreme precariousness of their endemic existence.

Simon Morgan embarked on a passionate argument to try to convince Sommers of the need to postpone the inevitable verdict, to give him time to prepare the people for the catastrophic upheavals that would befall the city and its inhabitants.

I am not trying to excuse the crime of my son. I regret bitterly that the odious conduct of this monster could not be punished now, with utmost severity. But, given the circumstances, Dr. Sommers, I ask you to rise above human conventions, to show generosity, selflessness, magnanimity, not towards my son, but toward those bigots, thousands of them would die of despair, of shame, if you removed suddenly, what they considered the most in the world: the atavistic pride of their supposedly superior race.

I understand what you're saying, Mr. Morgan, said Sommers. This individual almost kill me, and I am afraid that he is a recidivist, he could get me one day, if I stayed any longer in this rabid den. I am not seeking revenge, but, I think I have paid, quite expensively, the right to protect my life and all those who such a retrograde and criminal philosophy, put at risk. I will no longer be both accomplice and victim of this insane society.

I give you, Dr. Sommers, formal guarantees, that nobody, will try to undermine your life. Dr. Merville and I, took the necessary steps to ensure your safety. I beg you! Dr. Sommers, grant us this favor, we will avoid this disappointing debacle. I swear to you that you won't regret your generosity... Now, nobody will spy on you, you are free to communicate with who whatsoever, provided it be done discretely...

For more precautions, Dr. Sommers, intervened Dr. Merville, I'll get you another shot. Don't worry too much, the healing process has already begun. You are young and healthy, in a week, at most, you'll be on foot.

I will let you know my decision in three days. I need to reflect and to consult my lawyer

I beg you, Dr. Sommers, hastened forward Simon Morgan, I beg you, don't speak to anyone about the incident... to anyone. .it could result in devastating consequences for you and for me, in particular.

They helped Dr. Sommers to descend and took leave of him. Dr. Merville promised to return the next day to survey the wounds. Sommers feed the cat, and drank a glass of orange juice.

It was evident, now, that Simon Morgan knew about his escapade in New York; according to his insistence to emphasize his formal obligation of confidentiality on the criminal incident which he had been the victim. He knew that he was communicating with Isabella who especially ought to ignore the cruelty of her brother.

Sommers telephoned Dr. Morton to tell him that he was prevented this week from coming to work. He asked him to schedule his surgeries for the next week. He called his friend Ricardo, to say nothing of importance, just to hear a friendly voice. He spent the rest of the day reading and dozing off.

Humiliating and painful scraped that he had been administered by the minions of Harry Morgan, had plunged Dr. Sommers into a frustrating dilemma.

Revenge against Harry Morgan, (which could go rot in prison), put him in open conflict with the entire family. This approach would expose the city to vicious scrutiny of nosy activists. The inquisitorial harassment of journalists on the lookout for scandal. The ridiculous laughter of well-intentioned people and the hypocrite bigots.

Revealing the existence of this archaic society, immobilized in an illusory bygone, enclosed in a cocoon of prejudices and ridiculous taboos, without a preliminary psychological preparation, would be imposing a collective punishment, with all its traumatic rigor, to the entire Montjolian community.

The shame that would result, (because the press would not fail to cover them with ridicule), might alienate the affection and esteem of Elsa and the passionate love of Isabella. He was torturing his brain to foment weird syllogisms whose false premises still referred him to the same unacceptable conclusion.

The brilliant dialectic deployed by Dr. Sommers in his solitary cogitations, could not convince him, himself, of the validity or the consistency of his problematic synthesis.

His lengthy cogitation was most often expressed in abstruse ranting with no concrete connection to the reality of his situation. Sommers didn't give up yet, and hoped to find a solution to the crisis. His love was at stake, his life depended on it.

A week after his mishap, Dr. Sommers took his courage in both hands, and arming themselves with two mirrors, looked at his covered back striated with long scars. Dr. Merville had done his best to repair the damage caused by the swift beating by the bandits of Harry Morgan.

He remembered, then, reading in the book note of Cedric Vaudreuil, an ointment formula recipe, capable, according to the author, delete in a few days, the deepest scars.

Illico presto, he went to the library and opened the secret drawer of the glass cabinet. He immersed himself in reading the recipe and went up to the laboratory to search in the varied inventory accumulated by the ship-owner, looking for the ingredients he needed to succeed this medicinal preparation.

Sommers immediately began to work; measuring, mixing, grinding in the small wood mortar, the recalcitrant roots and grains of rye; adding aloe, garlic and other ingredients.

The preparation cooked in a water bath turned into a sticky, yellowish substance with a strong smell of herbs and spices. He added flavorings, of plant resin perfume.

Sommers plastered his back with the slime and, bare-chested, continued to read other recipes contained in the voluminous notebook.

The ointment was dried on his back. He felt a terrible itch, an irresistible urge to scratch, which bothered him fairly. He concentrated more on his reading.

Using his mannered writing skill, embellished with flourishes and arabesques, Cédric Vaudreuil had chronicled, in this valuable book, one of his adventurous trip aboard his yacht: Aventura.

We hastily left Cartagena, my companion and me; wrote Vaudreuil, as bandits hired by drug traffickers wanted to steal our precious loot. Systematic excavations we made in the Renaissance Cathedral, and above all, in the Church of the monastery of Saint John of God, had produced an unexpected result. In possession of a rich archaeological treasure, we returned to the Aventura and sails to more hospitable water along the Peruvian cost.

We went in Callao, a port best equipped and the busiest of Peru. My friend the colonel Francisco Bilbao who resided there, offered me the hospitality in his beautiful countryside villa.

Colonel Bilbao lived as a prince in his superb red brick villa, surrounded by a beautiful garden. He treated me royally. He commits three girls to my service. Fed me exotic and delicious food; made me drink cocktails of his composition, strong enough to cut your small intestine. I spent a wonderful week in Bilbao's abode. I had, like Ulysses in Calypso Island, I had to exercise violence upon myself to leave this idyllic Eden and the three nymphs, three languorous Calypso who were taking care of only me day and night.

Leaving the Aventura in the custody of two sailors, I proceeded to Cuzco where I had an appointment with a native antiquarian, specializing in the sale of pre-Columbian bronze statuettes.

A friend had recommended him. His name was: Santiago Cordoba. He had a solid reputation of honest businessman and competent... Arriving on the scene, I learned that this individual had been arrested for fraud. He made, all antiquities that he was selling to museums and collectors.

Frustrated and upset by the turn of events; cursing myself bitterly to having wasted my time in a disappointing trip; reluctantly I initiated my journey back to the ship at the wheel of my rental Land Rover Defender.

I had not travelled 100 meters, when a man, wearing a faded color poncho and a large sombrero that hide his face, waved his hands to stop me.

What do you want from me hombre? I asked him in a gruff tone. I can tell you where you can find what you're looking for, replied this guy, approaching the car. How do you know? I saw your disappointment at Córdoba shop, Señor.

I looked the man in the eyes a moment, hesitant to catapult myself, once more, in a mad adventure. The man supported my gaze, then, I motioned for him to ride in the vehicle. Where are we going? I asked him point blank. To Machu Picchu he replied calmly.

The Land Rover easily ascended steep and unpaved slopes. The narrow way bypassed the peak of Machu Picchu bordered by a dangerous cliff. At some distance from the summit, on the edge of a rocky outcrop, the man who was with me! Ugolino his name, showed me an embedment in the flank of the mountain, where I parked the vehicle.

We continue on foot, he said laconically. I took my leather jacket (because it was really cold at this height) and crept in my pocket my revolver, to be ready for all eventualities.

I followed Ugolino for 10 minutes on a narrow path that descended down the side of a cliff. We arrived in front of a cavity obstructed by intersecting branches. Ugolino moved some, and we went in a sort of rectangular gallery, apparently without issue. Without hesitation, Ugolino crossed the dark cellar, and drawing with both hands on the rough wall, hit a toggle joint and a section of the wall cleared a fairly wide opening.

The opening closed as soon as we were in the cramped hallway, which extended the gallery. Ugolino lit a resin torch and proceeded in silence.

Arrived at the end of the corridor, he repeated the same maneuver, he had made in the gallery, this time however, the wall turned on itself in unmasking a staircase which was sinking into the mountain.

Soon, we were in a circular hallway, lit by torches planted on the ground. Ugolino walked to a bronze gong hanging from a hook in the wall and knocked five strokes with a wood mallet resting on a sort of rudimentary stool. He waited a minute and struck four times on the gong sound. At intervals, he strikes three, then two, then a great shot and deposited the mallet.

A door opened, immediately. A dazzling light blinded me, momentarily. This profusion of light seemed to come from a break on the high Vault's cellar ceiling.

Ten colossi armed with spear, blocked us the passage. Ugolino pronounced, then, something, that was without any doubt, the password, and the men sided with respect, in both sides of the door, ready to escort us to a personage seated on a throne at the end of the large room.

Welcome, Señor Vaudreuil, to the refuge of the Inca emperors, he said, smiling. I am Emperor Yupanqui XV, son of the rising sun, undisputed master of this empire usurped by the Spanish invaders. The time finally came, he continued to recover for the slave nation, the ancestral heritage.

I have selected you, among many others, to help me accomplish the mission that fate invested in me since the beginning of time. The ancestors's spirits have imposed you to us. We must trust you.

I stood amazed, stunned. But you don't know me sir? I articulated in a hesitant voice. I do not think I can help you achieve your grandiose and revolutionary projects... I'm only a poor ship-owner without political ambition.

I course the seas as a dilettante, aimlessly as a wandering Jew.

Señor Vaudreuil, continued the emperor Yupanqui XV, the task that the ancestors entrust you, requires no particular talent, or a personal commitment in the struggle of the Mayan people against his old age enemy. The signs of destiny are visible in the stars. The avatar of Viracocha (the civilizing God of the Inca nation) is among us. He is the one, the ancestors want you to protect for a time, until he can take in hand the helm of power and destiny.

Come, said Yupanqui, standing up, you must be hungry. The guards of honor holding high their ivory spears surrounded the sovereign and escorted him with a ceremonial deferent slow pace, to a contiguous room, less spacious, but richly decorated.

We sat down on lama skin's pillows, posed on the ground. Emperor Yupanqui uttered a few words in his vernacular language and one of the guards went out hastily. He returned a few minutes later, accompanied by a veiled woman and two teenagers. The woman made a brief bow and sat down to the left of the ruler. The girl, all intimidated by my presence, sat without saluting; the boy joined his palms on his forehead, bowed his head and came to stand in front of the emperor.

Young maids, armed with jugs, tubs and towels, washed the hands of the guests. We ate in silence. They served a wide variety of dishes, each more tempting than the other. The food was served in vermeil plates which shone as the sunsets. The meal ended, the maids came rinse our fingers and left the room, the guards of honor did the same after a ceremonial salute to the emperor...

Then, Yupanqui introduced me his third wife Tikaa, his daughter Quinoata and the avatar of his ancestor Viracocha, the heir apparent of the throne of the Inca nation, the son of the rising sun: Huayna Tupak.

I don't have the time to explain to you everything in detail (because you must leave before nightfall), but I will convey accurately what the ancestors are wait from you. Detailed instructions will be provided to you before your departure.

Senor Vaudreuil, you are going to hide my family in France. My wife and children will travel on your yatch. You are right now the official guardian of Quinoata and Tupak. They will study languages, administration and law. No one should know their true identity. You will establish accounts in a Bank in their names of adoption, and those accounts will be fed by our care.

The empress Tikaa will reside with her children and ensure their education. The ancestors humbly beg you to grant them this great favor and promised to ensure, from now on, your interests and those of your family.

Emperor Yupanqui then rang a Bell which stood near him. Two maids appeared immediately and bowed their head, waiting. He said a few words in their language. They went out promptly. A few minutes later, Ugolino entered the room. Take care of the preparations for departure, said to him, the emperor, who stand up. He kissed his wife and his children who followed Ugolino out of the room.

Two guards came to place a medium sized trunk, at the feet of the emperor. The wooden trunk cover, circled with iron strings was removed, and the emperor pulled out two gold statues, saying: nothing could never, compensate the service you are granting to the ancestors; in gratitude, receive these two authentic pre-Columbian golden artifacts.

He then gave me a cassette containing fifty antique gold coins, inestimable in value and a sumptuous emeralds finery. The money is for your expenses and the adornment for your daughter Elsa; He told me. The empire will be eternally grateful to you.

May I ask you a question? But of course, said Yupanqui. It seemed like you know everything about me? Obviously! I knew that you will be coming at Cuzco... We know everything that is happening around the world; do not ask me how?

One thing still puzzles me... by what process do you get this beautiful coloring of your carpets in lama skin? I have never seen such bright, lustrous coloring carpets anywhere else.

Señor Vaudreuil, he said, it's a secret. This process involves altering the pigments in the basic cells requiring simple chromophores to adopt genetic sequences of melanin, which is responsible for the spontaneous staining: human and animal skin and hair.

Three days before the slaughtering of the animal, we make him drink a drop of a chromophore formula Icteric for yellow; chlorophyll for green; flavonoids for blue and violet; hemoglobin for red and Brown. Genetic manipulations operated at the level of the nucleus, slow down the speed of electrons, and cause an artificial photosynthesis of the tissues of the derma. This polarized mutation serves as a vehicle to the processes of innervation and desensitization of the skin cells, which become receptive to the desired specific staining.

We use these same processes to manufacture cotton fabrics adorned with luxurious flowers. He clapped his hands, a servant appeared immediately. Yupanqui said a few words, she went on to get the wanted item. She returned a moment after and handed a rolled scroll to the sovereign. He took it, unwound entirely the scroll and removed in the middle of the manuscript, some yellowed pages filled with a fine and tight writing. Make good use of it, he said, handing over those pages.

It was a complete and detailed description of the process of artificial coloring of the skin, by alteration of melanin at the level of the dermis. This alteration causes aberrant mutation of disturb chromophores. The wording of the chemical formula needed to succeed the process was enclosed between the last page and the cover.

Ugolino entered the room, greeted the emperor and said in his language : your Majesty, everything is ready, you are expected in the throne room.

It was a moving sight. The throne room shone a solemn radiance. Dignitaries in ceremonial clothes stood on both side of the throne. The honor guards in parade uniforms, lined up in two rows, formed a kind of steel vault with their ivory spears tipped high. The sycophant ladies in traditional costume escorted the princess Quinoata and empress Tikaa, hieratic in her sumptuous Imperial dress, sitting like a goddess on a golden throne.

The new avatar of Viracocha: prince Huayna Tùrpak made his entrance in the Hall, escorted by a praetorian cohort. He walked under a steel arch, followed by his comrades, to the throne.

Huayna Tupak puts a knee on the ground and prostrated himself as a sign of respect and submission. Yupanqui stepped forward and touching his son's shoulders with his scepter, says aloud:

The ancestors spoke the higher spirits dwell with us. I consecrate you, Viracocha Huayna Tupar, emperor of the Inca people. This saying, he placed the heavy crown on the head of his son. Yupanqui took his crimson cloak and put it on the shoulders of Tupak.

Viva el imperator! Viva el nuevo Viracocha! shouted Yupanqui. The enthusiastic assistance repeated in chorus: viva Viracocha! May the ancestors grant him long life!

Hooray! Hooray! cried the guards of honors who hoisted him on a palanquin for the traditional parade around the throne room.

I left Machu Picchu, charged with a delicate and dangerous mission: provide for the welfare and education of the emperor of the Inca empire. The Land Rover was unstable on the windy and bumpy road lined with cliffs. Ugolino, who had put again his peasant clothes, was sitting in the front with me. Empress Tikaa and her children, beholden on the back seat, roughly dressed, as the mountaineers.

Ugolino was eager to stowaway his people, and undertook to return the vehicle to the rental agency...

The story ended there. Dr. Sommers would have wanted to know what had become the family of emperor Yupanqui; but, Cédric Vaudreuil, God have mercy of his soul! had carried with him into the grave, the sequel to this exciting adventure.

Dr. Sommers found, taped to the inside of the cover of the book, handwritten pages that Yupanqui had delivered to the ship-owner. After reading, he cried: Eureka!

Releasing the flange of his imagination, Dr. Sommers absorbed himself in a deep reflection. The Yupanqui formula offered him the opportunity to remove the barriers and eliminate the major objections because of his skin color. However, he feared the devastating impact that this psychological trauma would produce on the Aboriginal population.

Dr. Sommers, as a man of science, was aware of the gravity of his decision, whose unpredictable consequences, could extend beyond the framework of his inductive logic.

However, he was determined to try the experiment. He spent sleepless nights, torturing his meninges, looking for a solution, without finding a smart response to his confusing dilemma.

Enough procrastinating, said Dr. Sommers, who headed to the laboratory, resolved to implement the Machiavellian plan he had conceived spontaneously, reading emperor Yupanqui chromophore formulas.

He understood now why Cédric Vaudreuil had installed this sophisticated laboratory at the villa. He began to work, having found on the spot, all he needed. Mikado, sitting on a stool, carefully followed the development of this fiendish operations.

Dr. Sommers collected carefully the ingredient mentioned in the formula . He broke the granular ingredients, poured the organic acids, and mixed them all until it become a dough soft and smooth. He then lay the dough in the bottom of a large crystal bowl, poured one quart of distilled water and covered the bowl with a dark fabric to facilitate fermentation of the mixture.

The ointment he had placed on his back dried and glued on the wounds, causing a severe itch to Dr. Sommers. He took a shower and found with great relief that the scars had almost disappeared. He made a new application of the magical ointment, hoping to get rid completely, of the pale lines still on his back.

According to the instructions provided by the Inca experts, the fermentation process could last at least three days. Dr. Sommers was impatient and restlessly walked in the house, like a lion in a cage.

Dr. Sommers, although he tried to hide his nervousness, appeared, concern nevertheless, about the dramatic turn of event that would occur. He didn't know how these ingrown racists are going to react, when they would lose the sole object of their arrogant pride: the whiteness of their skin.

He imagined already, the rage of this fool of Harry Morgan , when he will worn the nigger' slivery. Sommers was tortured, however, by the thought that Isabella, she might also suffer from this vexatious situation.

Although Isabella had demonstrated in none equivocally way, that she didn't attached any particular importance to an individual skin color; still, he feared her reaction when strikes by that vicious fait accompli.

On the third day, the dough having absorbed the distilled water, had become a murky hue, viscous liquid. Translucent cells, corollaries of rapid fermentation of the mélange, under the catalytic action of organic enzymes, jostling on the surface, as in a boiling liquid.

The process described by the Inca priests for manufacturing the "Occult Aguardiente", required the use of a still alembic. This glass alembic, consisted of three parts: the splitting column, a condenser and a receiver. A Bunsen burner with high heating capacity, complemented the functional equipment of the laboratory.

Dr. Sommers, poured the mélange in the condenser, settled the Bunsen to the required five hundred degrees centigrade temperature, and sat down, a little concerned, to monitor the distillation of the aggregate.

A slight steam Journeying through the splitting column, turned into fine droplets falling into the receiver. The catalytic process allows a considerable reduction of time spent for the distillation of alcoholic products: wine, cognac, whisky, rum, ect... It is also used in the refining of crude hydrocarbon.

Dr. Sommers collected the final product in a graduated container. It was a colorless and odorless liquid, presenting no particular characteristic.

He buried outside the walls of the villa, calcined waste at the bottom of the condenser. He methodically rinsed the instruments, removed the residue on the alembic.

Dr. Sommers had taken extreme care to avoid contact with "Occult Aguardiente" as it was called. its scientific name: chromophore melanin potion. According to the Incas, the potion was not toxic, ingested in low doses.

The information provided by the Incas, on the use of this product, did not allow him to objectively assess the level of toxicity of the potion, nor the safest manner to administer the Aguardiente to humans.

A drop of liquid was enough to change the color of the skin and hair of a lama. He had found, nowhere in the yellowed pages of the emperor, indications on the weight, the size, the age of the animal brought to the slaughterhouse.

He wanted to teach a lesson to the racists living in this stupid society, but, not exterminate them all. The life of his beloved was also at stake. He didn't want either, this vicious joke been transformed into an irreparable tragedy.

Dr. Sommers made a comparative research on toxicology, studied the effects of some harmful ingredients, incorporated in the mixture, learned about all aspects of Montjolly demography: number of persons in general, the number of men, women and children...

With all these data, and somewhat reassured by his careful investigation, he passed from theory to practice.

Mikado began to sleeping in Dr. Sommers bedroom, since the unfortunate incident that brought to the villa, a lot of strangers who had scared him to death. Sommers left the door of the room open, otherwise, the cat would wake him up, regularly, every morning at five o'clock to go attend to his ordinary business.

Sommers awoke early morning that day. He filled bottle with a pint of fresh water, and added a drop of the famous liquid: the Occult Aguardiente, and went down in the kitchen followed by Mikado, very surprised to see him downstairs that early.

Dr. Sommers put half a cup of milk in the cat bowl and poured a drop of saturated aguardiente water, placed two slices of bread in the bottom of the bowl. Then he put a bit of jam in Mikado saucer and went up in his room take care of his person.

Anxiety somewhat gnawed him inside. He was taken advantage of the cat friendship, who manifested a deep and sincere affection towards him. He had however, made the necessary evaluation, assessed the risks, and was persuaded that he had given the cat the innocent animal the appropriate dose.

It was very hard for Sommers to concentrate his thoughts on any trivial chores. His mind was fixated on a single idea: the success of its risky business. Mikado served as involuntary guinea pig. If the cat died, Sommers would be compelled, either to entirely abandon the project or to provide a less vulnerable guinea pig. It should then revise his false assumptions and modify his inept toxicological methodology.

Sommers ambled along in the villa like a wandering Jew. He was watching every move of the cat, and woke him up, when he judged that the animal sleep extended unduly. He was convinced at the end, Mikado appeared to experience no discomfort, or any clinical symptoms of a known pathology. Alea jacta est" he said to himself, going to bed.

Dr. Sommers slept all night. He woke up fresh and rested, ready to cope with the vicissitudes of life and the challenge launched by this retrograde and racist community who opposed

his happiness.

The first rays of the rising sun, penetrated in profusion in the room in this beautiful spring morning. The blooming chestnut scattered its petals with each breath of the breeze. Through the open window, he watched the clear bright blue sky, where a few white flakes of cloud were clung.

A small cat's meow pulled Sommers out of his morning reverie. Then, saw with an incredulous shock, Mikado entirely black sitting on the stool, looking at him with its big curious eyes. The cat had changed color. His pristine white coat became dark brown from head to toe.

A quick leap, catapulted Sommers from the bed, to examine, more closely the animal, He noted with surprise and relief that forced metamorphosis operated on the subject, didn't affected its external appearance, didn't altered its physical faculties.

Sommers examined the cat, its eyes, which retained their original color, checked its reflexes, and concluded, with satisfaction, that the complex process used to synthesize melanin, seeking a radical transformation of the pigmentation; had no negative influence over the vital organs of the animal.

Sommers went down to the kitchen to feed the cat. Mikado greedily swallowed its food, as if he had not eaten for three days. Its screening, revealed to Sommers a clear difference between the color of the coat of the animal: a very glossy dark brown, and its skin: a very light brown.

He took a sample of hair, to analyze its content in saturated pigments and determine, then, the gradual fading of impregnated tissues.

His phone rang suddenly. Dr. Sommers thought that Dr. Morton needed him urgently; No one called him in his cell phone. Hello! he said in a firm voice.

"The beach, three o'clock, someone whispered softly. The person hangs up immediately.

Dr. Sommers didn't know this female voice. He wondered, puzzled, what that's mean? Was this a joke? Who else had his number? He could not trace the origin of the call. He was completely lost in this imbroglio.

The clock in the kitchen marked noon. There was a chance in a hundred, he thought, that Isabella had initiated this call. He decided, immediately, to honor this strange and intriguing rendez vous.

Dr. Sommers, when he was ready, went to the library, to choose a weapon in the arsenal of guns of sir Cédric Vaudreuil. He took his precautions, in case, this wicked crazy Harry Morgan, had prepared an ambush to achieve, what he had promised him to do.

He arrived on the beach before the time of the rendezvous. He hid his car behind a bushy shrub with a watchful eye, hastily surveyed the surrounding area. He didn't see anything suspicious, everything in the surrounding appeared safe and quiet. He squatted behind a tree and, all senses in alert, he waited.

Soon, he heard the sound of an engine approaching. Nestled against the prominent roots of the oak, Sommers risked a glance from the side where the car had stopped.

He recognized immediately, Elsa Mercedes and leapt to meet her. Isabella, wearing a white dress with yellow flowers, a leather pumps of the same color; she ran like a desperate teenager to her lover, whom she hugged with all her strength.

Sommers grimaced in pain and jerked under the light embrace of the girl.

"Did I hurt you my love?

"Oh! No, my dear love, he replied, a little hesitant.

"What happen to your back? She Insisted, let me see.

"This is nothing, he said, kissing her on the mouth.

"You are hiding something from me, Carl? you have no confidence on me? Let me see your back, I insist...

Dr. Sommers resignedly removed the loose shirt he was wearing; exposing his bare back, still stained with the fresh scars, the flogging the minions of Harry Morgan had inflicted on him.

Isabella let out a horrified scream and nestles on her breast her friend to mourn. Who did that to you? she asked, still sobbing, eyes bathed in tears. You must have suffered, my love?

She looked at him right in the eyes, come on, answer me, who beat you so savagely? I don't know, really, he replied, a little hesitant. Five individuals have beset me last Sunday, I tried to flee, but they have caught up with me. One of them had guessed my ploy and blocked me the road with his car. I was going to hide in the hospital. I was breathless. They tied me to a tree; They beat me with a three leather stripes whip and I lost consciousness.

When I regained consciousness, I was at the villa, Dr. Merville was doing his last stiches?

He gave me a powerful sedative. The pain was unbearable.

Isabella sobbed more profusely. She touched gently Dr. Sommers's scars as to delete them off. Have you seen Dr. Merville since Sunday? He returned Monday night to renew the dressings. I took care of myself since. I made an ointment, according to a recipe of your grandfather... This gave me, as you can see, an excellent result. In a few days, every trace will vanish completely.

They were sitting, closely entwined on the dead trunk where he saw Isabella the first time. They were holding each other waist, and were constantly kissing. Isabella eyes still fogged with tears, glittered, sparkled with emotion and love. Don't be so sad, my love, my darling, said Sommers, deeply moved by the grief and despair of the young girl.

"Carl, she said to him, suddenly: this cannot last forever. We must make a decision. I need you to live... What do you want us to do? Said Isabella.

"I have analyzed the situation, long and wide, I developed original assumptions and extravagant theories, but I haven't yet, found one appropriate solution to this dilemma almost insurmountable. However, I don't despair...

"Carl my darling, I beg you, don't let me languished all alone, without your presence, without the heat of your love. I don't know what happens to me, but I am ready to abandon everything to follow you, anywhere you go. You see, I might compromise work security of my friend: Lisa Troy, she is the girl who has phoned you. I wouldn't miss this chance to see you again. Max Hollemberg and his wife Joyce are organizing a reception to present their daughter Mona Lisa to the Montjolly posh people. We were invited, but I claimed an indisposition. I noted with relief, that my father resumed his ascendancy on his son. This superb matador had balked in vain, he has been forced to go. Especially as Simon nourishes matrimonial projects for his idiot son.

She was leaning against his shoulder and the cascade of blond hair, stroking at each slight movement, the bruised and sensitive back of his friend. Carl Sommers, immersed in his thoughts, ruminated unachievable projects.

"Carl, my darling, said suddenly Isabella, you have not told me the truth isn't it?

do you know the name of your main aggressor?

"What do mean? My darling, my love...

"Look me in the eyes, Carl, tell me the truth.

"I already told you everything... I don't know the people here

"Carl, insisted Isabella, I know that you have not told me the truth. I have my doubts about it. Because, if It was Harry Morgan, the instigator of this coward attack, I would have ripped his eyes.

"I can't, unfortunately, assure you of the identity of my attackers; In addition, I don't know your brother.

"You would have recognized him; he looks like Simon.

"I'm sorry, my dear, I can't help you.

Isabella took again her position leaning on Carl shoulder. This intimacy languished her, she huddles more and more against him, she felt a sensation of panic inside her body that scared her tremendously.

Isabella stood up, painfully, saying: my darling I must go. People shouldn't be noticing my getaway, especially mother, to whom I said nothing. She tells her husband everything now.

Dr. Sommers led her to her car and kissed her passionately on the mouth. It is ironic, said Isabella, when she was sitting in the car; We behave like school children who meet at random circumstances, without hope to meet again anytime soon. Darling, she said, lifting up his face to kiss him again: don't stay on the deserted Beach, Carl! I fear for your safety. I don't want to woe you! I am very concerned. Well! take care of yourself darling.

Isabella eyes were still fogged with tears. She went with a heavy heart, her heart full of grief, unable to contain her passion, to muffle her desires, in the state of physical softening she was.

Dr. Sommers waited a few minutes before leaving on his turn. Those two hours spent in the company of Isabella, had done him good. He had read in the eyes of the young girl, a passionate supplication, a desperate and pathetic call for help.

He remained decided, more than ever, to try, without delay, this dangerous experience. It was the only asset he had, for the moment, to move closer to Isabella.

Dr. Sommers spent the rest of the evening, plunged into complicated computations. He wanted to be convinced that the potion would not endanger the lives of the people. The only way to be sure, really, he says, was to administer a dose of the potion, equivalent to that individual in Montjolly would inevitably absorb during the incubation period of the experimentation.

Dr. Sommers poured a drop of saturated liquid, that he had prepared for Mikado, in a large glass of water and swallowed it. He wanted to test himself, the effects of this dangerous mixture on the human body, analyze the symptoms of possible clinical pathology, establish a preliminary diagnosis, assess, in a scientific manner on his person, the risk that would incur the Montjolly city's population.

His business was a hilarious and cruel farce, black humor pushed to the extreme, a scholarly hoax, a deadly comedy; everything for joking, but he did not want it to become a macabre tragedy.

Changing a racist community's skin color, who boasted of its racial superiority; already, was a reprehensible action. To eliminate completely (through ignorance or negligence), the entire population; would be tantamount to an abominable holocaust; a monstrous and unforgivable slaughter.

His beloved, the Apple of his eye, the love of his life, his raison d'etre, his dear Isabella would be in the mix of the victims of his dark machination. It was necessary that he should be sure of the absolute safety of the melanin chromophore philter.

Dr. Sommers was aware of the seriousness of his approach and the catastrophic consequences that would ensue. But he had burnt his ships, already crossed the Rubicon and, despite doubts that enfolded his heart, anxiety that caused him the possibility of a bitter failure. Sommers was determined to play all for all, to achieve its goal.

He didn't sleep, that night. The outpouring of love that Isabella had lavished on him, her manifest disturbance of the girl; upset him thoroughly. He was anxious and resolved at once, having reached the point of no return.

He woke up tired. He went to feed the cat, as usual, and made the daily taking of hair and tissue for analysis under the microscope. He had to follow the regressive evolution of the pigmentation of the animal skin.

He noticed a slight discoloration of hair and in addition, an imperceptible degradation of the color of the cat skin. He remembered that he had swallowed, likewise, the magic potion.

He examined himself in a mirror, head to toe, without detected a significant change in his physical appearance. He made a brief analysis of his blood and urine, to control the functioning of his kidneys, detected possible changes in the normal secretion of the endocrine glands, quantified the level of hemoglobin in his blood.

He auscultated his heart, examined his sight, felt the sharpness of his hearing, determined the speed of his conditioned reflexes. He was satisfied with this preliminary examination.

Dr. Sommers went to his work at Biloxi, the next morning. He stopped at the rest area 23, but did not find in the mail box. Dr. Morton greeted him effusively. A heaps of surgical operations had piled up, during the brief absence of his protégé.

Dr. Sommers spent the week in a state of agonizing suspense, disconnected from the ambient reality, with a sort of daze, however, plagued by a feverish impatience.

He carefully prepared the operation planned for next Saturday. He knew that employees of the new drinking water distribution and purification station, were absent every Saturday from noon to six o'clock in the evening. He had to perform his task during this time.

He had taken steps to succeed at the first attempt.

Since his mishap, Sommers never went out without been armed. He feared a new altercation with Harry Morgan and his minions. He had borrowed a pistol from the panoply of weapons of Cédric Vaudreuil, to be ready for any eventualities.

He placed the vial containing the aguardiente in a cardboard box that he sided with extreme care at the bottom of his backpack. He carried with him, his binoculars, a bottle of water and a pack of biscuits.

Dr. Sommers clambered with utmost difficulty (because his back was still in pain); the winding and steep slope that leads to the top of the massif forest. He settled comfortably at the end of the promontory to observe the crowd of carefree swimmers in the sea.

He stared, with his powerful binoculars, each blonde that he could see, hoping to identify his dear Isabella in the middle of this joyous crowds; although he knew, that his fiancée didn't mingled with this people.

He sat in the shade of an oak tree, when he could no longer stay in the Sun. He sank into a melancholic reverie. About one o'clock, he began the descent to the reservoir, located on the lateral side of the mountain.

He walked slowly, not wanting to arrive too early and risk meeting a late employee. Near the distribution station, he stopped to listen to detect any suspicious noises or echoes of any human activity.

Sheltering from tree to tree, he approached with caution to ensure the complete vacuity of the distribution station. Hidden behind a Bush, panting, stifling his nervousness under apparent calm and irreversible determination. Sommers waited a few minutes, then marched resolutely to the ajar gate and walked without hesitation to the trap which was useful, usually, at the taking of water samples to measure the chlorine content in the tank. He squats to be within reach of the narrow hole, poured the content of the bottle, and immediately walked away his work accomplished.

Dr. Sommers went home, felt an incomprehensible discomfort. He has a burning fever.

He felt oppressed, his throat tied by emotional tension which flared up all his nerves.

He understood, because he was a doctor, this reaction of the body, caused by a very intense physiological stimulus: fatigue and anxiety.

The incubation period of the potion, did not exceed twelve hours. However, Dr. Sommers couldn't pinpoint the exact moment of the appearance of the symptoms; due to his inability to assess the flow from the tank to the urban distribution center.

He took a few pills and lay down, head on fire, mind tormented by anxiety and anguish. Sommers was really afraid to have opened Pandora's box and poured on the Montjolly city, carefree and happy, a litany of unknown and terrifying evils. He finally fell asleep in the early morning, floored by fatigue and a slight mental disorder, resulting from the abstruse rantings of his foolish thoughts. Mikado, as usual, awoke him the next day. He was hungry. The fever had subsided. He felt a little perked up.

CHAPTER VI

The reverend Ted Vogel, the parish priest, had codified a grandiose ceremonial to celebrate Palm Sunday. The Church was decorated with palms and flowers. He built around the municipal square, votive altars, triumphal arcs made of Palm leaves interlaced with branches of yellow bougainvillea and scarlet flamboyant flowers.

Mounted on a white donkey, caparisoned with a red blanket, the parish priest, bearing the gold monstrance for special occasions, strutted at the head of the procession. Two altar boys, in red cassock and lace surplice, drove the animal, two others were blessing with frankincense the Holy Eucharist at every step. The crowd happy and collected, was singing an incantation: the solemn Hosanna. They haven't done better in Jerusalem, for the triumphal entry of Jesus in the city.

"Hosanna! Hosanna! In the highest heaven and peace on Earth to men of good will" ...

It was a beautiful spring morning. The sun shone in a clear sky. The square spread out its bloom bushes with ostentation. The atmosphere steeped in strong flowers perfume, exuded a sweet intoxicating odor.

The procession had already toured the square and was on its way to return to the Church; when someone shouted: look! Oh! Watch! Grace! Mercy! Lord! Have mercy! the reverend Vogel went black... Oh! Oh! Oh! Lamented some ladies, echoing those who were nearby. People jostled to see this strange phenomenon.

Father Vogel jumped to the ground and hurriedly entered the Church, followed by his panicked and confused altar boys. At the same time, a terrible clamor arose outside, parishioners entered in turn the Church pushing frightful cries, heartbreaking and desperate cries: they had all become dark brown, men, women and children.

The curse of heaven is upon us cried a woman. The plagues Lord had inflicted to the proud Egypt, are threaten us all, advanced a disconsolate bigot. What have we done Lord! to deserve this severe punishment?

People were crying tears of blood. Heartbreaking complaints from parishioners stunned by this tragic occurrence filled the consecrated walls with sadness and despair.

The priest ordered the ringing of the tocsin to announce to the entire city, the sad news of this epidemic which blackened the skin and seemed to have struck the entire Montjolian population.

The reverend Ted Vogel, after this moment of panic which caused him to flee the crowd, ascended the Chair to exhort his flocks with quiet resignation. It is, he said, a transitory phenomenon. I believe that some morbid gas escaped somewhere and brought by the breeze. This infection would not last, according to the parish priest, in two or three days, everything will return to normal.

The faithful were not at all convinced by the prosaic explanations of the priest. They were facing for always the agonizing, the horrible prospect of endorsing, forever, the abhorrent negritude of the despised race.

Dr. Joe Merville was overtaken by the events. He was the physician in service for this weekend. The other two were attending a medical convention in Jackson, Mississippi.

An endless stream of patients had invaded the hospital in an indescribable hubbub. The rooms were packed. People slept, in the corridors, unoccupied offices, everywhere where there was an empty space, accessible to the public.

It was a true Capernaum. He sent some paramedics looking for the trained volunteers, to help him cope with this catastrophic mess. The police alerted, was guarding the hospital gates and no more people were admitted now.

Cries of rage welcomed the closure of the barriers. A kind of riot triggered spontaneously, extended to the street keeping the police at bay. Volunteers arrived on the scene, persuaded the crowd to disperse by promising to keep them abreast of the latest developments of the situation.

His helpers out of town and feeling faint under the weight of his responsibilities; Dr. Merville went back into his office and called Dr. Sommers to the rescue.

"Dr. Sommers, here Dr. Merville, he said, don't ask any question... I'm awaiting for you at the hospital immediately.

"I am coming, said Sommers, without hesitation or comment.

Dr. Sommers courageously, was determined to attempt the impossible, to save lives threatened by this terrible scourge that slammed on the horrified people of Montjolly. He didn't know yet the extent of the damage. But he remained convinced that the situation was very serious.

Simon Morgan, Mayor of Montjolly, dispatched heralds throughout the city, to announce to the inhabitants the provisions taken by the town hall to ensure the physical and moral welfare of the population.

The mayor, in addition, asked the citizens for moderation and begged them to stay at home. The proclamation of the Mayor affirmed peremptorily, that this outbreak did not affect the overall health of the individual. The black curse, (as will be known and called this strange blackening of the skin), caused only a transient alteration of the color of human skin.

Dr. Sommers identified himself to the police who opened the gate to let him cross the main barrier, at the wheel of his yellow Cadillac. He parked his car in the area reserved for doctors, seized his Kit and entered the vestibule of the jam packed hospital.

"I am Dr. Sommers, he said at the reception desk, Dr. Merville had called me, can I see him please?

"Come Dr. Sommers, I will lead you to his office.

In the elevator, the receptionist smiled at the doctor and whispered with a shy voice: I am Lisa Troy, I am glad that you came to help us to break this bad deadlock.

Lisa, said Sommers with gravity, I am indebted to you. I thank you for the terse message, but how eloquent, it was last Sunday.

The girl knocked on Dr. Merville office door; no answer. She opened it and saw Dr. Merville laying down, full length, on the carpet. Dr. Sommers ran toward his colleague and bent to examine him more closely. He is alive, he told Lisa. I need two stretcher bearers, ask a nurse to prepare a room for the Director. Okay Lisa! Hurry!

Obviously, Dr. Merville suffered an emotional shock. He was unconscious, he had a burning fever, glassy eyes and seemed to be quite dehydrated. He was in a pitiful state.

Dr. Sommers made him breathe a powerful alcohol to revive him. They carried him on a stretcher, up to his room. Dr. Sommers injected a saline solution to lower his blood pressure, gave him a few drugs and left him in the care of a nurse.

Sommers requisitioned the help of two police officers to remove people who had settled in the corridors and in the rooms of the hospital. He made them understand that they were not really sick, that this weird phenomenon, albeit very boring, presented no real danger, no latent threat to their health.

He ordered Lisa Troy to recall all the nurses and all the staff available. He visited the operating room and asked the anesthetist to stand ready for all eventualities.

During this time, the ambulances, accompanied by volunteers, patrolled the city, neighborhood by neighborhood, from house to house, to reassure the elderly on the benignity of this disease.

An elderly couple thrown themselves to the ground from the top of their balcony. An ambulance brought them to the hospital with broken legs and cracked rib cage. A couple of pioneers, Hélène and Jeff Graham hung themselves. Other couples were rescued, in extremis; by the volunteers who drove pass their doors.

As pioneers, Elsa and Isabella were early on the streets of the city and have brought heaps of wounded victims, people of hysterical trauma. A lot irreducible old pioneers, proud of their racial superiority, whose collapsing scaffolding of their absurd and shabby theory; had set fire to their home, to avoid this humiliating and unimaginable defeat.

Let's go see how aunts Joan and Cathy are doing, told Elsa to her daughter Isabella. I almost forgot them in the excitement of that tragic morning. Isabella and her mother went down from the ambulance, leaving Baptiste, the driver and Jacquelyn, his assistant, sitting on the front seat of the vehicle. They rang the doorbell, in turn, for more than five minutes. No one answered. The two men came knocking with all their strength at the windows, the house was apparently empty.

Mother, looks, said Isabella, looking through a gap in the garage door. Aunt Cathy's car is here. This is strange, said Elsa... It's funny! usually, these ladies never went out on foot! Baptiste, called Elsa, break a glass on this window and see what happens inside please...

With Jacquelyn help, who made him the short scale, Baptiste climbed nimbly and stepped over to the window where he had broken one of the glasses. Once inside the house, he felt a strong smell of propane gas. He opened all the windows and doors before he called for help.

Jacquelyn, Elsa and Isabella rushed in the house. Baptiste was already descending the stairs with one of the sisters on his back. He cried, by the way, hurry up, the other has lost a lot of blood.

Jacquelyn, accustomed to these kinds of situation, saw at first glance that the lady had cut off her wrist and was bleeding profusely. He tore a strip in the sheet that covered the bed, made a tourniquet to stop the bleeding, put the woman on her back and ran, as fast as he could, to the ambulance that was waiting, engine running.

Baptiste started out with a bang. Jacquelyn was busy near the victims, trying to revive them, to stop completely the bleeding. In less than ten minutes, the ambulance was at the hospital gate. Stretcher bearers carried the Morgan sisters, to the operating room. Isabella! What are you doing here? You look so sad? My aunts have tried to commit suicide... My god! exclaimed Lisa Troy appalled by this news... Where is Dr. Merville? Asked Isabella worried. Dr. Merville is very sick... But, who, therefore, is caring for all the injured people we brought to the hospital? insisted Isabella... How! you don't know? What should I know Lisa? tell me... Dr. Carl Sommers is doing surgery nonstop since this morning, the poor man... He must be hungry?...

Isabella didn't wait for the elevator. She rushed at full speed in the staircase which she climbed two steps at the time.

She arrived short of breath on the second floor and ran straight toward the operating room.

Her aunts were already in surgery. Elsa came to join her daughter, who told her the great news.

Elsa, as usual, woke up early this Sunday morning. She had the impression, in the half light of the room, coming from a small bedside lamp that her husband's face had burnished considerably. She lighted the ceiling lamp and let out a shrill cry. Simon woke with a Jolt and saw his wife who was shaking like a leaf in the wind, on the edge of a hysterical crisis.

What Elsa? You are all black... She went crashing on the dressing table mirror and undressed completely. She remained dumbfounded as paralyzed by this sudden and unexpected metamorphosis. Then she broke down in tears, looked again and laughed. Simon, stunned by this scourge, which slammed his family, was crestfallen, prostrated in a kind of morbid daze.

She endorsed a bathrobe and told Simon still planted as a crane, in the middle of the room: I'm going to see my daughter. Elsa entered silently in the bedroom. She leaned on her sleeping daughter and saw Isabella hair, had become light brown; color that enhances the brilliance of her brown skin. Isabella was as beautiful as before, and, why not say it? More beautiful than ever.

Isabella opened her blue eyes, color of sky and smiled at her mother. Oh! Mother she said suddenly you darkened overnight, what happened to you? You are also black. Sweetheart, retorted Elsa; you too, you become black.

The girl looked at her hands, her arms, her legs... What that's mean? Are we the only ones? It seems that everyone in Montjolly suffered during the night, this inexplicable metamorphosis... Dress up, Darling, said Elsa, we are going to see what happens in the city.

And father, how he took at the thing? Your father didn't want to leave home; his pride took a blow... Hurry up; I'm going to speak to the house staff, to reassure them... Amélie is a weak head...Jules is a stupid guy…

Dr. Sommers entered the surgical section waiting room, to announce to the parents of the two women that he had done an emergency and successful intervention.

"Isabella! He exclaimed, what are you doing here?

"I came with my aunts...

"These ladies? Asked Sommers

"Yes! Replied Isabella, nodding gracefully.

She was dying to embrace her virtual fiancé, but was retained by the presence of so many people who knew her.

Suddenly, Dr. Sommers saw Elsa who looked at him with a mocking smile.

"Elsa! He says, approaching toward her, he took her hand and kissed it. Excuse me, but I didn't see you at first Elsa.

"Is it because I'm a Negress now or, because you have eyes only for Isabella?

"Touché! But I noticed with great pleasure that you wear your negritude admirably well. Trimmed with a halo of juvenile grace, a mysterious aura radiates your colorful dyed hair, your wonderful somber complexion and renders both of you more beautiful than ever.

"Dr. Sommers, said Elsa, you are an incorrigible flattering tongue... Tell me how my sisters-in-law are doing?

"They are very lucky. They are still, in the recovery room. One of the sisters has lost a lot of blood. I had to infuse into her, my own blood during the surgery. We haven't found the positive 'o' in the blood bank. Who else in the family has the same blood type as these ladies? They still need a massive transfusion of blood.

Lots of people had surrounded Dr. Sommers to inquire into the state of health of their parents. He answered, that all his patients were doing pretty well, despite this unfortunate occurrence. He recommended them to petition the hospital administration to find out where they could visit their parents.

Dr. Sommers took leave of Elsa telling her that her sisters-in-laws would soon be, on a private room on the third floor. He nodded to Isabella who followed him out of the operating room.

Sommers headed for the elevator, he went to his provisional office located in the fourth floor. The elevator was packed. He had to shrink into a corner in the elevator to provide a small place for his companion. Dr. Sommers opened the office door and stood aside to let Isabella in.

They kissed passionately like two desperate, without a word. They remained hugging a moment, and then, Sommers pulled away from the loving embrace of Isabella. She smiled at him. He said to her: Dear love, you're still the most beautiful girl in the whole world. I don't know something magical happens during your metamorphosis; your brown hair your brown skin and the brilliance of your blue eyes light up your face and enhance your incomparable beauty... I love you my love. Isabella answered, but tears of joy and happiness fill her eyes. She suddenly realized that an incredible miracle had fulfilled her secret dream. The obstacles that prevented her to be happy had disappeared and that she was free to love, in the open, the man of her life.

"My cherished love, said Sommers, I'm hungry. I haven't eaten since this morning. Not even coffee...

"Isabella laughs. Nature is talking, my love, Isn't it? Carl

Darling, I'll ask Lisa to prepare something, I

will invite mother to share our snack. OK!

"Love Darling, I have to go, they expected me at the operating room, a long time ago.

Do the necessary arrangement and just call me within an hour.

"An hour! But you won't be able to hold until then, my love...

You are already tired.

"You know sweetheart, I can't complain now; They are making me work to justify, in a single day, the wages that I received for nothing. It's fair…

The lovers kissed before leaving the office. They parted at the second floor, Sommers was going to the operating room, Isabella went to the kitchen on the ground level of the hospital.

Dr. Sommers led Elsa to her sisters-in-law in room 312. She told him that Simon and Harry have the same blood type as the Morgan bridesmaids. Simon is on his way, but Harry refuses to leave his room. Already! Said Sommers. By the way do you want to join us, Isabella and me, in an hour, for a snack? My dear Carl, how can I refused, I'm starving.

Dr. Sommers consulted the record of these ladies. They had no more fever, their blood pressure became normal, and their heart beat at a steady pace. We read, however, in their watery eyes, a feeling of shame mixed with fear. They were happy to receive Elsa visit, which provided them a great comfort at this difficult time of their lives.

Everything is going well, said Sommers, I'll come to see you tonight. Simon made its appearance in the chamber at this time. He kissed his wife and shook hand with Dr. Sommers, and thank him for the special care given to his sisters. I'm leaving said Sommers, they expected me for surgery.

Simon Morgan refrained a terrible urge to admonish his sisters, for their stupid action; their behavior unworthy of the solid reputation of selflessness and courage, in the face of adversity; that characterizes the Morgan family.

He lingered long with them. He left to go the plant, see what was happening there. Harry didn't want people to see him in this lamentable state, he said to his father. He was contemplating the collapse of his arrogant ziggurat of pride, his ontological belief of his racial superiority and vanish his grandiose dream of establishing, in this enchanted region, an Eden of bliss and harmony for some privileged souls of the Aryan race.

Dr. Sommers was exhausted. He worked, without interruption, since his arrival at the hospital the morning at nine o'clock. Lisa, Elsa and Isabella were waiting in the waiting room for dinner. He had already removed his blouse, washed his hands and his face, when he heard, an infernal din and screams in the hallway.

Max Hollemberg and daughter Mona Lisa walked in front of a stretcher carried by four men. Joyce Hollemberg, the wife of the entrepreneur, Livid as a cadaver, moaning painful complaints. Her daughter, lamented noisily. People appeared at the footsteps of the doors to watch this pathetic show.

"Where is Dr. Merville, asked Max Hollemberg, in a shaky voice?

"Dr. Merville is unavailable, I am Dr. Sommers, may I help you?

"My wife was the victim of an accident...Take care of her, please doctor, for the love of God... She is dying…

Sommers brought the wounded lady directly in the operating room. He requisitioned the nurses and the anesthesiologist who were leaving, their work completed.

Elsa, lead Max and Mona Lisa, to sit in the waiting room. She told them, to ease their anguish, her own setbacks and the tragic effects of the emotional trauma resulting from this awful drama.

Mona Lisa was inconsolable. She lamented the lost of her delicate complexion, the disappearance of her provocative beauty (according to her), and the desperation of her mother who thrown herself down the stairs. She covetously, however, sneak an eye on Isabella; she knew at first glance, that this gorgeous girl, adorned with that stunning beauty, would be for sure, a dangerous rival in Montjolly.

Elsa who observed the curious gaze of the young girl, hastened to present Isabella. Max! Mona Lisa! do you know my daughter? I present to you Isabella. Happy to know you said Mona Lisa. Max just nodded.

This Dr. Sommers asked Mona Lisa, you know him? Can we trust him? Asked Mona Lisa. He is an excellent surgeon, specialist in neurosurgery. Your mother is in very good hands. Don't worry unduly, he will do the impossible for her, I am sure of it.

Max Hollemberg had remained silent, lost in his thoughts. He didn't or couldn't explain the origin of this scourge, this satanic calamity that was unleashed upon the city of Montjolly. Joyce, his wife, despite the care he had taken to make her understand the provisional character of this skin aberration, threw herself from the top of the stairs, rather than suffer the shame of this ignominious debasement.

At first glance, Mona Lisa had laid eyes on this young doctor, elegant and handsome like an Adonis. She flew on the wings of her dream to the enchanted shore of flowery love. This innocent reverie was a slight distraction to her sadness and grief.

After an hour and a half, which seemed to have lasted an eternity for the Hollemberg, husband and daughter; Dr. Sommers reappeared in the waiting room. Mona Lisa immediately ran to the doctor... How is mother? she asked anxiously... Max Hollemberg embroiled in a debilitating weakness, painfully, joined his daughter talking to the doctor.

Everything has gone well, said Sommers. I have fixed all that she had broken. I did my best, given the extent and the severity of her injuries. However, with a little luck, I think she could recuperate without great damage.

In ten minutes she will be transported to room 316, where you can go see her.

They thanked Dr. Sommers with heat and went forward to the specified room. Carl, said Isabella: We are going to eat now. The dinner is served a long time ago.

They went, all three: Elsa, Isabella and Carl, to the staff dining room, where a hearty meal prepared by Amélie, (the housekeeper of the Petit Palais).

Eggplant soup with gruyere, appetizer, grilled chops lamb, macaroni au gratin were the day's menu. Amélie had brought a bottle of a Moselle wine, Luxembourg origin, to accompany the dinner and strawberries jam for dessert.

I think, said Elsa, this meal will offset the one we couldn't have in New York. Bon appétit my children. They ate in silence, a moment, not knowing where to begin the conversation.

"Carl, said Isabella, have you an idea of the gravity of this black curse? Is it a permanent mutation or a transient phenomenon?

This black evil curse, my dear friend, has already altered the Psychic health of the frantic population; it will affect also the physical health of people?

"I can't state categorically, the absolute faithfulness of this strange mutation; since I haven't yet received the results of the analysis that I have ordered. However, my love, I can assure you unequivocally, this found from many of my patients, that black curse doesn't have any pernicious influence on the normal functioning of vital organs.

"The parish priest, father Vogel, said Elsa, is trying to propagate the idea of a heavenly reward, a deserved punishment, like the plagues of Egypt to punish in their foolish pride, those who believed they are superior because of the color of their skin. If in adventure, we would not find a rational explanation for this bizarre phenomenon, the casuistic thesis of father Vogel would be accredited, in the popular consciousness, isn't it?

"Anyway, adds Dr. Sommers, divine intervention or no, this drama will have a profound impact on the vulnerable psyche of the white race, which, for the first time, had experienced the coercive effects of the genetic theory of the monk Gregor Mendel.

"Someone misfortune is a blessing for someone else, said Isabella.

This awful tragedy allows us dear friend of my heart, to see and love each other without hiding, in the light day, in the eyes of everyone. I regret bitterly the lost of human lives, even if the most traumatic scourge strikes harder in the future... but I am profoundly pleased, that this gift of the providence has already clear the way for me... People can call me selfish and heartless; this makes me, neither hot nor cold. On the contrary, I thank heaven which answered my prayer.

One may believe, said her mother, hearing you talk, that you liked the woe that struck the city.

I won't shout it from the rooftops, mother! but I'm not a hypocrite, I am pleased and thank the black curse which bring me closer to the man I love, the man of my life... I know... It's wrong, but I am fulfilled beyond my wildest expectations.

Dr. Sommers, Dr. Sommers, shouted in the dining room speaker, you are expected in 302. He stood up, took leave of the two women, saying: the risks of the trade!

We must go home said Isabella. We don't know what's happening over there. Simon hired a nurse to take care of his sisters during the night. Dr. Sommers went to the room where he was needed, despite himself, the call to duty.

Dr. Joe Merville, still convalescent, was sitting on a chair stuffed with plush cushions. He presented his family to Dr. Sommers: his wife Bernice, daughter Rachel and his son Brandon. He thanked him for the titanic work he had done. Dr. Merville told him that he would take over for the night, he could go to rest.

You are not in condition to initiate the resumption of your duty, Dr. Merville, said Sommers. You must wait at least, the results of the analysis, before taking any decision. Incidentally, I have many patients who required a diligent surveillance and regular care; I can't entrust this task to you, in the dizziness state where you are in.

Dr. Merville, although the blood pressure came back to normal, it is no less true that I couldn't diagnose the origin of this malaise, that the risks of complications are still exist.

Dr. Sommers took leave of the Merville, and went to room 312, to see the Morgan sisters. They were sleeping peacefully. The nurse made him a detailed account on the status of the patients. Joan received again, a pint of blood and appeared to be regaining some strength. Cathy was more alert, but, much more self-conscious, embarrassed by her reckless and shameful action.

Mona Lisa and her father remained at the bedside of their love one throughout the day. Max Hollemberg was somewhat worried, by the torpor in which his wife was immersed. Dr. Sommers reassured him, telling him that he had administered a massive dose of painkillers to the patient to allow her to withstand, without failing, excruciating pain caused by her multiple fractures.

Mona Lisa revolved around Dr. Sommers, like a butterfly fascinated by the dazzling brightness of a lamp, she swirls around him. He didn't notice the languorous glances of the young girl staring in his direction. Busy and preoccupy, Sommers ignoring this kind of flirtatious game; Sommers left the room without noticing the tearful eyes of Mona Lisa.

Dr. Sommers visited his patients until two o'clock in the morning. He was exhausted. He went to the villa Vaudreuil, feed Mikado who had inherited a solid appetite since his metamorphosis. He threw some clothes, in bulk, in a suitcase, pocketed the pot of ointment miracle, and returned to the hospital. There, he took a shower, changed from head to the toe, and lay down on a couch in Dr. Loran's office, his provisional refuge.

Dr. Sommers awoke around 6 pm; he shaved, borrowed a fresh blouse in Dr. Loran cabinet and went down to the front desk.

Lisa Troy had not yet arrived. Nancy Gray, the alternate, made him a comprehensive account on the admissions of the night. The number of fatalities had increased significantly. Three other suicides. There were two serious injuries that were waiting in the operating room.

When he entered the operating room, Dr. Sommers saw Dr. Merville, who was preparing to operate one of the wounded. It is not reasonable Dr. Merville, said Sommers, in a tone of reproach. You will do me the pleasure of returning to your room, I'm going to take care of the rest.

Dr. Merville didn't try to resist. He went without protesting unduly.

After taking care of the wounded, Dr. Sommers visited his patients. He remodeled the bandage on the wrists of the Morgan sisters. He applied a layer of magic ointment on their wounds to clear, in advance, any scars.

Joyce Hollemberg was writhing in pain. She was alone, the nurse was gone looking for Dr. Sommers. He gave the lady a morphine shot, and wrote her a prescription for other drugs.

Dr. Merville had not returned to his room, he was at his office, calling the provincial medical authorities, announcing the strange epidemic unleashed upon the city of Montjolly.

The Director general of health in the city of Jackson, promised to send him illico presto, an epidemiologist, to assess the seriousness of this infection and gather samples: water, earth, air, animal hair, plant leaves and human roots, human skin; to investigate thoroughly, this black plague, which could contaminate the entire population of the country.

Sommers informed Dr. Merville of the result of his analysis. Everything was normal. He recommended, however, to consult a cardiologist. Because, this kind of sudden fainting, was symptomatic of an anomaly in the brain or in the heart. I heard a murmur in your heart rhythm that could lead to unforeseen complications in the future.

Dr. Merville was a little embarrassed by the presence of Dr. Sommers at the hospital. Saint Cecile staff had complimented the Director on the choice of this excellent Organizer, who in a jiffy had put the order in this shambles that had become the hospital. He demonstrated, in addition, his skills as an outstanding surgeon, operating successfully, all those requiring urgent surgical intervention.

Dr. Merville, said Dr. Sommers, responding to a proposal of the latter: take care of administrative matters, I will call you, if I need your help. You are not yet very firm on your two legs.

Joyce Hollemberg was out of the comatose state where she stood since her operation. When Sommers entered the room, she was with her daughter and her husband. She told them that she was sorry. That she had lost her mind under the emotional shock...

Don't talk with my patient, said Dr. Sommers in a jovial tone. I'll remove the bandage from her jaw, she could, certainly, better express herself afterward. The bandages removed, left an imperceptible scar on the cheek of Joyce Hollemberg. I have operated, especially inside the mouth, he explained, so precisely to avoid disfigure a so cute face. Joyce sketched a shy smile saying: thank you doctor. Sommers put on her cuts his magic ointment. In two or three days all traces of the operation will disappear.

Max Hollemberg took him aside in a corner of the room and handed him a check. What is that? asked Sommers intrigued. This is a check for ten thousand dollars; credited to the total cost of the operation of my wife. I'm sorry, Sir, but I didn't do anything for you personally; I am an employee of the hospital and as such, I do not have the right to collect money from the patients or their representatives.

Mona Lisa wanted to outbid the generous offer of her father, but, Dr. Sommers cut her sharply off. It is not worth insisting, believe me! The hospital administration is normally in charge of these kinds of financial transactions.

Simon Morgan came to pick up his sisters who had expressed the desire to go home. Dr. Sommers had redone their dressings. He noticed with satisfaction that the magic ointment had performed wonders again. He promised to visit in the evening, his job done.

Dr. Sommers didn't see or hear from Isabella all day. He went down to the reception desk to ask Lisa Troy about her. Lisa smiled at him a complicit way and told him, without waiting for a question; that Isabella had travelled with her mother and one of the assessors of the Town Hall, in the African area of the city, where the xenophobic and raging zealots, (despite the presence of an armed police contingent) wanted to set fire to the houses and chase the residents out of the city.

These pioneers made the new comers, responsible for this satanic epidemic plight, this horrible curse that blackened skin and exposed us to ridicule and sarcasm from around the world.

Isabella, standing on the hood of the Town Hall car, spoke to the rioters. She told them that South Africans were also victims of this disease. That was not the time to create a climate of division, suspicion and hatred among the population. Don't look for scapegoats to blame for the sins of Israel; they wouldn't whiten the conscience and the skin of nobody. She urged them to calm and weighting, for the sake of unity and solidarity which must prevail in this difficult period of the montjolian family.

The crowd dispersed, according to the talk reported; continued Lisa Troy, all proud of the achievement of her girlfriend. Isabella and her mother remained at the scene to reassure the foreigners, commiserate with their suffering and soothe their concern about their status in the community, after this unfortunate incident.

Dr. Sommers declined the dinner invitation of Dr. Merville, pretexting some urgent chores at the villa Vaudreuil: feeding the cat, a priority. He went, in fact, home, to take a bath and change, in order to be presentable to and elegant at the Morgan sister's house,

Sommers endorsed his beige suit, which according to the glowing opinion of Elsa, gave him an air of refined elegance. It was the same outfit he had brought in New York, to go dancing with Isabella at Fiesta Latina.

Back at the hospital, Dr. Merville introduced him to the epidemiologist: Dr. Suzanne Birmingham, who had just arrived. She was gloved and she took ridiculous precautions to avoid touching anything. She had suffered a shock upon learning that all the people of the city had caught this strange disease. She regretted, already, coming and accused Dr. Mervill, to having unnecessarily exposed her to contamination.

Sommers didn't linger with them. He toured his patients, visited the new admitted to alleviate Dr. Merville labor, because Dr. Merville (still weak and confused) was providing the service that night.

Leaving, Dr. Sommers gave Nancy Gray, the night receptionist, his mobile phone number, and recommended that she call, without hesitation, if an emergency occurred at the hospital.

The Morgan villa at the White Lily Avenue was an old building in red bricks, two-story high, ill-defined bombastic style. A large driveway paved with squared stone slabs, bordered on both sides by a dense hedge of white lilies leading up to the porch of the entrance. The gate was open; Sommers entered the courtyard where a sweet smell greeted him without mercy.

Dr. Sommers parked his yellow Cadillac in front of the garage door and rang. What was his surprise on seeing Isabella, eyes sparkling with joy and happiness, her spellbound smile on her lips, open the door. She jumped on his neck, and kissed him madly.

Isabella took his hand saying: let's go darling, they are expecting you. She led him through a sumptuously furnished living room to the dining room where already sitting, around the table: Cathy, Joan and Elsa Morgan and three others individual he didn't know yet.

Dr. Sommers, called Isabella emphatically, I present to you the singer Michelle Morgan, the Principal of the high school: Nancy Morrice, Admiral John Dexter and the parish priest: reverend Ted Vogel. You have already met mother and my aunts Joan and Cathy. Dr. Sommers greeted everyone and sat down at the place reserved for him, between the priest and Michelle Morgan.

Dr. Sommers had thought making a visit of courtesy to these ladies; he didn't expect, but not at all, this meeting and this ceremonial dinner. Isabella was sitting just in front of him and smiled to give him insurance.

Responding to a discreet sign of Cathy Morgan, the amphitryon, the priest stood and recited grace. Amen! said the guests at unison.

All these people came each week, to dinner at the Morgan sisters whom proverbial hospitality was a family tradition. This impromptu evening was in appreciation for the many testimonies of sympathy and affection that he had given them, their parents and friends, affected by this traumatic ordeal.

The cook had prepared a simple, but delicious menu. An onion tart and foie gras patties for entry, green salad, a duck fried in orange and Apple sauce, as the main course and for dessert, crepes Suzette flavored with mandarin syrup.

Dear friends, said father Vogel, after having tasted a few patties and drank two glasses of wine: heaven has permitted, for our sins, this misfortune), as would say Mr. Lafontaine. This plague, dear friends, is a scourge, a divine punishment, meted out to all, without exception, to cast off our pretensions to racial superiority. To destroy overnight, the reason of our stupid pride and rendering void our systematic refusal to recognize the undeniable humanity of people of color.

I propose, me, to appease the wrath of the Almighty, a rogatory procession throughout the city, in bag of penitent, to implore God's mercy. The prayer of a contrite heart and a sincere repentant sinner; can attract the favor of heaven and deliver us from this insulting and shameful leprosy.

You, church people, intervened Admiral John Dexter; you see the divine hand in all the mysterious phenomena, not yet explained by science. I do not believe that the providence has interfered in our small seedy business, for revenge, especially of the montjolian population. Other (much more guilty and cruel) with impunity violated the laws of God.

The Lord perhaps wanted to draw an example, replied Fr. Vogel; the Lord has always taken in horror the false pride of man. This is undoubtedly; this evil black curse is a just retribution...

Before embarking on the wings of mystical religious speculation, said Admiral Dexter, ask science to light our lanterns. Dr. Sommers, can you give us your opinion on the subject?

Dr. Sommers, introduced abruptly in the conversation, sketched a shy smile to give him confidence and said with his male voice: preliminary analysis carried out in local laboratories, didn't revealed the presence of any pathogen in samples collected everywhere. Dr. Merville asked and got an epidemiologist attached to specialized research centers. Nevertheless, I can assure you definitively that the evil black curse does not affect the vital organs and does not alter the physiological functions of human or animal.

But then, asked Michelle Morgan, a little embarrassed, doctor, do we have even a small possibility to become normal again? Have we a chance to recover our original pigmentation? Can we find an antidote to fight this terrifying plight?

Unfortunately, mademoiselle, replied Sommers, I cannot answer all your scary questions. This virus that disrupted the nuclear synthesis of melanin and chromphores (the pigments responsible for the coloration of the skin) has not yet been isolated.

However, I am convinced that this anomaly is fleeting, and soon, your complexion will regain its original coloring.

I don't see, you haven't demonstrated on which bases you utter this categorical assertion? Doctor, said Nancy Morice: the high school's principal: you declare conclusively, a probable end of our miseries, without making any tangible evidence available to support your assertion. Would it be to put to sleep our apprehension or to give us a false hope?

Of all those present at the dinner, Isabella and her mother only knew the true identity of Dr. Sommers. Everyone assumed, in fact, that he too was, a victim of this terrible evil. Sommers looked at Isabella who sends him an encouraging nod.

Admiral Dexter asked me my humble opinion on the subject in question and I answered as best I could. I am not trying to gild the pill for anyone, or mitigate potential and unforeseen risks incurred by the entire population of montjolly... My opinion is that of the reverend Vogel, are just assumptions. Mine is supported by scientific observations obtained by operating on injured patients victimizes by the virus. But, above all, developed from the preliminary results of analysis not less conclusive and revealing. As long as we have not found evidence of the origin of this evil and an antidote to neutralize the toxic effect of the poison; the conjectures made by Fr. Vogel are as valid as mine.

How doctor! Exclaimed Cathy Morgan, indignant; we have been poisoned?

Excuse me, Dear Miss! There is a misunderstanding in the interpretation of my thought. What I meant is that this virus is, as would be a poison in the body. In this case, the physiological responses caused by the substance, (if there is substance) have not disturbed the normal functioning of the vital organs of the human body. Such disruption would result in certain death... Fortunately, the substance in question is bound around the enzyme tyrosine, whose synthesis produces melanin. I didn't use medical jargon of high pseudoscientific speculations to give my opinion on the matter... It would seem that people has misunderstood...

Oh! No, on the contrary, we understood, strongly your point of view, said father Vogel. You didn't exclude yet (as a good Christian) the possibility of divine intervention in the granting of this awful fate that afflicts us all. We must each do our mea culpa, continued the reverend, (caught in the excitement of the moment), and recognizes, in a spirit of humility and penance, that we have sinned against God and men.

Elsa and Isabella had kept, (as unproductive academician Conrad) a prudent silence, during the entire meal. Isabella, would have wanted to ask a lot of questions, she refrained, to avoid engaging in conversation on a slippery slope where it could reveal the true identity of her lover.

We are going to drink coffee in the lounge, suggested Cathy Morgan, we have two great musicians that will brighten up the evening and hunt for a brief and precious moment, our worries and our dark thoughts.

Michelle Morgan was the niece of Cathy Joan and Simon. She was raised by these ladies when her father, their little brother Georges, was killed in a car accident. The family had sent her studying in Switzerland. Her studies completed, she didn't return to Montjolly for the great disappointment of the family. She got a contract with La Scala in Milan. She pursued her career, without worrying about the, scornful disapproval of her parents. She just came to see her Aunts, when misfortune knocked at her door. She has been compelled to share the ill fate of her relatives.

Michelle sat down at the grand piano that stood in a corner of the large living room; hesitantly she strikes a few syncopated chords and began to sing the aria: E strano e strano! Sempre libera! Taken from Verdi's La Traviata. Her brilliant voice filled the living room with a pathetic accent. The poignant melody, jerky, at times sad tremolos, accompanied the wrenching complaint, of the desperate Violetta, obliged under oath to renounce the love of her lover Alfredo. The audience utterly under the bewitching charm of this extraordinary voice broke out in applause. Sommers, sitting with Elsa, on a red velvet sofa, threw a circular glance but didn't see Isabella at the living room. He was worried.

Michelle Morgan sang, back-to-back, two other arias: Vien diletto in heaven the luna!, I Puritani by Bellini and Ardon Gli Insensi in the opera Lucia di Lamermoor of Donizetti. Everyone began standing up to applaud the soprano. Her aunts had never heard her in concert. Montjolly city, reveling in his xenophobic isolation, had completely ignored the success of the dissident, who set a very bad example for Aboriginal talent. Michelle's career nipped in the bud, Isabella's dreams.

Dr. Carl Sommers observed, with a growing amazement, the casual attitude of these people, confronting this tragic occurrence, which had not only changed their physical appearance, but also, transformed the ordinary practice of their conceptual theory of living, which constituted their objective reality. Dr. Sommers felt less remorseful for his bold and nasty action.

Sommers, himself, was on the edge of panic the first day of the visible manifestation of the effects of the potion. Seven people had committed suicide, he expected many more.

The panic of the population in the first hours of the tragedy, the disorderly crowd rushing to the hospital, had made him fear the worst: a horrible massacre and hundreds of deaths. Naturally, he deplored the lost of human lives; however, the phlegmatic casualness of these people to the suffering of others, took any regret he could had have out of his mind. He could not imagine this scenario in which he had to play a very important role. His talents and compassion were involved.

Although it has been possible to save the wounded and the poisoned, he felt, nonetheless guilty of having caused the death of seven innocent victims. A glimmer of sadness clouding his eyes.

What are you thinking, doctor? Elsa asked him. Elsa who was following on the worried physiognomy of the doctor, the evolution of his melancholic thoughts. She was obviously, mistaken on the subject of the sad reflections of the young man... Isabella went to change, she spilled coffee on her dress... She will be back in a few minutes.

I was worried, really, by her prolonged absence. You look tired, said Elsa, you can't afford the luxury to get sick. You are the only healthy doctor of the city...

Isabella smiling appeared in the room at this time, dazzling in white velvet, princess style dress. The dress was tight at the waist, with a flared bell shaped skirt.

Excuse me for making you wait, I had a small accident, said Isabella with a smile.

Before sitting down at the piano, she threw a glance at the people and stopped briefly on the nonplussed Dr. Sommers. When Cathy Morgan had announced the presence of two great artists, he did not suspect that his beloved Isabella was one of them.

Isabella played the sonata No.3 in F minor by Robert Schumann, highlighting with wistful emotion, the pathetic seriousness of the passionate recurring leitmotif throughout the piece.

The assistance was stunned, appalled even, by the incomparable verve with which she performed the sonata. She bowed under a thunder of applause. She had to order silence in order to continue.

Isabella then played studies Tableaux op. 33 of Sergei Rachmaninov. She poured her sore soul, wounded by the shocking drama that plagued the community. She evoked with the intimacy of her impeccable artistry, the nostalgic regret of the past that reflected the musical composition. Those musical décors were translating also, but enshrined in a setting of sadness and foreboding, the undecided awakening of a new dawn, full of promises, joys and happiness.

It was a triumph. Even those who had heard her the last time, at the party given at the Petit Palais: Admiral Dexter, Nancy Morrice, her aunts, marvelled the elegant virtuosity of the artist. Her brilliant play was superb. Love had metamorphosed the chrysalis into a wonderful butterfly.

For who had Isabella played with both fever and passion? asked her cousin Michelle Morgan, intrigued and jealous. She discovered in Isabella a dangerous rival, talented, able to overshadow her reputation and tarnish her career.

She did not look too long; it was for the young and handsome doctor, certainly, that her dear cousin deployed the captivating variety of her artistic charms and an irresistible arsenal of romantic feelings.

Michelle observed with much more attention, then, the attitude of Dr. Sommers, who riveted on Isabella, as fascinated by an eerie glow, seemed to hover in a prohibited sphere, beyond the prosaic reality of life.

This presented no more mystery for Michelle; Isabella and Sommers loved each other madly. But, where were have they , encountered? She asked herself, bewildered. Female curiosity awaken, Michelle wanted to know all the details about this intriguing romance. She proposed to check with her aunts and, if necessary, with the protagonists themselves.

The highlight of the evening was the 23 sonata of Beethoven: The Appassionato. Isabella broke loose, literally, in the interpretation of this difficult score which ended in apotheosis. She played, despite the presence of other guests, exclusively for Carl.

She wanted with this recital to impress him, as much, or even more, when he had seen her on the beach during their first encounter. She was engaged, body and soul, by revealing all the excessive ardor of her feelings.

I am going to thank our hosts, said Sommers to Elsa sitting beside him; I must go visit my patients at the hospital. I spent a wonderful evening with you, he said to the Morgan sisters, and I thank you from the bottom of my heart. I brought you a little ointment to help you erase all traces of the scars. I left the pot in the car, I'll be back in a moment.

He took leave of the Morgans, greeted around the other guests who tried to hold him back a little more. I will show you the way, Dr. Sommers, said Isabella, who walks toward the front door.

Outside, the Moon shone in a clear sky, interspersed with silver stars. A cool breeze caressed the face of the lovers. You never told me, love dear, that you were such talented musician? you are too secretive my love... What do you know about me Carl? All...All? Said Carl...I know everything about you, insisted Carl, I know that I love you madly, and my life depends on your love. This is enough for me! They kissed.

If people see us? Said Carl, suddenly anxious... I don't give a damn my darling. Carl, my love, said Isabella who became pensive, I have a lot ideas in my head... I will come to the hospital, one of these days, to implement our projects.

Love honey, said Carl, I must go. The Hollembergs are waiting for a final prognosis. See you tomorrow...

You'll never know how much I am pleased to hear you say: see you tomorrow? I feel able to splurge, because my heart is full of joy and happiness. Tomorrow my love.

CHAPTER VII

Dr. Suzanne Birmingham, epidemiologist, sickened by the heartbreaking spectacle of all those people, she met, according to her, the black plague, avoided contact with the affected population. She sent volunteers across the city to provide the samples she needed to fulfill her mission.

Mayor Morgan housed her in a kind of luxury hotel, private property of the Town Hall, where he usually hosted the important personalities who visited the city. She walked to the toilet as soon as she was in her room, cleared promptly off all her clothes, took a shower and washed her hair.

Dr. Birmingham put a pink silk pajama, carefully examined the sheets and cover and lay down. A few minutes later, a maid knocked on the door. The maid asked her if she wanted to go down stairs to the dining room; or take her dinner in her room?

If this doesn't bother you too much, she answered, still lying on the bed, I would better eat here. Immediately, Madam, replied the eager servant.

Indeed, the servant returned soon, pushing before her a wheeled table loaded with dishes.

Can I help you madam? No thanks, curtly answered Dr. Birmingham, you may withdraw.

Dr. Birmingham ate of bon appétit, drank some drugs as a

prophylactic, nudged the table across the large room and lay down.

She called her friend Roland Peterson, a CNN reporter, to tell him about the strange phenomenon, this strange disease which affected the population of an entire city. I could send you all the details on this case, she said to him, but she advised him to come take a look. There is, perhaps, promotion in this exclusive, sensational scoop.

She was soon in the arms of Morpheus, wrapped up in the white sheets of this cozy nest.

She woke early in the morning to go home. Because she didn't want to extend her stay in this unhealthy climate, to breathe the air of this morbid atmosphere, where people could catch this naughty black plague.

She went to the toilet, lit the lamp, and mechanically, began to brush her hair. Lost in her thoughts, she didn't even look in the large beveled mirror which occupied a whole wall. Suddenly, raising her eyes, she saw her face in a diffuse darkness, where her features become blurry, indistinguishable like a shadow. She lit the dazzling stream of neon light bulbs surrounding the mirror.

Dr. Birmingham uttered a wild ripping scream triggering a sudden hysteric attack. Her screams and calls for help, brought the servants who rushed, illico, to see what was happening.

The servants found her, naked as a worm, in the middle of the room, prancing with a desperate rage despite, showing off, without shame, her beautiful burnt mahogany body like an authentic creole. She shivered with indignation, sobbed bitterly and impotent tears run down her browned cheeks.

Janet, the servant who had brought her dinner the day before, consoled her as best she could, dressed her and carefully combed her blond hair changed auburn.

Janet made her understand, in prosaic, but appropriate terms, the futility to express any resentment toward fate dictum. Useless, madam, to languish, trapped, alone in this room, chewing black ideas.

Madam, said the servant, encouraged by the passive attitude of Dr. Birmingham: Dr. Merville told us that the black curse is a transient disease and very soon, it will disappear. Janet made her drink a cup of very strong coffee and recommended to Dr. Birmingham to take it easy; everyone had suffered the same fate. Nobody died expect the one that have committed suicide.

Her panic attack healed, Dr. Birmingham called the Director of health in Jackson, making him aware of the seriousness of the situation in Montjolly.

The Director fearing the spread of this scourge, according to the alarming story of Dr. Birmingham; obtained an immediate interview with Governor Rogers, to give an account of the situation; but above all, to develop a plan of action capable of stopping the progressive race of this terrible epidemic.

The Governor gathered his emergency cabinet, and with the vote of the majority of his advisers, decided to quarantine the city of Montjolly. This measure was taken to contain the epidemic in a specific region, easy to control. He deployed on the field, a contingent of the National Guard, equipped for battle: helicopters, tanks, drones, to insure the surveillance to stop any fugitives.

These measures in place, Governor Rogers called the White House, the Secretary of State, The Secretary of Human Services, the Pentagon, the Defense Secretary, the Speaker of the House of Representatives and the Senate Majority Leader.

Then, he telephoned the Mayor of the city, Simon Morgan, to blame him for his negligent incompetence. You failed to inform the concerned authorities, about a so dangerous occurrence? You say that this epidemic has been raging for two days? Eructed the Governor, visibly angry, and it is only today, that someone else, a stranger, brings us to speed? You put me in front of a fait accompli, isn't it? I am completely distraught, without any possibility to avoid the unprecedented scandal of the sordid history of your small, shabby hometown.

I'm not happy, continued the Governor, very angry. Morgan, you're an incompetent and a fool. You should have thought that this strange phenomenon would inevitably extend beyond the narrow confines of your mediocre jurisdiction. I will be responsible for all the troubles that will befall on my back because of you. Governor Rogers hang up loudly.

Simon Morgan remained crestfallen, surprised by the unworthy way the Governor had admonished him. He felt, a little guilty. Precisely, he didn't alert the provincial authorities, for the simple reason that he feared spreading the news, which would inevitably have attracted experts, specialists, the press, in his little corner of paradise.

Roland Peterson, of CNN, warned by his friend, Dr. Suzanne

Birmingham, had immediately gathered his team: Britt Home, his driver and Jeff O'Neil, his cameraman and, without losing time, sailed on for Montjolly.

James Nadowsky, a Fox Television reporter, followed Roland Peterson as his shadow. He walked on the heels of Perterson everywhere he goes. James started, headlong the pursuit of his competitor.

The two teams arrived in Montjolly, just in time. As soon as they were onsite, the National Guard took position around the town and the Commandant, General Collin, sent a communiqué to the population to inform them about the quarantine established by the provincial authorities.

General Pete Collin intimated to the city, the formal order, under threat of severe penalties: interdiction to use the River, either for fishing or swimming. The beach access was forbidden to them. The maritime cabotage service was suspended until further notice. The utilization of the roads are interdict. Anyone caught disobeying the orders stipulated in the communiqué, will be imprisoned for one year, without any form of trial whatsoever.

Simon Morgan, visibly upset and disappointed, had to send heralds throughout the city, announce the sad news of the quarantine.

Upon his arrival, Roland Peterson contacted his friend, Dr. Suzanne Birmingham who advised him to speak to the Mayor of the city: Simon Morgan and the Director of the hospital Sainte Cécile, Dr. Joe Merville were the only people able to provide him with the information's he needed to warn the public about this weird phenomenon, the evil black curse.

Wolf Blizer of the CNN network, in his four o'clock news program, created a feverish anticipation on the mind of his audience by announcing, in flash, the discovery of an epidemic that had infected all the white people of a small town in Mississippi.

Roland Peterson, CNN onsite reporter, was going at five o'clock, to present a comprehensive and exclusive picture of the situation.

The issuance of Peterson began with a brief presentation of Montjolly city. Peterson exhibited the streets floral designations; rustic and elegant houses. He highlighted the architectural achievements of various styles: modern and rococo. He showed the breathtaking panorama that served as a framework to the city, incomparably original.

Peterson had recorded the picturesque scenes which was taken place on the square. Old people, sitting on granite benches, warming themselves in the Sun, absently following the noisy antics of unruly kids, chasing a white ball, uttering wild cries. The old gentlemen, looks pale and tired, played chess in silence; others slowly wandered on the sidewalk paved with bricks. Everything seemed normal. People apparently were in good health, nothing really suspicious or unusual in this charming picture.

The Mayor, Simon Morgan, laconically, answered questions of Peterson. Morgan was visibly on his guard, he didn't want to reveal to the curiosity of his interlocutor, the underside of the case.

Simon granted the interview to CNN, despite himself, on the peremptory insistence of his wife Elsa, but that put him in straight jacket.

"Mayor, asked Peterson in an anodyne tone. Why have you subscribed to the imposed quarantine in the city?

"The Governor Pete Rogers, without consulting the experts, without seeking the advice of physicians who are familiar with the epidemic; physicians who are dealing with the affected population, took unilaterally the decision to impose this disastrous quarantine. This ill-considered action has the potential to ruin, forever, the prosperity and peace of our city.

"I have been told, questioned Peterson, that only the white people have been contaminated by this unknown and virulent virus?

"To what I know, it seems that this virus attacks only whites, replied Morgan to the incredulous reporter.

"Do you know, sir, the percentage of the population affected by the disease?

"Everyone in Montjolly has contracted the evil black curse, as doctor Carl Sommers call it.

"How! said Peterson, a little bewildered I thought you said that only white people were victims of the evil black curse?

"Yes!

"But then, insisted Peterson, there is a blatant contradiction? If all the inhabitants of the city had caught the evil black curse, that means blacks, also, have been infected? logical deduction, isn't it?

"There is no black in Montjolly, replied Simon

Morgan, a bit embarrassed. "There is no black in Montjolly?

Said in echo the reporter from CNN. Not a single one?

"Not one! said Morgan looking with an air of aggressive challenge, the stunned reporter.

"How many people are there in the city?

"After the last census, the Montjolly population Was estimated at more than twenty-five thousand.

"How the population has responded to this unforeseen disaster?

"The epidemic has caused a moment of panic in the community. Panicked people, not knowing what it was, invaded the hospital seeking help. Thanks to Dr. Merville and Sommers, who make them understand the benignity of this strange disease, sent everyone home, with a little less fear and apprehension.

"Have you regrettably unregistered losses of human lives?

"Dr. Merville can provide these statistics to you. He has all the data.

Wolf Blizer announced for the next hour, the sequel to the show, with an interview with Dr. Joe Merville, Director of Sainte Cécile hospital. It was, literally, bombarded with enquiries about this unknown locality, that was not on the map of the State of Mississippi.

Dr. Joe Merville, during his interview with CNN reporter, Roland Perterson, provides more details on the ravages made by the evil black curse to the population. He lamented the psychological trauma caused by this sudden change in their physical appearance, which resulted in a profound alteration of the collective psyche.

Well-known personalities have tried to commit suicide. There were seven dead and many injured people. We deplored the number of suicide attempts, aborted thanks to the boundless dedication of Dr. Carl Sommers.

Dr. Merville made a brief exegesis of the evil black curse, to explain to the public, in appropriate and simple terms, the relative innocuousness of the virus responsible for this pigment mutation. No symptoms were discovered, which would reveal a pernicious effect of disease on the human body.

Preliminary analysis carried out in our laboratories, did indicate, in addition to the elementary metamorphosis of the color of the skin of contaminated individuals, no alteration structural, physiological or functional of the vital organs.

The epidemiologist: Dr. Suzanne Birmingham, sent by the authorities of Jackson, (she also have contracted the black curse) collected samples, that she sent to specialized laboratories. I hope soon, continued Dr. Merville, we could unveil the intriguing mystery of this unholy plight.

The Black Caucus, the association of legislative black members, within the American Assembly, through its Chairperson, the representative Barbara Lee, wrote to the Governor of Mississippi, a very stern letter, in which, she asked him to justify the drastic measures taken by his administration, to impose a quarantine in the town of Montjolly.

The representative Barbara Lee pointed out to Governor Rogers, that he had endorsed a great responsibility to the community in question. That he was obliged to provide supply for the population until the lifting of the quarantine. He would have, in addition, not only compensate workers and patrons, for losses incurred, but also, all those whose profitmaking activities have been interrupted unnecessarily.

She made him know, that she would discuss the issue in the House, to ensure the rule of law covered his hasty and inconsiderate action. The Black Caucus immediately introduced a Bill, calling on the federal Government to support expenditures for the city of Montjolly, during this quarantine, with no defined duration. The news of this leprosy that blackened the white made Headline in the national and international press. The White House was flooded with calls, from especially, European countries. The population, rightly alarmed, required from their respective Government, the quarantine American products. They demanded and obtained the imposition of an embargo on the United States, the ban, until further notice, of ports and airports to vessels and Yankee's aircrafts.

France reported at a later date, the meeting of the Eight most industrialized countries, which was to be held in Paris. Russia informed the U.S. delegation, led by Secretary of State Condeleezza Rice, that she was not welcome in Moscow, for the time being. The talks, aimed at reducing the number of ballistic missiles pointing towards one another; had to wait for more favorable circumstances.

Vice President Dick Cheney, for once, lost his phlegm and his cynicism. No one couldn't evidently provide information on this scandalous quarantine that threatening to break the relations of the country with the allies.

He telephoned, personally, to the Mississippi Governor Pete Rogers, asking him to provide explanations, so he could, in turn, informed, foreign Governments, alarmed by the publicity around this "evil black curse" and the quarantine that Rogers had imposed on the population of this unknown village.

Have you sent some experts to the scene? inquired Cheney, very circumspect.

"The Director of health has delegated an epidemiologist...

"What was the result of his investigation? cut him off the Vice President.

"We haven't received yet the results of the analysis entrusted to specialized laboratories.

"And then, on what criteria have you based to cram America into this dirty mess?

"The epidemiologist has been contaminated, she said that the situation was very serious and we had to act with diligence to prevent the contamination of the entire country...

"Governor Rogers, said Cheney, who began to get excited. I don't give a damn about of your epidemiologist opinion; You should have consult the federal administration, before taken this ill-considered decision that engages the whole nation.

"But I acted in the public best interest...

"In the public interest, my butt! You acted as an idiot. I give you an hour, to send me the results of the analysis, imbecile, moron.

That's the way it was, like second nature, the Vice President Cheney, who was, the real power in Washington, ordinary deal with those subordinated to him. He always dealt with a scornfully arrogant and insulting manner, with all those who do not slavishly submitted to his dictatorial rules or haven't obey his orders, much of the time, absurd or inconsistent.

James Nadowsky, for his part, as professional freeloader, had interviewed the doctor Joe Merville and a few other personalities of the city. In his ten 'clock show, led by Greta Van Susteren, the Fox network, transmitted on the air a story much more alarming than that of CNN.

Juicy details, on the social life of the city, made surface

unexpectedly. In fact, it was learned that the town of Montjolly housed no person of color. That the entire population was affected by this evil black curse. The only means of communication with the outside world were reduced to the strict minimum. They have no television nor telephone in the homes. This society immobilized in an inveterate archaism, rejected any contact with the world and forbade its members to evolve outside the narrow and retrograde sphere of this xenophobic community.

In addition, the Montjolians lived in relative safety, free from the scourges, controversies, social conflicts, and this satanic polarization that destroying with small firearms, the American society.

AIDS, homosexuality, shameful diseases, were unknown to this community, retrograde, admittedly, Puritan, obviously, but healthy and natural, exempt of the vices and defects which infected modern society corrupt and supposedly civilized.

In the next newsletter of the CNN reporter, journalist, Roland Peterson, he communicated a panic scare to stunned viewers, horrified, eyes riveted on their small screen; at the sight of their favorite reporter converted into a nigger.

Peterson had to admit that his crew (Britt Home and Jeff O'Neil), also were infected with the evil black curse. He said, with some emotion in the voice and a growing concern in his eyes, that the thing had occurred during his sleep. He felt, he said, no physical pain. He experimented no significant decrease of his mental faculties, or a weakening of his skills in the fields of cognitive thinking and energetic action.

While deploring his forced imprisonment at Montjolly, Roland Peterson promised to his viewers, to explore the history of this community, to say the least, bizarre, keeping them abreast of contemporary activities of the people during the quarantine.

James Nadowsky, of Fox Television, took refuge at the hospital Sainte Cécile, citing imaginary ailments, to avoid exposing his blackness to the racist fanatics of this radical and polarized network. James Nadowsky, in doing so, left the field completely open for the CNN representative.

The vice president, Dick Cheney, telephoned the Speaker of the House of Representatives: the incompetent Dennis Aster. Who was miraculously raised to this high office, through threats from Larry

Flint, who scared to death, the best qualified, most capable, but unfortunately, who had eel under rock, skeleton in the closet, to hide shamefully or risk been exposed by the vindictive Larry Flint.

Cheney intimated him the formal order to hold the quarantine in place, the quarantine of Governor Rogers; although tests had not revealed any real danger to the proven population. But the idea that all the whites in this country could become black was an intolerable prospect, we must fight with utmost determination and resolve, Cheney told Dennis Aster.

Barbara Lee introduced a drafter law calling for the immediate lifting of the quarantine (because the evil black curse presented no risk health), according to the results of the very elaborate analysis obtained in sophisticated laboratories in the country.

Furthermore, this Bill stipulated that the State of Mississippi should compensate the city of Montjolly and compensate its people for the losses incurred.

Dennis Aster entrusted to a Member of Parliament: John Boehner, the stewardship of the debate on the Democrats bill. They were confronting the maneuvers and the intrigues of the Republican majority, to punish the Montjolian population by fear and ignorance.

John Boehner was an ambitious reactionary, an ultraconservative, fiercely opponent to any innovation in the rigid system established by whites to protect their privileges and prohibit any active participation of people of color, in the management and distribution of the wealth of the nation.

Barbara Lee opened the hostilities in the House, accusing the Governor of Mississippi (a confirmed racist) of unnecessarily imposing this abject quarantine to this small community with limited resources, unable to resist the heavy machinery of the provincial administration, and the vindictive wickedness of the federal Government.

Governor Rogers, continued Barbara Lee, made this stupid decision, subjected to an irresponsible panic. He had no information on the seriousness of the evil black curse, nor its ability to spread, nothing that could justify this action hasty and thoughtlessly taken, which put America in a dirty mess, in an embarrassing and perilous situation. This arrogant fool has tarnished the reputation of our dear country by associating a stigma of shame with this benign evil, without any danger to the health of the general public.

We demand, continued the Representative, the immediate repeal of the decree and the support by the federal Government, of the effective control of this quarantine for its lifting, without objection or delay.

"The representative of the Democratic Party said John Boehner, in taking the floor; comes once more, to spread, big time, her politic immaturity, her civic irresponsibility and her blatant disregard for the constitutional rights of the provinces. These people, I mean the Democrats, are full of contradictions. They would be the first to shouting loudly against inaction Governor Rogers, if that evil black curse was raging among the population of the other cities of the State of Mississippi. As long as we have not found a cure for this terrible disease, as long as the community in question will be infected by this evil plague; we recommend to the Government, the nonintervention in the ordinary management of State affairs. Prematurely, or not, I praised Governor Rogers to having taken these preventive measures, to stop the epidemic from spreading everywhere.

"The Democrat: Ed Pastor of Arizona, took the floor to refute the false allegations of the reactionary John Boehner. Firstly, evil black curse is not contagious. Everyone in Montjolly has caught the evil at the same time (with the exception of a doctor and several journalists arrived the next day) Secondly, the evil black curse, according to any clearly stated analysis, presents no real danger for the health of the people. The pigment cell mutation didn't alter, in anyway, the normal functioning of the organism. Thirdly, Mr. Boehner is a hypocrite. When his party favored the action of the federal government, circumventing the exclusive rights of a State, to impose its retrograde ideology; the Republicans brandished the starry banner of democracy with one hand, the constitutional weapon of stupidity in the other, they find a way to justify, even, the most outrageous abuse of power. I quote by example, the case of lady Chiavo decided by the Republican Senate and the atrocious appointment of George W. Bush to the Presidency by the Supreme Court.

"What are you picking up here? Protested Ileana Ros-Lehtinen, republican representative from Miami, (impregnable bastion of Cuban landowners) what's mean this incoherent rant?

The representative of Arizona has restated the same discordant catch phrases, him and his colleagues uttered regardless of the subject matter, since the election of President Bush. We are discussing a very precise issue, the risk of contamination, of all inhabitants of the country by this deadly virus, which threated of extinction the white American population.

"The representative, Ros-Lehtinen, has no reason to alarmed, said, Kendrick Meek, also from Miami, tongue-in-cheek, dialectician feared for his compelling synthesis; the evil black curse has the possibility of recognizing the nigger, even when they dye their hair blond and use cosmetics products to whiten their skin.

The president, per tempore, of the House struck with force his gavel on his desk and recalled to order Miami representative Kendrick Meek. The most basic politeness requires, the rules of this House demands a strict decorum of all its members: the respect of his colleagues, restrain from offending with abusive and backbiting comments their susceptibility. In addition, it is forbidden, to engage in any personal dispute at the expense of the steadiness of the parliamentary debates.

"Excuse me, Mr. president, of the Assembly and to the Member Ros-Lehtinen, but it is inconceivable, Mr. president, inadmissible, that people can still, today, impugned the sigma of shame to the color of my skin and equate it with an horrible disease. I protest strongly against this outrageous allegation.

We, nigger, are wearing, today, physical and moral scars of the excruciating torture an inhuman humiliation that the Aryan race has inflicted upon us, with contempt and cruelty.

If their skin became black, (their only different attribute from the other races, their only brand of distinction) discrimination and abuse will cease immediately. This aberrant complex of superiority, the first instigator of the criminal holdings of people of color; of wars of aggression against the people judged inferior, of the crusades being preached by the Church and the affluent societies, to destroy the unworthy civilization that should need disappear to extend the influence of the Arian race all over the world.

"This bombastic rhetoric is an absurd fallacy, declared Mike Ross of Arkansas, in taking the floor. Mr. president, the Florida representative harps the same worn refrains, the same preposterous and irrelevant ideas. His bombastic and inconsistent tirade, is complacent in his ranting of one dubious dialectic, like an illuminate exalted by his own whims... The decision of the Governor Rogers to impose this quarantine on Mont jolly city, should be the object of any criticism on the part of the Liberals. This is a preventive measure taken upon the advice of health specialists, to avoid the spread of a contagious disease. Those who ask the lifting of the quarantine, are irresponsible. They don't have any evident data: on the brood period of this unknown calamity. They don't know the effects, in the long term, that this strange mutation can produce on the human organism. So, I recommend that the House abstains to intervene in the State of Mississippi affair, until further order, to allow time to the experts to assess the safety or the malignity of the mutation, in the affected population.

"The evil black curse sowed havoc in the Greek camp, said Maxime Waters, Member of the California delegation, Whites are afraid. Panic hates the idea of losing their badge of superiority. To do this, they are willing to sacrifice the wellbeing of a whole community, to throw at nettles prosperity of a small provincial town, victim twice; crushed by the evil black curse which upsets his life and by the stupid and racist reaction of the authorities of Mississippi.

Jo Benner of Alabama, who chaired the meeting, deeply outraged by the inflammatory comments and the inappropriate language of the proponents of lifting the quarantine; suspended the proceedings until further notice.

Mr. Bonner made it clear to the protagonists, their excesses of language and their vicious personal attacks were not part of the code of conduct of a member in the legislative Assembly.

The excessive passion of the Democrats helped the Republican majority, to avoid commenting openly on this thorny controversy.

Although they sympathized to the cause of the Montjolly racists, Republicans did not (in good sheep of Panurge) oppose the decision taken by the Governor Rogers, decision endorsed by Vice President Cheney and his clique of drafters without scruples.

The meeting at the legislative Chamber, leading to an impasse, created even more confusion and fear in the public. The television networks, uninformed, related all sorts of stories, each more extravagant than the others.

CNN announced the arrest of two individuals with the evil black curse syndrome, who were trying to flee the contaminated town. Fox talk about the arrest of six women in Australia, with the visible characteristics and the stigma of this black leprosy. The Wall Street Journal, required daily, in its editorial page, that the federal

Government must reinforce the quarantine, give local authorities the necessary resources: (money, troops, logistic) everything they need to support the siege for an indefinite period.

A fool from the Weekly Standard advocated even more drastic measures. He wanted to exile the entire Montjolian population on a deserted atoll in the Pacific Ocean; to reduce to the minimum the chances of contamination for the rest of the country. It was necessary, at all costs; avoid this unprecedented disaster, this abominable fate, this terrible calamity, this deplorable eschatology. This occurrence would be tragic: the complete eradication of the white race from the surface of the Earth.

Rush Limbaugh, the eminent guru of the Republican party thought ossified in stupidity; the anointed interpreter, of the conservative absurd philosophy; the shabby theoretician of racism and hatred; the spiritual master of the brotherhood of the unrepentant reactionaries; Rush Limbaugh evil instinct (activated by drugs) set the evil black curse in a context much more cynical and frightening, however, closer to the reality that all logical and reasonable, assumptions made by the so called experts.

"Who gained profits from the crime committed it!" said Boss Limbaugh, as Keith Olbermann called him, host of television output: Countdown with Keith Olberman. I think, I am almost sure, advanced Limbaugh, in one of his stormy emissions, that the Latinos are the instigators of this Machiavellian plot to eliminate the White majority, spread their retrograde culture and impose the use of their archaic language to the Anglo Saxon quintessential civilization.

These people have invaded our country in a clandestine manner, penetrated the secrets of our science and acquired the knowledge necessary to concoct this awful evil black curse that attacked unrelenting only the whites.

Religious fanatics, blinded by centuries of systematic brainwashing, invoking divine mercy every Sunday in their temples (real insane asylums) continued the Boss; attributed wrongly, without evidence, that evil black curse to some heaven retribution.

The Government must investigate, this weird phenomenon with all the sophisticated means in its arsenal of counterintelligence weapons to prevent and combat terrorist attacks like this one, wherever they come from.

Because, I am convinced, lamented Rush Limbaugh, an attack against the Aryan race, a plot hatched by the frustrated invaders: niggers, Latinos, Arabs, natives, inferior race, the gent degenerate: homosexuals or perverts, the dregs of the marginal population, all of the parasites who lived at the expense of the authentic sons of the nation.

These absurd comments highlighted the congenital buffoon character of the drug addict, the moron, obese, swell up to silliness. His audience (white men, false devotees and racist) love him as a God.

These sheep of Panurge follow to the letter, without discernment, all the recommendations that he made them. That's where was born and spread, the abominable idea to exterminate all the inhabitants of this cursed village, to avoid this terrible catastrophe: the Arian race outright annihilation.

The Senate did not want to commit immediately, in the controversy. No one knew, really, what going on. Again, the inconclusive analysis results, done in many specialized laboratories, added to the general confusion.

Water, air, soil, human tissues, blood samples, plants and flowers, everything was doing fine. But the traces of the volatile virus, despite frantic searches undertaken by the despondent scholars were not found.

The U.S. Government, unable to provide credible and reassuring explanations on this diabolical epidemic, was in turn shunned by the concerned countries, i.e., the European, Australia, and Argentina. Smote banned U.S. trade and tourism. Aircraft and boats, already on route, have to backtrack.

This case took a catastrophic magnitude.

At the request of Ambassador Bolton, the United States, the Security Council meets in special session, to decide on this thorny controversy, which could disrupt the order of things, upset free trade between nations and threaten international peace.

Ambassador Bolton, in a speech loaded with arrogance and defiance, launched an ultimatum to the European Union, the Australia and Argentina. The U.S. Government demanded the immediate lifting of this offensive banned and threatened with terrible reprisals those who dared defy the only major world power.

We have added Ambassador Bolton, taken all necessary measures to contain evil black curse and prevent its spread. We enhance the aerial and maritime surveillance set up by the Governor of Mississippi. We increased to ten thousand, the number of soldiers who are maintaining the siege of the city.

Our Government offers to everyone, the formal guarantee and unequivocally the absolute safety against the evil black curse. "Nobody died, we have not yet isolated the pernicious virus, but it will be soon. Don't worry and take confidence in American science.

France, in the person of Ambassador: Jean Lavigne, refused to comply and opposed a categorical veto to the Security Council resolution, prepared by the only great power of the world.

One of your president, I think Ronald Reagan, repeated all the time, his favorite mantra: "Trust and verify" trust, but verify! As long as the threat of contamination exists, as long as an antidote to this virulent poison is not found; our ports and airports will be closed to U.S. boats and planes. With courage, pride and determination we assume our responsibilities to our people; We are not surrendered to any blackmail, wherever it comes.

The situation became more and more difficult. Vice President Cheney, who had dictated, himself, the speech to his sidekick: Ambassador Bolton read; didn't expected this violent reaction on the part of the European countries. Cheney, the rage in the heart, resigned himself to change his approach. He pretended to accept, in principle, the idea of the embargo, but a mixed embargo which would not involve a drastic disruption of trade between the United States and Europe.

He tried, in addition, to entice poor countries of the European Union, offering them attractive bribes. He wanted to break the weak links in the chain, circumvent by the tangent the opposition of the great Manitou. This bold attempt stillborn because of the horrible propaganda made around the issue by the American media.

Panicked reporters, unable to investigate, on background, this contentious subject, dangerously extrapolated on the true nature of the evil black curse. The CNN team led by Roland Peterson, caught in the trap of its legitimate professional curiosity was victim, also of this dreaded black curse; realized alarming reports, broadcast during a new nocturnal emissions. The sinister face, the scowl, the gruff tone of Roland Peterson would suffice, alone, to give the jitters and to sow panic among anxious viewers, their eyes riveted on their television sets

The hideous metamorphosis (according to the epithet given

by Limbaugh to this skin darkening), frightened, even more, the leukoderma species, already terrified. The article of the prominent dermatologist Marc Stanley, (published in the Wall Street Journal), scared the daylight out of Arian people.

This eminent professor of Johns Hopkins, Washington University placed the appearance of this evil unknown in a context that embraced both the purely pathological and clinical aspect of the epidemic, but also, the context of its holistic integration into the existential drama that is the frenzied pollution of the planet, by emissions of toxic gases and volatile chemical waste.

Professor Stanley listed first, many skin infections due to defects or agents' pathogens disturbing, as exposure to ultraviolet rays, the lack of melanin in cells in the dermis, etc.

He quoted Addison's disease to indicate that skin infections might be caused by a slight modification of the cell structure.

Albinism was taken to exemplify the severity of a lack or absence of melanin (pigment responsible for the color of human skin) in the skin cells, in the dermis.

Professor Stanley brushed a fairly bleak picture of the wide range of skin conditions. Jaundice characterized by an excess of bile pigments in the blood. He reviewed, dermatitis: benign inflammation of the tissue epidermal endemic (such as allergies) caused by the toxic, industrial pollutants or natural, by plant or animal poisons. He also mentioned the proliferation of skin diseases: (syphilis, eczema, smallpox, measles, scarlet fever, and many others) in the pathology affecting the cells of the dermis and the epidermis tissue.

These diseases that I listed, said Professor Stanley in his presentation; have been the subject of in-depth studies and, in most cases, treated successfully. But the mutation that occurred at the level of the enzymes and melanin remains a troubling mystery, in the case of the evil black curse.

These enzymes serve as catalyst for melanodermic pigments that are responsible for the protection of the skin from the harmful sun rays.

The unfortunate reduction of the ozone layer in the stratosphere, leaving our biosphere without real defense, opened the door to dangerous particles from solar flares and the pernicious ultraviolet rays, which attack the immune system of the skin tissue and make them vulnerable to awful pathogens.

It is in this context that we must consider the bizarre phenomenon, the incongruous appearance of this evil black mutation, added Professor Stanley. Whether we like it or not, the chemical industry fighting against our ecosystem, with repeated attacks, lead us, slowly, but surely, towards a predictable and inevitable disaster.

I am convinced, continued Professor Stanley, that this inexplicable mutation, even enigmatic, because it occurred outside the scientific standards, the natural process and progressive alchemical transmutation of innervated cells.

I might, conclude, said Professor Stanley, that the Earth has already exhausted its arsenal of hermetic protection against vectors of interstellar dust and cosmic rays. This polluted pollen waste, a heterogeneous mixture, composed of mesons, of hadrons, quarks and antiquarks, who came from the absolute gravitational collapse; have the potential to alter the genetic structure of the human chromosome, duplicate the phenomenon of evil black curse, anywhere in the world, and create all kind of hideous monsters, capable of destroying civilization and life on Earth.

The article of the Professor Stanley was severely criticized by the conservative class. She fustigated verbally the eminent dermatologist for taking, categorically, the party of the Liberals, like Al Gore; by advocating the ambiguous idea of a gradual warming of the planet.

The insignificant increase in the earth temperature, recorded by meteorologists, is due, according to the conservative scientists, in a cyclical phenomenon, caused by solar explosions, produced at regular intervals, but remote from each other.

The Republican nomenclature rejected the thesis of Professor Stanley condescendingly. They contemptuously called it childish naiveté. The exponential growth of the capitalist economy was for these blind and stubborn fanatics, the sole valid criterion, in the rational evaluation of a scientific theory. A respectable theory, said the paid scholars and the idiot conservative nomenclature, must states in any egalitarian equation, the fundamental and proven values, taking into account the interests of the ruling class.

They followed, to the last iota, the methodology of ancient techniques, repelling any innovation that challenged or threatened with contempt, their archaic way of thinking and their outdated dialectic.

The preservation of the tradition in all aspects of life, was for this predatory companies ossified in pride and stupidity, the unique way the rational development of a progressive and thoughtful dynamic structure of knowledge transformation could occur. Greed is the only compass that guide this class to his destiny of selfish greatness and stingy prosperity. These people here have endorsed no science, no theory that could curb their selfish greed, their hedonism of inveterate epicurean, their lust for power and wealth.

The universally accredited idea that industrial pollution, the emission of carbon dioxide and other toxic products, reducing the ozone layer, could threaten life on the planet was unbearable to the conservatives.

The Bush administration, led by Vice President Dick Cheney, did his best to reassure the O M S, the recalcitrant countries, who were, virtually, less confident in the United States of America.

CHAPTER XII

Montjolly, small picturesque and unknown town, became, overnight, the darling of the media from around the world.

A flotilla of brightly painted helicopters, bearing logos of the newspaper it represented or very famous television channels, patrolled the sky above the proven city, which, despite this constant uproar, and this feverish agitation, had resumed a semblance of normal life.

The schools had reopened their doors. The shops were busy again. The factories, although unable to receive orders from the big firms, struggled, however, to provide labor to the workers. Business owners had decided to remain productive, to enable mother and father to meet their family's obligations; but, above all, to give them an outlet for their idle miseries.

Farms and agro industries were the most affected by this unexpected embargo. The town hall was forced to provide immediate assistance to lay off workers.

Farmers free of charge, distributing the surplus of milk that they could no longer sell at Biloxi, Fulton and the Gulf Coast City.

The U.S. Navy helicopters provided the supply for the city. They parachuted at regular intervals, on the large esplanade, located behind the hospital Sainte Cécile, heavy containers of essential goods for the survival of the community. Mayor: Simon Morgan had identified and listed a number of items the public needed, and given to the federal authorities to fulfill.

Trucks from the City Hall, carrying foodstuffs were dispatched to distribution centers, placed at strategic locations around the city. People went about their usual business, watched by hundreds of intrusive cameras. Some television stations, broadcasted, permanently to their viewers the boring scenes of the ordinary life of this unfortunate village.

Simon Morgan had protested to the military authorities (who administered the quarantine) so that, at least, to reduce this frantic air traffic, to enable people to rest during the night. Everything was fair game. Children going to school, workers going to the factory or their farms, the contrite bigots, dragging towards the Church, while clinging on their rosary, the impassive old men, playing chess on the public square, the disgruntled old ladies, warming up in the morning sun, you name it.

Already resigned Montjolian, remained indifferent to any such defamatory publicity which they were subject. They had neither radio nor television. They completely ignored the scandalous commotion around the epidemic and the offensive comments from the national and international press.

The Morgan Bridesmaids: Joan and Cathy had, (under the urgent demand of their nieces, Michelle and Isabella), formed a Committee of aid and leisure which main task was to ensure the physical and mental health of the population.

Indeed, the ordeal was difficult to bear for these people anchored in their ineradicable belief of racial superiority.

Most of them suffered from a nervous breakdown and languished miserably in deep prostration, with a melancholic lethargy nearby daze...

The Committee of the "Public safety" as referred to it, Matt Potter. The Committee recruited young volunteers who are sent to visit families and report to the attention of the Committee, all cases of disease, depression that they encountered on their way.

The Public Safety Committee although having a clearly defined role, was going beyond its powers to initiate a genuine revolution, upsetting the archaic structures of the Montjolian society.

Cathy Morgan won by Isabella ideas, and deeply disappointed by the turn of events, had recruited a host of young people who, at one time or another, had expressed their desire to reform, modernize, the social life of the city.

Complete isolation where Montjoliam youth mustered, deprived of a plethora of opportunities: in the field of education; significantly limited his chance to flourish in contact with advanced minds; knowingly, reduced its ability to acquire practical and scientific knowledge and skill, not taught at the Montjolly high school.

Cathy Morgan was the Chairwoman of the Committee. Elsa, her sister-in-law was the Treasurer. Lisa Troy, recommended by her good friend, Isabella, was chosen as Executive Secretary of the association. Lisa was a dynamic, competent, talented, possessing a friendly temperament and a secret charm.

Matt Potter, Harry Morgan, Samuel Rutherford, Ronald Commins, Jack Spencer, Charles Lewis and Robert Carlson, participated in the first meeting of the Committee.

On the side of the ladies there were: Michelle and Isabella Morgan, Mona Lisa Hollemberg, Christel Baldwin, Samantha Sandford, Dr. Suzanne Birmingham and Grace Norris.

The first meeting of the Committee of Public Safety (this name was adopted unanimously by the Assembly) was animated. Each proposed a different project. The best were voted on and adopted by a majority of the votes.

Joan Morgan insisted on inviting the reverend Ted Vogel, because she made it clear to the Committee that father Vogel can mobilize, at a glance, the entire city. In this same vein, Dr. Birmingham advocated the candidacy of reporter Roland Peterson and his team, the only opening available to the outside world.

Mona Lisa Hollemberg suggested the recruiting of all the doctors present in the city. Inevitably, we will need their service, she said, smiling and, looking right at Isabella's eyes. Isabella remained impassive, affecting a fake indifferent attitude to the implication of the equivocal words of Mona Lisa. It was agreed that Dr. Merville and Sommers, would be invited to the next meeting.

Lisa Troy brings to the attention of the Committee, the fact that they haven't included Bernice Merville and her children: Rachel and Brandon, in the list of potential members of the Public Safety Committee. Brandon was studying medicine and Rachel law at

Harvard; they were retained in Montjolly, like everyone else, by the quarantine. Their integration was approved immediately, as well as that of Nancy Morice.

Isabella, knew two rivals in the group: her very beloved cousin Michelle which, during the dinner hosted by her aunts, had deployed a battery of discrete simpering, languorous making, to attract and retain the attention of Dr. Sommers; and the lovely Mona Lisa, who had covered the man with her

Insistent and cuddly looks.

Isabella didn't want Dr. Sommers to participate in the Committee of Public safety, to avoid the inevitable clashes between her brother and Carl, but especially to save her fiancé from the aggressive kindness of single bridesmaids seeking a suitable party. She couldn't, either, ask him to apologize to the Committee, for fear of offending the susceptibility of her lover, who would think that she did not trust him. So, she didn't attempt to influence his decision, one way or another.

Lisa Troy, the Secretary, was entrusted the task to announce to the doctors, their selection to the Montjolian elite society. Fr. Vogel welcomed this initiative with enthusiasm and proposed (before any worldly activity) to implore the divine mercy, performing a rogatory procession where the entire city should participate, with humility and contrition.

Dr. Joe Merville declined the honor, but accepted willingly, the involvement of his wife and his children. His multiple obligations and the limited number of doctors at the hospital, he said, did not allow him to devote a minute of his precious time to these frivolous activities.

Dr. Sommers was really flattered, they had thought of him. Sincerely, he wanted to join this young, dynamic group which, according to Lisa Troy, wanted to change the antiquated infrastructure and outdated mores of the Montjolian society. But when he learned that Harry Morgan was a member, his instinct in alert, recommended him to abstain.

Despite the insistent and passionate arguments of Lisa Troy, sparkle in her eyes, she told him, he can play a leading and unique role. He could be a catalyst in the radical transformation of the behavior of the natives. He argued the weight of his responsibilities to the hospital and the lack of physician, to deny this honor.

However, he promised to Lisa Troy to participate, (if necessary), in his sphere of influence, to the activities of the Committee of Public safety. Lisa Troy, frankly disappointed, complained of the failure of her embassy to Isabella, believing her friend would have a compassionate ear. Isabella was pleasantly surprised by the decision of her fiancé, but she played that she was upset, to give the change to Lisa.

Because she feared, with good reason, the permanent climate of tension and the inevitable opportunities for conflict between her brother, aggressive and vindictive and her lover, man of principle, reluctant to yield to anyone.

Roland Peterson, made arrangements with CNN who consented to retransmit some spectacles emanating from Montjolly. These events would serve as a vehicle to solicit funds to finance the grandiose projects of the Committee.

James Nadowsky, Fox reporter, having suffered severe admonitions from his Director and furious threats from Rupert Murdoch, resurged and offered to the Public Safety Committee, the antennas of the Fox television network, in exchange for exclusivity on the first shows and some preferred interviews.

The FOX offer was much more generous than CNN. The Committee opted for two uninterrupted hours, live, on the waves of this chain of stations devoted to the conservative, racist and retrograde propaganda of the Republican Party.

The Montjolly people were, by no means, resigned to their fate. They were constantly harassing the officials, of the besieged city hall, petitioning the State authorities, claiming loudly, an antidote to this insidious poison that threatened to exterminate them all.

Every morning ambulances brought to the hospital, heaps of old people, suffering from depression, who attempted to end their lives. The hope that the evil black curse would be short in life gradually faded to make way for a deep despair. An atmosphere of sadness and melancholy draped the city in this mourning period. This city once so happy.

The rogatory procession organized with solemnity by the parish priest, didn't produce the miracle awaited by the population. It had depressed them more.

The Committee of Public Safety, aware of this harmful situation and the secret and poignant drama that had plagued in families; decided, (despite formal objections from a few diehards), to cover the city with a telecommunication network, and the use of the telephone, radio and television.

The unexpected announcement of this initiative created a happy diversion in the public. The reviews went well. It has been said, that this radical isolation had lost its raison d'être, since the wolf broke surreptitiously into the fold, without warning, under the cover of darkness.

On the urgent request of James Nadowsky, Fox parachuted, ten giant TV screens and the necessary equipment to a live satellite broadcast. These screens were placed at strategic points: the square in front of the Town Hall near the church, on the esplanade of the hospital, at Silver Linden Park, located north of the lilac avenue; to enable the population to participate in the Festival.

The Public Safety Committee would take advantage of this bargain, to seek financial assistance from all the viewers, to financing major infrastructure works and development projects planned for the city of Montjolly.

CNN, to save face, sent to the Town Hall, Twenty telephone lines, and electronic gadgets necessary to ensure the solicitation and transfer of funds, the Committee hoped to collect for the duration of the show and beyond.

Matt Potter was chosen unanimously as the host of the evening. Indeed, Matt Potter was an ideal choice. He was a handsome guy, full of innate skills, a daring story teller who has an intellectual look jaded with an irresistible smile.

He had a dual personality: half gentleman, half gigolo; living in dilettante with too gullible women money. In a few years, he had squandered the fortune that his parents had bequeathed to him. He had only the villa des Eglantines Street and a meager income from a bleed investment in the electronic factory, under contract with the Pentagon that his father ran.

James Nadowsky, under threats of Rupert Murdoch: his boss, had eventually display to the general public, his Adonis face, ravaged by the evil black curse. He presented, in a sober and elegant style; a summary of the tragicomic drama that was played in this lost Mississippi town. This ridiculous and heartbreaking drama once, already, was changing completely the hostile, abusive, hateful, racist whites, behavior toward people of color.

This epidemic, for the time being circumscribed, could quickly, spread like wildfire and completely change the optic of the so called superior race.

The host of the evening: Matt Potter, announced by Nadowsky, appeared on the small screen, impeccably strapped in a black tuxedo, a provocative smile on his lips.

The city of Montjolly, under the unrelenting yoke of this terrible evil and besieged by the National Guard, presents this variety show to entertain the population, poised to sink into the throes of a collective madness. The Public Safety Committee, with the assistance of talented artists, offers this entertainment to raise funds, to the improvement of the living conditions of the unlucky population.

The organizing Committee, thanked the representatives of the two major TV channels: (FOX and CNN) sequestered arbitrarily, and victims, too: James Nadowsky and Roland Peterson; whose generosity and knowhow, enabled the Committee to realize this program; said Matt Potter with his voice of Stentor. .

For your donations, ladies and gentlemen call number: 987 654 3210; very easy to remember, this is the countdown.

And now, I leave you in the company of the delightful and famous singer of la Scala in Milan; (native of Montjolly, obviously), who will interpret arias by Verdi, Donizetti, Rossini, Bizet and Puccini; accompanied by the beautiful Mona Lisa Hollemberg at the piano.

Ladies and gentlemen: the soprano: Michelle Morgan.

The two girls came to the scene under a frenzied ovation. Three hundred handpicked guests who sat in the Star Theater and the tens of thousands of viewers gathered in front of the giant screens, had never even heard Michelle Morgan.

The Habanera from Carmen was a smash hit. Michelle had to sing this aria three times, to appease the mob and calm the excessive enthusiasm of the spectators who were cheering without stopping and chanted loudly: Mi chel Mor gan, loud enough to tear their throat.

Money flowed profusely into the coffers of the Public Safety Committee. The time allocated to Michelle brought them the tidy sum of nine million dollars. The young girls attending the phones were extremely busy. Calls flowed incessantly in the conference room of the town hall which served as a switchboard.

After many commercials that followed the uninterrupted recital by Michelle Morgan; Matt Potter complimented the artist, made a summary account of the parallel activities taking place on the sidelines of the concert.

The Public Safety Committee, he said, has already collected nine million dollars. He encourages viewers all over the world to assist generously the Committee of Public Safety, which strives to find an antidote to this virulent poison that plunged the city into anguish and despair.

The popular Orchestra of Montjolly City: the Roms, (under the baton of maestro Renalto, with JeanLuc on cello and Manolo on violin) will play a few tunes of his vast cosmopolitan repertoire.

Everything goes: the beautiful blue Danube, the Emperor a Strauss Waltz; (la vie en rose) Life in pink, dead leaves, (from France) O Solo Mio, the addio a Napoli, Santa Lucia, (from Italy); Guantanamera, (Cuban) and many other nostalgic works of the same ilk.

This was a popular treat, much applauded by people on the street and millions of viewers worldwide, who witnessed the tragedy (heroically supported) that plagued this charming, this rustic town, bruised by the curse and the quarantine as a pestiferous evil.

Matt Potter announced that the fund rose to eighteen million. Time flies, he said and we have still two artists in the program.

Without further delay, dear friends, I present to you the great pianist Mona Lisa Hollemberg in a few Chopin waltzes.

Mona Lisa, molded into a white, very low-cut dress with a high hairstyle, (the Roman), caused a sensation by entering in scene. The public in the Theater of The Stars made a triumph to this statuesque beauty, with a refined elegance, who smiled with confidence and charm.

Her artistry was impeccable, but without poetry. She had performed masterfully some waltzes of Chopin, without however engaging her soul, without printing on this brilliant music the patina of her intimate emotions. Her exceptional virtuosity largely compensated for her lack of sensitivity.

The musician was forced twice, to replay the piece she had been interpreting. She got five enthusiastic recalls on the part of the public.

During the commercials, James Nadowsky informed, the organizers of the evening, that they have only fifteen minutes remaining time. Matt Potter converge this unfortunate news to Isabella Morgan who was preparing to enter the scene. But, I need twenty minutes, you know Matt? He told the girl who pretended to be very disappointment. I can do nothing, answered Matt with a embarrassed look.

Isabella suggested the organizers to end the show with the musicians of the Roms, in the interpretation of two pieces of Pablo de Sarasate: Romanca Andalouza and Caprice Basque. Manolo was more grateful for the opportunity that was providentially offered to play for this select audience, and display his Gypsy violinist virtuosity.

Manolo surpassed himself and made the Theater of The Stars vibrate with pathetic emotions and sentimental nostalgic Gypsy music.

The concert proved to be a success, both artistic and financial. The Public Safety Committee had at the end of the show, Twenty-three million dollars. The Committee was on his way, already, to realize some of its large projects.

The party went on until three o'clock in the morning for the autochthons. The Roms orchestra played exiting music tunes, retransmitted on the giant screens, the whole city dances in the streets this popular ball. It is with regret that people were dispersed when the music stopped.

Dr. Carl Sommers who expected to hear Isabella was very disappointed. Isabella made him understand, however, that this setback represented an opportunity for him and for her, to perform together in a show that she intended to organize in the near future.

But, cherished love, he said, in a derisive tone, I am not musician, I can't sing, I'm real good at nothing.

Do not talk nonsense, my dear friend; you will give a conference on the strange disease the evil black curse and its brood development in the human body. And me, I will interpret the concerto in D major by Rachmaninoff or the concerto no. 1 by Sergei Prokofiev.

But then my darling, you are not at all disappointed; I would say even more, you are glad you didn't play last night, isn't it?

This telephone conversation inaugurated a new phase in the relationship of the two lovers. They spoke all day long. Isabella had always something to say. She interrupted him, sometimes, in the middle of a surgery to tell him that she is madly in love with him; to what he replied, laughing: I know you're crazy, no need to reiterate it when I am in the operating room, sweetheart!

His work done at the hospital, they met either at the Morgan sister's house, where they regularly ate, either at the restaurant Le Grand Meaulnes, venue of the wealthy people of the city.

Isabella despite her swarthy complexion remained a radiant beauty. She was happy and her happiness put a nimbus of mysterious halo that lit up her face, transfigured by an ineffable grace.

I am telling you, Carl darling, let's realize this show. What do you say about that Carl? This is a great project. You had evidently planed the whole thing carefully; even if I wanted, it would be very difficult, impossible to refuse to you my complete collaboration, because I love you?

I knew you were an intelligent man, I'm glad you're also a very wise one. I was expecting protests, and excuses, pretexts; and I had prepared an arsenal of compelling arguments to convince you.

Come on, Isabella, you still doubt the depth of my love for you? For me, and this, as long as I live (I hope a very long life) your desires will be my orders. Don't forget, I promised to Elsa, and I pledged to her maternal affection, to make you happy...

So Carl, this is it, you love me for the sake of Elsa affection?

Naughty child! Do you want to hurt me? And if I had made objections to your project?

Your punishment would be even more severe. That must serve you as a warning, retorted the girl.

Isabella, my love, I must leave you now; see you later, at your aunts house!

I'll be waiting for you, goodbye my love.

The installation of the telephone network was progressing rapidly. But already, they had increased the capacity of the existing embryonic network so; important people can communicate during the crisis.

Moreover, Motorola and AT & T had established a relay on the mountain, outside the military cordon ensuring the strict observance of the quarantine. They were anchored at the limit of the prohibited area, to reserve the lion's share in the market of mobile phones that would open, no doubt about it, in the town of Montjolly, once freed from the yoke of the quarantine.

Indeed, the fundraising conducted during the show, had been made possible thanks to the mercantile foresight of these two companies. Dr. Sommers possessed a satellite phone; he paid a fortune, which could put him in communication with the whole world.

The circle of guests at the weekly dinner of the Morgan sister's house was expanded considerably. Mona Lisa Hollemberg, Dr. Suzanne Birmingham, Bernice Merville and her daughter Rachel, Lisa Troy, Christel Baldwin (sole heir of a colossal fortune), just graduated from La Sorbonne, Samantha Sandford (daughter of the wealthy Éric Sandford) on the women's side.

Matt Potter, Harry Morgan (persuaded by his favourite: taty Cathy) Roland Peterson and James Nadowsky (for their valuable contribution to the cause) Jack Spencer and Robert Carlson (two authentic specimens of the Monjolian idle and pretentious elite.

To accommodate this entire beautiful people, the hostess pitched a buffet table in the dining room, where each could serve themselves, without ceremony. Several servants were circulating through the crowded grand salon, offering cocktails and snacks, to the guests, sitting or standing, who were chatting with animation.

The undeniable success of the televised evening was the object of all conversations. Michelle Morgan was surrounded by a large group of admirers who welcomed her warmly.

Mona Lisa Hollemberg, sitting a little away, (in a corner of the grand salon) received lots of compliments of eager guests, like a queen receiving the homage of her dedicated royal court.

Dear friends, said Cathy Morgan, welcome. We have prepared a buffet in the dining room to make weekly meeting less formal and friendlier.

Those who love the great outdoors will be able to sit under the veranda, where are arranged tables. Each person may serve oneself, the servants are responsible for the drink.

The reverend Vogel, as usual recited grace. He went in the dining room, where people followed him. Most of the guests were foreign to this traditional ritual.

Isabella, sitting on a long couch, absentmindedly chatted with Lisa Troy and Rachel Merville. She was surprised by doctor Carl Sommers delayed. She monitored the living room door hoping to see her lover.

When everyone left the dining room, Isabella quietly eclipsed herself to call Carl. When she had him, at the other end of the wire:

Carl! Where are you? I am waiting for you, my darling! I am really worried.

I had an emergency at the last minute. I apologize to you, my darling, I just left the operating room... I'll be there in half an hour. I am going to change immediately... I'm sorry...

Isabella was visibly upset. But she had to make good heart against bad fortune, and solicited by her friends, participated in lively conversations and passionate discussions.

When Dr. Sommers opened the salon door, Isabella's mind absorbed in deep reflection, didn't see him. Her aunt Cathy who observed carefully everything that was happening around her took his arm to present him to the other guests.

Dear friends, she says, with her beautiful tenor voice, I present to you the Dr. Carl Sommers, who saved the city from a disaster much more awful than the epidemic of evil black curse. He operated the crippled, sewed up the wounded, boosted the morale of the population taken by panic, only one doctor available during the first hours of the crisis.

Dr. Sommers has worked for three days without sleeping, almost without eating. The doctor apologizes for his late arrival ; but he had a surgery at the last minute.

Isabella smiled and her eyes sparkled with joy. Cathy Morgan, still holding Sommers's arm, went through the dining room, designating each guest by name. He honored the ladies with a tilt of his head and a smile. A firm handshake, greeted the men seated within his reach.

Mona Lisa Hollemberg, got up from the table where she sat in the middle of her admirers and stretched out her hand to the doctor. How is your mother? Sommers asked her in a friendly voice.

The scars on her cheek have almost disappeared. She asks me every day when they would remove this annoying plaster.

Furthermore, she needs another jar of ointment.

I will bring the ointment tomorrow, said Dr. Sommers.

Matt Potter came to greet the doctor telling him:

I had a burning desire to know you! They have been talking about you a lot.

In positive terms, I guess? Said Sommers laughing.

In good and in bad, doctor, said Potter, a sneaky look in his grey eyes, full of malice and curiosity.

Sitting next to Mona Lisa, Harry Morgan, stood impassive, and staring with insistence and wickedness at Sommers, who pretended been unaware of him. He completely ignored the aggressive attitude of Isabella's brother. But, Cathy Morgan the aunt that accompanied Sommers in his tour; noticed with surprise and disapproval the manifest hostility her nephew shown to the doctor. It must be said also that she knew nothing of the terrible blood feud between the two men.

Sommers greeted Robert Carlson, Jack Spencer, who, with the other two, formed the inner circle of the appointed suitors of the alluring Mona Lisa.

There was, in addition, to the table: the beautiful Christel Baldwin and Samantha Sandford: two intimate friends of Mona Lisa.

Dr. Sommers shook the hand of Admiral Dexter and the reverend Vogel and bowed to Bernice Merville, Nancy Morice and Joan Morgan. Cathy sat down in her place, on the same table and pointed out the last table, saying: you already know those people; I don't need to present you.

On Isabella's table, were: Rachel Merville, Lisa Troy, Grace Norris, Roland Peterson, James Nadowsky. Sommers greeted around and sat down on the seat Isabella had reserved him.

A servant came to ask the doctor what he wanted to drink. Isabella asks to come at her side. She whispered a few words in the servant ear. The servant returned after a moment with a loaded tray of hors d'oeuvre, she placed in front of Dr. Sommers.

Barely had he bitten in a pâté de foie gras, that Admiral Dexter, sitting nearby, called him: tell me doctor! You bring us some good news? Is the evil curse begins to subside?

Science didn't find yet an effective response to this terrible evil. However, he added, I am now convinced of the ephemeral nature of this evil black curse so much dreaded.

You have, therefore, found an antidote to the epidemic? Said ironically laughing, the reverend Vogel.

The rogatory procession, didn't produce the expected miracle, reverend Vogel, therefore, I went back to the scientific observation; replied Sommers without a wink.

Don't get angry, doctor! Said Nancy Morice, father Vogel was joking.

I'm not angry dear mademoiselle. Only me, I don't mess around with a nitty-gritty.

Carl! You're not in your element tonight; what's wrong, my darling? Asked Isabella softly.

I am okay. But this delay has irked me. I promised you to come early.

These are the risks of the trade, see! Carl! I don't believe you are telling me the truth.

Grace Norris, seated next to Isabella, followed with a growing curiosity, this very intimate conversation between two people, that she supposed, barely knew each other. Rachel Merville smiled at the obvious embarrassment of the doctor. She stared brazenly, at him without stopping. Roland Peterson who seemed to be a little tipsy, (he drank lots of cocktails) speaking to Isabella, said to her:

I have contacted those gentlemen in Atlanta; they agreed, in principle. The only condition; (sine qua non condition) was that this show is given on a Saturday evening between nine and ten o'clock.

It is fine with me, answered Isabella laughingly. What do you think Dr. Sommers?

I believe that this is a good arrangement. This suits me perfectly!

Have you decided the date? Asked Roland Peterson. I have to know at least, a week in advance.

It will be done, replied, very enthusiastically, Isabella.

Dear friends, said Cathy Morgan, we're going to the living room, for the artistic entertainment of the evening. We will have coffee and liquors over there.

As people rose from their table, maids carried the chairs and placed them along the walls of the living room where there were not enough seats to accommodate everyone.

Leaving last the dining room, the people sitting at Isabella's table, were put in the farthest corner of the living room, far from the grand piano center of attraction of the moment.

Seated at the piano surrounded by admirers, Michelle Morgan attacked at the outset a difficult aria, to induce a thrill among her suitors and give the extent of her talent: "the young Hindu, the air of the bells from the opera Lakmé by Léo Delibes...

Her voice flooded the lounge with a stream of enticing harmonies and stood, effortlessly, in the stunning high pitch notes, shaking slightly in the ornamental trills and the passionate tremolos that plunged the audience into an extreme rapture.

Michelle saw the number of her admirers increase significantly. James Nadowsky and Jack Spencer went join, Charles Lewis, Ronald Commins and Samuel Rutherford who stood on each side of the grand piano.

Everyone noted the dramatic defection of Jack Spencer, who concluded he had no chance with Mona Lisa, preferred to try his luck elsewhere.

Michelle performed, in turn, two other arias, who received warm thunderous applause: Casta Diva of the opera Norma by Vincenzo Bellini and Col sorriso of innocenza, from 'Il Pirata' by the same author.

The entire table of Mona Lisa followed her on the piano.

Smiling, she played with a surprising brio, a nocturne by Chopin, melancholic and languorous. The face of Harry Morgan, scowling from the arrival of Dr. Sommers, unbent a little smile toward the young pianist.

Five minutes after Mona Lisa regained her place; Cathy Morgan approached Isabelle and said:

I thought you were going to play something for us?

I'm too nervous tonight Taty Cathy, it will be for another time.

I have seen that you weren't feeling good... What wrong sweetie?

Don't worry Taty, this is nothing. I promise to play for you next week.

Cathy Morgan glared at her niece with sustained attention and saw in her eyes an unusual sparkle, a languorous and passionate look, she was convinced, at once, that Isabella was in love.

The guests departed. In small groups, they came to salute the Ladies of the house and thank them for a wonderful evening.

Everyone was gone. The only people remaining in the living room, were Isabella and Dr. Sommers, waiting for Grace Norris who was using the toilet.

As she looked at her friend right in the eyes, nothing around her existed any more. She didn't see her brother coming right at them. Sommers whispered, in the midst of the conversation: your brother coming toward us.

Isabella turned abruptly, like a tigress who protects her cubs and waited, with a scornful eye, nerves tensed, ready to pounce.

Isabella! Go home immediately! Said Harry Morgan in an imperative tone.

You have no rights to give me orders! Harry Morgan, go your way...

I do not want you to talk to this man...

Who do you think you are? You're pushing your audacity a bit too far. I talk to who I want and I am not accountable to anyone. Put this in your stupid head, once for all brother.

You will pay dearly this impertinence, Isabella!

Harry Morgan took a step forward her, Sommers by a rapid movement steps in front of Isaella, in a defensive position. This gesture stopped short the aggressive momentum of Harry Morgan.

Get out of my way! Said Isabelle's brother at the height of anger, furious as a madman.

Harry Morgan, you are a coward. You attack only women, and poor defenseless fellows. Where are the bandits who usually accompany you in the accomplishment of your dirty misdeeds?

Beware Sommers! Do not immerse yourself in my family's affair.

This concerns me intimately. Because I give you my word, things wouldn't be easy for you like the last time.

The loud voices had attracted a few retarded hosts: Bernice and Rachel Merville, Matt Potter, Grace Norris, but nobody dared to intervene in this family feud. Everyone was eagerly looking at this scene, with amazement and curiosity. It was thought, from their belligerent posture, that the two men would violently attack each other.

Cathy and Joan Morgan, rushed at this point and interposed themselves between the two adversaries.

What does this mean, Harry? Asked his aunt Joan who was boiling with contained anger? You shouldn't have done this uproar

in my house. You are disrespectful and rude... But,
Taty, tried to explain Harry.

I don't want to hear your explanations, cut him off his aunt Cathy. I beg you, leave my house immediately.

Taty, insisted the young man.

Go away! I am telling you? Don't aggravate further your situation....

At this moment, Matt Potter grabbed Harry by the arm and led him out of the room. The other women approached and Grace Norris asked her girlfriend to tell her what's going on.

My brother wanted me to leave, illico. As I refused to comply, he wanted to hit me. Dr. Sommers objected. He became furious why did he want you to go home, immediately? Asked her aunt Joan...

Because he does not want me to talk to Dr. Sommers. Replied Isabella...

You are shaking my darling, come sit down, you also doctor...

Bernice, her daughter and Grace Norris manifested their desire to leave...

Stay a little while, if it doesn't bother you too much.

Cathy beckoned a servant: Julie, bring coffee for everyone.

After drinking the coffee, the Merville went home. Grace kissed her girlfriend telling her: Isabella tomorrow, I'll come see you.

Cathy accompanied her guests under the colonnades porch and kissed them good evening. Then she returned to sit near her niece who sobbed nervously.

I am so sorry, she said, speaking to Dr. Sommers; for the deplorable behavior of my nephew. I ask you to accept my apology.

You do not have to apologize, Miss Morgan...

Pamper me, doctor, call me: Cathy. Tell me, so why Harry does not want you to talk to his sister? I really do not understand. Have you ever had problems with him?

Isabella, seeing the apparent reluctance of her friend to divulge their secret, hastened to reply:

Taty honey, mother and I met Dr. Sommers in New York. It was he who had diagnosed the real cause of the rampant eurhythmy of mother and saved the unfortunate lady from the fatal knife of those morons Harry had hired to care for my mother.

Professor Peter Grant, said Dr. Sommers, who I called, suspended the preparations for the surgery and proposed instead the treatment that cured Mrs. Morgan.

Moreover, added Isabella, Professor Grant wouldn't accept compensation, saying he had dune his favorite student a favor. The satisfaction to be helpful to Carl, said Professor Grant, largely offset any other kind of compensation. He should rather be thanking Dr. Sommers, whose intuitive diagnosis had saved his mother's life; in extremis.

The two sisters were not at all satisfied with the explanations provided. They did not understand why, after having saved his mother from a fiery death; Harry could display such hostility toward Dr. Sommers. They promised to investigate fully this incomprehensible story.

It is getting late, Isabella, I bring you home.

I have my mother's car, she replied to her aunt.

I am driving you home, leave the car in the garage.

Dr. Sommers took his leave and went to the hospital. He wanted to ensure that the road was clear before going to the villa Vaudreuil. He was taking precautions in case Harry Morgan would have set a trap. He sent the ambulance driver over there to observe the surroundings and report to him any suspicious activity.

The ambulance driver, when he returned, told him that he saw a car moving slowly in avenue des Eglantines. Another vehicle was parked at the exit of the impasse which led to the villa.

It would seem, according to an obviously deduction, that someone wanted to block a possible escape from the villa.

Sommers knew now what to do. Harry Morgan thinking that he would not be on his guard, had pitched this mousetrap; this crude trap, to make him swallow the epithet of coward he spat out on his face.

Cathy and Joan accompanied Isabella home. They told Elsa, the unfortunate incident of the evening, deploring the hostile attitude of Harry towards Dr. Sommers. They wanted to know more, but Elsa remained cautious, not knowing what her daughter told her aunts.

These ladies, a little disappointed by the evasive response of their sister-in-law, went promising in good journalist to shed light on the issue.

Isabella got directly into her bedroom and lay down all dressed.

The next morning, as soon as he learned the arrival of Dr. Merville at the hospital, Dr. Sommers requisitioned a driver to take him home. He was trying to avoid, at all costs, a confrontation which could be an unbridgeable gap between him and Isabella.

When he introduced his key in the lock, it presented an unusual resistance. Someone had wanted to force his door. He called Lucien, the driver, who was waiting for him to get in; and asked him what he thought of all this?

Let me try, doctor, step back a bit, please, you never know.

Lucien opened the door with difficulty, penetrated the villa and made a summary inspection of the premises.

No one has entered the house, doctor, but it will require that you replace the lock. I am returning to the hospital, I will come back with a much stronger lock and the padlock to consolidate the closure.

CHAPTER IX

D r. Sommers in turn entered the villa and double lock the door . He went immediately feed Mikado. The cat ran down the stair and came to rub, as usual, the leg of Sommers.

It's OK Mikado! I know I didn't come home two days in a row... But this isn't a reason to Meow, so desperately!

Dr. Sommers gestured to abscond to the caresses of the cat and let out a cry of surprise. Mikado was back to white and seemed to be aware of the fact.

He examined the cat from head to feet. The cat purred with obvious pleasure and looked at Dr. Sommers as to thank him for this sudden transformation. Mikado didn't touch his food and followed Sommers in his room.

Sommers consulted his notes. Exactly ten weeks went by since he had administered the potion to Mikado. The effect was instant, the incubation period was brief; in one night, the cat was completely transformed.

The resorbing process was completed without any apparent symptoms, at the level of the characterized pigments, innervated by the poison. The melanin was cleared, little by little, the polarized constraint of the enzymes misled by the power of the chromatophoric potion.

The preliminary calculations that Dr. Sommers had made, had

brought him some indications on the likely duration of the synthetic blackening of the fur of the animal.

Now, with this new data, he would be able to fix, very roughly however, (between seven to ten months), the incubation period of the evil black curse. He based his deductions on the assumption that a week of incubation in the cat was equivalent to one month of incubation in humans.

He was sure to have the time to carry out his projects.

The phone rang, it was Isabella.

How are you this morning my darling? Asked Sommers.

I just wake up Carl, I am still upset by last night incident.

Don't worry, my love, I am taken precautions. Forewarned, forearmed, as tell this old saying. Your brother opened the hostilities and aggressive scared you...

It is you that he wants to hurt, Carl darling! I know I know my brother; he's vindictive, a villain, a bully who will stop at nothing to make you suffer...

Don't worry darling!

You say that to strengthen my confidence isn't it? I don't want you to suffer like last time.

What are you saying there Isabella?

Carl! Don't attempt anymore to hide the truth from me. You have betrayed yourself yesterday evening, when you tell Harry that this will not be like the last time. I wasn't born yesterday, my love.

I'll put a stop to this stupid antagonism, I'll inform my father.

I do not believe this is necessary...

You don't know Harry I say? He has made you responsible for the fact that he has lost any influence over Elsa and me. He considers you as a troublemaker, a dangerous character, a subversive element that came from who knows where, to upset the established order of his community. He even accused you of having caused this epidemic on the city, retaliatory punishment for having ostracized you because of the color of your skin.

I am going to the hospital, said Sommers to change the subject. You join me for lunch?

At the Grand Meaulne? Asked Isabella.

Yes! We have lots of things to set forth before the show, I prefered the restaurant, said Dr. Sommers.

Then, see you later. I kiss you.

Dr. Sommers called Lucien, the hospital driver, to pick him up. He slipped a revolver in his pocket and put another with a supply of ammunition in his Kit. He did not want to be caught unprepared, if an attack were to occur. He recommended that Lucien comes with his Cadillac; he didn't want Harry Morgan to think he was afraid of him.

Despite this threat of conflict, Carl Sommers was jubilant with the turn of events. He was sure, now, that people would regain their natural skin color, that the virus would leave no ill detrimental effects to the health of contaminated individuals.

Sommers was at the bedside of a patient, when Lisa Troy came to tell him that Mayor Simon Morgan expected to see him in about one hour at City Hall; to discuss a very important matter.

Try to find Isabella, ask her if she is aware of this interview?

The time of the appointment was approaching; Neither Lisa nor Sommers, could join Isabella on the phone. Nevertheless, he decided to attend this impromptu meeting.

Simon Morgan greeted Sommers with a firm handshake and led him immediately, without saying a word, in a spacious room, already full of people: in addition to the Mayor, Dr. Merville, Cathy and Joan Morgan, Elsa and Isabella. Sommers refrained a gesture of surprise and bowed to the ladies. As usual he kissed Elsa hand and came to sit at the place Isabella had reserved for him.

You looking very good, Dr. Sommers told Elsa, to break the awkward silence regrettably prevalent in the room since his appearance.

We are expecting someone else, said Simon Morgan looking at the time on his watch.

On entering the room, Harry Morgan, opened wide hid eyes and took a step backward.

Harry! told his father take a seat, we have to talk.

The man, crestfallen, not knowing what to do, obeys without saying a word.

Dr. Merville spoke first.

We live, dear friends, a really difficult period. The situation is bleak and uncertain. It requires no aggravation, no drama that would make it even more unbearable. Harry, by his obnoxious behavior; wants create more hassles, worse than those created by the evil black curse.

Harry opened his mouth to protest, but his father told him, in a tone without reply: shut up, let Dr. Merville finish.

I was saying, continued Dr. Merville, I bitterly regret the aggressive attitude of Harry against Dr. Sommers. About three months ago, I saved Dr. Sommers, in extremis, from certain death. Responding to an emergency call, I went to the hospital, when I spied a man tied to a pole near the barrier that four guys flagellated with rage.

I approached, and by recognizing Harry, I intimated him the order to stop this cruel flogging. He refused and encouraged his henchmen to pursue their dirty job. So I pulled out my gun and threating the bandits to shoot them on the spot, if they continued. The cowardly fled without warning.

Not willing to damage, even more, the dismal state of the wounded (which I had not yet identified) I requisitioned the driver of an ambulance to help me.

We transported Dr. Sommers at the villa, where I gave him proper care. I requested Simon presence, in order to see the wonders of his son.

We stood at the bedside of the injured until he has regained consciousness. This prolonged fainting, although it has allowed me to operate without too much suffering, worried me, however fairly.

The neck and the back of the doctor were shredded under atrocious bites of a tipped swift's lead whip. I stitched, sewed gaping wounds, it took me, sixty points of suture to repair, somehow, the damage of the whip.

However, despite the harassment of all kinds, inflicted to Dr. Sommers, despite the abuse, he didn't hesitate one second, to respond to my desperate call for help at the hospital in distress.

Dr. Sommers is an exceptional man, an outstanding surgeon, posses a refined education, a perfect gentleman, (such as the chevalier Bayard) is without fear and without reproach.

Dr. Sommers accomplished a colossal work at the hospital, the first day of the crisis. And, he is more essential today, because it is he who hold the helm of the boat. Anyone who tries to touch a hair of the doctor will answer to me personally

I met you here, to explain the situation. Since yesterday evening, Harry Morgan, that behold, wanted to recur his strike. Fortunately,

Dr. Sommers was on his guard. He sent an ambulance ride to survey around the villa. He reported seeing Harry's car just below the entrance to the impasse and another blocking the exit.

This is the situation, what do you say? Harry, he said looking around.

Isabella sobbed softly, throughout this long monologue. A flood of tears rolled down her brown cheeks. Her large blue eyes reddened by tears, were dilated even more. Sommers passed her his handkerchief to wipe her swollen face of grief.

Is this true? Simon asked his son, that you have attempted to assault Dr. Sommers, last night?

Harry Morgan, kept silence. He looked at his mother, his sister and his aunts then bowed his head.

Answer golly! Shouted Simon angrily. I thought you were a man; Obviously, I was mistaken greatly.

After a long time thinking, Harry looked up and said:

This man has insulted me, in front of everybody, I intended to give him a lesson of knowhow and make him swallow the qualifier of coward he threw in my face.

And, in doing so, said his father in a contemptuous tone, you have hired five bandits, isn't it? Dr. Sommers has reason to call you coward. Did he insulted you the first time you have tried to assassinate him?

Dr. Merville, stood up, took his hat that was lying on a chair and took leave saying to Simon: the rest is in your hands.

Sommers stood up, too, ready to go. But Simon Morgan motioned for him to stay. We have a score to settle.

I don't want to interfere in your family discussions, said Sommers, still standing, wanted to go no matter what...

Sit down, ordered Simon Morgan, with authority, this dispute particularly concerned you, whether you want it or not.

Firstly, continued Simon Morgan in the same tone, I demand, you hear me Harry? I require that you make a public apology to Dr. Sommers. That you cut short this ridiculous vendetta against the doctor. Beginning today, I don't grant you hospitality any more at the Petit Palais. Take your belongings and go live somewhere else.

How father! You hurting me to please the nigger?

You, Harry Morgan, you make me laugh, you're also as nigger as everyone and a fool on top of it. Have you look in a mirror lately?

I'm not a nigger, and I hope to regain my original color... I will not deny my philosophy, the conservative tradition of the family, the way of life of the population; I will not abandon the values and virtues that characterized our society; to please this individual, this hacker, who believes he had already, overpower our society and our family...

Shut up Harry! Cut him off Simon Morgan, furious. You do what you been told or, I immediately denounces you to judge Crampton.

You won't dare Vociferated his son, really stupefy.

Try me, Harry Morgan. Do you want to spend the rest of your miserable life in prison? Do not obey my injunctions.

Harry Morgan left the room in grumbling; almost break the door, slamming it with violence. An awkward silence gave way to this lively discussion. Joan and Cathy Morgan questioned with a stunning gaze, their brother, still embroiled in a terrible anger.

What's going here Simon? Asked Cathy. You're hiding things to us, eh! She said, including her sister in the outrage she felt to have been kept out of this family secret.

I haven't hidden anything, replied Simon. It is not a family secret either. Only us knew the true identity of Dr. Sommers. Telling us included: the sheriff, Dr. Merville, big Luc, Elsa, Harry and Isabella. Dr. Sommers lives in the villa Vaudreuil, following an arrangement agreed between us. You have heard the words of Dr. Merville, I have nothing to add.

His sister Joan told Simon: I do not understand why Harry was whipping Dr. Sommers?

Elsa and Isabella may answer your question. I have to go; I have things to do at the factory.

He shook the hand of Sommers, kissed his wife and went out.

My dear Elsa, said Cathy, with a bit wrathful voice; you are too secretive. How! Do you think I am unable to keep a secret? Or unworthy of your confidence?

What are you insinuating my dear Cathy? Sweetheart! Simon didn't want people to know about the existence of Dr. Sommers in the city. it was before the municipal elections, and the appearance of Dr. Sommers at the Church, had already put the bug in the ear of some voters. He did not want the propagation of the news.

In all this tedious rant by Dr. Merville, I only have withheld: that

Dr. Sommers is a black man that had saved your life; sparing you a useless and dangerous surgery; that you took him in affection; that your son was offended and that he beat him to death?

This is not all, replied Isabella.

My faith! This becomes more interesting, retorted her aunt Joan in an ironical and scathing voice.

Taty honey, I know that you would have not approved my friendship with Dr. Sommers before the tragedy that shook our archaic design and our unjustified prejudice. When I ventured on the deserted Beach one Sunday, for the first time, after three years of voluntary confinement; Carl, who also went there for the first time, appeared to me suddenly. A strong emotion crippled my whole body, I was shaken from head to toes by a violent earthquake. Eyes wide open; I only saw the rapid lightning of his gaze that fascinated me. I do not know how I recovered my senses, but, I ran up to my car to dress in my bathrobe, because I felt naked and vulnerable. Carl approached the car, picked up my book I had dropped. He said: I am the doctor Carl Sommers and you, what's your name?

I replied spontaneously: ah! It is you? He had perfectly understood and answered: it's him...

I have to go I told him, because his presence disturbed me incomprehensibly.

He looked at me a moment, then he told me: I found you today, I don't want to lose you never. Like what, he had already known me!

I answered nothing. He asked, then, if I could give him: a pen, a pencil, something to write. I held out a pencil, the touch of his fingers made me the effect of an electric shock. A strange thrill ran through my spine and I nearly fainted. Carl wrote his phone number on the last page of my book and gave it to me saying: call me, keep in touch... I remember saying, at this time only: I am Isabella Morgan.

Her aunts had followed with great interest the story of the young girl. The emphasis and passion with which she narrated her first encounter with the young doctor, indicated to them, unequivocally, the nature of the feelings of their niece for Dr. Sommers.

They understood, now, but didn't approve, of course, the feelings of hatred and contempt that Harry professed toward the doctor and the reasons which had led him to act as a bandit.

Dr. Sommers, overwhelmingly touched by the story of Isabella, stood up to leave. They are expecting me at the hospital. He kissed the hand of Elsa; but she attracted him towards her and hugged him. Cathy and Joan made similarly. Isabella accompanied him out of the room.

What a story! Exclaimed Cathy Morgan, when the young people left the room. What do you say about this Elsa? Asked her sister-in-law, a little intrigued by her complacent attitude. I see that you are on very good terms with Sommers

You figure out, my dear, said Elsa; this man has saved my life.

How! You knew him before? Inquired Joan.

Listen, this Sunday, when Isabella returned from her escapade, she entered my room tottering, the face Livid, bewildered like someone who had just seen a ghost.

What happen to you my darling? I asked her, leaping to meet her. She lay down on the bed without saying anything. With an alarming nervous spasm ridden and scared me a lot. I am taken you to the hospital I told her? She beckoned me not. Anxious, not knowing what had happened to my daughter, I was going to call for Dr. Merville when she sat down and told me naturally: I feel fine now mother.

Then, she narrated to me the story of her encounter with Carl. She told me about the paralyzing emotion that gripped her; the strange sensations that she felt in the intimate regions of her being which upset her. Mother! She told me, have you ever experienced such a thing? I laughed and quite simply I said: my darling, you have been suddenly struck by lightning. Sweetheart, I am afraid, you are fallen in love! That's the only plausible explanation...

Are you kidding me, Elsa? This is relatively nonsense! How could I be in love with this man? I don't know, and, more importantly, he is not like Us.

For me the incident was closed, I thought. Eight days later, (it was about midnight) Isabella came into my room and lay down, all dressed, without saying a word to me. She thought maybe I was sleeping. Are you feeling well sweetheart? I asked her.

Can I sleep with you tonight? She told me without answering my question.

Gladly! I replied.

Isabella then removed her shoes and slipped under the sheets, cuddled in my bosom. After a brief moment of silence she said:

Mother, you know, this man's face haunts me. His voice haunts me day and night. I cannot sleep. I have lost interest in life...

This is serious, I said; even very serious. What do you want to do? Anyway, it is necessary that you get rid of this intolerable obsession.

But, how?

Until we can contact him personally; try to find the most information as possible about the person.

Her girlfriend: Lisa Troy gave her the first information on the subject. Information derived from the folder provided by Carl in his application. We quickly built on the character and the personality of Dr. Sommers. In addition, Simon and Harry provided a rich account of very important details. They often referred to the hacker (as they called him) by ridiculing his boring activities at the villa that big Luke reported to them. They laughed, of his wanderings at Biloxi, volunteer at Biloxi General Hospital. You know why. When I went to Jackson, en route to New York, where they were going to fix a supposed congenital heart defect. Taking advantage of the unexpected absence of our two guards, Isabella telephoned Biloxi General Hospital where was Dr. Sommers. She told him: listen to me, I don't have much time. Mother and I, we are going to New York. She must undergo surgery. We will be at the Marriott in Manhattan for eight days. I had not forgotten you. She hangs up suddenly when she heard the footsteps of these gentlemen in the corridors of the hotel.

At this time, the caretaker of the town hall said to Mrs. Morgan that her husband was waiting for her to go dinner.

I am leaving, dear Sisters; the rest at the next meeting!

The ladies went on their way, moved and shaded by the account of the exciting adventure of Dr. Sommers in Montjolly city.

When Elsa returned home after diner at Grand Meaulne with her husband, she found her son waiting for her, wild-eyed and crazed looking.

Mother I have to talk to you, let's go down to the garden...

What's so urgent Harry?

Harry took his mother's arms and led her towards the flowery and fragrant garden of the Petit Palais. They walked a few moments in silence, entered a driveway lined with roses and sat on a granite bench under the shade of a beautiful bloomed chestnut tree. Harry had lowered his head, under the weight of a deep prostration. Elsa watched her son, struggling with a sense of helplessness and frustration, burden by the ultimatum of his

father.

Thus, mother, you let my father kick me out of the Petit Palais without intervening? You must oppose him ... Do it for your son, I beg you mother. Only you can force Simon to reverse his decision; you know that very well. If I leave home under these conditions, I'd be finished. I wouldn't be any more a leader in the community, I couldn't be a respectable family member, I'd be the laughing stock of the city, a subject of scorn and derision.

Elsa had listened without interrupting the desperate rant of her son. This hasty expulsion put him upside down. The prospect of enduring this shame was unbearable.

You know, Harry, you're asking me, an impossible thing, isn't it? Since the misunderstanding that had driven us apart during three years; my influence over your father has diminished considerably. I have no more grips on him.

You have to try, dear mother, implored her son, watery eyes, face ravaged by grief and defeat.

Harry, said his mother on a stern tone: you're no longer a child. You can understand that your heinous behavior could exasperate your father. You also have to accept the consequences of your bad actions; be a man. Harry, you don't move me anymore with your histrionics, you have threaten me as enemy and destroyed once, already, the legitimate and honorable aspirations of your sister. Why? To satisfy your pride and prove your ascendant over your father and the city? Your father condoned all your whims. Frankly Harry! I am not at all inclined to help you.

What I am going to become? Mother! You can't abandon me to my fate...

You are walking on an evil way without thinking, one moment, about the terrible consequences for others of your actions. Have you ever thought about my pain, the three years where I held and kept your father away? Do you think that coming whining like a baby in my skirts, I was going to tenderize myself, as in the past, and plead your case against my husband?

You're right; mother, to belittle me as you please. I agree, I did stupid things, but you are not as vindictive as I was cruel towards you and Isabella. I ask for your forgiveness on my knees, dear mother.

Elsa Morgan, fine psychologist, had obliged her son (without asking specifically) to make amends. She knew that it would be very difficult, this crisis passed, to obtain concessions from this man, convinced of his superiority, arrogant and stubborn, who wanted to impose his stupid ideology to everyone.

I would venture to make such a risky approach with Simon; only if you agrre to accept (without baulk) my conditions I'll stipulate to you.

Yes mother! I agree in advance.

You better make a deep analysis of my conditions before commit yourself; because if you betrayed your oath, the consequences would be even more devastating than your expulsion from the Petit Palais. I am listening mother.

First, you apologize, not only to Dr. Sommers, but to your sister.

Secondly, you got to curb your aggressive temper to silence your jealousy and your selfishness in welcoming with kindness (even if this causes you aversion) Dr. Sommers at the Petit Palais.

Thirdly, you must be married within three months to Mona Lisa Hollemberg.

Harry Morgan remained astounded, unable to articulate a word, stunned by the extravagant request of his mother. He wanted to protest this last condition.

Mother, I do not know if...

Take or leave. She said getting up. I don't have anything to add. She returned to the house, leaving her prostrate son, trembling of anger and frustration, facing an agonizing dilemma.

Elsa went to the library where her husband was working. He was surprised to see his wife. Since their misunderstanding she never went there when he was present. She sat close to him around the large table of studies, where they had spent so many studious hours in the comfort and warmth of the marble fireplace that stood at the end of the room.

Simon, said Elsa with her most tender voice, I just promise to Harry (subject to conditions, of course) that he could remain at the Petit Palais, and I was going to plead his cause with you.

You shouldn't have done it, Elsa. Your son became a vulgar thug. He is involved with a band of rascals to sow terror in the city and the surrounding area. It was a just punishment inflicted on this scam. You shouldn't have interfered in this mess...

You don't even ask me the conditions that I imposed?

He acquiesced? Asked his very anxious husband.

Not yet. But I know that he wants to save face. I told him to think; because once its decision taken; I told him, he will not be able to disengage. He will accept, I am sure.

In this case, Elsa, you have my approval.

She jumped on the knees of her husband, embraced him and kissed him tenderly. Since the reconciliation Simon strove to regain the affection of his wife. She had, little by little, indeed, smothered her resentment towards her husband and resumed her spontaneity, her surges of tenderness, her passionate ardor and her customary good humor.

Thanks, my love said Elsa rising. If someone saw us? She broke out into a crystalline laugh and walked out of the library.

The next morning, before going to the factory, Harry Morgan went to his mother to tell her that he accepted her conditions and he promised to change his behavior.

On his way, he met Max Hollemberg whose car broke down in the middle of the road. He packed his Mercedes and came to offer his services to the contractor, who didn't know, really, what to do.

Harry opened the hood of the Ferrari and saw immediately what was causing the failure. He went and took a tool into the trunk of his car, and in a few minutes, reestablished contact between the motor and the battery terminals.

Try to ignite, said Harry Morgan.

The engine started at the first turn of the key. Me, I don't know anything in terms of mechanics; It is an unforgivable gap, said Max Hollemberg laughing, satisfied. By the way, he added: can you recommend someone to install my satellite dishes that I just received?

You forget, sir, that I am an electronics engineer? You've come to the right place. When do you want me to come fix them for you?

This afternoon, about four o'clock? Asked Max Hollemberg, a little hesitant?

I'll be there, without a doubt.

The two men exchanged a handshake and went each on his way.

Harry Morgan landed in the Hollemberg before four o'clock. He was accompanied by two technicians of the plant he had requisitioned to help him. He was greeted by a servant who hastened to announce the absence of Mr. Max who had not yet returned from his office.

Is Miss Mona Lisa at home? He inquired casually.

Who should I announce to mademoiselle?

Harry Morgan, he said, by presenting a business card to the servant.

After a moment, the girl appeared, casually dress, her long dark hair streaked with thin auburn reflections scattered over her bare shoulders. She wore jeans that ground her slender hips.

Harry Morgan! What a pleasant surprise! But, sir, you realize, that it is the first time, you deign to venture in the wilderness, since the reception offered by my parents to introduce me to the Montjolian society? And without notify me of your visit, It's indeed the climax of astonishment!. Don't stand there, like a clown, Harry; she continued laughingly, and come embrace me.

Harry stepped forward, looking shy and embarrassed, and kissed the girl on both cheeks.

You should have notified me of your visit Harry? She told him in a tone of reproach. Father is not there, and you know that my mom does not want people to see her in the plaster. Will you be kind enough to get in the living room?

I'm going to disappoint you more, Mona Lisa, I owe you certainly a visit, and it will be coming soon. But today, I came, at the request of your father to install the satellite dishes which will allow you to receive TV signals via satellite.

You have disappoint me greatly, Harry Morgan...

I promise that you will not have more opportunity to be disappointed by me. If you want, I'll be happy to spend my entire life to repair this odd irreparable blunder.

Suddenly, Mona Lisa became very serious. She did not believe her ears. She asked Harry, still standing on the doorstep:

Have I understood the meaning of your words? Are you sure that you want to live with me the rest of your life? Mr. Morgan, express yourself more clearly; I do not understand innuendo, I am not an expert in conundrum.

This is not how I had imagined this scene. I would like to choose the circumstance and the time for an approach so important. But, the hazard requires a prompt decision:

Mona Lisa, I love you with all my heart, with all my soul, I deposited my life and my happiness at your feet. Will you marry me?

The girl did not answer, she was moved to tears. She took Harry's hand saying: enter!

She dropped herself in the first available chair in the hallway and began to sob nervously.

Harry Morgan threw himself on his knees in front of her and, taking Mona Lisa's hand in his, and kisses them passionately. I'm sorry if I hurt your feelings, but this declaration was burning my lips for a long time.

- Stop Harry! I heard my father's car. I'll give you my answer tomorrow.

Mona Lisa wiped her eyes, nimbly, and composed a serene face to greet her father.

Good evening, my darling, ah! You received engineer Morgan

in my absence? That is very nice of you. Then, turning to Harry, he said to him: I'll show you the equipment.

Where do you suggest me to place them? Asked Max Hollemberg?

I do not know your house, replied Harry.

It's just; we're going to rectify that omission, right now.

His daughter, clinging to his arm, he showed the house to Harry Morgan. Who recommended the appropriate places. Mona Lisa wanted a screen install in her bedchamber. She loved watching TV.

Harry worked diligently and, aided by his two employees to fix the satellite dishes on the roof, slipped the cables under the heels of the walls, so they are not visible and hung large flat screens at designated places.

The satellite's reception was perfect. Four televisions set functioned perfectly. I thank you, said Max Hollemberg, you did a great job.

I have to go, said Harry Morgan, they expected me for dinner. Do not hesitate to call me if you have a problem, I am very honored to render you service. Thanks, again, I appreciate the offer at its fair value. Max Hollemberg handed him an envelope saying: a small compensation for your men...

I already take care of that, dear sir, see you soon.

Mona Lisa had disappeared during the installation. He didn't see her again, before leaving. However, he welcomed the favorable circumstances, which allowed him to anticipate the fulfillment of his oath, without having to pass for a savage on the girl eyes, it seems, very attached to the etiquette.

Mona Lisa had received a terrible blow. She did not expect this declaration of love that she had herself provoked, by the biting irony of her condescending remarks.

She had gone to seek refuge in her mother's room and lying on her back, she was trying to make the point about the situation. Before the abrupt appearance of Dr. Sommers in town, it was on Harry Morgan that she had set her sights.

Her parents had even made her understand that he was a very good party. Despite her secret tocade for Dr. Sommers, she had retained in her heart, a privileged place for her first love.

However, like many other young girls of Montjolly, she had fed the hope to conquer this handsome and affable gentleman, basking in the glow of a mysterious charm.

She had promised Harry to give him a response the next day, she needed to know immediately, the availability of the doctor and her chances with him. She didn't have time to lose investigate; she called Isabella.

The phone rang at the Petit Palais.

Here the Morgan residence, said Amélie (the housekeeper) may I help you?

Amélie, Mona Lisa, can I talk to Isabella please?

Wait a minute, Miss, I'll see if Miss Isabella is available.

Mona Lisa, after a minute of waiting; heard the charming voice of Isabella:

Mona Lisa sweetheart, how are you? Your mother is doing well, I hope?

She is doing wonderfully. Isabella, I called you to ask you a question that you will find, perhaps, incongruous or indiscreet; but, hold a crucial importance for me.

Mona Lisa honey, you can trust me. We are all immersed in the same mess, and nothing exists that I cannot do to alleviate your obsession and your anxiety, which I share, believe me, I beg you.

Isabella, are you in love with Dr. Sommers? Is he in love with you? Answer me frankly, I beg you.

Mona Lisa honey, you have no need to beg me. Dr. Sommers and I are practically engaged. I say almost, because the thing has not yet officially approved by my parents. It's the only thing you wanted to know?

Yes, the only thing. I'm going to make you a confidence. You got to keep it secret until further notice. No one else is aware. I want you to be the first to know, darling sister. Harry asked me to marry him.

Oh! The wonderful news! I am happy for you. Welcome to the family. Already, I promise to you my affection and all my love.

When have him proposed to you?

This afternoon, only.

Congratulations dear sister, I feel that we will both get along beautifully.

I hope so with all my heart, said Mona Lisa. See you tomorrow... and thanks again.

See you tomorrow repeated Isabella...

Isabella was burning with the envy to announce Elsa the surprising news. But she could not betray the secret that Mona Lisa had heartily entrusted to her and under promise not to reveal this to anyone.

Isabella knew, why Mona Lisa had asked this question. She wanted to be sure of the nature of Dr. Sommers feelings for Isabella, before abandoning the race. In addition, Isabella knew that her man had sown disorder in the camp of the Greeks. That most of the girls in the city, had eyes only for her dear Carl.

Because her brother had not responded to the repeated advances of Mona Lisa, a little, discouraged by Harry's haughty and condescending attitude, would also seek compensation for her disappointment. But, basically, she really loved, her brother. Isabella wondered, all perplexed, what could have precipitated her brother into the arms of the girl?

Elsa certainly knew. Because she had seen them, (from her room), on the rose granite bench, talking with animation. She could not hear what they were saying, but she had noticed clearly the upset face of her brother and his eyes watery, red with anger.

Mona Lisa didn't go to dinner the night, claiming a terrible migraine. She didn't even turn on the big screen TV that had just been installed in her room.

Lying on her stomach, her face buried in a pillow, Mona Lisa was trying to put order in her thoughts. The dream that she had cherished since her return in Montjolly, suddenly was realized. She had suffered at the thought to be scorned by the man whom she loved, only because of her African origin?

Her father, Max Hollemberg, who could settle anywhere in the world, had received a cold reception of the pioneers of the city. Elsa Morgan was the only one who had pleaded in their favor and demanded that they accept him, and his exile companions, in the Montjolly xenophobic community.

At the election of Simon Morgan as Mayor of the city, Max Hollemberg received permission to build his industrial complex, on the model of the one he possessed in Pretoria. His expertise in navigation of ballistic missiles: such, Solaris, the Poseidon and Trident and his knowledge in aeronautics which had enabled him to improve the performance of high-speed rocket technology, had assured him, without too much difficulty, the renewal of his lucrative contracts with Boeing and Lockheed Martin.

Her parents worshipped particularly the Morgan and had a special devotion for Elsa. Did Mona Lisa misjudge the behavior of Harry Morgan?

She preferred to believe that the evil black curse, putting racists and xenophobes in a situation, at least, embarrassing, had pulled the pride of noble caste and claims of arrogant elite from Montjolly. This disappointment brought Harry Morgan to the reality of his human condition and the acknowledgement of his true feelings.

By the way, said Mona Lisa, the evil black curse, (although it made me suffer bitterly) would have contributed, however, to my happiness. "At something evil is good" she thought, smiling.

Mona Lisa got up and went into the room of her parents to tell them the great news.

She knocked on the door. Enter! Said her mother who was reading a novel. She was sitting on a Louis XVI chair, her cast leg was resting on an antique stool adorned with a red velvet cushion. Under the lampshade that strained the dazzling glow of the light, Joyce's face appeared to be sheer and shone with health.

I thought that you were suffering, my darling?

Mom, I feel better, much better now. Where is father?

You know! He is immersed into its paperwork, as usual.

Very well said the girl in a playful tone. Anyway, I wanted you to be the first to know the news.

What news? My Lisa, tell me quickly.

Harry Morgan asked me in marriage.

Joyce Hollemberg dropped her book, seizes by a sudden dizziness and closed her eyes under the pressure of a strong emotion.

Don't faint mother! Whispered anxiously Mona Lisa who grasps the hands of her mother. Joyce attracted her daughter on her heart and embraced her with all her strength.

I am happy for you, she said to her daughter, slightly, loosening her grip. When had he proposed to you my love?

 Did you already say yes?

My mom! You know I couldn't do such a thing without consulting you and father. If you agree, I ask for your blessing.

I fully agree, if you love him. Well! Have you consulted your heart?

I always liked him, despite his reluctance and his prevarication.

Go get your father; he is in his office.

Max, my friend, said Joyce, when her husband entered in the bedroom; I just heard great news.

Father, said Mona Lisa presenting an intimidated smile, I have been asked in marriage. I request your consent before responding to the person.

Don't make me languish, my darling, tell me who it is.

Harry Morgan...

Ah! I am happy, really happy that he finally decided. When it happened? You didn't speak to him, not a word, while I was visiting the house this afternoon? That was already happened?

When I received him, in your absence, I was so surprised, (not knowing that he had promised you to come fix the antennas) that I have accosted him wryly, telling him: he finally consented to visit the savages in the wilderness! He should, at least, announces his visit; but that it was still welcome in my poor straw hut. I remember telling him that he deceived me fairly. Confronted at the boundary of disappointment; He told me he was going to disappoint me even more.

That it was not the visit that he planned to grant me soon, I had reason to hurl abuse at him, but if I allowed it to him, he would spend the rest of his life to repair the irreparable blunder he had committed.

I asked him to explain himself more clearly, I did not understand well innuendo, that I was not an expert in the art of deciphering riddles.

Then, he declared that was not how he had imagined this solemn moment. But, as the circumstances are obliging, he could no longer wait for a better opportunity.

Mona Lisa, he says, I love you with all my heart, with all my soul, my life without you would be unbearable for me. Do you want to marry me? And voila.

Max Hollemberg took his daughter on his heart and asked her:

What have you told him?

I told him that I will give him my answer tomorrow.

Good! Sighed Max Hollemberg after a long pause. Let's talk about serious things, now, when is the engagement?

Max, you're going too fast extrapolating. Firstly Mona Lisa must send her consent to Harry. Then, Simon and Elsa will come make the official presentations. All this before you can fix the date of the engagement. Be reasonable, my dear, control your impatience.

That's won't be for next week, either, because Isabella's recital is scheduled in exclusivity at CNN. For lack of time, she couldn't play the last time, added Mona Lisa

I understand, chained Max Hollemberg, in a resigned tone: the thing is in the hands of women, consult me if it is absolutely necessary?

I knew you were a weighted and understanding man, said his wife, laughing out loud. Something she hasn't done since her accident. Don't worry, my darling, said Joyce, still chuckling laugh, nothing will happen without your consent.

Mona Lisa woke up the next morning, about ten o'clock. She stayed lying in her bed, giving free rein to her loose imagination.

She felt a sense of profound wellbeing. She was already swimming in a pool of sweet and balsamic euphoria. She was immersed in the early thrill of unexpected happiness. Since the accident of her mother and the appearance of this horrible leprosy, she had lost her enthusiasm and gaiety, but strove to give change (especially her mother) to encourage her to live and survive her disappointments and her despair.

Mona Lisa dressed with elegance and sobriety. She put a corsage of pink organdy and a scarlet chiffon skirt, tight to her waist of wasp, by a wide leather belt, of the same color. She wear transparent and red leather pumps.

Her long disheveled hair on her shoulders, framed her lovely face that revives a touch of carmine on her fleshy lips.

Mona Lisa went into her mother's room. As soon as she crossed the threshold, Joyce exclaimed: you are beautiful my darling, you are radiant of grace and beauty, it is obvious, you are in love!

You make me blush, my mom! I thought that Dr. Merville was coming today, to remove your plaster?

I believe he is already on his way. Replied her mother, always in ecstasy of admiration in front of her daughter. Turn around sweetheart, so I could better see you.

She executed a swirl on her heels, making a cheeky complicity pout, as when she was a little girl.

Have you already called Harry?

Not yet mom. I will call him after the removal of your cast by Dr. Merville, because I would like you to go out with you. We are going to have lunch at the Grand Meaulnes, all three of us.

Oh! No, my dear: you'll take lunch with your fiancé, all alone. You don't need a chaperone. Moreover, you can trust me; you don't share these moments with anyone. These are unique and precious memories an inexhaustible treasure that you must keep at the bottom of your heart, to maintain the fire of love through the vicissitudes and during difficult moments of life.

Someone knocked on the door at this moment. Enter, shouted Mona Lisa, the maid came and said:

Madam, the doctor arrived. He is waiting in the vestibule.

Thank you, Laura, I will take care of it;. Answered Mona Lisa. Mother, do you want me to bring him in your room? Or did you prefer to go downstairs?

But, of course, my Lisa. It will be more comfortable for him and for me in my room, obviously.

The girl went downstairs and stopped at the last step, hesitantly. Dr. Sommers was standing in the middle of the room, gazing at a painting depicting a hunting scene, painted by Antoine Watteau.

Did I scare you? Miss Hollemberg? You look very afraid. I am sorry. But you still look more beautiful today.

I was not expecting to see you, said Mona Lisa blushing. Dr. Merville...

He had suffered a slight discomfort. It irks you that I replaced him?

The girl had recovered from her emotion, she told Dr. Sommers:

Before I lead you to my mother, we have to settle down something: now you call me Mona Lisa, me, I'll call you Carl. We are friends, isn't it? Looking straight in the eyes of Dr. Sommers. Then, no more ceremony and protocol between us.

It is understood, Mona Lisa.

Good! Let's go liberate my mom from her shackles!

Joyce Hollemberg was lying in her four-poster bed, a yellow cover on her legs. She was wearing a slight make up, to hide, her pallor and her apprehension.

Hello, dear Madam, said Dr. Sommers on entering the room. How do you feel?

Apparently, I am well enough. But I await the verdict of the doctor to make sure.

The most recent x-rays indicated a complete and flawless welding of the broken bones. I think you'll be happy with the result. Get up please Madam!

Dr. Sommers then, removed the casts on Joyce, all exited and Impatient.

Perfect! The doctor exclaimed: the skin is smooth, without any scar. The magical ointment has done wonder! Now, let's walk. Try these new legs, joked Dr. Sommers. He helped her take a tour of the room, supporting her arm, and then asked Joyce Hollemberg to do so alone.

No pains, dear Madam, are you uncomfortable?

She approached the doctor, suspended herself to his neck and rested her head on his chest. Thank you! Thousand times thank you, whispered Joyce swallowing her breath. You have restored my life. I am infinitely grateful.

A little embarrassed, Dr. Sommers gently resolved Joyce Hollemberg hands, clinging to his neck and said: if it is so, you call me

Carl, I'll call you Joyce. This is the formula enshrined by Mona Lisa, who kept watching them with an amazed air and softened look. Right now, added the doctor, joking: you can dance all night without been tired; I hearsay that you loved the dance.

I take you at your word, Carl! By the way, I am reserving my first dance for you; at the evening reception we organize to celebrate...

She stopped abruptly. Mona Lisa was making warning gestures behind the doctor back.

My mom she said: you cannot invite Carl now, you do not know when it will be possible.

Joyce understood immediately that she was committing a blunder by revealing, prematurely, to Carl, the engagement of her daughter.

The two women accompanied Dr. Sommers, on the doorstep and said goodbye kissing him on both cheeks.

Mona Lisa telephoned, Harry telling him she is coming at his office to take him to lunch at the Grand Meaulnes.

I waited for your call all morning.

I will be there momentarily, my love.

The same evening, Harry told his mother that Mona Lisa has accepted to marry him. He hoped that Simon would accompany Elsa for the marriage proposal, according to the custom in usage in their society. He wanted that to be done in the shortest period of time; because Mona Lisa wanted to set the date for the engagement, the Saturday following the presentation of the show featuring Isabella on television.

CHAPTER X

The Morgan's sisters house at the white Lys Avenue, had become a center of attraction. In addition to the weekly evenings, held regularly, and attended by a selected elite; Michelle Morgan brought together, each evening, a small group of friends: Dr. Suzanne Birmingham, Christel Baldwin, Grace Norris, Samantha Sandford, around which revolved an Areopagus of idle suitors in search of adventure. Matt Potter, and Robert Carlson, were courting Michelle Morgan and Grace Norris; James Nadowsky (Fox reporter) courted seriously, Dr. Suzanne Birmingham. Charles Lewis (the surrealist poet) wrote cryptic sonnets to Christel Baldwin (who boasted of literature), and subtle madrigals to Michelle Morgan.

They had elected homes in the small library of the villa of white lilies; Playing Bridge or Chess, watching avant-garde esoteric movies, ordered by Michelle. Cathy Morgan joined a few times the band and provided the supply of cognac and liquor.

We saw, less and less, Suzanne Birmingham and James Novomeský, since Dr. Merville had asked her to help him at the hospital.

James, obviously interested in Dr. Birmingham came to the villa, when Suzanne was present.

Isabella had, literally, disappeared from the scene. She deserted even the weekly meetings, so she could rehearse for the concert and to help Carl polish the text of his lecture. Isabella taught the tango to her preferred partner, for grandstanding, at Mona Lisa betrothal's ball.

The arrival of doctor Birmingham at the hospital Sainte Cécile, had eased somewhat, the work of Dr. Sommers and allowed Dr. Merville to take a few days off.

He complained, regularly now, of an unbearable migraines which incapacitated him for hours. Dr. Sommers urged him to consult a specialist but he refused. Sommers was worried and share his concern to his wife Bernice, who he had managed to convince of the imperative necessity to take care of his health.

Dr. Sommers, by doing a summary inventory in the surgery room, found a lot of unpacked surgical instruments.

He sterilized them and stored them in a glass cabinet.

Dr. Sommers took the great bulk of the job at the hospital; and divided the rest between Birmingham and Merville, so that that D. Merville could stay home longer to rest. Dr. Merville was not at all happy with this arrangement, but, he couldn't dare complain because Dr. Sommers had threatened him of an early retirement.

CNN had made the promotion of the show throughout the past week, and prided itself rightly, for his selfless contribution to the effort of the Montjolly's youth.

Roland Peterson had put the network in the obligation to carry out this program, for two reasons: to eclipse Fox success and stimulate an exponential increase in the number of the network international viewers.

Peterson did not dare mention the main reason that incited him to plead the case of the city in distress with passionate conviction. He secretly loved Isabella, and was ready to do everything to please her.

To be fair, Roland Peterson was not the only one nourishing similar expectation. Robert Carlson, Charles Lewis, not to mention Matt Potter, who despite suffering a stern rebuffs, didn't despair to conquer, one day, this untamed heart, this impregnable fortress.

Nine o'clock sharp, the smiling image of Matt Potter appeared on the screen of millions of televisions, connected in anticipation of an interesting show, like the last time.

Matt Potter congratulated the CNN officials on behalf of the Committee of Public safety, thanked the viewers who had contributed so generously to the success of the last presentation. He asked them to be even more generous this time.

You remember the number to call: (987) 654-3210. The countdown.

I don't want to make you wait any longer; I leave you in the company of the beautiful and talented pianist, Isabella Morgan, (accompanied by the local Orchestra, the Roms), who will interpret the concerto in A major by the great Portuguese composer: José Vianna Da Motta.

The theater of the Stars welcomed Isabella with a burst of applause. She was dazzling in her sequined yellow dress. She sat down and made a slight nod to Renalto who raised his baton of improvised conductor.

The audience was captivated from the first notes. Isabella attacked the "moderato" with exquisite fluidity, harmonious flexibility, and ran the syncopated chords the Orchestra brass punctuated vividly.

With the «Largo» Isabella gave the measure of her mastery of the piano. She exuded her passion for music through all her pores. Her phenomenal virtuosity was exalted in the execution of difficult passages. She permeated her impeccably balanced play, a dizzying sensation of communicative euphoria. The audience amazed, won by this poignant emotion, immediately endorsed the birth of an exceptional artist.

Isabella had chosen for this work of Da Motta, she had studied in Switzerland, instead of the first concerto of Prokofiev, she proposed to play initially; because she didn't want to leave people with the impression that she was a snob, a dilettante looking to promote her talent. She chose this work for his passionate romanticism that suited well her exalted nature. This concerto allowed her to spread out the perfection of her style and her prodigious talent.

Renalto, the conductor and the musicians of the Roms hoisted their virtuosity at the height of the circumstance.

They had a subtle affinity with this music with a strong mystical coloring, similar to the pathetic and visceral complaints of the Gypsy music.

Backed up by the impeccable artistry of the Orchestra, Isabella let slip her fingers on the ivory keys; sometimes stroking them with pleasure, sometimes beating them with delicacy, to snatch the aesthetic and harmonic accents that characterized the emotional decor of the masterly work of Da Motta.

From time to time, the camera presented on the small screen, the dazzling piano keyboard, on which ran the girl fingers. The Topaz and diamond ring she wore at her ring finger of the right hand, projected sporadic sparks in all directions.

Sometimes, she shook her head in a graceful, elegant and short gesture to prevent her hair on her face to obscure her view.

Isabella began with an exceptional flair, the five variations of the second movement. She completed the piece in apotheosis, alternating (according to the wish of the composer), crescendo chromatic scenic and diminuendo of descriptive arpeggios, until the dramatic climax of the finale.

It was delirium! The room exploded literally. The audience unleashed, threatening to break everything, it was impatient and called loudly: bis! bis! bis!

Isabella received three enthusiastic recalls. But this didn't satisfied the excited crowd. She received three wreaths, and then left the stage to the great disappointment of the dissatisfied fanatics.

Matt Potter, after consultation with interested stakeholders, i.e., Roland Peterson and Dr. Sommers, who agreed to shorten a few minutes the time of his presentation; announced to the public

The incomparable Isabella Morgan, in the Ballade for piano of José Vianna da Motta.

This ballad dramatizes the sentimental and melancholic journey of a lonely soul in the unknown regions of dreamlike meditation. In mystical language, it describes the mandatory and successive steps taken by the loved soul seeking the sublime metempsychosis.

The tortured soul of a haunting embrace, revolted in a distraught explosion, full of blazing spontaneity, tried to get rid of the heavy drowsiness that clogs the happiness. But the feelings that overwhelms him, and torment, as a leitmotif haunting, brings every moment, to the sad unreality of his voluptuous and impossible transmigration.

It was an extraordinary triumph. A true apotheosis. They had to lower the curtains to prevent the assistance from invading the podium.

People telephoned to compliment the artist. The most renowned Philharmonic Orchestras: London, Paris, New York, Tokyo, Sydney, Moscow, made her pressing offers. Money rained into the coffers of the Committee.

Parents and friends had stormed the scene of the municipal theater to congratulate this brilliant star who appeared like a meteor in the dark sky of the city.

Everyone wanted to kiss her; they had undone her hairstyle and crumpled her dress.

Elsa, enjoying a slight respite, coached her daughter out of the hustle and bustle her into her car and led her at the Petit Palais.

As soon as they arrived in the vestibule, Elsa, without saying

a Word, pressed her daughter on her heart. They remained there, welded by an exclusive connivance of thought and a miraculous joy.

It was a brilliant revenge, a complete defeat for Simon and Harry who believed they had, forever, killed Isabelle's musical ambitions.

Let's listen to Carl on TV!

Meanwhile, Matt Potter was trying hard to restore order to the theater. Dr. Sommers has an important communication for you on the evolution of the evil black curse; he said, striving to stay calm.

He was booed and whistled. It was impossible, to announce Dr. Sommers. The audience was chanting in a dreadful clamour: Isabella, Isabella, Isabella...

Dr. Sommers entered the scene, smiling, casual demeanor, chanting with the crowd: I sa bel la, Isabella. After a moment, he raised his hands, the thunder subsided immediately.

Dear friends, began Dr. Sommers, I ask you, before bringing you to the prosaic reality with my presentation; to applaud, once again, the incomparable artist who sent us (with her extraordinary performance, her emotional interpretation of the Ballad of José Vianna da Motta) to the enchanted region of dream and fantasy.

The assistance broke loose again. But Sommers had thawed the atmosphere. Now, he could present his lecture without too much trouble.

He realized at that time that he had left his text on a stool behind the scenes. He did not hesitate a second; He would improvise.

Time fails me, but I shall try to be as explicit and brief as possible. I ask you, however,

To heed the information that I am going to give you. I exhorted the Aboriginal population to be patience, because, very soon it will be free of the humiliating stigma of the black plague. I want to especially, address the politicians and panicked Arian executives and worried citizens, who are languishing in the dreaded expectation of a horrific mass contamination.

I can say authoritatively that the evil black curse is not, I repeat, is not contagious.

Evil black curse does not affect any vital organs, and does alter only the skin pigmentation.

I can also guarantee almost conclusively that this strange virus incubation period, extends, (according to my clinical observations, and the study of the analysis submitted to laboratories around the world), extends I say, from nine to twelve months.

I do not exclude the appearance of this weird phenomenon in other regions of the globe, but it would not because of what was happen here in Montjolly.

I will in a moment present formal and indisputable proof, the relative safety of the evil black curse does not spread by contagion.

Dr. Suzanne Birmingham, whose valuable assistance, has been a priceless help at hospital Sainte Cécile; came the same day when the epidemic was declared. Roland Peterson and his team which was boundless dedication has made possible the organization of this event, suffered the same fate as well as James Nadowsky of Fox and his invaluable companions.

This contamination was not due, as formerly believed, a contagious transmission of the evil black curse; but, as I am sure now, by primal and direct impregnation.

Dr. Sommers turned and motioned to someone behind the scenes. A, young man, dressed with short pants, torso naked and bare footed,

Holding the leach of a white fox terrier, stepped onto the stage.

I present to you, ladies, and gentlemen, Fred Curtis Hunter, farmer by profession who lives with his wife and two daughters and has not been contaminated by them.

Fred Curtis went to hunt Partridge, on Friday morning before the spectacular eruption of the evil black curse and returned home Wednesday after the epidemic was declared.

Fred Curtis is the only white person locked up in the inhumane enclave of the quarantine. I am convinced, (you also I guess) speaking to the federal authorities, that these barbaric measures present a danger for the population.

Fear to become black, you cannot in any way, justify the systematic depletion of this flourishing region and the plight of the people who are dying with hunger.

Since the federal Government has taken an active part in the imposition of the quarantine, it should at least have the basic decency to feed the starving population.

I called on the Senate of the Republic to plead the cause of this doubly hit town. That Senate must help us break this yoke that stifles us.

Dear friends time is running out, I will not be able to develop the other two points in my presentation.

He took Fred Curtis by the arm and was preparing to leave. Matt Potter entered at that instant and muttered a few words in his ear.

Then, Sommers thanked Fred Curtis who left the theater in the company of Potter.

Dear friends, at the request of some officials of the Government, the direction of CNN give us a break to finish our presentation.

The audience listening Dr. Sommers statements, surprised by the appearance of Fred Curtis, had remained silent. People were cheering, now convinced of the veracity of the speaker who ignited in their hearts the hope of recovering their congenital pigmentation.

The evil black curse, is not the only weird phenomenon recorded in the global history of strange and cursed facts. But since it affects a particular breed, physically and psychologically, in what they considered the most precious wealth in the world: the color of their skin; this affection, at the very least, benign, has sown panic in the camp of the Greeks.

Charles Hoy Fort, in his "Book of wretched" (book published in New York in 1919) had compiled more than forty examples of these unusual phenomena, drawn from scientific and serious magazines from around the world: black rain, heavy red rain of live fish, a storm of periwinkles, cinder of frogs and so on. Those pesky facts have disappeared from memory, since no one, except this wacky Fort, was concerned to these taboo incongruities, which disturb the Cartesian logic of the self righteous scientists.

It is likely that the evil black curse, came from, who knows where, either one of these aberrant manifestations of nature, disturbed by the harmful agents generated in laboratories, the blast furnaces of petrochemical plants.

The gradual warming of the planet, the accelerated reduction of the ozone layer in the stratosphere, which protects the Earth from harmful rays from elsewhere, have created ideal conditions for the emergence of such an aberration.

Evil black curse is a warning, a harbinger of an impending catastrophe that threatens the world.

The melting of the glaciers of the two poles is not due only to the alarming increase in the Earth's temperature, but more importantly, a significant loss of the original weight of the Earth.

The indiscriminate extraction of minerals of all kinds, the systematic draining of oil wells, on all continents; ore and oil vanished into thin air consumption, and dispersed by evaporation, beyond the stratosphere; did tip the precarious balance that tilted earth on its virtual axis.

The dangerous rectification of the curve of attraction of the planet, (initiated less than fifty years ago), to satisfy the materialistic demands of a selfish and decadent civilization; has resulted in:

The loss of a significant portion of the protection offered to us by the ozonosphere, shredded in some spots, porous in others, infinitesimal (but extremely perilous) have initiated an acceleration of the axial rotation of our biosphere.

The imperceptible acceleration of the rotation of the globe, causes a considerable decrease in gravity. This negative factor destabilizing the balance of the solar mechanics, which governs the gravitational forces inversely proportional to the square of the distance from the Earth to other planets; but proportional to the constant mass of the globe; endangers the Milky Way and who knows? The entire universe.

We are dancing on a volcano, said Louis the XV. Man is trying to poison the Earth. As cobra venom can kill a stone, chemicals and artificial fertilizers poison the soil.

Toxic and carcinogenic residues contained in foodstuffs for consumption, (assimilated by the human body), in turn, affect health precarious and current human living in this polluted environment. Long time survival of mankind, has been forever compromised.

I stop this extrapolation in the hypothetical and real field of the possible; the inevitable extinction of life on the planet, by the insane and dishonest human action.

I reiterate my urgent appeal for the immediate lifting of the quarantine. I urged the leaders of all countries of the world to find other energy sources than those that endanger the existence of the Earth and the other planets in the Galaxy.

Prevailing over his own resolution, despite himself, flying on the wings of improvisation, Dr. Sommers had ventured an hazardous foray in the hermetic forest of pseudoscientific premonitions and overflowed the framework for his briefing on the evil black curse.

The audience had applauded softly, it retained of this incomprehensible verbiage that hope to soon resume its natural coloration.

But the interest in the theory of a relative and systematic the diminution of the gravitational force exerted by the earth; was translated by an avalanche of phone calls. Call demanding more informations about the probable duration of the epidemic and its potential harmfulness; others protesting bitterly against this absurd theory, which might terribly impair the projected expansion of the mining and oil prospection in Alaska by the industry.

Exxon Mobil, Shell, Total, British Petroleum, pressured Dr. Sommers to produce formal proof of his fanciful allegations or abjured immediately, his inept and misleading heresy.

Spontaneously, a group of scientists organized, via the internet, a network of researchers, experts in geophysics, specialists in geology, Geodesy; to promote and resolve the theoretical equation of the weight lost of the planet.

The professor, Saurel Chaussonnet, eminent Geophysicist of the Sorbonne, validated in a brief declaration on French television, the principles on which the young American scientist, had built his brilliant theory.

Professor Chaussonnet, himself , continued the research on the subject. He had, he said, already made a similar theory (unfortunately still unpublished) which he has named: «theory of the no compensation of the dispersed energy.

Professor Chaussonnet, advocated without spirit of rivalry, (although the author of the theory, had delivered only a simple overview of his work), and promised his full cooperation, in cases where the doctor would refer to his notes on the matter.

Dr. Sommers telephoned Professor Chaussonnet to thank him for his invaluable support. He answered, until late into the night, to the numerous emails from the four corners of the globe.

Isabella had followed on television, the improvised presentation by Carl. She was very surprised by the outlandish theory which he had never mentioned to her.

You become a celebrity! My darling, said Isabella to Carl.

I am return the compliment, my dear love! The world is cheering you and praises you. They vituperated against my theory, disputed its legitimacy with aggressiveness, they said I shouldn't never have emerged from my unhealthy darkness.

Carl darling, said Isabella, you never told me about your theory, matter of fact, nothing about your projects, your research, nothing important? What are we talking about all the time, then?

About the most important thing in the world; our love. Everything else is only illusion and deception. If one lives with love and tenderness; It succeeded his life; No matter who you are or what you become!

The lovers chated all the night long, until dawn. Each formulated its plans for the future. Isabella wondered if she should pursue a career as a musician. As long as you book me a little place in your heart, I am ready to follow you everywhere, said Dr. Sommers. But, Isabella, wanted to have a large family. She cannot imagine how to reconcile her eventual career and her family obligations. Carl made her understand that she had plenty of time before taken this decision.

Now that the thing is official, I can reveal you a strange conversation I've had with Mona Lisa. She had made me swear to say nothing to anyone, as long as she would not release me from my oath.

She asked me, continued Isabella, what was the nature of my relationship with you. I told her bluntly; we are madly in love and that we intend to get married soon. She thanked me, warmly, promised me a sincere and eternal friendship.

The next day I learned that she was going to marry my brother.

Carl, do you understand what that means?

I expect that you are going to explain to me, my darling!

Firstly, Mona Lisa wanted to be sure that you were not available to commit elsewhere. Because as long as there was a chance of conquering you, she would have remained in the trenches. I will reveal you a secret, my darling. All the girls in Montjolly have a crush on you, every single one of them without exception. I would not make you this confidence, if I didn't effectively know that you're already familiar with the issue.

Secondly, I don't like, but at all, the idea that this pretentious of Suzanne Birmingham is at the hospital every day. Really, you shouldn't have required her help!

Ah! Ah! Ah! Laughed Dr. Sommers. You're jealous darling love? Don't laugh at me Carl!

Isabella, my darling, calm down... I didn't know you in this light... You know that you have no need to be jealous... Did I give you a reason to be?

Isabella didn't respond and changed abruptly the topic.

Carl darling! Are you sure the black curse will not last any longer? Are you really certain that in a few months, everyone will resume its natural coloration?

Yes, my dear love, clinical observations of vital organs, made in the course of many surgical procedures, have led me to this conclusion. I promised that in about five months, the evil black curse will disappear as it appeared as a hideous nightmare in the morning

Carl! Asked Isabella, what Orchestra should I choose, if I decided to pursue my career as a musician?

That will depend on the circumstances, I might choose: the Orchestra de Paris or the London Philharmonic.

But I'm not at all sure I want to embark myself on this vagabond adventure. There was a time, I could have said yes! No more now. My outlook and my priorities have changed.

When is the engagement of your brother? Asked Carl, who did not want to dwell on this matter of her musical career?

The engagement is for next Saturday. We must practice again the tango steps. It will make them jealous. Especially my dear cousin Michelle, who had accused you of being a dolt. We will make her swallow her tongue of viper and retract her backbiting, in front of all these stuck-up who had applauded her.

You know, my love, I am going to sleep. Before, I must feed Mikado.

Mikado! Who is this?

How! I haven't yet mentioned Mikado to you? It's a white cat who adopted me. The cat of a patient of Biloxi General Hospital. Two days before the eruption of the evil black curse, it had sneaked illegally into my car. As I can no longer go to Biloxi, I had to take care of him, until I can bring it back to its owner.

Carl Sommers, you are an unmitigated secretive, said Isabella in a tone of reproach. Now, dear sir, I want you to tell me everything. The small facts and the important events in your life: past, present and future.

Simon and Elsa went to the Villarossa, the sumptuous residence of the Hollemberg, located at the top of the avenue of Cherry Trees, in the new districts of the city.

The contractor had built a beautiful house on the model of a villa of the Roman countryside that he had visited with his wife during their honeymoon in Italy.

In the middle of a natural park of oak trees and spectacular chestnut trees, the villa, a two story building, was built in the shape of horseshoe. The main facade was adorned with a columned porch supported by ornamental pilasters.

A spacious vestibule, kind of Gallery of mirrors, led to the monumental staircase serving the first floor. There was on the ground floor, the grand salon, the small reception room, the dining room, the music room, a small theatre, a large kitchen, filled with all the modern gadgets, and billiard room, equipped with large panes glass, which opened at the side of pool. The seven rooms were upstairs.

Joyce and Max Hollemberd received the Morgan with a great outpouring of joy. They were really happy that finally, Harry Morgan decided to marry their daughter, a suitable match up, even for the Vaudreuil Morgan.

They settled in the small living room, a setting more respondent which this kind of intimate occasion.

My dear Max, said Simon Morgan, I have been instructed by my son, Harry, to ask your charming daughter, Mona Lisa's hand. I do it with all the more fun, because I learned and appreciated the invaluable qualities of Mona Lisa, her dedication without reserve for her parents, her generosity of heart and spirit, coupled with an education like no other. Her incomparable musical talent adds yet a wonderful luster to her stunning beauty. I am telling to you, without false modesty: I believe that the Morgan win much more in the exchange.

My dear Simon, said Max Hollemberg with good communicative mood: I gladly agreed to extend the hand of my daughter to your son. I know that she will be loved and pampered within your family. My dear friend, I know that Harry is a hard worker, a weighted and serious man, the heir of two illustrious families; Joyce and I are flattered by the choice of your son and we wish him to be happy.

Joyce rang, a servant appeared.

Go tell Miss Mona Lisa she is expected into the living room and tell Ferrer to bring the champagne.

Yes, Madam replied the maid.

Mona Lisa kissed Elsa who pressed her a long minute on her heart, telling her: I am filled with joy, today, and welcome you with all my heart, in our family. I love you and I am willing to do anything to make you happy.

Mona Lisa moved by the poignant words of Elsa, sat down near her father crying. She stayed a few minutes hanging on the neck of her father which stroked the hair with a gesture of tender affection.

When she recovered her composure, the girl greeted her future father-in-law. Then they drink champagne and eat crunchy almond and hazelnut Praline. Max and Simon exit the room, left those ladies and went out.

 Elsa said, Joyce dear, have you already sent out the invitations for the engagement party?

I was expecting your visit to do so. Upon your arrival, Max has ordered the improvised mailmen to distribute the invitation cards.

My Dear Lisa, said Elsa with deep tenderness in her voice: have you retained a date for your wedding?

Mother! Propose me a date? Replied the girl taken by surprise.

With this black evil curse quarantine, making things more difficult, I do not think we can choose a date now.

 Why not? Inquired Elsa.

They are a lot of things to prepare: the wedding dress...

Joyce dear, say no more, I think you need to choose a certain date and work accordingly. Harry is the sole male heir of the Vaudreuil family; my Lisa will wear the traditional dress that my great-grandmother had wear, that my grandmother, my mother and I had all dressed on our wedding day. I would suggest to you December 21, but this evil black curse, doesn't help.

Elsa honey, said Joyce, it will be done as you pleased.

Are you satisfied, My Lisa darling? I do not mean to shove you. You will have ample time, in four and a half months, to learn to know and deepen your love.

Dear Joyce! You will need someone to organize and prepare the reception. I am sending you Amelie (our housekeeper) and two maids, they are knowledgeable. I'll come, too, on the morning of Saturday, to take a look, to make sure that everything is ready for the event. Joyce honey, I don't like the idea of you working. You must rest, you need to recuperate fully.

You are too nice Elsa, I had been told that you were an extraordinary woman, they were not mistaken.

Elsa got up and went to sit on the sofa by Mona Lisa.

My darling said Elsa to the girl, by removing a silver cassette, inlaid with motifs from her handbag. This cassette of jewelry is the first gift that received, traditionally, the girl who married the heir to the Vaudreuil family.

Elsa took a diamonds necklace and put around the neck of Mona Lisa, on her slender wrist she placed a matching bracelet and on her ears the earrings that complemented the adornment.

You are so beautiful! said Elsa, you look like a Queen. I am really happy to steal you from Joyce.

You are now the vestal virgin of the family and by agreeing to marry Harry, you become the legitimate guarantor of moral and spiritual virtues of the Vaudreuil: honor, loyalty, love and compassion. The fortune of the Vaudreuil is, today, at your disposal. But knows that fortune is little in exchange for the unspeakable joy, the immense happiness your affection brings to us. We are delighted beyond the possible.

Mona Lisa hugged Elsa and wept tears of happiness.

Max brings Simon in his office to discuss the modality of the wedding. Simon Morgan proposed a marriage contract to Max Hollemberg who refused saying: we have nothing to consider, only matter, our children happiness. Your son is not an adventurer, not a gigolo; it would be insulting to the Morgan family the request of a marriage contract.

They talked over the decline of the country's financial institutions. Lamented the imminence of a severe recession that would significantly decrease the influence of America and relegate its hegemonic ambition in the attic of uncertainty and improbability.

Max Hollemberg sensed already, as the Pentagon is out of

resources, (because of the inevitable budgetary restriction imposed by the economic situation), was going to take drastic measures, eliminate war and atomic submarines aircraft orders, in order to continue its disastrous adventure in Iraq and Afghanistan. We can join forces to combat this difficult period that points on the horizon, said Max at Simon. Harry could easily transform a section of his plant to accommodate the clutter of works accumulated in a corner of my factory.

This is an excellent idea, replied Simon, I will inform my son. I am sure that he will accept the generous offer, you're giving to him, to diversify his production and provide new sources of revenue to his employees.

Simon and Elsa went home late in the evening, after (on the suppliant insistence of their future daughterinlaw s) shared the hearty dinner of the Hollemberg family.

There were now only a single topic of conversation in town: the engagement of Mona Lisa Hollemberg and Harry Morgan. It was an event not to be missed. One hundred twenty privileged people who had received an invitation, were running from shop to shop through the heavy traffic of the city looking for a suitable toilette to wear for the occasion.

At the weekly meeting of the Committee of Public safety, there were outstanding absentees: Mona Lisa, Harry, Isabella and Elsa. They had been excused for one reason or another; but everyone knew that the engagement of Harry Morgan and Mona Lisa Hollemberg was the cause.

The huge success Isabella recital was mentioned only because of the 60 million dollars it had collected. As Dr. Carl Sommers, who became a world celebrity overnight; he had completely disappeared from memory and conversation of people.

However, the popularity of Sommers increased exponentially. The Gazette of Mississippi published the controversial thesis, causing uproar and a public outcry which forced the Senate to introduce legislation to speed up the lifting of the quarantine.

The theory of "No Compensation of dispersed energy" had created stormy controversies and an unbearable existential malaise in the scientific circles around the world.

The endorsement of the theory by the Sorbonne Professor Saurel

Chaussonnet, had cut the grass under the feet of critics and detractors who thought they could ridicule Dr. Sommers and his inept theory.

Scientific journals, specialized magazines, as well as a few large circulated newspapers, had ordered unpublished articles from Dr. Sommers who was reluctant to engage in this risky business.

The controversy raised around his theory, put him under an obligation to respond to its critics, to formulate more precisely the results of his research on the subject.

This was not news to Montjolly. Everyone was concerned about the betrothal and the lavish party offered by the Hollemberg.

It was raining lightly. Valets in red livery, gloved white, armed with large umbrellas, wre receiving guests. They drove them under the shelter of the porch, where the hostesses took them in hand.

Other valets, white dressed, parked cars behind solid flowering bougainvillea shrubs.

The façade of the Villarossa was illuminated like in daylight. Projectors placed on remote spots, flooded the walls of a crude light. Lampposts staggered along the circular entrance, added their dazzling luminescence to this blinding profusion of light.

The hostesses drove the guests to their assigned seat. A very elaborate protocol established by Mona Lisa, herself, assembled her friends by couple, hoping to see knotted romances.

The tables were arranged in a horseshoe shape in the living room extended to the billiard room which they had removed the decorative panels separating them.

Under an improvised canopy, a little below the opening of the horseshoe, stood the table of honor reserved for the families: Hollemberg and Morgan.

A vast dance floor was laid out between the branches of 'U'. The room was plunged into a dark colored, dimly light by multicolored lanterns placed on the tables.

The Roms Orchestra under the baton of Renalto, famous now, hosted the evening. The musicians already onsite, were playing muted outdated American folk tunes.

Dr. Sommers was one of the last guests to penetrate into the large living room transformed into a reception hall for the occasion. That happened because he had to check if everything was in order before leaving the hospital.

He was surprised to meet Dr. Merville at the hospital, he believed he was at the Hollembergs with his wife Bernice and his two children.

Dr. Sommers, in vain, insisted. Dr. Merville pretexting an urgent report needed to be provided to the provincial authorities opposed a definitive refusal to his colleague who wanted at all costs, to bring him to the party.

Leaving Merville, Dr. Sommers went to the Lobby, where he recommended to Nancy, the night receptionist, to have an eye on Dr. Merville. Do not hesitate to call me, even for a hitch.

About eight o'clock, the betrothed couple took place around the table of honor, as well as Max Hollemberg, his wife Joyce and his old aunt Hélène on one side; Simon Morgan, his wife Elsa, his two sisters Cathy and Joan and niece Michelle.

Dear friends, said Max Hollemberg: thank you from the bottom of my heart, for enhancing the brilliance of this small reception we offered to, not only, celebrate the engagement of Mona Lisa and Harry Morgan, but also, to give thanks to God and a vibrant tribute to Dr. Carl Sommers, who had saved the life of our beloved Joyce from a terrible accident.

With outstanding skill and boundless dedication, Dr. Sommers has sewed up, mended, plastered, in a word, rehabilitated the beauty of my wife Joyce, who recuperated without a scratch, nor a scar.

Thanks Dr Sommers.

Joyce stood up under a thunder of applause, went to the table of the Merville where sat the doctor and gave him a loving hug. Thank you! Whispered Joyce moved to tears. You will always have a special place in my heart.

While Joyce Hollemberg regained her seat near her husband, Harry Morgan taking the arm of his fiancée, stepped forward in turn near the Merville table saying:

As one looks at the record of Dr. Sommers, I must admit that I, too, have a dispute to settle with him; but of a different nature than that of my future mother-in-law. I had publicly offended the doctor, it is publicly, as a man of honor, that I want him to accept my apology. I regret infinitely my awful conduct. Do you accept my apology Dr. Sommers?

He didn't even look Isabella sitting next to him, stood up and stretched out his hand to Harry Morgan. The two men gave themselves the accolade. Mona Lisa also kissed the doctor.

I asked my little sister to forgive my despicable behavior, relying on her generosity of heart and spirit.

Harry pressed his sister on his heart as to stifle her. Then it was the turn of Mona Lisa tightens Isabella on her heart.

The champagne put the guests in an excellent mood. The dinner was served by experienced maids who anticipated the need and the wishes of the guests. After dinner, (caviar, lobsters, crayfish, seafood, steak, leg of Lamb, rabbit).

Harry knelt down and made his formal request. He passed to the finger of his fiancée a huge diamond and kissed her for the first time in public.

The atmosphere was relaxed. People chatting loudly and laughed out loud, drinking the champagne, sipping wine and cognac.

Isabella had taken refuge at the Merville's table where she had reserved a seat for Dr. Sommers, arrangement approved by Mona Lisa who was a little intrigued.

The generous gesture of Harry Morgan had surprised everyone, Simon and Elsa, excepted. They were (despite his humiliation) satisfied, at least, the elegant way he had fulfilled the task.

Isabella albeit skeptical, would finally be able to impose the presence of Carl at the Petit Palais.

Mona Lisa opened the ball in her father's arms and Harry danced with his mother. Joyce, as she had promised, came to make a short bow to Dr. Sommers who make her Waltz gracefully.

Couples formed: James Nadowsky and Suzanne Birmingham, Robert Carlson and Samabtha Stanford, Matt Potter and Christel Baldwin, Charles Lewis and Michelle Morgan, and so on.

These gentlemen had the hope to win the jackpot, by marrying one of these wealthy heiresses.

But, nothing really serious on the horizon, except for Dr. Suzanne Birmingham, who seemed to have taken the bait. She was flattered by the respectful attention of James Nadowsky, his loving kindness and his great erudition. She had conducted a discreet investigation which revealed the elegant modesty of the unique heir of one of the largest fortunes on Wall Street.

Dr. Sommers, sought by all the girls had not yet danced, once with

Isabella. She slip away a moment and went to say a word to Renalto.

When the last dance ended, the musicians took a break, to allow themself to rest and drink.

Christel Baldwin approached Dr. Sommers who was conversing with Matt Potter. Dr. Sommers! said Christel, you have danced with all the girls, isn't it? Book me for the next one...

I regret that dear Christel, you'll have to wait a little longer, hastened to answer Isabella. I booked the next dance and it's my turn now.

What entitled you to monopolize the doctor? Nothing empowering you to claim the right to speak for him. You're not his interpreter as I know? You have to allow him to make his choice, replied Christel, in a scathing tone.

Dr. Sommers has already made his choice. I'm his partner for the rest of the evening. You don't have any luck, my darling, go accommodate yourself elsewhere.

Isabella! You think you can make fun of me? But laughs well who laughs last. Christel angrily went back to her seat.

Matt Potter and Dr. Sommers attended, wary and perplexed at this altercation and without doubt, resembled a scene of jealousy.

It was the first time that one of these golden stuck-up, dared arguing openly about

Dr. Sommers, thought Isabella, nonetheless, satisfied to have put this pretentious checkmate.

Her nerves skin deep by this unexpected altercation, slightly tipsy, Isabella was swimming in a bath of euphoria. She was feeling an intoxicated joy that had overwhelmed her heart.

Are you ready Carl? It will make them swoon with envy and faint with jealousy?

At this rate, my dear Isabella, we'll have the whole Montjolly on our back!

Don't worry, darling, I will take care of these bad girls...

Maestro Renalto raised his baton. The lascivious melody of Carlos Gardel famous tango; ''Por una Cabeza'' invaded the living room. Sommers stretched out his hand to Isabella who lithe and graceful leap on the empty dance floor, to the beat of the music colored with frantic passion.

Isabella offered her svelte figure with a discreet sensuality. But more often she evaded, mocked the man who was pursuing her with his caring gallantries. She swirled, gripping the neck of her partner who dragged her, turning in circles, trying unsuccessfully to get rid of her.

The haunting refrain, true leitmotif, marked the resumption of elegant and rhythmic steps and stylized figures imposed by the choreography.

Then, abruptly, she slides down making lascivious splits. She recovered her blushing cheeks and her inflamed gaze revealed her unbridled passion. She was turning around her partner, as a butterfly fascinated by a flame.

He attracted her towards him. She moves back with sharp and threatening hand gestures. Their legs intersect by drawing artistic arabesques on the wax dance floor.

Their steps aligned, sometimes down, sometimes face to face. They draw an arc with their arms high, under which they, in turn, are able to buttress back to back.

The male dancer, unable to retain this wisp that slid his hands tense and suppliant, ran here and there after his partner, who swirled, breathless, elusive as quicksilver. He eventually snatched her hands and pulled her towards the exit.

People gawked, stunned, flabbergasted, and not believing their eyes. They just attend an extraordinary performance that would dazzle any professional dancers.

The room exploded suddenly. The applause punctuated by cries of admiration, the bravos roared loudly, a racket of sharp clink of champagne glasses hit with the silverware filled the room with a deafening din.

After a short break, the Orchestra resumed with a joyful tcha tcha tcha. Carl and Isabella went back to the dance floor, swinging in cadence from one side to the other, to the frenzied rhythm of the joyous melody.

Isabella executed jerky hip movements from the original choreography of this Latin dance.

Holding hand, the dancers skipping nicely made a stylish walk around the floor. Isabella smiled at the crowd and from time to time pulled back her auburn hair, in a gesture of extreme elegance.

The assistance applauded the loudly, chanting at each refrain: Tcha Tcha Tcha, Tcha Tcha Tcha, Tcha Tcha Tcha.

The round ended in apotheosis. People invaded the dance floor to congratulate the couple in the spotlight. The triumph of Isabella was complete. She had, without declaring to anyone, announced to this select assembly, unequivocally, the nature of her feelings for the elegant and handsome doctor with whom she came to dance.

The atmosphere was joyful. The Orchestra sought his vast cosmopolitan repertoire to maintain the general euphoria.

The young and the less young played madly. This unexpected interlude created by the spectacle offered by Carl and Isabella, had brought a surge of excitement to the party.

Isabella was dizzy and slowly walked into her partner's arms. As she had announced to Christel Baldwin, she had sequestered her lover in the jealous circle of her exclusive affection.

Although she felt a little eclipsed by her sister-in-law; Mona Lisa, drunk of joy and happiness, was not offended by Isabella success.

Michelle Morgan, Isabella dear cousin, was dying of jealousy. Her chagrined mood did not escape the people sitting in her table, especially Charles Lewis who danced with her from time to time.

Far from discouraging the bridesmaids who aspired secretly to seduce Dr. Sommers; the spectacular exhibition of his spectacular talent of dancer, had kindled their passion and reinforced their desire to compete, tooth and nail, with this pretentious Isabella Morgan who coveted the love of the enigmatic doctor.

CHAPTER XI

At two o'clock in the morning, Elsa Morgan, seeing the effervescent gaiety of the party getting dull; organized a Scottish quadrille to restart the declining animation and recreate the fantastic ambiance which existed without interruption, since the beginning of the evening.

For this figures dance, the girls chose their partner. Mona Lisa, the principal protagonist of the evening, gets the privilege of choosing first. She took the arm of her fiancé and led him in the middle of the dance floor area, up until the moderator of the quadrille assigned them their position in the square.

Seeing Christel Baldwin coming on their direction, Isabella, guessing the aggressive intention of the girl, whispered to Carl: accept!

Indeed, Christel made a deep bow to Dr. Sommers saying loudly, so the whole room can hear: Dr. Sommers do you want to grant me this dance?

With pleasure Miss Baldwin, I'm really flattered. He stood up, presented his arm to the girl and went to lineup in the formation.

Isabella was afraid that Christel, already furious against her, started a scandal to spoil the rest of the evening.

When the dancers were ready, the Orchestra began to play a nostalgic tune, from the Scottish folklore.

Elsa named the dancer who would execute, the diverse configuration

(along with their partner)

By complex cross hunts which drove them to an opposite

Place.

Those who did not participate in the quadrille, surrounded the dancers, and teased the blunder of these inexperienced amateurs. They laughed. The atmosphere relaxed, once more.

In the midst of this hubbub, this communicative hilarity, trying to follow the convoluted route ordered by the moderator; Dr. Sommers felt the vibration of his cell phone.

He apologized to his partner and went to the silent vestibule to answer the call.

Dr. Sommers, it is Nancy.

What wrong Nancy?

Dr. Merville fainted. I found him on the ground in his office...

We transported him on a stretcher to a room of the third floor.

I am in my way said Sommers. Asked the nurse to administer an electro-encephalogram, and monitor the blood pressure of the doctor every ten minutes, and to control the regularity of his breathing.

Sommers informed Bernice who was dancing, greeted the Hollemberg explaining the urgency of his departure. He alerted Bernice and her two children under the porch. He gave his token and a ten dollars bill to the valet parking telling him: I am in a hurry.

He was joined by Isabella very worried, who wanted to know what was happening. I'm going with you, she said, after hearing the news of the sickness of Dr. Merville. Did you tell your mother that you are leaving the party? Time is running short, hurry up.

Dr. Sommers opened the rear door of the yellow Cadillac and brought up Bernice Merville, and then he held the door for Isabella. Brandon Merville helped his sister and in turn entered the car.

Sommers made the journey in less than twenty minutes. He recovered his Kit in the trunk and without worrying about the people who were in the vehicle, hastened to the hallway dimly lit and completely silent.

He retained the elevator for the people who rushed to catch him.

Upon entering the room where was Dr. Merville; Sommers asked the nurse who was watching him: how is he doing Miss?

As you can see doctor, answered the nurse who handles him the patient's record.

Bernice approached the bed, visibly panicked.

She took, the frozen hands of her husband rubbing them furiously. Joe! Joe! Joe! She was screaming on the edge of tears?

Dr. Sommers affectionately dismissed Bernice to the bedside of her husband, to consult him. After a quick review, he declared to Bernice and her anxious children:

I'm afraid that Dr. Merville suffered a stroke.

Is it serious Dr. Sommers? Inquired Bernice, eyes reddened, bathed with tears.

Ordinary, Yes! But the case of your husband seems to be different; the obstruction was caused by a swarm of tumor cells, which did not tightly clog the artery. Do not worry. I will do the impossible to save his life.

He send, illico, Dr. Merville to the operating room. The surgical staff, absent, at this late hour into the night, he solicited the services of Helena, a private nurse who was taking care of a rich patient.

I need someone else, he told Isabella. Are you scare of the sight of blood? Of course not, she said. So just get ready.

Brandon offered his help. But Sommers made him understand that he would be too emotional for him given his close relationship with the patient.

The nurse Helena shaved Dr. Merville head and sprayed his skull with a antiseptic solution. She was responsible for monitoring: blood pressure, heart rate, temperature and breathing of the patient, for the duration of the operation.

Loris, the nurse, promoted anesthesiologist, controlled the administered of low dose narcotic flow, to induce the desired localized anesthesia...

Isabella, dressed in white, masked, gloved, the hair retained under a plastic cap, was to take care of the sophisticated surgical instruments: laser scalpel, ultrasonic devices, classified and numbered, stored carefully on a table placed nearby.

With his laser scalpel, Dr. Sommers cut the skull of the patient, and gently, using an ultrasonic instrument, removed a square of the skull bone, in the frontal region of the brain.

While he carefully ranked the bone in a sterilized container, tightly closed; Isabella was sponging the cavity with sterile cotton. Blood squirted in profusion in the walls of the cavity.

As soon as the bleeding stopped, Dr. Sommers, equipped with a special plier, raised the primary layer of the frontal lobe at the level of the Rolando calcarine, which separates it from the parietal region.

Isabella dabbed with a compress, the bloody seepage that rose to the surface of the wound.

This manoeuver exposed immediately, the tumor, big as a marble, greenish outgrowth which seemed to link the primary frontal lobe with the secondary parietal lobe.

The method usually used in such operation was to remove the tumor (malignant or not) by delicate incisions. But, in so doing, are also removed part of the neurons which attached them.

These lesions at the level of the left frontal lobe, resulted, inevitably in apraxia or difficulty moving. On the side of the parietal, the lesion causes a loss of language and other essential motor faculties.

Usually, the patient after such an intervention, remained paralyzed on one side, lost the use of an arm or a leg; had difficulties in expressing themselves, you name it.

The lucky ones recovered somewhat, after months or years of assiduous rehabilitation.

Sommers already knowing the result of the conventional method, decided to practice on his colleague a new technique of his own invention, to try to save not only his life, but spared him a debilitating situation giving him a fighting chance of total recovery.

Without hesitation, he took a tool generator of ultrasound and placed it on a kind of syringe at the end of which he adapted a tiny, pointed device that looked like a needle.

Dr. Sommers introduced with infinite caution, the tip of his cells vacuum at the tumor and activated the device.

Silently, under the watchful eye of the surgeon, ventouse, and disintegrated the malignant cells accumulated in the narrow receptacle on the bottom of the ultrasonic syringe.

This delicate operation emptied the inside of the tumor and left intact the rough walls welded to the neurons of the secondary frontal lobe and parietal.

In the meantime, the nurses controlled the vital functions of the patient. At regular intervals, they announced his condition to the doctor.

Isabella placed the stained instruments in a special box and exhibited promptly on request the object listed by the doctor.

Sommers injected into the empty cavity of the tumor, a nuclear dissolver whose functions were: the complete elimination of the tumor's cells and the preservation of superficially damaged neurons.

At a sign of the Dr. Sommers, Isabella brought him the part of the skull bone, which he replaced with extreme precision. He welded the bone with laser and asked Loris, the nurse, to apply a dressing on Dr. Merville's head.

As soon as they had removed the intravenous containing the anesthesia, doctor Merville opened his eyes.

You're again among the living said affectionately, Dr. Sommers; who recommended to him: don't speak yet, nevertheless.

It was, indeed, a very good sign. Dr. Sommers after having sampled the tumor cells to be analyzed, he took off his dirty blouse and gloves wash up and hastened to announce the good news to Bernice and the children. All went well, he told them. I believe that he will get away with few problems. Hopefully, if my prediction is confirmed, he will resume his ordinary routine in a couple of months.

They carried Dr. Merville in one of the suites on the third floor where his wife and children could spend the night with him. They found him awake and received them with a shy smile.

How are you darling? Asked anxiously Bernice.

Well! he replied in a barely audible voice.

Do not talk! Said Loris, the nurse. He is still under the surgical shock.

Rachel kissed her father and took his hand, squeezed it affectionately. Bernice pulled a chair and sat at the bedside of her husband.

Are we spending the night here? Naively asked Brandon.

Brandon darling, replied her mother, it is already seven o'clock in the morning. Do you mean the day?

In any case, me, I sleepy. I'll rest in the room next door.

Dr. Sommers, accompanied by Isabella, came to pay a visit to Dr. Merville, before leaving the hospital. Let him sleep. The nurse will come every hour, to control his blood pressure and take his temperature. Feel free to call me at the slightest irregularity.

I don't know how to thank you Dr. Sommers. Thank you! Thank

you thousand times.

How! Asked Isabella to Dr. Sommers, what do you do to stay as alert, after such an eventful night?

Love of my heart, it's very simple: practice!

I am tired, I cannot keep my eyes open. You are bringing me home?

Do you think that's a good idea, Isabella sweetheart? What will tell your parents?

Carl darling, don't worry about such trifles. The whole city is aware of our relationship. You know that mother trust me. As for Harry, he has been neutralized and domesticated by Simon. Heard! You haven't even kissed me for the excellent performance of your preferred operating room nurse.

What was I thinking? You are right my love; I owe you more than a compliment. In the elevator he took her in his arms and kissed her passionately.

The sun shone in a cloudless sky. A flock of birds fluttered from branch to branch singing their joie de vivre. It was really nice this morning. Sommers brought up Isabella onto the yellow Cadillac, lowered the hood and resolutely headed to the Petit Palais.

Isabella with her remote control opened the monumental gate of the Petit Palais to let the car slowly enter the beautiful and lined with flowers, the alley that led to the threshold of the house.

It was the first time that Dr. Sommers saw closely, this impressive and beautiful building. The elegant colonnades façade, decorated with marble statues of the nine muses, looked surprisingly as the entrance of a Greek temple.

Dr. Sommers stopped the vehicle outside the front door and opened the door. He helped Isabella get off the car. Isabella retained the hand that Carl had stretched to her and looking straight in his eyes, with an air of defiance, punctuated by an irresistible smile, she said: you are going to take coffee with me, dear Carl!

He wanted to escape, fly away, pretexting the fatigue of a long and traumatic night, the incongruity of such intrusion in the privacy of people...

Say no more Carl! I stress... You are going to take coffee with your fiancée. Isn't it my darling? This house is my house, I am inviting you home, just that...

Isabella opened the carved door and took his friend's arm. They penetrated in the vestibule. Isabella flooded the room with a crude spring light. Dr. Sommers remained stunned, dazzled by the display of elegant luxury, antique furniture, paintings, art objects.

The girl without paying attention to the doctor lost in admiration of a painting by Canaletto: depicting St Mark's square in a grandiose perspective. She struck a bell placed on a mahogany table which issued a melodious sound.

A servant appeared immediately. She said with astonishment in her voice at the sight of Dr. Sommers, what do you need miss Isabella?

Go tell Amélie that I am taking coffee with a guest in the living room; tell her to prepare breakfast for two. Do you understand Laura?

I understand! Miss Isabella.

The small living room (which was not so small) was even more luxuriously furnished. Isabella sat Carl in an armchair Regency, an authentic work of Charles Cressent, who introduced this style of lightness and fantasy, to attenuate the marmoreal rigidity of the classical style.

I saw that you admired the Canaletto of the vestibule said Isabella, sitting in a similar chair.

It's not every day you find a Canaletto from the pre English period. Mr. Cédric Vaudreuil, didn't lose his time sailing the oceans.

I noted with pride and pleasure, naturally, that Dr. Carl Sommers, fine dancer in the face of the Lord, like King David in front of the Ark of the Covenant; eminent surgeon, inventor of new process and operating procedure, is also a great connoisseur of art.

Isabella, did you know that you are a flattering tongue?

No, replied, it is the first time someone dare tell me that face-to-face. I am greatly offended, sir! She says, bursting into laughter.

Mademoiselle is in a good mood this morning, advanced Amelie, who brought the coffee on a silver platter. She put the platter on a coffee table between the two of them. Dr. Sommers said Amélie, how do you take your coffee?

Isabella didn't let him answer, she said: you can leave us dear Amelie, I am serving Dr. Sommers myself.

Well! So what should I cook for you Dr. Sommers?

My dear Amelie, said Sommers, this time: I trust your talent and your exquisite taste in the matter.

Despite her dark coloration, Amélie became red like a poppy. She gave him a deep bow and retired.

My dear Carl, nobody ever told you that you are such a flattering tongue? Teased Isabella chuckling.

Oh! No, you are the first and I'm outrageously offended. They twisted with laughter.

Isabella pour a cup of black coffee, and said: Carl my love, how do you take your coffee? No milk or cream and two sugars. Isabella, drinks hers with lots of cream and very little sugar.

Isabella told him, how she was impressed by the dexterity and the assurance with which he had performed this delicate operation. She marveled to see the striking contrast between the casual and relaxed attitude of the man who danced with her last night, and the personality of the professional with the seriousness and competence which transcended all other considerations.

Miss, the table is served, said Laura, who kept leering through Dr. Sommers.

Come honey, said Isabella taking the hand of her fiancé. She led him to the regular dining room.

There were two tables, a round with four seats, and the other rectangular surrounding by eight seats.

To make it more intimate, Amélie had prepared and decorated the round table. It was covered with a pink tablecloth embroidered with flowers and fruits. A beautiful bouquet of red roses, white carnations, yellow orchids (favorite of mademoiselle) sat in the middle of the table, in a crystal of baccarat vase, chiseled like a piece of jewelry.

Amélie adorned the table with a particular care. She set the plates side by side to create a more intimate atmosphere and facilitate the tete-a-tete conversation. Plates, cups and saucers, painted by Gregor Horold; bore the signature of the Melssen manufacture. For this casual breakfast, Amélie deployed an incomparable luxury for grandstanding.

Carl Sommers was not accustomed to this Lucullus like luxury, but he pretended to find it all natural and familiar.

Amélie herself was serving the couple. She brought first an herbs omelet and Buttered toasts. Isabella put a large portion on her fiancé plate and poured the rest into hers.

It's delicious! says Sommers after having tasted the omelet. You know honey, he continued, I think you've had the lucky hand selecting me. But I got so far all the benefits. You corrected my lame speeches, help me in my work, you revealed yourself an excellent collaborator in the operating room, you make me dance like an acrobat; when you get home in the morning you received me like a prince, you could, at least, thank me for having discovered your fairy talent?

Carl! You are an irredeemable prankster. Said Isabella bursting with laughter. I thought I would hear something serious? Anyway, you are not entitled to anything for the service. But I am forever grateful to you for having giving me back my life and my joie de vivre.

They ate Crepes Suzette flavored with orange syrup, which Isabella liked. They drank white wine and finished the meal with a wild cherry jam.

Dr. Sommers didn't linger after breakfast. Isabella accompanied him to his car. Present my compliments to Amelie. In your company, Isabella my love, I relished the most succulent breakfast in my whole life. Goodbye, love, see you soon.

I feel so happy, at this moment, that I wouldn't let you go. Your departure will break the magic spell which filled me with happiness since yesterday evening.

The song of the siren is less melodious than yours. If I listened to you Isabella my love, you locked me in the enchanting prison of your beloved presence. I wouldn't be able to exorcise the love spell that retained me.

At the villa Vaudreuil, Dr. Sommers telephoned the hospital Sainte Cécile. Anything salient to report, said Lisa Troy. Everything run like clockwork.

How Dr. Merville is doing?

He was sleeping when I saw him in the room. Everyone was asleep. Bernice on a chair, at the bedside of her husband, the children in the other room.

Thanks Lisa, I will come at two o'ckock.

Dr. Sommers took a shower and lay down.

Isabella as usual, was sleeping completely dressed in the middle of her four-poster bed; exhausted by fatigue and frantic happiness.

CHAPTER XII

Dr. Sommers woke up at one o'clock. He was feeling relaxed and refreshed, ready to get back to work. But Mikado wouldn't let him go. His companion was absent too often, could have said the cat who liked to stay around the doctor and keep him company when he was working at room.

After parking his car, Dr. Sommers went directly in the suite where Dr. Merville was.

He was awake and speaking to his wife (with great difficulty). This effort was, however, encouraging index in the evolutionary process of timidly spontaneous rehabilitation. I see that our patient has made progress Sommers Said, entering the room. Bernice, you may go home. Do you want to take my car? Or do you prefer that someone drive you home?

I would like somebody to drop me home, Said Bernice.

I will keep you abreast of the results of your husband's physical and psychological assessment and will share with you my prognosis on his chances of recovery.

Dr. Sommers executed a battery of tests on the patient: reflex, perception, sensation, motion, coordination, and etcetera.

He studied samples of blood and urine, to controlling the functioning of the liver, kidney and thyroid. He redone himself, the dressing, applied, this time, his miracle ointment, to activate the healing of the skull bone.

Dr. Sommers helped his patient to sit down. He asked him if he feel dizzy? He answered in the negative. Can you stand? Sommers ask him if both his legs can support him. He walked a few steps with doctor Merville around the room, then took him to bed, extremely tired.

Dr. Sommers could not be more pleased with the progress made in such a short time, by Dr. Merville. Preliminary tests carried out so far, seemed to confirm in praxis, his daring surgical method.

His hypothesis, formulated to take the opposite view of the conventional method, which handicapped inevitably the patient seemed to have filled, beyond expectation, his most secret wishes. The operating protocol in use, paralyzed, render the subject partially amnesiac, incapacitated   significantly decreasing his faculties of language.

Dr. Sommers had concluded that the best way to proceed, would be to avoid, at all costs, the unnecessary ablation of neurons that transmit nerve impulses. Preserve from destruction the synapses, which facilitated the transmission of information between the neuron and the cells.

Dr. Sommers was imbued with the fact that he was playing his career in this dangerously risky adventure. The excitement of the moment, did not allow him to reflect on the disastrous consequences of a failure.

Whatever happens, he mused, failure or success, I will never regret having tried to spare the wheelchair and years of reclusive life to a colleague.

But if he succeed; he could be famous and would have the possibility to offer Isabella the same luxury and confortable existence she has always known.

Since his visit at the Petit Palais, Sommers had become more aware of the amazing disparity between his miserable condition and that of this incomparable goddess, at any point, blessed by God and nature.

He decided to make arrows from any wood, snaring all the opportunities that were knocking on his door. He had hitherto neglected enticing offers from scientific magazines, trade publications, large circulation newspapers. He would immediately remedy this unforgivable gap.

For now, he focused on the case of Dr. Merville, which had the potential to provide, if not fortune, but at least a comfortable life to offer to his fiancée.

Preliminary analysis carried out in the laboratory of the hospital Sainte Cécile, revealed, firstly, the benign nature of the tumor; Secondly, very little damage to the liver and kidneys; Thirdly, a perfect functioning of the thyroid gland and the endocrine system in general.

Less than 24 hours after his dramatic intervention, Dr. Sommers, full of apprehension, doubts over the success of his risky endeavor.

He called Bernice to communicate the good news. I firmly believe, he said, that Dr. Merville may, in a month or two, and without too much difficulty, return to work.

I'm keeping him in the hospital for a week; the time to monitor, the evolutionary stages of the recovery process and, especially, to control the absorption, through the liver of the radioisotope, vector of the provisional substance, which supplies to the function of chemical synapses, in polarized transmission impulses from axon of a neuron to the dendrite of another.

I have committed to the care of Dr. Merville, an experienced nurse. You won't be any more obliged to stay overnight at his bedside.

Dr. Sommers, said Bernice: Joe and I, are forever indebted to you. Be assured of our eternal gratitude.

The portable of Dr. Sommers vibrate in his blouse pocket. Allo! he answered neglectfully, occupied to read the record of a patient.

Carl honey! I just woke up. Mona Lisa and Harry invite us to eat at le Grand Meaulnes, tonight at eight o'clock.

I do not think that I can get away; I still have many patients to see.

Where is Dr. Birmingham? Asked Isabella.

She has not yet giving sign of life.

Call this fainéant; insisted Isabella, they are abusing you in this hospital. You are killing yourself at work.

My love! Dr. Birmingham is a volunteer who has no contractual obligation with the hospital. If she comes before seven o'clock, as provided by the schedule; I will pick you up, otherwise, I regret that miss opportunity.

Do your best, beloved Carl. Whatever happens, I'm going to get beautiful and wait for you.

At six thirty, against his usual behavior, Sommers telephoned Dr. Birmingham.

Allo! Suzanne...

Oh! What an honor! Exclaimed Doctor Birmingham recognizing Dr. Sommers voice. Is there fire at the hospital? She said sarcastically.

Sommers ignored the persiflage and asked her: are you working tonight?

What do you need from me doctor? What's wrong?

I have to leave for a few hours; I would like you to take care of doctor Merville during my absence.

What happened to Dr. Merville?

I had to operate on him urgently last night. A benign tumor between the frontal and the parietal, which caused a partial embolism.

I am coming immediately Dr. Sommers.

Dr. Sommers put on his light brown suit, one of the attires he had purchased in New York, too match up next to the elegant and charming lady he accompanied everywhere.

Dr. Sommers went to the Petit Palais. The gate opened on his approach, expected, obviously. Laura, (the servant who had received him the last time) led him to the small living room saying: mademoiselle will come down in a minute. Can I offer you to drink Dr. Sommers?

No thanks Laura but, thanks anyway.

A few minutes later, Isabella, molded into a carmine red, low-cut at the back, skirt slit to mid-thigh, entered the small living room, resplendent of beauty and refined elegance.

You are lovely my dear love, said Sommers rising. You are really chic this evening, he said, kissing her on the cheek, not wanting to disturb the splash of red on the lips of his fiancée

You are not bad, either, said Isabella. Let's hurry. We'll be late.

They found Harry and Mona Lisa, waiting at the entrance of the restaurant. Mona Lisa squeezed her sister-in-law on her heart with affection. Carl and Harry exchanged a solid handshake. The ice was broken between them, however, the visceral hatred that had opposed them and the instinctive antipathy they experienced one for the other, were still muted; despite the public apology of Harry Morgan, on the night of his engagement.

The restaurant owner of the Grand Meaulnes: Madame Preschyl, had booked them the table of honor, in the center of the main room.

They were greeted by a standing ovation. The whole room began standing to applaud the fiancés and express their congratulations.

Harry Morgan thanked them, and invited everyone to drink champagne, at its expense, in honor of his fiancée.

One should rended him justice; although Harry Morgan was known as a hard and vindictive man, his friends regarded him as the most generous fellow man in the world.

Harry Morgan never mind at the expenses, and always treats people royally. He handed one hundred dollars to the duo (a pianist and a violinist), to play romantic and popular tunes that his fiancée loved.

These gentlemen ate the superb meal. The girls drank more that they ate. Both were quite tipsy at the end of the meal.

Isabella wanted to accompany Carl at the hospital. He opposed categorically. You need to rest, and what are you coming at the hospital for? asked Carl. I could help you and be with you. It is understood, I bring you home, illico presto. You should have studied medicine, my darling! If you love so much been at the hopital.

Don't you dare laugh at me Carl! I am seriously going to be mad. Love honey! You are becoming too sensitive. You know I love you, but I can't really take you with me to the hospital.

The Birmingham will leave at midnight, I must hurry.

Isabella arriving at the Petit Palais, refused to get out the car. Carl asks and begs, and cajoles and coax, she stubbornly remained in the Cadillac, firm in her decision. I'll ring the doorbell, he said, as his last argument.

You can't do that Carl! You'll wake up all the personnel.

Love darling, I'm already late. Sorry if I have to take this extreme measures. Be nice, sweetheart, let me go.

You don't love me anymore Carl?

Now more than ever. But I try to be reasonable for two

Dr. Sommers stretched out his hand, Isabella ignored him, but got out of the car. She walked resolutely towards the door. She opened it and entered the house without looking back. Dr. Sommers shook his head, confused and baffled. He went, shocked by the incomprehensible attitude of the young girl.

Dr. Birmingham was in the lobby waiting for the return of her colleague to leave. Everything is in good shape she said to him before disappearing. Dr. Birmingham displayed certain hostility towards Sommers. He pretended haven't noticed it. This attitude excited doctor Birmingham anger even more.

Dr. Merville was not asleep. Good! Here you are, he said seeing Sommers entering the chamber.

What wrong doctor? asked him.

I feel a discomfort at the level of the parietal, and an itch in the area of the liver, preventing me to sleep.

Dr. Sommers examined the patient's record and said:

You should know, sooner or later; I used a process of my invention, during surgery. To save you the trauma of a problematic rehabilitation, or even more serious consequences: like a paralysis. I crushed the aberrant cells within the tumor, then flushing them out with a ultrasonic vacuum. I introduced a radioactive halogen into the cavity of the hollowed tumor. The halogen is slowly resorbed and eliminated through the liver.

Two antiallergy tablets will do the job tonight. Tomorrow, I will assess the state of the organs affected by the process and will apply appropriate therapy.

Dr. Sommers visited three other patients, and then went to his office, where, for some time now, he slept regularly.

Barely had he settled on the sofa who served as a bed, that the phone rang.

Allo!

She hesitated at the other end of the wire.

Here the Dr. Sommers! He Insisted.

It's me Carl, whispered shyly Isabella. I thought you were sleeping, I didn't want to wake you up.

I just finished my tour, I didn't lie down yet.

I call you Carl darling to apologize.

Apologize for what?

For this stupid scene I pulled on you in front of the house.

My love, believe me if you want, I haven't thought more about that. Remember! You have quarreled me the same way twice, in New York; because I had paid our first head to head dinner; and for daring to offer you the Topaz ring. I infer (since I'm no expert on the subject) that's possibly the way young romantic girls behaved.

Do not think, Carl darling, I'm a capricious girl. I do not know what happens to me, since the engagement of Mona Lisa, I feel helpless. I would like it to be me the bride to be...

A little patience Isabella my love. Our turn will come soon.

Carl! I want to marry you right now. I want to be close to you, day and night, do you understand?

Don't forget the promise you made to Elsa. Promise to which I subscribed myself? You see Carl, the barriers are fallen under the strength and purity of our love, one after the other, swept away by the irresistible passion of a mutual feeling.

How long it will take? You have predicted that the city will be rid of evil black curse, very soon, can you be more specific than that? Your visit at the Petit Palais has upset me. I cried with joy and sadness.

Listen to me well Isabella my love! According to my observations, according to my own deduction, the event will take place in mid-December. Everyone will regain its natural coloration. Because I do not want to marry you disguised as a fake white man; we are going to wait until this occurrence to set a date for our wedding.

Another four months to wait?

Time flies when people are madly in love my cherished sweetheart. In addition, I must, during this relatively short period, deploy my talents and my ingenuity to earn a lot money, to be able to offer you, a decent life worthy of you my princess. I can't promise you, yet, the luxury and comfort you are accustomed to; but I bring you my overflowing gratitude of my heart, and the fabulous wealth of my everlasting love...

Carl Sommers! Cut off your superlative rhetoric, said Isabella in an irritated voice: do not talk nonsense. I beg you my love, banished these prosaic considerations from your concern. This shouldn't give you a pretext to postpone our wedding. I'll be happy drunken with joy everywhere your love will lead me: in a palace or a poor cottage.

My love is yours for life. But, I think about the future Bella my love...

I don't want you to worry about those things. I beg you honey. I want you to pursue your research to become a great writer, a great scholar; won a Nobel Prize, is my ambition for you.

By the way, said Sommers, to steer the conversation on a different track, Vanity Fair offered me twenty-five thousand dollars for an article of five thousand words.

On what subject? Asked Isabella.

A topic of my choice.

Have you already accepted?

I was waiting for your opinion.

It is an excellent and lucrative offer. I will help you in the writing. Do you think you have enough spare time? You are doing more than your fair share of the hospital work, isn't it? You don't have time for anybody else.

Bad girl! You know that you pass before everyone and everything. But I do still need to meet the obligations that fell on me.

Good night Isabella, I must wake up at five o'clock, I have a surgery early morning. Sweet dreams!

I love you, good night my darling.

Orders of food and products of necessities, made by the Committee of Public Safety, were finally dropped by the U.S. Navy helicopters.

Strategic centers of distribution were reactivated. The members of the Committee travelled the city and the surrounding countryside, in the trucks of the Town Hall, to supply the depots which facilitated the distribution of the goods.

Harry Morgan and his fiancée Mona Lisa Hollemberg, appointed by the Chairman of the Committee: Cathy Morgan, controlled the proper functioning of the operation. Max Hollemberg began an active campaign among his friends in the Pentagon and in the administration, so they could put pressure on the men of law, which seemed to be unconcerned, by natural inertia, with the lifting of the quarantine.

Max Hollemberg was still eager to distribute the invitations for the wedding of his daughter. He expected that action by the federal Government, or a miracle from heaven, would allow him to achieve the grandiose celebration that he intended to offer, to mark with a milestone this extraordinary event.

The black curse had no defender in the Senate. The bubonic plague hadn't as bad reputation. The only black senator: Barack Obama of Illinois, did not want to engage in this fight alone against all; without hope to influencing the frightening vision, (deeply rooted in the horrified psyche of the white man); of an imminent apocalypse of the Aryan race.

Senator Trent Lott of Mississippi and Jeff Sessions of Alabama, were adamant opposed to the introduction of an amendment to modify the rigid structure of the unnecessary quarantine imposed on the Montjollian community.

Dr. Joe Merville convalescent at home, gradually recovered well. Symptoms of brain disconfort and internal itch disappeared completely.

He experimented no postoperative sequel. He walked every day, with his wife Bernice, who fostered him as a spoiled child.

The association of English neurologists had wind of the operation and invited Dr. Sommers in London, so he could introduce the members of the association, to his revolutionary therapy.

Dr. Sommers sent a detailed plan of the clinical process, but, retained the exclusivity of the radioactive serum, a powerful additive in the limited arsenal of vested chemical drugs in the treatment of cancerous or benign tumors of the brain.

The prompt and total cure of Dr. Merville, served as a testimony to the effectiveness of his innovative methodology.

The pharmaceutical firm: Bristol Myers, which lost lots of money in expensive unpopular drugs development; proposed a contract to Dr. Sommers. He argued forcefully that the quarantine imposed on the city of Montjolly, to deny, momentarily engaging himself in such an endeavor.

Two months after his surgery, Dr. Merville (which felt in great shape), completely restored, according to the diagnosis of Dr. Sommers; made a triumphant return to the hospital.

The staff greeted him at the vestibule, with flowers, and shouts of joy, noisy demonstrations of affection, and a whole shebang wishes and compliments.

Dr. Sommers assigned a very flexible schedule to allow him to gradually readjust to the arduous tasks and long hours of work.

The return of Dr. Merville helped Sommers to be absent for a few hours every day, to take care of his personal affairs.

He finished writing the article promised to Vanity Fair and handed the manuscript to Isabella for correction. Sommers, now quite often went to the Petit Palais. He assiduously frequented the library of more than fifteen thousand volumes gathered by Mr. Cédric Vaudreuil.

He consulted old documents and rare editions of classical works of famous authors: english, french, Italian and german.

Sometimes (when he was present) Sommers played chess with Simon. Everyone seemed to have accepted his presence, as a fait accompli. Without openly declare, Carl Sommers (with the tacit complicity of Elsa and Isabella), became a member of the family and was welcomed as such, with esteem and affection. Sometimes, when permitted by his obligations at the hospital, he ate dinner at the Petit Palais or took Isabella to the restaurant.

On Sunday night, Mona Lisa and Harry joined them to go dancing in La Romanichelle, Renalto's chic night club.

Dr. Sommers article: capitalism or neo-feudalism, appeared in 'Vanity Fair' and made sensation. He lifted a terrible controversy within the conservative nomenclature.

Dr. Carl Sommers brushed a synoptic portrait in which he compared the current socioeconomic system operating in the capitalistic scheme put in place by the neo-feudal.

At all points similar to the feudal method, capitalism uses the same processes of enslavement and exploitation, with superficial changes.

The serfs attached to the glebe, working for a meager salary, barely allowing them to subsist. The capitalist disposed of them at will and make them chore for nothing. They became slaves in colonial plantations, treated worse than animals and burdened with contempt and indignity.

The workers of today: in factories, in mines, in the industries, working for a paltry salary, are no better off than the serfs.

Businessmen, bankers, the barons of industry, corrupt politicians, men without scruples, the exploiters of all stripes; have replaced the great lords, and the fierce clique of noble parasites.

Europe army of bloodthirsty and cruel conquistadors, the gospel and the cross, has enslaved the people of other continents, has systematically looted and massacred, on behalf of the civilization and the church.

The Catholic Church, in 1891, during the glorious reign of his Holiness Pope Leo XIII, ranked itself on the side of the exploiters, with his Encyclical: Rerum Novarum.

In the eighth paragraph of this pastoral letter, the Catholic Church, under the pretext of fighting communism, (its material interests being at stake, as one of the world's richest institutions), invokes the right granted by God himself to the more capable, to the most ingenious, the privileged race; the right to own, operate and enjoy private property by subjugating another individuals too weak or inferior. This natural law of the jungle is, according to the Church, in the plan of the universal concern of God towards his creation.

An example of sophistry used in this Encyclical letter to hide the enormity of the contradictions inherent in such argument. The Encyclical appealed to the generosity, to the charity of the haves, to compensate for the lack of fairness and justice in human society.

The Church preaching not by example, the socioeconomic condition of the masses, far from improving with the spectacular progress of material technology; deteriorated miserably under the complacent gaze and cynical pity of rich and holy preachers of acceptance and resignation.

The Church has condoned the iniquity of men. Humanity is divided into upper and lower race. The society being divided by class and caste, ignores with ostentation and contempt: the weak, the poor, the sick, people of color or foreigners.

It's really sickening (wrote Dr. Sommers in his article), to see the number of people dying of hunger, lack of food, disease, lack of care, in the richest country which ever existed on Earth.

According to the famous aphorism of Alphonse Karr: 'more things changed, the more it remained the same'; capitalism is the neo feudalism, disguised, but as fierce, as reactionary and as criminal as his alter ego.

Dr. Sommers article raised a public outcry. Administration, the men of law, business leaders, the press, the Church; everyone was upset and protested vehemently, against this odious comparison, which did no justice to the progress made by the workers of the world, organized, unionized, insured, who lived and their families with respect and dignity; with the product of their honest labor.

Cardinal Archbishop of New York published in the New York Post, a very angry article lambasting the ignorant attempt of this small countryside doctor, to put on trial the social doctrine of the Catholic Church, which has released the worker from the shackles of poverty and humiliation.

The Encyclical Rerum Novarum, continued the wrathful prelate, is an inspired work, which was the point of departure of the liberalization, a significant change, in the relations between the employers and the employees. Pope Leo XIII, in his infallible wisdom, has recognized the individual right to private property, the natural disparity between races and individuals, and has recommended a fairer remuneration for workers.

This controversy gave additional notoriety to Dr. Sommers. The theory of dispersed energy, the spectacular success of his bold surgery, and the Vanity Fair article, made of Dr. Sommers, a world celebrity and a very respected and important character in Montjolly.

Suddenly an obsessive craze for the young doctor, spread among the old ladies of the city. They demanded to be visited by the eminent doctor who had literally resurrected Joyce Hollemberd and spared the wheelchair to doctor Joe Merville.

The ladies of a certain age, informed by the Morgan sisters: Joan and Cathy, harassed Dr. Sommers to provide them this miracle ointment, which had operated wonders for the Morgan.

Isabella was worried, with reason, for the prolonged absence of her fiancé at the Petit Palais. He was rarely there now. He came as a gust of wind; still having a patient to visit, or caring for such or such old sick lady, unable to go to the hospital.

Jealousy gets involved in the mix, since the illness of Lory Baldwin: the mother of Christel. Dr. Sommers had crushed the awkward desire manifested by Isabella to accompany him in his patients house.

What do you want me to do darling love? I am the only available doctor in the community. When Dr. Merville will be restored, we will share the task and everything will be in order.

Carl darling, I hardly see you. You spend more time at the Baldwin house than at the Petit Palais. It is an untenable situation, I need your presence to live...

You're right, I have been abused. Today, we are going to remedy the situation. We are going to have lunch every day together. I will be at the Petit Palais at eight o'clock every night. On Sunday, (except for an emergency), will be dedicated only to you.

How honey! You do not answer; you are not satisfied with this arrangement?

You have already overlooked me for your work! I am afraid that your profession, already, has become my first rival. It could have put a shadowy stain on our happiness. Replied Isabella with an intonation of sadness in her voice.

As soon as we overcome this ordeal; life will be back to normal, I promise to follow you everywhere your career will lead you. You can banish this fear of your mind, nothing, but nothing can ever take your place in my heart. You are the reason for my existence, the happiness of my life, the love of my heart...

Carl darling, you got to beholden your promise. From now on, I am supervising your schedule, so you can have a little more time for yourself. I understand that the exceptional circumstances, in which we find ourselves, require self-sacrifice and dedication; but don't ask me to sacrifice everything?

Doctors, Suzanne Birmingham and Joe Merville will never know why their share of duty at the hospital, has exponentially increased suddenly.

The old ladies of the city could not be more disappointed to receive less and less their favorite doctor visit. They complained to Dr. Merville, who had to find appropriate excuses each time, without being able to convince them.

Dr. Sommers was forced to put an extra effort at the hospital to free himself in time, to please his fiancée.

Isabella imposed, de facto, the daily presence of her lover at the Petit Palais. This was a bit embarrassing for him at the beginning; eventually he got adapted to the codified ceremonial and the routine etiquette of the house.

Dr. Sommers dined regularly with the Morgan, and very often took lunch in private with Isabella. She did not understand why Dr. Sommers didn't officially make the demand, so she can fix the date of her engagement.

Isabella constantly harassed Carl to make his move. But, Dr. Sommers remained inflexible on this issue. He would await the end of the ordeal, this degrading scourge to make his presentation.

Carl, what makes you so sure? Do you think really that the black curse will disappear suddenly and soon?

I have my doubts on it; you say it to make me wait as a docile child. Isn't it? I do not know, I do not understand...

Isabella my love, I noticed with pain and disappointment that you don't attach any credence to my words. Did I ever lie to you?

No! answered Isabella, but unless you have something to do with the spread of the black curse epidemic, you couldn't predict with certainty the date of its resumption.

Are you afraid of the dead Isabella?

Why do you ask me that?

Yes or no?

No, I'm not afraid of the dead or the living, matter of fact. Don't try to change the topic of the conversation Carl...

Just! I'll show you conclusively, by clinical observations that I have made lately, the scientific nature of my assertions.

Dr. Sommers brought up Isabella in his car and took her to the hospital. They went down to the basement where the morgue was located. The guardian greeted the doctor and asked him if he needed his help.

No, Jeff, I'm just going to observe something.

Isabella shivered from cold when entering the dark and frigid room. The doctor took off his jacket and put it on the shoulders of his beloved.

Thank you! She said, simply by leaning heavily on Carl's arm.

Dr. Sommers opened a drawer and uncovered the corpse of a old man, whose limbs were visibly broken.

He died before the burst of the black curse? Asked Isabella.

Oh no! This is one of the first victims of this terrifying evil. He threw himself down from his balcony.

And then! exclaimed the girl, he regained his color dying?

It took him seven months. Death accelerates very little the period of the black curse incubation. But, it still exerts a significant influence, eliminating abruptly the flow of venom with the stopping of the blood circulation.

Dr. Sommers opened another drawer. Angelina died five months ago, yesterday she regained her natural coloration. That one, he said, had passed away two months ago; his skin became white the day before yesterday. Cornelia, she died yesterday evening. Come see.

The corpse of the old lady was whiteness, not a stain, not a scar, not even a winkle on her pale face.

You understand now why I could predict categorically, the

imminent end of this black curse. I know, this evil phenomenon had operated in depth and deviant mutation of the psyche of the people of Montjolly.

Harry had said that you were the instigator of this attack against the people of the city, to punish them for not having welcomed you with an open arm. Futher more and especially to be able to freely, integrate yourself in our aristocratic society, closed to people of color and the vagabond.

And you believe him?

No, replied Isabella. But, I was feeding my own suspicions. You had promised to move heaven and Earth to make possible and accepted this love like no other, this passionate and eternal love. That didn't surprise me at all, that you have found this extreme way to overcome the taboos and prejudices that hindrance our love.

Love honey, according to my latest calculations and recent clinical observations; we have yet, at least for a month.

A long month! Said Isabella, you make me languish beloved Carl.

Yes! One month to punish you for having doubted my words. That will be a lesson. Now you will have to accept my words, like those of the gospel, without discussion...

Never in the life, said Isabella, not so fast, my friend, you are still obliged to provide me valid explanations at every opportunity. I will not give you a pass, I love you too much already.

Thanks anyway for this lack of confidence you disdained to testify to me.

That evening, during the family dinner, Mona Lisa raised the question. She asked Dr. Sommers if he thought that the quarantine would be lifted before her marriage.

What do you say Isabella? Questioned in turn Dr. Sommers. Talk about what you have observed today.

Too long, advanced Isabella, I have harassed Carl to officially make his demand, so we can set a date for our engagement. Still, he argued that he would take such a decision, only when the black curse will disappeared and his true identity buried in shambles, being restored.

What do you mean Isabella? How! Dr. Sommers is not what it claims to be? Does he assumed a false name? What do you want to insinuate there?

What! My Dear Lisa, Harry didn't introduced you yet in the gods secret?

I would never divulge people's secret; exclaimed Harry in apologizing.

Tell me Isabella!

Dr. Sommers, that behold, has not been, blackened, like us, by the black curse. This is his natural color. He has become a little darker, that's all.

Ha! I see, Mona Lisa contented herself to say.

Today, continued Isabella, he took me to the hospital morgue, where I found, visually, the corpses had resumed their natural pigmentation. They were all white as snow.

Should we wait until we died to resume our coloration doctor? Laughed sarcastically Harry Morgan in a derisive tone.

No sir, said Sommers. This means that the incubation period of the venom came to an end. That the withdrawal mechanism began an earnest. That the melanin have disposed of the insidious virus and was ready to operate the synthesis of the enzyme tyrosine. This enzyme is a powerful catalyst that ensures the normal functioning of the chromatophores in the epidermis cells.

The dead regained their color at the same time; those who died seven months ago and those who died yesterday. I can, therefore, assure you, dear Mona Lisa, that your guests will be at the wedding in Montjolly.

You are sure! cried the girl radiant with joy.

Absolutely. Said Sommers.

Can you be more specific Carl? Intervened Elsa who had followed with growing interest the explanations of Dr. Sommers.

Today is September 2, isn't it? In all probability, on the first or on first November, the black curse will be no longer in existence.

Then replied Elsa, we can begin preparing for your engagement, if the black curse was holding you back?

Sommers, said Simon Morgan with a playful tone: don't let us down, answer the question ...

I agree in advance with everything you decided Elsa. I wasn't trying to decline myself, Simon. But I have throat tied by your testimony of affection...

This saying, the doctor apologized to the guests and got up from the table. He left the dining room. Isabella followed him. Dr. Sommers took refuge in the sitting room to hide his emotion and his tears.

I knew, said Isabella in approaching him, I knew that you were a shy guy, but at this level? She sat down next to him and put her head on his shoulder, in a move that had become familiar. Isabella wiped with her small batiste handkerchief scented with lavender, the tears that flowed along the face of her fiancé.

Let's go Carl darling, she said, moved up by the emotion. We are returning to the table...

You'll apologize for me to your parents, I'm going home, my love, said Dr. Sommers who stand up abruptly.

You are returning to the dining room, dear sir, she insisted. You're going to wash your face.

Sommers followed Isabella without protest and returned to sit in his place.

Amélie was waiting for you to continue the service. Everything is okay' Carl? Asked Elsa.

He was a bit embarrassed. He understood immediately why Isabella was so eager to bring him back to table.

Carl, I have to talk to you, said Elsa at the end of the meal.

She took him by the hand and led him in the middle of the illuminated garden filled with an intoxicating scents. She made him sit next to her on a granite bench.

They remained silent a long moment. The light breeze rustled through the foliage. You could hear the muted murmur of the fountains of marble and the melodious sound of artificial waterfalls.

Carl, I felt a great reluctance in your reply to my question. Don't you love my daughter anymore?

What are you saying here Elsa? You break my heart. How can you think of such a thing? Isabella is my whole life. I cannot imagine my life without her...

You left us, Simon and I with the impression that you hesitated to become involved. That Isabella and I are forcing you...

Don't say no more Elsa. You have been misled by your imagination. I'm still more eager than Isabella. But I wouldn't want that later, people reproaching me my intrusion into your family through a misunderstanding. I would like to let everyone know that I'm black and that the Morgan family has accepted me as such. I don't want to pass for an impostor. If it's pride, I plaid guilty...

I will concede this point of view, although I am not quite agree with your argument; However, this does not answered my question. Do you want me to fix your engagement date, yes or no?

Elsa, before answering your question, I have to reveal a secret to you. One of my patients told me, under the seal of secrecy, that Joyce Hollemberg naive, generous, manipulated by a swarm of interested parasites accuse you of having eclipsed her...

Joyce, advised by these instigators; now, complains of having been thrust into the background, because you have assumed the lead role in the preparations for the wedding of her only daughter.

It is absurd. From time to time, Joyce telephone me to ask my opinion on any decision taken; but I never take the initiative to recommend anything.

This is not all, my dear Elsa, continued Sommers. These wives have told her, that Isabella and I did express to overshadow Mona Lisa the night of her engagement. That Isabella was jealous of the happiness of her daughter. That is why I had marked this hesitation. I believe mother, that we should wait until the end of this episode before proposing anything.

You're right dear Carl, we risk to inflame things, unnecessarily, by alienating the spontaneous affection of my dear daughter-in-law.

I hope mother, that you'll reason Isabella about the delay?

No, dear sir, you are in charge of convincing your fiancée. It would be too difficult for me. In any case, I wish you good luck. Carl, continued Elsa, after a moment of reflection, I am proud of you, Isabella was lucky selecting you, I love you.

Carl Sommers, for the first time, kissed Elsa on both cheeks saying: dear mother thanks a lot.

They returned home, walking slowly and silently along the alley of orchids. Without admitting it openly, an intimate phase of their relationship had begun.

When they entered the small living room, Isabella was reading, under the halo of a lampshade that wrapped her auburn hair highlighted with golden stripes. She pretended not to see them.

Mademoiselle is pouting? Exclaimed Elsa.

What have you been concocted? You never finish speaking? You look like two conspirators.

Elsa bursted out laughing, saying: those things: gloomy mood or sad pout; no longer works with me my dear. I won't tell you what we discussed, Carl and I. Secret of grown up.

Dr. Sommers said nothing. Isabella closed her book and deposited it near the lamp on the table.

Mother, I'm going on a ride with Carl.

Of course, honey, you're trying to squeeze him to extort information's? Carl continued Elsa, don't reveal our secrets, I count on you?

Come, my darling, said Isabella taking the arm of Carl. And facing her mother: we'll see which one will prevail.

 Don't be so sure my dear, retorted Elsa who made a faint sign of collusion to Dr. Sommers.

Where are we going? Asked Carl as soon as they were out.

It is so nice tonight; let's go to the public square. We will follow the lovers trail.

They went up in the convertible Cadillac. The gentle breeze caressed their faces. Thousands of stars shone in a clear sky. The perfume of the flowers filled the atmosphere with strange and sweet odors.

They left the car in a side street near the parish church and followed the walkers who wandered around the square.

They held each other by the waist and walked in silence, each lost in his thoughts. Near a stone bench, a crowd had formed to listen to the melodious serenade of a volunteer guitarist.

They stopped for a moment to hear the poignant lament of a lover, abandoned by his beloved lady. The song, though sad, aroused the admiration of the crowd.

After touring twice the square, Isabella wanted to sit. All the benches were occupied. If you are tired, said Sommers, I am bringing you home? We are going to sit on the base of the Virgin Mary's statue behind a bushy bougainvillea; said Isabella, pointing the finger the place.

Carl darling, she said, as soon as they were seated. What have you decided with mother? Have you set the date for the engagement?

No, love of my heart. Mother has concluded that we better wait until we finish with Mona Lisa and Harry, before starting the preparations for our engagement.

You disappoint me a lot Carl! How could you make such a decision without consulting me? me, the most interested? I am no longer a child...Mother and you can't decide for me. My opinion counts as much as yours.

Isabella honey, calm down. There is no reason to get so angry. Your mother has her reasons, valid reasons that compel us to slow things down and act cautiously.

What is it? What happens Carl? Why I shouldn't be aware of the situation?

We have learned, your mother and I, that people who gravitated around Joyce, have convinced her that we were determined to outshine her daughter. We had, you and I, managed to do this during the engagement and we would try again on the wedding night. The apple of discord was thrown into the garden of the Hesperidia. The gods are angry.

Is Mona Lisa aware of this nonsense? I wouldn't like a cold between us, said Isabella. She's a nice girl...

I don't believe she knows this shenanigan. This why, I urged you to be patient. We could if we were doing anything, now make the situation worse by validating the backbiting of the gossips who extorted money from the gullible and vulnerable Joyce Hollemberg. It will be necessary, my darling, that you seemed more interested with the activities of your sister-in-law, to defuse this bomb that could burst at any time.

You are exhorting me to be patient, a long patience isn't it?. But, me, I can no longer wait. You do not understand, you can't understand me.

I'm also looking forward as you, my darling. But I have my reason. You see, a year ago we didn't known each other. Ten months ago we couldn't even talk to each other; eight months ago we were on the edge of despair, to look for a way to live our love in broad daylight. Things have improved significantly since; You agreed, isn't it?

I don't disagree, answered the girl on the edge of tears. The wait is much more difficult for me than for you.

What makes you think that?

You are a man and I know that men always experimented before marriage.

I am in this case, dear love, the exception that proves the rule. You're the first girl I ever kissed in my life, aside from Monique (my mother) obviously.

Do I understand correctly what you just say Carl? Is it true that you have never known other women? Asked Isabella, her eyes enlarged by emotion and incredulity.

I swear to you on my honor and before God who hears us. You are and you'll always be the only love of my life.

Isabella threw herself on Dr. Sommers lap, laughing and crying at the same time, mad with joy, frantic with love and gratitude. Isabella repeating like a mantra: I love you, I love you my love, I love you my darling, I love you...

People are looking at us, Isabella...

I don't really care, she said, hugging her fiancé increasingly stronger. I was counting on you to teach me... she was laughing, that should serve me as a lesson... I'd let loose flange to my imagination... It has played a bad joke on me.

Isabella, stop that, people are looking at you... We are going house.

Dr. Sommers tore the grip of Isabella's hands from his neck and forced her to follow him out of the square. He was crestfallen and embarrassed, afraid she was generated gossip of old ladies sitting nearby and curious walkers who smiled mischievously. Isabella saw nothing, didn't care, she was in an indescribable state of joy. She walked painfully, suspended from her fiancé, who rushed her in a hurry towards the car...

Don't go just now; said Isabella soon arrived at the Petit Palais. You know sweetheart I have to go make my visit at the hospital.

I beg you Carl darling, stay a moment more with me.

Isabella laid her head on the shoulder of Dr. Sommers and remained motionless and silent. For the first time, with light and timid gestures, her companion stroked gently her hair and her face, to show her, his deep affection. Isabella shivered from head to feet under this light caress. She felt faint, invaded by an unknown and ineffable feeling that opened for her, the awakening of wonderful enrapture of the libido and her modest introduction to erotic pleasures.

I have to leave, love darling, said Sommers who felt enthrall by the fever of desire; interrupting, by design, the dangerous enchantment of that moment of bliss.

He presses her strongly on his chest and kissed her with increased passion.

Goodbye, my love, said Sommers.

Good night my darling replied Isabella.

CHAPTER XIII

The following Sunday, after the mass, Elsa Morgan took reverend Ted Vogel aside, and persuaded, without revealing the deductions of Dr. Sommers, on the likelihood of a sudden disappearance of the black curse, to organize, once again, a rogatory procession at the celebration of all Saints on the first of November.

Everyone went to the Morgan sisters for the traditional Sunday morning snack. Max and Joyce Hollemberg, Harry and his lovely fiancée Mona Lisa, Simon and Elsa, Carl Sommers and Isabella; and all familiar faces in search of the latest news. Charles Lewis was making an assiduous courtship to Michelle Morgan who rejected him with resentment and disdain. Now, she sported a sullen and contemptuous face. Matt Potter had received a similar reception to his advances.

Michelle was ostensibly jealous of her cousin Isabella. She thought, in the first instance, she could be able to prevail over Isabella: the naive provincial girl, without luster or fame. But she was quickly disappointed and her love for the young doctor converts into a fierce hatred for Isabella.

Dr. Suzanne Birmingham, resigned her pursuit of the good doctor. She had found a respectable suitor, in the person of the elegant James Nadowsky. Christel Baldwin, in spite of the advice of her mother, didn't waived and continued to harassing Dr. Sommers with her untimely phone calls, impromptu visits to the hospital and invitations to private dinner.

She wanted to provoke Isabella. She knew the exclusive and jealous temperament of her alleged rival. She knew the extreme blindness that characterized the feelings of this passionate, of this exalted Isabella; crazy enough, who wouldn't hesitate one second to expose herself to defend her possessions. But Sommers, had uncovered the perverse game of Christel, but he never say a word to his fiancée.

All those beautiful people, invited to dinner, then, went to the Hollemberg house. Michelle declined the invitation, claiming a terrible migraine. She felt incapable to sustain the presence of Carl and Isabella. She couldn't bear to hear the soft and coaxing voice of her cousin, calling for about anything: Carl darling, Carl darling, without interruption.

The words and gestures of her cousin literally tear her heart. The velvety tenderness of Isabella's gaze surrounded and captivated, (the man whom she, the famous singer Michelle Morgan, adored in silence), in a passionate magic spell.

Mona Lisa was in verve that day. She told crisp anecdotes gleaned from her studious years at the Sorbonne University. She accompanied on the piano, Christel Baldwin, in conventional popular songs: life in pink, the autumn leaves, the hymn to love, don't leave me and much more.

Christel had a lovely voice and imitated nicely the sensual tremolos of Edith Piaf. The guests were cheering with passion, while enjoying the delicious meal offered by Joyce Hollemberg.

Max Hollemberg took over after his daughter and started to explain, with data in support facts, the losses that had endured the Monjollian community, through this horrible scourge that had fallen unexpectedly on the city and its immediate surroundings.

He felt (if the black curse does not subside soon) that the region, strangled by this abominable quarantine, would be completely devastated and ruined.

The plants: Morgan, Hollemberg and Baldwin, were out of breath. There were no more orders. The wellbeing of our workers and their families, advanced Max Hollemberg, was the only reason we were maintaining some semblance of activity in our abandoned businesses.

The telephone of Dr. Sommers vibrated in his pocket. He apologized to the guests, to respond. He returned two minutes later: I must leave at once, he said, there is an emergency at the hospital.

Isabella rose from her table and ran after him. I am going with you Carl?

No, stay with your parents, replied Carl, who walk faster toward the exit. The hospital staff is at hand, my darling, I do not think I will need your help.

It doesn't matter, said Isabella, I will accompany you anyway.

Dr. Sommers had to bend a docile front before the stubborn determination of his fiancée. He didn't want to upset his beloved fiancée who, since the evening on the square, became sensitive to the extreme, getting angry for anything.

Carl darling, life will require that you give up this profession, said Isabella, very seriously. You never have time to enjoy yourself. I apprehend with anxiety that you won't be able to devote time to your family.

What do you want me to do Isabella? Said Sommers, a little upset. Professional ethics requires self-denial. My private life must not, in any way, constitute an obstacle to my inalterable dedication to my patients.

Don't be angry, my love; said Isabella a strand contrite. I do not ask you to completely leave the practice of your profession, I would say even more, your vocation; but only, to practice less the duty that absorbs you day and night and prevents you from living.

Watch out! Carl, cried suddenly Isabella, on a dangerous deviation of Dr. Sommers. Look where you are going, my friend...

You drive too fast.

The receptionist told to hurry up.

You shouldn't, however, risk your life? My love. Where is Dr. Merville?

Exactly, it's him. He fell like the last time, I fear serious complications. It is for this reason that I have to hurry.

Dr. Sommers entered with a bang in the courtyard of the hospital, stopped outside the main entrance, rushed out of the car, asking Isabella to park the vehicle before coming to join him.

Dr. Merville was barely breathing. Despite his dark skin coloring, he clearly distinguished the hue yellow subcutaneous, symptomatic of an acute hepatitis.

Dr. Sommers ordered an emergency dialysis and collected blood samples. He went himself analyze them at the hospital lab.

He found an excessive amount of bilirubin in the blood. He feared that Dr. Merville has failed to take the drugs he had prescribed to him to supplement the inevitable destruction of the erythrocyte cells responsible for the oxygenation of the liver.

Dr. Merville regained consciousness, as soon as they had completed the dialysis. He confessed to have really failed to take his medication.

You're very lucky, said Sommers. Your body weakened by the repeated onslaught of the toxins from the brain tumor, has given up under the first attack. We could have pernicious cirrhosis on hand.

I beg you Dr. Merville, pleaded Sommers, please follow my recommendations. Take better care of your health. We have overcome the most difficult phase; do not lose the gambit for trifles.

During this time, Isabella had alerted Bernice that ran at the bedside of her husband. We have remedied the urgent crisis, said Sommers; we are keeping him for the night under observation. Lisa Troy entered the room where Dr. Merville was, and pulling Dr. Sommers in a corner, she whispered a few words in his ear. He rushed out the room and ran toward the elevator, Isabella on his heels.

What happens Carl? Asked Isabella anxious.

Your cousin Michelle, she is in the emergency room. I don't know yet what happened to her.

Isabella gripped Carl arm to avoid falling. Her legs shamble, her soul hurting and failing, filled with a terrible premonition.

Michelle was lying on a narrow bed, pale and almost lifeless. Take her to the operating room immediately ordered Sommers. Follow me he told the nurse who was taking care of Michelle.

Dr. Sommers proceeded himself to a gastric lavage and administered, back-to-back, by the nurse, two enemas to remove all residues of the powerful sleeping pills she had swallowed.

Isabella paralyzed by emotion, sobbing silently, sitting in a chair in the corner in the room. Dr. Sommers had forbidden her to call her parents who were at the Hollemberg's. Wait until we got a positive result, before alarming these people.

Michelle's pulse was, now, at fifty beats per minute. Her breathing seemed to regularize. Her cheeks were regaining color.

Dr. Sommers injected intravenously to the girl, a purgative to remove all traces of the narcotic in her blood. Michelle! Michelle!

called Sommers, patting her cheeks. Wake up! Michelle, wake up!

Isabella, still within the scope of emotion, joined the party: Michelle! Michelle! Michelle! She shouted increasingly loud; while tickling the soles of her unconscious cousin feet. After a minute or two of this rudimentary maneuver, Michelle let out a deep sigh and opened her eyes briefly.

Michelle! Do you hear me?

yes, do an acquiescence nod.

Open your eyes. Very well! You see me? Who am I?

Michelle opened her eyes again, and whispered in a slurred voice, almost inaudible: Dr. Sommers.

You recognize this person to your left?

She leaned her head aside and said, with a little more clarity in the voice: Isabella, my cousin.

Now, said Sommers, you're going to walk around the room. Isabella and I, will support you. You must stay awake?

Dr. Sommers, taking both hands of the girl in his own, to help her sit on the edge of the bed. Then passed his arms around her waist to get her off. He touched slightly, inadvertently, the tip of her breast. She shivered feverishly.

When the Morgan landed in the hospital, Isabella and Dr. Sommers, was busy cheering Michelle to eat some crispy buns or to drink a sip or two of a creamy chocolate, placed in front of her on a plate.

They came as soon as Lisa Troy had telephoned Simon to transmit the unfortunate news. Joan and Cathy, Elsa and Simon, Harry and Mona Lisa; all rushed to the girl bedside, bombarding her with a lot of questions.

Please! Interposed Dr. Sommers; Michelle is not in condition to undergo this collective questioning. Do me the favor please! leave the room. Isabella will keep you informed. When Michelle recovered her faculties, she will tell you, herself, the circumstances of this whim, which she is the only one to know the cause.

Isabella took her folks in Dr. Sommers office, for more privacy; and, especially for their removal from public curiosity.

Isabella told them that Dr. Sommers hadn't suddenly left the dinner for Michelle. Dr. Merville had relapsed. Carl has stabilized his case.

He feels better now. The prognosis is quite favorable.

While Carl was still busy attending Dr. Merville, Lisa came to announce the arrival of unconscious Michelle, in the emergency room. He rushed illico and diagnosed, at first glance, the nature of the ailment.

Michelle had swallowed a massive dose of sleeping pill. Carl washed her stomach. The nurse administered two or three enemas to get rid of soporific residues in her bowels, not yet digested, which could have maintained her state of deep lethargy until final sleep.

Everybody is going home. Carl told me and I understand that your presence at her bedside, now, could generate a debilitating psychological climate for Michelle. Shame and remorse, allying themselves with regret to having caused you so much trouble could delay her complete healing. Her inconsiderate action, symptomatic of serious mental disorders and a sense of guilt, inevitable in such cases; would negatively affect her personality.

I am staying with my cousin, said Isabella. Dr. Sommers will take care of Dr. Merville. Michelle is sleeping peacefully. Her respiration a little panting remained the only visible evidence of the terrible drama that she came to play at the expense of her life.

Isabella settled on a longue chaise at her cousin bedsides, removed her shoes to be more comfortable and fell asleep, exhausted by fatigue and emotion.

Back in the room, after his usual tour to check on his patients, Sommers found the two cousins in the arms of Morpheus. He carefully covered Isabella, because of the cold, with a wool blanket, and went out tiptoeing to avoid waking them up. He went to lie on the sofa in his office, which served him as a bed, very often.

Dr. Sommers called Morgan sisters to reassure them. He asked them not to worry unduly, as Isabella spent the night with her cousin.

Elsa was the most affected of the group. In the outline she knew why her niece wanted to commit suicide. She had followed with apprehension the evolution of the young girl crush on the doctor and her fierce, jealousy toward Isabella.

I don't think Carl, said Elsa, it's a good idea to leave to Isabella the custody of her cousin? I think that you are more or less aware of the reasons that pushed my niece to that extreme desperation?

Of course, little mother, said Carl, anxious. I believe that we must beat the iron while it is hot, as they say. I trust the insight and the wisdom of your daughter. She will burst the abscess once for all and reconcile with her cousin.

Good! I trust you. I'm not an expert psychologist to assess the chances of success of the test entrusted to someone as inexperienced as Isabella...

Experience and psychology count for nothing in this delicate undertaking. Love and the compassion remain the only viaticum in those circumstances. Isabella has this exceptional charisma.

About three o'clock in the morning, Michelle woke up, still all numb, and unaware of her whereabouts. She opened her eyes, trying to identify, in the diffuse half lighter room; the familiar objects of her own room at the villa at White Lily's street.

She flooded the room with a profusion of dazzling light coming from the ceiling. Isabella woke up immediately.

I'm hungry, murmured Michelle; I feel a vacuum at the pit of my stomach.

It is not surprising, replied her cousin. They had emptied you literally yesterday. What do you want to eat?

Don't leave me! I'm afraid to stay alone. Thank you for staying at my bedside tonight.

Isabella rang the service nurse who came immediately. What can be found to eat at this hour? My cousin and I are hungry.

Bring us some black coffee, exclaimed Michelle. If it's possible an omelet for us, toast or brioche, a piece of gruyere, finally everything you can find that is good in your kitchen.

I'll do my best, said the nurse.

It is just now that I find out, I haven't eaten since yesterday, began Isabella. We were barely seated at the table when Carl was forced to leave. Lisa Troy called for an emergency at the hospital.

Dr. Merville has collapse once again.

How is he doing? Asked Michelle, anxious.

Good! He is doing pretty well, I think. He had regained consciousness and discussed with Carl, who rumbled him for having neglected his recommendations. Carl criticized his casual attitude regarding the treatment he had proposed. As soon as your presence had been reported by Lisa, Carl rushed to the emergency room to treat you.

The nurse returned at that instant, pushing a table of victuals.

Thanks, said Isabella, I will take care of the rest.

Isabella helped her cousin to get off the bed and sit her in a chair and placed the table in front of her. Isabella fills a cup of steaming coffee, and handed it to her. Drink! It'll do you good. Isabella put a large portion of the omelet on a plate, cut a slice of Swiss cheese, butter a few toasts, eat my dear, you have to get your strength back.

How! You don't eat yourself?

I'm taking my coffee first.

The omelet is delicious, said Michelle.

You love him that much? So much you choose to die, Michelle?

Taken aback by the brutality of this attack, Michelle lowered her head and cried without restraint. A steady stream of tears run down on her pale cheeks.

Don't stir the knife in the wound! I beg you Isabella. I bitterly regret my stupid action; I do not want to talk about it... I am ashamed of myself... I'm still in shock. I'm confused...

On the contrary, Michelle darling, we must beat the iron while it is hot. No one can better understand you than me. Let's make the argument and find a way to reconcile things, so we can both live without rancor, according to our family tradition.

Everything collapsed around me. Look! I became a Negress; my career is suddenly been interrupted or ended permanently. I do not know, and the man who could bring me a reason to live, in this lost Montjollian hole, (that I fled, to avoid this poor, petty, idle and dull existence) which disdained me and treated me like a pestiferous pestilence...

But, Michelle, you kept the room when Carl was at Aunt Cathy's. I have always observed that Carl treated you with courtesy and respect. Where do you find that he disdained you?

Isabella, you're a naive, blinded by your love, you do not see what is happening around you. Are you aware or do you pretend to ignore this fierce struggle by some girls from the supposedly high society, decided to grab your prey, one way or another?

Why should I bother? I have absolute confidence in Carl.

Don't be too pretentious Isabella? Others may succeed where I failed.

Could it be too pretentious to trust the man I love?

Have you been to the villa Vaudreuil Isabella?

Of course, when I was little. I would often go see my grandfather.

I mean, since Dr. Sommers resides there?

No! It would be inappropriate, don't you think?

Improper or not, my dear cousin, countered Michelle, I went there two times revive your Carl. The first time he received me with kindness. He offered me a cup of vanilla ice-cream. I wanted to visit the house, but he refused politely; pretexting that he didn't have this right, stipulated in his lease. The second time, it was in the evening; he didn't let me enter the house. I stayed more than one hour in the courtyard, disappointed by the distant and reserved attitude, observed by this cold and phlegmatic individual. I rang at his door, unnecessarily, several times again. I had learned by Suzanne that he was probably not at home when the yellow Cadillac was not outside the front door of the villa.

What role played Suzanne in this story? How come she was aware of these details? Inquired Isabella, really intrigued.

Ha! Ha! Ha! Laughed Michelle, externalizing a fun hilarity. Let me tell you my dear cousin: your man kicked her bot out at his door two or three times. Dr. Carl Sommers don't mess with his reputation. I have suffered to know it.

You learn it well good! Michelle

Let me spare you all the Machiavellian machinations engineered by Suzanne and Christel, to snatch her man from this little silly, this false ingénue, this naïve and dumb Isabella; this exceptional man, absolutely unique.

I suspected this plot, but I didn't really know the magnitude of the cabal; because Carl never blew me a word of it.

Carl was right to keep secret this sleazy affair. He spared you a lot of problems. He controlled the situation. Things would become explosive, if he had put you in the midst. Mona Lisa, your future sister-in-law resigned first in her hunt. She loves you a lot you know?

I love her too, said Isabella, very moved by this confidence.

Suzanne quickly comforted in the arms of James Nadowsky. As soon as the quarantine is lifted, they are going to get married... you know? Christel Baldwin is spoilt for choice. All the idle bachelors are at her feet, coveting her hand and her fortune.

And you, Michelle, asked Isabella, what do you want to do with your life? Before you answer me, I'll confide into you two secrets. What am I saying? I'll make you two confidences. Can I ask you an intimate question?

I have nothing more to hide in the dilapidated physical and moral state I am. What do you want to know my dear cousin?

Would you agree to marry a nigger, Michelle?

Funny question? I do not understand what you mean.

I don't ask you to understand, but simply to answer my question. Would you accept to marry a man of color? Yes or no.

Michelle remained silent. She invoked with pain the long family tradition that ostracized those people, and refused them all humanity. These taboos rooted in her psyche, since childhood; didn't allow her to consider the possibility of such a mésalliance.

My parents will never accept such a marriage.

And you, Michelle, do you feel capable of marrying a man of color? An exceptional man; i.e.: educated, talented, learned, courteous, kind, devoted, handsome as Adonis, a perfect gentleman what?

Michelle nodded her head as a sign of disapproval and said: I do not think that I can introduce a nigger in the Morgan family. My dear cousin, it is only in your dreams that you met this rare individual who you have described. This type of man you have described, doesn't exist in color and rarely found in white.

You're mistaken, your assertions completely false, said Isabella.

Your prejudices, Michelle honey, have put blinkers on your eyes. My first confidence, meant to widen your field of vision, to make you understand the inherent absurdity of any action, which does not aim to surpass one selfish interest. The generosity of heart and spirit and the dedication to the human cause should be the guide of one's existence.

I confess that I do not understand your cryptic verbiage. I'm not savvy in Riddle, dear cousin. Explains your thoughts better than that.

You wanted to commit suicide for decoys. For things whose ephemeral existence fascinates us or frighten us; mirages that will disappear tomorrow from our limited horizon. Dr. Sommers has predicted the end of the black curse for the first of November second, that is to say in ten days.

Your man is also prophet or a magician? Let us be serious Isabella, you are telling me that to make me suffer.

What formal proof do you have? Don't repeat those absurdities. Said Michelle.

I believe in his science,I trust him with my life! Replied Isabella.

Are you speaking true Isabella?

Why should I be lying? Elsa, Simon, Harry and Mona Lisa were present when he said it to me.

You have eliminated suddenly, the two reasons that led me to despair.

Your fantasies were transformed into a tragic reality. You ran after a chimera. Dr. Carl Sommers is and will remain a black man when the entire population of Montjolly will resume its original pigmentation.

You are lying Isabella! You lie! You lie! Tell me that you lie!

He will confirm the fact himself...

It is not true Isabella, you try to make me regret my foolishness, isn't it?

Michelle honey, I swear on what I have the most precious in the world, on the head of my fiancé, I told you the truth, the whole truth and nothing but the truth.

Did you know it before falling in love with him?

Listen; after three years of voluntary seclusion, I went on the beach one Sunday, to be alone, between the sky and the sea. I wore, I remember, a flesh colored bathing suit. I had spent the morning splashing around in the water as a child. I had stepped on the deserted Beach, barefoot on the burning sand.

Tired, I sat on a fallen tree, sheltered from the curious gazes, by a bush of bougainvillea and wild buttercups. I was reading a St John Perse book of poetry, mother had bought for me. Absorbed by the reading, I was paying little attention to the singing and the tweeting of birds fluttering, nor the muted rustling of the wind in the dry leaves that littered the sandy soil, nor the constant lapping of the waves that licking the golden sands of the beach. I saw him suddenly very close to me. He looked at me with his big brown eyes; his face radiant, imbued with a surprised delight, made me wince with unspeakable joy. I was shaking from fear, unable to take my eyes off his stare that fascinated and make me dizzy.

He then told me: you are one hundred times more beautiful than

Botticelli's Venus. You could be the love goddess herself? Am I dreaming or what? I was shaken by a delightful earthquake. His ardent looks undressing me, literally. I ran toward my car, to endorse my bathrobe and break the spell that kept me trapped under his magical spell.

In my panic, I had dropped my book, he picked it up. What's your name he asked me, always peering me with an expression of pure ecstasy and surprise? Me, he said, I am the doctor Carl Sommers. It is you? I cried, with the spontaneity of a little silly. It's me, he replied, relentlessly, I am glad to know that you were already aware of my presence? What's your name? He insisted. You're not from Montjolly?

Who cares! Since I found you today, you whom my heart was longing for, I don't want to lose you ever again.

He begged me for a pen to write, I gave him a pencil. He wrote his phone number on the last page of my book and handed it back to me. I must go, I said in a murmur. I'm Isabella Morgan.

This event shocked my life radically. I didn't say anything to Elsa in the early days. But she quickly noticed a profound change in my behavior. I could hardly eat, I couldn't sleep at night. This man's eyes haunted me day and night. As I couldn't call him, Elsa suggested that I make some research not to get into this adventure like a fishing expedition. Enough about me!

Don't you have, by chance, in the circle of your admirers, a substitute replacement for Carl? Where is your appointed poet: Professor Charles Lewis?

The poor man! I have snubbed him so often, he ended up deserted the Committee. I treated him with rudeness and disdain, thinking that I had a chance with Dr. Sommers. Among all my suitors, he is the only one that I liked. I know, for sure, that he will not come back to me.

If he loved you as you think, he will come back. Elsa could arrange everything for you, if you want...

Leave me the time to recover at least. Isabella, it was good to talk to you. We should have this conversation a long time ago.

Better late than never, replied her cousin.

The two cousins kissed tenderly. I want to go home; do you think it is possible? In a way, I could pass for your advisor, but I'm not your doctor, for sure, said Isabella. They burst out laughing.

The atmosphere is wonderful, said Dr. Sommers on entering the room.

I just needed you Carl! Michelle told him, I want to go home, is this possible?

How are you? Do you feel able to face your aunts? You're not going to recur in your madness? Are you sure to have exorcised your obsessions and your phobias? Although it is hard for you to answer those questions, I must make sure of your psychological balance before I let you go.

Isabella and I we have talked most of the night. She has boosted my confidence, removed my illusions, revealing her amazing secrets. She dispelled my dreamlike fads making me confront reality in a new way. Isabella told me that you were black, is this true, Dr. Sommers?

Of course, I am black. I didn't hide it to anyone? There was a misunderstanding, the black curse, alone, is responsible for.

Why didn't you reveal the fact to everyone? This would have saved you so many problems, and countless inappropriate visits.

What do you want to insinuate, Michelle? I am not ashamed of my race. But I could not shout on the rooftops that I was a nigger; in this explosive situation where, the panicked population needed someone to reinsure and take care of them. Lots of people knew I was black: Simon and his assessors, Elsa, Harry, Isabella, Dr. Merville, his colleagues at the hospital and Lisa Troy, the receptionist, the good friend of Isabella; judge Crampton, big Luke, the sheriff, the minions of Harry Morgan who flogged me to death.

The nurse will come to help you get ready, I'll bring you home, (Sommers looked furtively at his watch) probably in half an hour; time to grapple with this recalcitrant Dr. Merville.

One minute after the departure of Dr. Sommers from the room, Suzanne Birmingham landed there in a windstorm. She ran toward her good friend, already ready to leave, and pressed her on her heart with touching tenderness. What happened sweetie? I cannot stay; I'll come to see you at home. She looks up and down at Isabella and strolled with a decided step saying: see you later Michelle!

CHAPTER XIV

The frantic traffic prevailing in Montjolly's sky, had long lost its attractions. Onlookers gather no more to watch the Navy helicopters across the sky in a constant uproar. They had more fun following the slow flight and silent multicolored airships, which watched over the city. The fighter jets flying in formation, and drawing the maze of white smoke on their course, interested them no more.

Life was once again routine and monotonous. People little by little, and seemed not to realize, or worry about the color of their skin.

Thanks to the innovations introduced by the Public Safety Committee: TV, radio, phone, young people were turned to other poles of attraction. The old ladies flocked no more, every evening, over the square. They preferred to watch fun movies or listen classical music concerts, selected by the cenacle overseen the orthodoxy and the puritanical customs of this vulnerable society. The pioneers feared, with reason that exposed its austerity without transition, to the pernicious influences of the outside world would perturb the psychological health of the community. While regretting, humiliating and traumatic test of the black curse; the majority of the population, had welcomed, the radical transformations in the Montjolian society, rooted in its taboos and prejudices.

"At something, misfortune is good" father Ted Vogel, told the bigots who complained.

Father Vogel advertised through the media: radio and television, an urgent appeal to the people, to participate in a rogatory procession that he is organizing on the occasion of the celebration of all Saints.

I do not ask you to take the bag of the penitent, wear the cilices or crowns of thorns; but I would like to see you barefoot, dressed in humility, contrition and faith; to implore forgiveness and mercy for our sins.

Nancy, the receptionist at night, handed over two letters to Dr. Carl Sommers, who, his work done went to dinner with his alleged fiancée, at the Moulin Rouge: the new restaurant at Chrysanthemums Street.

You are late, said Isabella, opening the door for Carl. Elsa and Simon have been here a long time and Mona Lisa is waiting for us out there.

Excuse me darling, he told her while kissing her on the mouth. You know how absorbent my work at the hospital is. Dr. Merville is recovering slowly, I don't want him to work presently.

You don't look sharp my darling? Come I am going to fix you a bit better. You're frumpy today.

She led him to the toilet, she brushed his hair, redone the knot of his tie and cleared the pockets of his jacket from the papers that were there.

Wish! Exclaimed Isabella, you have received two letters from France.

It's true? Nancy just gave them to me. We will read them later?

The restaurant was jam packed. The hostess led them to the table of the Hollemberg, located in a sort of lodge artistically decorated, discreetly lit, dominating throughout the room.

Joyce Hollemberg (fine gourmet) composed a menu, much appreciated by everyone: a shellfish mousse with whipped cream, sprinkled with white wine; a timbale of seafood and vegetable, with a bottle of red Bordeaux; fillets of chicken with crayfish sauce; and a white chocolate mousse and Marie Brizard Amaretto liqueur, for dessert.

Mona Lisa's wedding was the subject of the conversation. Her father, Max, was reluctant to launched the invitations to personalities, friends and parents living outside the prohibited area. If, as predicted Dr. Sommers, the miracle happened really in November 1st; we could welcome our guests for Thanksgiving Day on the 23rd , continued Max

Hollemberg watching the doctor with insistence.

I'm not a miracle worker, Max, retorted Carl Sommers. I'm not omniscient either. But I can tell you with certainty that the black curse will disappear shortly. What I know is that the black curse will subside very soon. It could be that the event does not happen the day said, but I can assure you that it will happen in less than a week.

In this case, chained Joyce, why do we send the invitations for 23rd; me, I have absolute confidence in the predictions of the Dr. Sommers. Besides, we have nothing to lose. If the quarantine is lifted, we will have the crowd with us; with or without people from outside, the wedding will be celebrated with splendor and circumstance, isn't it Ma Lisa? Said Joyce nodding to her daughter.

Because Carl has confirmed the imminent end of our ordeal, said Mona Lisa, I proposed to Harry to have the wedding earlier instead of the choosing date; so we could come back from our honeymoon trip before the year end holidays.

Elsa honey, would you have any objections?

My Dear Lisa, I agree wholeheartedly, with everything what you decide, my only concern is that you are happy that your marriage (one of the major events in a woman's life) goes according to the secret wishes of your loving heart.

Elsa took advantage of the opportunity that was offered to her, to dispel once for all the rumors that Joyce false friends were already spreading in town. She flattered her future daughter-in-law and immunized her against any gossip of her mother's friends.

I heard, said suddenly Harry Morgan, that the Subcommittee on Family Affairs in the Senate, sponsored by the seventeen female senators, Democrat and Republican; will introduce Monday a law proposal to put an end to the quarantine.

It is more than time, said Simon Morgan, who attended with pain and helplessness, the dangerous deterioration of the standard of living of his city and the progressive impoverishment of the region.

Isabella didn't say a word during the entire meal. She ate almost nothing, either; lost in her thoughts. She imagined how profiting in a timely manner, from the wedding date change proposed by Mona Lisa's. I will notify Carl, as soon as he comes out, said Isabella with a sigh of relief.

Out of the restaurant, satisfied and happy to have spent a great evening; the family dispersed by couple. Simon and Elsa, Carl and Isabella, headed to the Petit Palais, Max and Joyce, Harry and Mona Lisa, to the Villarossa, the palatial residence of the Hollemberg.

Elsa and Simon went up in their room, immediately, Isabella and Carl settled in the small living room. Dear Isabella, said Carl, once he was sitting, you must eat more than that? That is wrong my love?

Carl darling, can I ask you a question? She said avoiding to answer.

Of course, my love.

 But I don't want to get you upset my love.

Why should I be upset? I promise not to get mad whatever you ask...

You heard that Mona Lisa has advanced her wedding date?

Yes! I heard...

What would you say if we get married on December 21?

What I'd say? Preferably, ask me what I think?

What do you think Carl?

I think it is a great idea...

He couldn't finish his sentence. Isabella uttered a cry of joy and threw herself at her fiancé. Thank you, thank you, I love you,

I love you…

 A little restraint, dear, you're going to disturb the entire house.

Isabella sitting on the lap of Carl, said to him: please remove the topaz from this finger?

Why? asked Dr. Sommers.

You ask too many questions my dear... Just removed! She said, presenting her hand. He executed the order. Place the ring in this finger. Very well! Now we're officially engage, said the girl radiant of joy, like a child who had just been given a coveted toy.

Isabella! Said Carl, a little embarrassed, please sit on your chair.

You don't have to be angry for that, my darling!

I am not at all angry… but let's see...

I'll report the good news to Elsa, starting tonight, so she could set in motion the preparations for the wedding and the engagement?

I don't want an engagement anymore, said Isabella, I want to get married.

It is not necessary, however, my darling, to get mad!

Touchée! Said Isabella, smiling... You pay me back, isn't it? You are a bad boy Carl!

By the way, said suddenly Isabella changing the subject; I almost forget your French correspondence. I'll look for the letters.

- Let's see! The first is from Professor Saurel Chaussonnet. She opened the letter and said:

Professor Chaussonnet invited you to Paris (all expenses paid) to a scientific symposium on the theory of "the Non Compensation of the Dispersed Energy". Six other scholars will participate in this conference. He presents his compliments and wishes to you, enthusiastically, whether you can be among his guests or not.

When is the Symposium, asked Sommers, not at all interested?

It is for 10th November, the 10th replied Isabella, enthusiastically... You must go Carl!

Not so fast my darling. I can't leave the hospital, I have no one to replace me.

When the quarantine will be lifted, one of your friends in Biloxi could reciprocate. You worked for them, you have helped them?

I am revealing a big secret to you, I don't have a passport.

Tomorrow I'll order one in emergency. It will be ready in three days. If all goes as planned, we will leave on Sunday the 7th and we will return on the 18th , just in time for my brother's wedding.

What did you said, said Carl? We leave... It doesn't matter, my darling... I will not endorse this responsibility. By the way, I didn't want to go anyway.

Joking apart no more discussions Carl..., my love, I will not let you lose this golden opportunity to make yourself known in the scientific world. Whether you like it or not, I take your future in charge.

You're taken care of my future? Are you kidding me? I know you have taken my destiny in hand, since I met you! What happens to my authority as head of the household in all this? What happens to my male pride in all of that?

Isabella burst out laughing. I note with a great pleasure that you understand perfectly who is in charge here. I am proud to marry a man as intelligent as you.

This not a proof of intelligence to abdicate his patriarchal prerogatives for the beautiful eyes of a beautiful girl; even if she is pretty inside and out, generous and compassionate.

Things became even more interesting! Said Isabella. You are expected, my dear, at Saint-Brieux in Brittany, by Auguste Lavignac, notary public. He said he spent more than a year looking for the son of Monique de Foix: Roger Sommers. It is through an article in Paris Match, he could, finally, find the whereabouts of Monique's son.

Your great uncle Gérome and your grandmother Simone died, tragically in an accident. The small plane uncle Gérôme was flying, fell into the Bay during a storm.

Where do I fit in this story? I don't know these people. What does he wants this Auguste Lavignac?

Auguste Lavignac is a notary; the executor of the viscountess Simone de Foix will.

You have until December 31st to enforce your legitimate rights to the estate and claim your share of the inheritance, which would be equivalent to your mother Monique de Foix. After this time, you lose your rights.

You think I should go to see what's all about? What do you think Isabella?

What woman wants, God willing Darling. I'll do my best so to have everything ready before the lifting of the quarantine. We must go first to New York to renew your wardrobe.

Dear love, replied Dr. Sommers, how to submit such a request to your parents? We are not even engaged officially.

You're wrong, Carl, we do since a one hour ago.

You're playing with the nitty-gritty Isabella.

No one can stop me to follow you wherever. Believe me dear Carl, Simon and Harry have learned their lesson, they won't dare express their opposition. Elsa loves me too much to frustrate me; even if, in her heart, she would not approve.

You put me in a quandary...

Eh! What are you saying? I am putting you in an awkward position! I know, you just have to deal with it. Would you ever have kissed me, if I hadn't done the first step? Handle your problems as you please; with embarrassment if you will, Carl Sommers, I want to go to France with you, it's as simple as that. I do not have the courage to be separate from you, for a minute!

Should I call Mister Auguste Lavignac, to acknowledging reception of his letter?

Don't you worry my love? I will deal with everything. You only have one thing to do at the moment: notify Simon and Elsa that we are going, to travel for a few days, a business trip in France with me. That we will return before Harry and Mona Lisa wedding.

As soon as Carl departed for the hospital, Isabella ascended in her mother's bedroom to give her the latest news and her decisions that she and Carl had taken about their marriage. If everything goes well Elsa, she asked her mother, do you think you can all arrange for my marriage on December the 21st?

Everything is ready a long time ago, my darling, the only thing I still have to do is send those invitations. You make me so happy, mother, that I am afraid of becoming too demanding? What would you say continued Isabella, if I accompanied Carl in France?

I would say that it is inappropriate for a girl to travel alone with her fiancé. "But me, I trust you and,": honne soit qui mal y pense (reviled is that ill think about it!) "To paraphrase King Édouard III of England, picking up the Garter of his mistress: the Countess of Salisbury, (under the mocking and equivocal of the courtesans amused smiles) during a ball at Windsor Castle.

Mother, can I reveal you a secret, to reassure you of Dr. Sommers good intention.

Keeps your secret, my daughter! I need no revelation to know that Carl Sommers is a perfect gentleman. Don't worry, sweetheart, I will speak to Simon on the pillow.

Parishioners responded in great number, to the invitation of reverend Vogel. The Church was packed as an egg. There were people everywhere: in the nave, the transept, the portal, even in the chorus, where notables agglutinated standing around the altar.

Old devout ladies, barefoot and all clad in white recited their rosary under the porch of the church. A huge crowd was massed on the square and in the surrounding streets, to monitor, on the big screens placed in strategic places, the religious ceremony.

Roland Peterson of CNN, had facilitated the retransmission of the mass and the procession that followed.

The psalmody of the parish choir was singing the litany of all saints in latin, with a monotonous and sad voice. The celebration of all saints, this year, took the aspect of lent. Anxiety and fear were on every face.

Dear friends, began father Vogel, we met on this day of All Saints in the spirit of penance and contrition; to entreat the favor of heaven through all the saints.

The chosen of the Lord, bow before the throne of Almaty God, worshipping him in spirit and in truth, saddened by our deep dismay can intercede for us if we humiliate ourselves in repentance, if we acknowledge in a sincere regret, that we have sinned against the transcendence, God and men.

This traumatic event must make us reflect on the futility of our pride without real basis, our prejudices of caste or class, our superiority complex that represents a sacrilegious affront to the infinite wisdom of God.

Indeed, my dear friends, overnight, by divine intervention or the result of hazard. We have become similar to those that we hated, we treated with contempt, which we avoid like plague stricken pariahs.

Today, nothing does distinguish us anymore from the outcasts. We are ostracized, isolated, humiliated, ridiculed the way we had humiliated and ridiculed people of color.

The black curse put us down our rotten pedestal of pride and complacency. The black curse had shaking the known superior race by dangling through his frightened eyes, the vision of its ontological vulnerability and the extreme precariousness of the human condition. We have built a beautiful ivory tower, whose prosperity was the envy of surrounding cities. We had built around it, a wall of vanity and arrogance, which has collapsed on itself (such as the city of Jericho); superscript in the eyes of the world, the spiritual nakedness of our proud hearts, the moral poverty of our hedonistic existence, the atavistic stupidity of our superiority complexes and the dismal baseness of our selfish feelings.

We have sinned against Heaven and Earth, brothers and sisters, united by baptism and communion; beat our mea culpa, skeptics, bow our knees as a sign of repentance, bend our docile fronts under the yoke of humiliation and shame, and ask God to deliver us from this scourge.

The moving and brief homily of Father Vogel plunged the faithful into a deep reflection. Each examined without indulgence, his misguided conscience on the royal road of a pathetic heresy. The entire

Montjollian community recognized its guilt, but complained bitterly, however, for the stringency of the fate.

The rogatory procession began an earnest, immediately after the mass. The group of notables, who attended the ceremony, followed the choir singing with it the anthems of the ritual liturgy of the feast of all saints.

At each crossroads, the priest stopped reciting the invocations to the Blessed Virgin and the supplication to the Holy Spirit. Someone from the crowd recited one of the seven Psalms of penitence, and the procession continued to a new stage.

At the fifth stop on the corner of Roses avenue and rue des Eglantines, (opposite the Sainte Cécile hospital), Isabella was supporting the painful walking of her mother, barefooted, bruised by the uneven bumps of the street; proposed to Elsa to take her to rest in the lobby of the building.

No sweetheart, said Elsa turning her to face her daughter.

Isabella! Isabella! Oh! Isabella!

What happened mother? Are you feelling okay ? Cried Isabella.

Your hair! Your hair is reverted blond... The miracle is accomplished for you...

For you as well mother...

They remained a time paralyzed by emotion and joy. Reverend Vogel was reciting an invocation. Elsa Morgan called on him:

Father Vogel! Father Vogel! She shouted louder; Miracle! Miracle! Heaven has heard our prayers.

Father Vogel looked at Elsa Morgan, gazed his eyes on Isabella, turned left and right and fell on his face, invaded by an extraordinary emotion, an ineffable sense of extreme rapture that stunned him literally.

The vicar and the altar boys hastened to make him stand. The parish rector was lead out of the crowd, toward a car parked on the side of the street; which brought him to the church.

Isabella was, with difficulty, dug a passage to the hospital gate where she brought her mother who was crying of joy.

The crowd unleashed an explosive sense of relief. People shouted of joy, crying, kissing, circling the pavement on the edge of vertigo, and, embroiled in a febrile delirium.

The bells began to ring joyously. The crowd dispersed with difficulty, still in shock of emotion. A deafening uproar replaced the calm and the fervor of the procession. It was an amazing show. An improvised parade of cars, vehicles of all kinds, ran through the city in an infernal noise: horn and roar of helicopters escorting from above the insane uproar, to prevent or put down a revolt of the population. Not knowing what had caused this sudden excitement; the army took its precautions.

A wind of madness swept the corridors of the hospital; It was a real shambles. Patients left their room, and ran from door to door to see.

Several went home, miraculously healed. But, still limping. Others wandered in hospital dress uttering wild cries capable of puncturing somebody eardrum.

Dr. Suzanne Birmingham against any professional ethics dropped her stethoscope in the midst of a consultation when she noticed her transformation. She uttered a wild inhuman scream and ran like a crazy woman up to her office, where she retreated and locked her door.

Dr. Sommers returning from the operating room, met Isabella and her mother, who went to his office. Isabella jumped at the neck of her fiancé and embraced him saying:

You were right Carl, my hair reverted to blond.

Elsa hugged very hard, her future son-in-law. She says nothing, but the ardor of her embrace reflected her feelings towards him, whose presence had upset the pattern developed by her family life, and transformed the obsolete and ridiculous behavior of an entire population.

Dr. Sommers took them in his office, shuffling, Isabella grasped his right arm and, supporting with the other, Elsa who was limping slightly.

Let me see the damage of the walk, he said, in a mocking tone. When Elsa sat on the couch. You shouldn't have nibble your feet like that Elsa?

Dr. Sommers poured hot water into a tub, carefully washed Elsa feet bruised and cracked. He dried her feet, wiped them with delicacy, dressing them carefully and wrapped them in a sterile tissue. Then, he proceeded to Isabella's. The washing of the feet of Isabella was for Dr. Sommers, an introduction to the practice of tenderness; and for the girl, a shy and disturbing awakening of sensuality.

We should be concerned at what going on now at the Petit Palais? I am taking you home. Give me five minutes.

He went out of the room and returned a few moments later, with a wheelchair. He helped Elsa to sit saying: You can walk Isabella?

Of course my darling,

He led them to his parked car behind the hospital, near the entrance to the service elevator. The street was seething. Dr. Sommers went through Rosehips street, less crowded, to get by detours at the Petit Palais.

The joy was at its peak, everywhere. Memory of man, we had never seen, an also extravagant demonstration of joy. People were crying, people laughing, kissing everybody, danced, sang; fallen under the bewitching charm of a jubilant hex.

Cathy and Joan Morgan and their niece Michelle went to the Petit Palais to embrace Dr. Sommers. Joyce and Mona Lisa arrived almost at the same time. They lavished on him their indefectible affection, thanking him effusively for his incomparable dedication throughout this terrifying ordeal.

Michelle Morgan experienced visually, the truth of of her cousin assertion. Cathy Morgan expressed astonishment that the miracle was not yet produced for Dr. Sommers. She signaled her concern to Elsa.

 Dr. Sommers will not change color, said Elsa, it's his natural color. This is not true! Shouted Cathy Morgan. Did you know it Elsa? I was aware of the fact and Simon and Isabella. And you told us nothing? Retorted Cathy Morgan in a tone of reproach. What it would serve you? Moreover it was not for us to unveil the secret of Dr. Sommers and raise the hostility of the people against him... Would you consent to let him took care of you, if you knew he was black? Do not hesitate to reply! Now you know why they said nothing to anyone.

Simon Morgan, (the Mayor) telephoned the Governor Rogers, asking him to lift the quarantine. He, in turn, communicated the news to Vice President Cheney, to make the necessary steps.

Cheney presented, immediately to the signature of president Bush, the decree ending one year quarantine imposed on the city of Montjolly.

He hastened to solicit the assistance of the State Department, through its embassies, for spreading the news of the sudden disappearance of this unusual phenomenon.

He demanded the lifting, without delay, of the interdict which hit the United States, and the restoration of trade, cultural and diplomatic relations, suspended because of this black curse.

Roland Peterson of CNN, communicated the news in flash. The news of this incredible metamorphosis, spread like wildfire around the world.

Senator Obama of Illinois, the only black Senator during debate on the new law, proposed to reform the administration of the health in the country; took a few minutes of his time, to report to the skeptics, that black curse settled, as predicted by this young doctor: Carl Sommers and, now, they could sleep without fear of becoming black in the morning.

The other members of the Committee welcomed the comments of Senator Obama with coldness and contempt. Senator Chuck Grassley of Iowa, did the remark that these words did not have their place in a serious debate on health. To what Senator Obama replied, with anger in his voice: that the health and wellbeing of an entire population were threatened by this insidious epidemic, and he doesn't appreciate the hostile attitude and contemptuous of the Senate toward this proven region.

The statements of this provincial doctor, weighed for nothing in the scale, next to the assertions of the prominent scholars, Nobel Prize in medicine, who predicted the irreversibility of this black curse and the permanent danger of contamination it was for the white population of the world; retorted Senator Grassley.

Your scholarly leading epidemiologists, replied the Senator Obama; are, in reality, that unmitigated morons. With their dubious science and their actual phobia, they have contributed to the suffering of these poor people, and to the maintenance of the quarantine that has impoverished and humiliated unnecessarily the city of Montjolly.

In doubt, the Government could not run the risk to the population. The pressure exerted on the administration (by friendly countries, embroiled in a crisis of paranoia) made it difficult the premature lifting of the measures taken to contain the black curse and prevent its spread throughout the world.

It is obvious that the Bush administration does react only under pressure, continued Senator Obama, that the interests of the people always stays in the background. We must, if we want to remain a great nation, take to heart, the cause of the poor, the sick, and children.

This is what we are doing here, Senator Obama, said Grassley, angry.

The people for whom you working, are big corporations, the wealthy, the moguls of high finance and industry. Everything else, the majority of the people does not count for you. Everything is too expensive for their dirty snouts...

Senator Olympia Snow of Maine, put an end to this venomous discussion, which could inflame the atmosphere already tense of the meeting.

Gentlemen! Gentlemen! She said in a severe tone. be moderate in your comments. The discussion has degenerated into personal feud. We cannot afford the luxury of such antagonism in the middle of an important meeting.

The fate of the people is even more important than these endless debates that lead nowhere. I am the product of the Plebs, declared Senator Obama. I take the defense of my brothers, everywhere and at all times. In this august Assembly, the voice of the people is mute. Nobody cares regardless. If they died for lack of medical care. It doesn't matter if millions of children are hungry... Excuse me said Senator Obama, who left the meeting disappointed and outraged.

Monjolly recorded a resurgence of collective delirium, when Mayor: Simon Morgan, announced on the radio and local television, the lifting of the quarantine. People swam in a nearby jubilation of madness.

The African district organized a veritable bacchanal. The wine flowed galore. The frenzied music woke up the passions on the back burner for a year.

On the square near the church and in the adjacent streets, a huge crowd had gathered to celebrate this auspicious day of deliverance and blessing. Renalto's orchestra was entertaining the enthusiastic joy of the people.

People flocked in droves in the Petit Palais. The grand salon and the lounge were stuffed with people. The regular guests at the house, moved to the library.

Amélie, (could not be more pleased to find her beautiful carnation) deployed an incomparable zeal to satisfy the hunger and thirst of the improvised guests. She was busy preparing hors d'oeuvres and cocktails, which the servants offered to the crowd.

Dr. Sommers telephone to Dr. Morton in Biloxi, asking for his help. He explained to him the situation as it was. He must leave and go to France, and I have a shortage of doctor at the hospital Sainte Cécile. Dr. Merville was still in recovery and could not ensure by himself, the service at the hospital. Dr. Suzanne Birmingham went home the same day the governor lifted the quarantine. It was not a big surprise. Dr. Morton promised to come personally with two other doctors; the time for him to put his family affairs in order.

Elsa Morgan enjoying the euphoric and joyful atmosphere that reigned at the Petit Palais, brought Charles Lewis. She talked to him for a moment and sent him to renew his courtship of her niece, Michelle. She was sitting alone, melancholic and miserable, in a corner of the library, in the middle of the general rejoicing.

Charles Lewis, poured cognac in two glasses and approached the girl saying:

Your sorrow in the middle of this explosion of joy and happiness broke my heart. I came, unable to live without your beloved presence, to renew my offer once again, and rekindle my love and drop my life at your feet to prove my affection.

I'm glad you're there, Charles! It's true I was bored terribly, bored here.

Hey, he said, presenting the glass to Michelle, will you drink to our newfound friendship.

To our friendship always, repeated in echo Michelle.

This sudden conversion had enhanced your beauty, Michelle, although it is a unique and effective incentive in the painful restoration of our collective psyche traumatized forever; I could never get rid of my deep sense of powerlessness; because despite my efforts I couldn't communicate to you the warmth of my love.

I love you Michelle, I need you in my life!

Come, said Michelle, let's go down to the garden; this cluttered library is not at all suitable for this kind of conversation. They walked a moment in silence, through flower filled walkways, breathing intoxicating scents of roses blooming under the tepid sun of this beautiful autumn afternoon.

Are you sure, Charles, asked Michelle suddenly? Are you sure you can give up your life of anchorite, abandon without regret, the studious and lonely existence you had lived in your isolated mansion; to follow me in my random wanderings around the world?

Michelle darling, I am ready to follow you everywhere. (Ubitu Caia, ego Caius) where you'll be Caia, I'll be Caius! I just reversed the roles in the marital rite of ancient Rome; but it is my heart panting and disillusioned that I offer you, do what you want with it, as long as you're happy.

Let's sit down on this bench she told him. I warn you, she continued, I'm a capricious, selfish, independent girl and jealous; don't adventure if you want to live your life in peace and comfort...

You say that to discourage me Michelle? I love you and all the rest is literature. I don't want to know anything else; I will devote my life to you. He kneeled he kissed the young girl feet, as a sign of complete submission...

What are you doing there Charles? Stand up!

Michelle helped the young man to stand up and kissed him passionately, moved to tears by this eloquent testimony of deep worship.

Charles and Michelle returned directly to the private office of Simon Morgan, next to the library, where were gathered the close family: Aunt Joan, Cathy, Elsa, Harry and Mona Lisa, Bernice Merville, Joyce Hollemberg, Carl and Isabella.

Michelle went to sit with Cathy and Elsa who were chattering head to head. These ladies interrupted their conversation, scoot over to create a small space for Charles Lewis.

Charles and I, we decided to get married soon, said Michelle raising her voice so everyone in the room could hear.

Congratulations, my dear, said Elsa, kissing her. The whole room did as such. They surrounded the girl, who did not expect this explosion of joy at the announcement of the news of her engagement. Isabella took her aside:

You got to tell me everything Michelle! Your poet came back to you as I predicted?

Come later at home taty has invited Charles to dinner... Take Carl; there we will be more comfortable to talk.

I don't believe I could come. I have so many things to prepare before my departure to Europe.

How! Petite secretive, you were leaving and you didn't tell me anything?

I am accompanying Carl, who must get there, to settle a matter of inheritance.

Carl, indifferent to all this brouhaha, to all this fuss, was writing feverishly (using notes gleaned here and there) an embryo articulated the scientific project that he intended to develop in the Symposium of professor Chausssonnet at the Sorbonne.

People came to greet him particularly. They were surprised to see he was still under the spell of this black curse. To those who hazarded the question to him, he answered, invariably: this is my natural color, I'll not become white.

Some people thought he was making fun of them. Others took offence of his so called, haughty attitude of this arrogant nigger. This treacherous impostor who had managed to win the favor of the elite society, through an unfortunate misunderstanding.

Dr. Morton, Chief Surgeon of the Invalids hospital at Biloxi and his team, was the first to cross the military cordon which applied the quarantine imposed on the city of Montjolly

He headed to the Petit Palais, where Dr. Sommers was awaiting for his arrival. Doctors Ashley Martin and Christina Henry, who accompanied Dr. Morton; took refuge at the Petit Palais. Dr. Morton, was housed at municipal villa near the Town Hall, in the room exit by Dr. Birmingham the day before.

Sommers led them to the hospital and left them in the hands of Dr. Merville. Sommers thanked his friend and went to rejoin Isabella who was already impatient.

Elsa and Simon wished bon voyage to the two lovers. Amélie brought a cup of coffee to Dr. Sommers, telling him:

You didn't have enough sleep; it will keep you awake on the road.

Thank you Amelie, said Sommers, you indulge me a little too much in this house...

Simon, visibly worried, was still making recommendations to Sommers, who nodded helplessly; pleading, glancing on the side of Elsa. Let go the children Simon, they must be at Jackson before two o'clock. They could miss their flight. Said Elsa to her husband.

Isabella kissed her father, Nestle her head on her mother's shoulder whispering: thank you Elsa, I'll be sage as an image.

The Cadillac was running at full speed, on the damp road, strewn with dry leaves, on that sunny, late autumn morning. Bare shrubs, spiky pointed arrows, lined the path. The naked and sad trees had not yet isolated the landscape, which protested the arrival of the winter season with all its strength.

I have long dreamed of making this journey with you, Carl! Sitting in your outdated old Cadillac. You will never be able to imagine how much happy I am!

My love, I will not even try. Said Carl Sommers, throwing a furtive glance at his companion. It is sufficient that you say it, I am convinced. Your blue eyes' sparkling shards have unveiled for me, unequivocally, the depth of your feelings and the intensity of your happiness.

Darling, do you think that the Director of the Bank will be there? You know him?

I had saved his mother, a difficult amputation. Jack Kurt promised me he would be there; I have no reason to doubt his word.

Indeed, the Director Jack Kurt was waiting for them sitting in his car, parked in the middle of the deserted parking lot of the imposing building of the Bank.

Kurt got out of his car and walked to meet Dr. Sommers as soon as he saw the yellow Cadillac stop in front of the Bank.

Punctual to the rendezvous, said Sommers, reaching out.

I'm glad to finally, help you at something, replied the Bank manager.

I present to you my fiancée: Isabella Morgan.

Ha! She is Simon's daughter. Pleased to make your acquaintance, said Jack Kurt, squeezing her hand. Let's go to our business, doctor! He said indicating the Bank doorway.

They went directly to the safes room. The Director introduced a key in the armored lock and told Dr. Sommers:

You let me know when you are finished; I'm in my office.

Carl Sommers unwrapped a few items remaining from his parents. Precious memories that had willed to him, aunt Hélène. A few yellowed photos, which told his happy childhood in the bosom of his family. His picture sometimes with his father, sometimes with his mother. Photos of his first communion, his first day of class; irreplaceable treasure he kept religiously. His diplomas, his sports trophies, and so many other trinkets that he cherished with devotion. He chose some pictures of him with his parents, especially with Monique. Took his birth certificate, an extract of the wedding certificate of his parents, put them in an envelope.

Isabella wanted to see, read everything... There is no time for it, sweetheart... You would do it upon our return. Sommers called the Director after putting the rest of his business in the safe.

I thank you once again, said Sommers handing his key to Kurt.

I wish you a good journey and success in your endeavor. Said Kurt preceding them towards the exit.

They arrived at Thompson Field, Jackson international airport, about one o'clock. After recording their luggage, they followed the long parade of travellers who would be subjected to a thorough and intrusive search.

This vexatious practice implemented since the tragedy of September 11th, don't facilitated trade or tourism, the two most profitable sources of revenue of the country.

From the Kennedy airport, where they landed about five o'clock; they went directly to the Sax Fifth Avenue. Isabella bought: A white suit by Christian Dior, an evening gown water green of De la Renta, a Pierre Cardin ash grey suit. She then accompanied Carl to the Ricks on Broadway, where she acquired two suits for her fiancé: a three pieces steel grey and the other dark blue with thin strands a bit clearer. Isabella became angry, because Carl insisted without receding to pay for those purchases.

Carl darling, this is the last time that we quarrel about this issue of money. I gave you my heart, my soul, my youth, my life, costless gifts that you have accepted with gratitude, which are worth more than any fortune, more than any wealth, more than anything material ... Money is nothing my love. What you brought me worth hundred, thousand times more than all the fortune of the world. Everything I have is yours for life. My love transcends the petty conventions, the narrow prejudices. Let's live our love in the ineffable fullness of a passion out of the ordinary. Elsa already told you that my grandfather left me a fortune. Let me pamper you, Mon amour, to my liking, it makes me so happy.

You're right, dear love. I offer you my apologies, said Carl embracing his fiancée. It will never be anymore an issue between us, I promised.

They went to dinner at John's restaurant. Where they had taken their first meal in head to head, during their brief romance in New York.

Contrary to the last time, Isabella ate with good appetite; while her companion eager, anxious, not knowing what a welcome his French relatives reserved for him, what a disappointment could be in the work for him; what about the testament; he drink and watch his fiancée who smiled to comfort him.

CHAPTER XV

A supposed breach in the security cordon at Kennedy airport in New York, delayed for a few hours the departure of air France airbus to Paris. The aircraft remained nailed to the runway, for five hours.

This stupid incident, (in fact, a false alarm) put the security services and the FBI agents, in a slaughtering mood which didn't facilitated things.

They forbade the control tower to allow takeoff or landing of any aircraft, as long as they wouldn't give the green light.

After much harassment and an endless wait, the plane flew, finally, at dawn.

It was impossible now, for Isabella; landing at Orly Paris, on Monday afternoon at two o'clock, to follow the itinerary she had built carefully with a railway employee help.

The train to Saint Brieux had already left Saint Lazarus station a long time ago. Carl and Isabella, a little upset, caught the monorail bound to the city of Rennes, their only chance to arrive on time at their appointment with Mister Auguste Lavignac, in Saint Brieux, the next morning at ten o'clock.

They did not have the courage to wait the departure of the train to Saint Brieux. They hired the service of a tour guide, who drove them to their destination.

Isabella had booked two rooms at the hotel Ker Moor, a luxurious building ultramodern, glass and steel, located at center .The medieval cathedral, massive and imposing construction, (a touristic attraction), that brought many visitors to Saint Brieux. Notary Auguste Lavignac's studio was closed.

An unpleasant surprise was waiting for them. The Director of the hotel, claiming their late arrival, had disposed of their rooms. The cause was a group of Italian tourists.

The tour guide offered to lead them to a better hotel, but very far away from their meeting place. They declined the offer and accepted the luxurious penthouse suite that the director put at their disposal.

Exhausted from fatigue and frustration, they felt still happy to finally take a well-deserved rest.

While still at the desk waiting for their key; another couple approached the counter with the same complaints:

I booked a room eight days ago. I gave you my credit card number, and you have the nerve to tell me baloney? I do not ask, I demand you to give me a room immediately.

Listen! Madam of Carcassonne, we have committed an unforgivable mistake. It is a very serious mistake, I agree, stammered the Director trying to justify himself. The computer seems, had not registered your reservation. I am so sorry of this embarrassing situation. I am sending you (at our expense), Green Oak Hall.

It is too far from the city center, replied Mr. Carcassonne, in an outraged tone, we have a deal in town early tomorrow morning.

Dr. Sommers! Called him the hotel manager, do you want to grant me a big favor?

As you can see, I'm caught in an unfortunate imbroglio. You alone can pull me out of this mess.

You flatter me sir. But I do not think that I can help you. Said Sommers, just amazed by the request of the man.

This is! He told him, pleading. Your suite has three bedrooms. It is obvious that you need only two. Do you want to make me the favor to host the Carcassonne in your suite?

What do you say Isabella? Said Dr. Sommers turning to his fiancée.

I do not know, she answered. Is the hotel manager a guarantor for them?

Of course, hastened to say Mister Thibaud the hotel manager.

Those are honorable people. They are in the region, I guarantee their respectability.

In these conditions, said Isabella, we gladly accepted to host your guests.

Mr. Thibauld himself, led the two couples upstairs. It was, indeed, a luxurious apartment with a comfortably furnished living room, a dining room of four seats, and three large bedrooms.

Isabella chooses the first bedchamber, Carl moved to the middle and the back room went to the Carcassonne.

About seven o'clock in the evening, Isabella came out of her room wearing an elegant pink organdy dress. She knocked at Carl door:

Are you ready my darling? I'm starving.

I am joining you in a minute, said Dr. Sommers, without opening his door.

In the meantime somebody rang at the entrance door. Isabella intrigued, asked:

Who goes there?

Master Thibauld, replied the voice hoarse and powerful of the director.

Enter! Said Isabella, opening the door.

Master Thibauld entered the apartment followed by three maids, pushing a table filled of victuals.

The maids covered the table in a jiffy. They lay down in the middle of the white tablecloth a crystal vase with a bouquet of red roses.

Leaving her room, Dr. Sommers remained amazed by the preparations for the meal. Master Thibauld invited Pierre de Carcassonne and his wife Adele to join his guests.

It will not been said, began Master Thibauld, (when everyone was sitting around the table) that I did a hitch in the good reputation of French hospitality, without repairing my blunder, by offering this dinner with champagne for my honorable guests. Bon appétit ladies and gentlemen, excuse me, once again for the inconvenience I have caused you and wishes you a pleasant stay at the Ker Moor hotel.

Master Thibauld opened the bottle of champagne, poured everyone a glass and proposed a toast to the health and happiness of his guests.

He then, discreetly, left, leaving two servants at the disposal of the guests.

The two couples became more acquainted. At the mention of his name, Adèle de Carcassonne exclaimed:

Are you not this doctor Carl Sommers who stunned everybody watching TV? Are you not the author of the highly controversial theory, praised in scientific circles: The Non Compensation of Dispersed Energy?

That's me! Replied Dr. Sommers a bit surprised. I didn't know people were interested in my theory?

Then, outbid Adèle de Carcassonne, speaking this time to the girl. Are you Isabella Morgan the great pianist who charmed the world by her artistry, both delicate and brilliant?

You flatter me dear Madam, replied Isabella who blushed under the compliments of the French lady; I am merely a dilettante; I don't deserve all these eulogized epithets.

Don't be modest dear mademoiselle, intervened Pierre de Carcassonne. We listened, Adele and I, to your Montjolly live concert. This little jewel of hometown had smoldering both your talents. It was a real treat. It has been a long time since I heard a so dazzling interpretation of the concerto for piano in A major by José Vianna da Motta. I was pleasantly surprised by the mastery of the execution and hopelessly charmed by the elegant simplicity of a subtle and passionate rendition.

Master Thibauld had offered a feast to his guests. It was little beside the huge profit realized, with their rooms for a large group of Italian tourists who wanted to stay at the Ker Moor for two weeks.

There was Salad Niçoise, a slab of bacon and potatoes with caviar, a dish of sauerkraut, a quiche Lorraine, crepes Suzette, champagne, wine, and liquor. A real treat.

The conversation centered on the town of Montjolly, quarantine and especially the black curse that flanked a terrible scare for the white population of the world.

Dr. Sommers had to explain everything in detail to Adèle de Carcassonne curious who kept asking questions.

The meal completed, the doctor gave each of the servants fifty euros. Isabella slightly tipsy and very tired was falling asleep, yawning ostensibly. She eagerly was awaiting this magpie of Adèle de Carcassonne to finish Jabber to get up from the table.

Pierre stood first and wishing a good night to his new friends, dragged his wife to their room.

Dr. Sommers led Isabella to her room, she took off her shoes and lay down all dressed. I am going to call Elsa to communicate the latest news.

When he got his mother-in-law at the other end of the wire, the girl was already deeply asleep. Sommers narrated to Elsa the vicissitudes of the journey, from Kennedy, the perilous airport incident, the crossing by cab from the city of Rennes to Saint Brieux, his misadventure at the Ker Moor hotel and his unexpected meeting with the Carcassonne.

Whom they hosted in their suite and shared their meals.

Isabella is sleeping all dressed in her room, said Sommers, answering a question from Elsa. I'm going to bed mother, we have a long day ahead tomorrow and I'm falling asleep.

He remained a few minutes still to contemplate Isabella who was sleeping curled up on herself. He bordered her, extinguished the ceiling light and left the room.

Dr. Carl Sommers rang the reception of the hotel and asked if they could make available, for the duration of his stay at Ker Moor; a luxury car and an experienced driver.

The receptionist replied that the hotel did not have such a service, but they could get him what he needed in addressing a specialized agency.

You can hang up Dr. Sommers, said the receptionist. I'll call you back in a few minutes.

Although he slept very late, writing down, the version of his theory on Non Compensation of the energy dispersed; Sommers awoke very early the next morning. He was already ready when he heard someone knock at his door:

Enter! He says the door is open.

It's me, Carl darling; I can't operate the zipper of my dress! Do you mind helping me?

She furtively kissed her fiancé and turned the back of her dress slit up to the belt.

Your bra is not closed either! Carl awkwardly, undertook to close the clip. His fingers touch the girl skin, soft as silk, and she shivered slightly. He then closed the zipper, rather uncooperative, pressing gently with his left hand, the light fabric on the hip of Isabella.

Thank you, she told him, usually Elsa takes care of these small things. I see that you can replace her fairly well like that, my darling. I'll finish to dress soon.

Fifteen minutes later, Isabella reappeared, dazzling of beauty, wearing a yellow dress (her favorite color) jolly and protocol. She wore red pumps and had in her gloved hands a matching red leather bag.

You are stunning, my beautiful love darling, Carl told her, while pressing her fiancée on his heart.

You're looking very handsome today, said Isabella. But, don't look at

me like that! You are making me blush.

Come on, sweetheart, he said, it's time to go. They went downstairs arm in arm.

Gladys the receptionist came to meet them as soon as she saw them approaching the counter. Dr. Sommers I settled everything. I present to you Rémy your driver.

Thanks Gladys told Dr. Sommers quietly sliding in her hand a one hundred euros bill.

And then reaching out to the driver wearing white uniform:

I believe we will get alone great Rémy, I present to you my fiancée Isabella.

Glad to know you miss, replied the driver by tilting the head, his way of saluting.

Rémy, said Sommers, we have an appointment with Mister Auguste Lavignac at ten o'clock, do you think we can make it in time?

 The notary studio isn't far from here, doctor, we have plenty of time.

Then! Let's go.

A convertible Rolls Royce was waiting for them in front the Ker Moor hotel. Rémy opened the door for Isabella. It is chilly this morning, that's why I haven't lowered the top; Rémy explained closing the door of the car.

Less than twenty minutes later, Rémy stopped the Royce before an old three story building on a street so narrow that the balconies on each side were almost joined. We are at destination doctor! Said the driver who hastened to open the car for Miss Isabella. I cannot wait for you here; this is my mobile phone number, call me when you done.

Very well Rémy, nodded Sommers taking the card the driver handed to him.

Supporting his fiancée who wore stilettos heels shoes, Sommers went up the narrow steps of the building porch. A sliding glass door (certainly, a recent innovation in the old building) opened before them.

They entered a fairly spacious vestibule where a few people (no doubt customers) were sitting waiting for their turn to meet Mister Lavignac.

They approached the counter where a young receptionist was busy storing documents in a large workbook.

I am Dr. Sommers, I have an appointment with Mister Auguste Lavignac at ten o'clock.

Follow me, doctor, says the girl who headed toward the stairs. Mister Lavignac was waiting for you.

It was a wide staircase with a slick ramp that led directly to a large room, summarily furnished with two rows of seats separated by lined driveway which lead to a large desk lifted on a stage.

 Dr. Sommers announced the receptionist with a singing Marseilles accent.

Mister Auguste Lavignac, immediately ran to meet the new comers.

I am glad to meet you Dr. Sommers, said Mister Lavignac, and happy to be able to contact you. Welcome to Saint Brieux... Hey Hey! As well as your companion...

I present to you my fiancée: Isabella Morgan, said Sommers, who had properly interpreted the hesitation of the notary.

Delighted to make your acquaintance dear mademoiselle. Come, I will present to you the interested participants.

A dozen people were sitting on lined up chairs. Some cast a furtive glance at the couple, but all remained silent, almost indifferent.

Dear friends began Mister Lavignac when he came near his desk with the new entrants; I present to you the Dr. Carl Roger Sommers, (son of Monique) and his fiancée, the talented and beautiful: Isabella Morgan.

At the forefront there were: Hugues Simonet, his wife Joëlle de Foix and his two children Hubert and Mireille. In the second row were: Pierre de Carcassonne, his wife Adèle de Foix, cousin of Gaston de Foix (Carl's grandfather) and Julienne Cassale (niece of Simone

Cassale: wife of Gaston de Foix;) (Grandmother of Dr. Sommers).

In the third row at the same aisle side, was the old Geneviève de Foix: a remote cousin of Gaston de Foix, André Cassale: Simone de Foix's brother and his son colonel: Henri Cassale.

Joëlle Simonet, eyes reddened with tears, holds the son of her sister, strongly on her heart. She was visibly moved and repeated: the son of Monique! The son of Monique! You see Hugues, she said, addressing her husband; Carl is the living portrait of father; to what, Hugues, pinched and dreary, agreed loosely.

Dr. Sommers greeted all the people around and presented with pride his lovely fiancée.

Pierre and Adèle de Carcassonne told everybody how they had shared the meal with these two charming young people and how much they had enjoyed the hospitality that they had offered them so generously, without knowing them.

The clerk's solicitor brought forward two armchairs and sited Carl and Isabella next Joelle, the aunt of Dr. Sommers. Mister Auguste Lavignac black dressed, lustrous

hair and moustache, opened a safe placed in a corner of the room

and withdrew a metal suitcase closed by a combination padlock.

The clerk opened the metal suitcase, took two large sealed envelopes and placed them on the desk of the notary.

Ladies, ladies and gentlemen, began Misster Lavignac in a solemn tone: the verbal instructions of the viscountess Simone de Foix, (before her death a few hours after this airplane tragedy) recorded in the presence of many witnesses; demanded that I waited at least a year before opening her authentic testament to allow the study Lavignac and son, to locate her grandson, (Carl Roger Sommers) the only child of her eldest daughter: Monique Thérèse de Foix.

The notary breathed loudly after this tedious output tirade with a monochord, professional voice.

His brother-in-law Gérôme de Foix, perished at the scene of the tragedy, in this terrible accident. The viscountess also asked me to postpone the execution of the will of her brother-in-law, as long as the prescribed period required.

The notary sought the presence of a member of the family, to check and testify the original authenticity of the seals on the envelopes containing the viscountess Simone and brother-in-law Gérôme wills.

Hugues Simonet was delegated by his wife to perform this role.

This October 20th , 2007 in the presence of the Justice of the peace of the section East of the town of Saint Brieux: Jules Pollidoc and Gontran Marcillac lawyer from the bar of the same location: I, undersigned, Mister Auguste Lavignac, having recorded the last wishes of Mr. Gérome de Foix, formulated in full knowingly and voluntarily...

Let's spared you the reading of the rest of this long preamble to enter the part that interested you the most, obviously. Forwarding the will, the notary Auguste Lavignac was smiling maliciously.

I bequeath to my lovely niece Joëlle and her devoted husband Hugues: The Valley Manor, my personal residence and the lands attached to it.

I leave also: one million euros to draw on my account at the Bank of France.

To my little nephew Hubert Simonet, I leave 10 thousand actions, my investment in the South Aviation business, over 20 thousand euro to allow him to continue his law studies at the University of Sorbonne.

To my little niece Mireille Simonet: I leave five thousand shares I own in the automotive manufacture company Peugeot and 40 thousand euros to complete her medical studies in an exclusive institution.

To Adèle de Foix, my dear cousin, I leave two hundred fifty thousand euros to draw on my account at the Bank of France.

To Geneviève de Foix, I leave one hundred fifty thousand euro to draw on my account at the Bank of France.

To my good friend and adviser: Mister Auguste Lavignac, I leave a hundred thousand euro.

To each of the clerks of the study Lavignac and son; I leave five thousand euros.

I leave sealed, the names of the persons to whom I paid a monthly allowance. I ask my principal legatees (in this case Hugues and Joelle) to continue, in my name, this charitable organization.

I'll spare you also the reading of the last part of the testament, in which my friend Gérôme had made a very accurate and well detailed, arrangement for his funeral. "Sic transit gloria mundi" sententiously declared the notary. "Man wishes but God accomplishes " as said the old adage.

Unfortunately, Gérôme de Foix never had any vested funeral oration. Despite this tedious curriculum that the old bachelor himself had written to his solemn last rite.

Mister Auguste Lavignac proposed a short interlude to the assembly, during which he offered: tea, coffee, wine and other strong drinks and a plate of appetizers.

André Cassale and his son, the colonel, drank three fingers of cognac, despite the early hour. Giulia ate mouthfuls of hors d'oeuvre and drank, back-to-back, three cups of tea. The Carcassonne drank coffee. Hughes swallowed a glass of wine to drown his disappointment and keep his phlegm. Genevieve, preferred biscuits that she crunched noisily, while drinking, swig after swig, soft sparkling white wine.

After chatting for about fifteen minutes here and there with his customers, the notary went up and sat down at his walnut desk.

The testament of the Viscountess Simone de Foix, recorded and our care; signed by the protagonist and countersigned by us and the identified witnesses.

The preamble to this testament is very important, so I will read it to you.

This Monday, January 3rd of the year 2000

I, Simone Cassale, Viscountess de Foix, in full possession of my faculties physical and mental, healthy in body and spirit, in full freedom, I write this testament to distribute (after my death) fairly and according to the ancient tradition of the family; the hereditary estate of the Visconti de Foix.

The death of my husband the Viscount Gaston de Foix, although it was a terrible rip and a disconsolate sorrow; it gave me the opportunity (since he was opposed in his lifetime) to search my grandson, Carl Roger Sommers, the son of my beloved Monique Thérèse, removed too early from my maternal affection.

Our research so far remained unsuccessful. I barely know him. I have seen him in some rare photos received in secret that my daughter sent me, (at the early days), at the address of my brother André.

If I die before you find him, I asked Mister Auguste Lavgnac to move heaven and Earth to contact and find him, so that he could enjoy the benefits and privileges granted to the heir apparent to the Visconti of Foix.

In the event that it would be impossible to contact Carl Roger before the deadline set by the law; the inheritance would go to the cadet branch, that is, my adored daughter, so good and so dedicated: Joëlle Beatrix de Foix and her husband, the incomparable Hugues Simonet.

The Visconti of Foix, including: the castle of Val d'Armor, the fifty thousand hectares of land utilized for forestry and agricultural enterprises that depend on and income from the leasing of land. The Assembly plants, the real estate agency; everything will be on the reading of this testament, the exclusive property of my grandson, Carl Roger Sommers, Viscount de Foix; exclusive heir (through his mother) my eldest daughter, the late Monique Thérèse de Foix.

The capital deposited in different banks amounted to 25 million.

Before I continue reading, I have to make a small correction to the figures in the testament dating back to the year 2000. Today, according to the latest estimates, the Visconti has thirty one million euros in Bank.

All of you know the tradition attaches to the Visconti: undivided trust, who has survived intact, from generation to generation, for the prosperity of the entire region.

To my daughter Joëlle I bequeath two million euros on the accounts of the Visconti,

To my stepson, Hugues Simonet agronomist I leave one million euros.

To my Hubert, the pride of the family, I leave five hundred thousand euros.

To the apple of grandma's eyes, the charming princess Mireille, I leave five hundred thousand euros.

It is now to the new Viscount or the new Viscountess; as we have found or not Carl Roger; to exercise his or her prerogatives; (according to a tradition dated from the time of the Crusades) to show generosity by allocating to the other members of the family gathered for the occasion, the amount as he selected to offer them.

I am calling on Viscount Carl Roger, said Mister Auguste Lavignac making a great sign of the hand. Come put your signature at the bottom of this document before proceeding to the second phase of the execution of the will.

Dr. Sommers was stunned, struck with this shocking occurrence. Paralyzed by this extraordinary reversal of fate that tormented his substantive life. His existence suddenly took a new and unexpected fate. Overwhelm by emotion, Dr. Sommers bowed his head and wept.

Isabella and Mireille surrounded him; their moving affection, made his eyes bathed in tears; while encouraging him to regain his senses.

See! My darling, said Isabella, also, on the edge of tears; the notary is expecting you, come on!

She took the arm and forced him to stand. Mireille supporting him on her side, they dragged him, more than anything else, to the desk of Mister Lavignac.

Facing the fait accompli, Dr. Sommers found the strength to regain his composure; and fulfill with dignity, the role assigned to him by this reversal of fortune.

Under critical eyes of his two charming guardian angels, Sommers signed the documents introduced to him by the notary Lavignac. When he finished, Mister Auguste Lavignac took his hand, lifted it and proclaimed with his doctoral voice:

Ladies and gentlemen, I present to you officially the new Viscount de Foix: Dr. Carl Roger Sommers.

A muted applause welcomed the words of the notary. Dr. Sommers who had taken over his senses, to excuse this moment of weakness, unworthy of a man who has survived so many adversities, known a lot of ups and downs in his life.

I firstly thank Mister Auguste Lavignac for his boundless dedication to the Foix family. His solicitude towards the Viscountess Simone de Foix allowed me to be here, surrounded by my loving parents instead of being this orphan without hope.

I am happy and proud to carry this prestigious title and I promise to all of you, that I will wear this investiture with honor and dignity for the greater glory of the family.

I want to share my good fortune with my parents, so this memorable day will be as auspicious and happy for you as it is for me.

To Adèle de Carcassonne born de Foix: I allocate Five hundred thousand euros.

To Pierre de Carcassonne two hundred fifty thousand euros.

To Geneviève de Foix: two hundred fifty thousand euros.

To André Cassale: Five hundred thousand euros.

To colonel Henri Cassale: two hundred fifty thousand euros.

To Julienne Cassale: Two hundred fifty thousand euros.

To Mister Auguste Lavignac: two hundred fifty thousand euros.

Each of the clerks of the study: ten thousand euros.

The signatories of the testament witnesses: Judge Jules Pollidoc and Mister Gontran Marcillac: five thousand euros to each of them.

The uptight atmosphere of the room unbent immediately. Everyone approached the desk to compliment, thank or give the embrace to the new Viscount de Foix.

Viscount! Called Mister Lavignac with a sententious bonhomie tone: we have to go to the Bank now, if you want the recipients of your largess to be able to cash or deposit their check.

I am calling my driver, continued Mister Lavignac, in five minutes he will be there.

I will call mine, preferably, I am going to vehicle you today Mister Lavignac, said Sommers, responding with kindness to the excessive politeness of the notary.

Gladys, the receptionist of the study, came personally announce the arrival of his driver to the Viscount and without taking notice of the severe apoplectic looks, of Mister Lavignac, threw herself into the arms of the Viscount to thank him.

Gladys! Gladys! Recalled her, boss very amazed.

Thank you! Thank you very much Mister the Viscount, says the girl who didn't give a damn to what, for the moment, could say or do Mister Lavignac.

The notary is visibly excited, because he wanted to lead Dr. Sommers, but, solicited everywhere, failed yet to take leave from his new parents, eager and grateful.

The old Geneviève de Foix, felt and immense joy. In human memory she said, to whom wanted to listen to her; it was the first time we could see so munificent legacy. This young man demonstrated an extraordinary liberality. That God lends him a long and happy life.

Julia Cassale, the neglected one, was stunned. As usual she came expecting a meager sustenance; and receiving what she considered to be a fortune: a trifling sum of two hundred fifty thousand euros; She threw herself at the feet of Dr. Sommers to thank him. He helped her standing and took her in his arms. Julia nearly faint from pleasure and gratitude.

Cassale senior lost his usual phlegm and came to make his oath of allegiance to the new master of the House, so generous and so unpretentious.

The colonel, put himself at the disposal of the Viscount. He had a great knowledge of the area and offered to the Viscount to guide him through woods and glades of the Viscounty.

Adele wanted the Viscount as host for dinner at the Ker Moor hotel, to celebrate this providential reunion. However, Joëlle announced to everyone that the reception will be held at the Manor du Vallon, and she was waiting for them at eight o'clock.

Mireille was fond of Isabella at first sight. You are so beautiful! She told her, I've never met someone as beautiful as you. To what Isabella replied: me either I've never met a pretty girl than you, Mireille.

Without flattery, I can return your compliment. You'll be the little sister I never had. I already love you very much, confessed Isabella.

Mireille asked her mother if she could accompany Isabella in her visit to the city. I can show them, the direction to the mansion when she and my cousin Carl Roger will come for the reception.

Mister Lavignac, anxious and nervous, finally led the Viscount to the exit. The notary sat in the front of the car, Mireille inserted herself between her cousin and Isabella.

The Bank of France, said the notary to the driver who drove away immediately.

First we are going to fill the administrative paper and give a copy of your signature, so the Bank could validate the checks. Then, we will go to the Credit Lyonnais Bank, then at the real estate agency (headquarters of the Viscounty administration), to present you to the director and the employees.

The highlight of the day will be the visit of the castle of Val d' Armor at Beauvallon, declared emphatically the notary in verve. I am an amphitriyon guide, said Mireille, I know very well the Castle. Before we are going to have lunch at the bistro of the elm, continued the girl; it is a picturesque and charming restaurant; In addition, to its excellent cuisine.

You are dear cousin my private amphitryon. I trust your gourmet taste and your talent of tourist guide.

Are you kidding me Carl Roger?

God forbid my cousin, I am not teasing; but seriously I am flattered to have one so charming and devoted cousin to guide me through this enchanted region; as Ariadne led Theseus to escape from the labyrinth.

Carl is a professional flatterer, Mireille darling, said Isabella, I didn't think that he would have begun so early with you!

See Isabella, this is not nice what you say there, you painted me with a very bad brush to my cousin. I have never laugh at people I am to a gentleman for that.

In this case, I apologize...

They arrived at the Bank of France. Mister Lavignac presented the Viscount to the senior employees of the institution; like he was his creation.

From there, they went to the Prefecture Le Goff Street, to certify his title and claim his French passport.

The extreme zeal of Mister Lavignac had been, already, royally rewarded. Really, he didn't expect such munificence on the part of this young man. His relationship with the Viscount started under favorable auspices. Also he deployed his science to initiate his illustrious client to the affairs of the viscounty, and ensure, by thus, his influence on this generous novice.

Leaving the Prefecture, Mireille asked Isabella, the name of the driver. His name is Rémy, replied the latter.

Rémy, called Mireille, do you want, please to switch toward the Cathedral? It is not far from here.

We don't have time to visit today, Miss Mireille, replied the notary.

Who spoke about visiting? I only want to show my cousin Isabella, this massive medieval construction, built as a fortress, with towers, battlements and embrasures.

I'll turn left. I'll do anything to please Miss, announced Rémy. Joining the gesture to the words, he made a sudden turn around and run into a narrow street lined with redbrick houses shaped with protrude balcony and wrought iron balustrade.

The Rolls suddenly arrived at the Cathedral square. Straight fairways planted giant Elms, which somewhat obstructed the view; we can't see well this impressive building, this magnificent masterpiece of gothic art.

Rémy was forced to bypass the immense square and engage in a side street, to allow his passengers to admire the imposing Basilica.

At the Real Estate Agency, the executive director: Raymond de Blezier, greeted with an affected deference his new boss.

He presented his employees to his improvised guests...

When he wanted to explain to the Viscount the vagaries of the Real Estate market down for the moment, because of the global recession; the notary was opposed outright, saying: we have to go elsewhere, Director; today it was a courtesy visit by the Viscount.

As soon as they sat in the Rolls Royce, Mireille said to Rémy: we are going to the Elm Bistrot at Beauvallon... All these visits, she, continued (speaking this time to her cousin), make me Hungry. Are you starving also Isabella?

I did not dare to complain, given the particular circumstances of this day; of course I'm hungry, I did not eat anything yet.

I do not believe Carl Roger has eaten either? He is too upset, continued Mireille, to think of the prosaic things of the daily life.

The patron of the Bistro, a statuesque woman with a prominent cheekbones, and red hair cut short, came to meet them as soon as the car crosses the entrance.

What a pleasant surprise! Says the redhead. Miss Mireille, even more beautiful every day.

Yvette replied the girl; I bring my cousins to taste your cuisine.

We are all very hungry...

You might at least introduce to your relatives? Yvette was outraged and pretended to be disappointed.

My cousin Carl Roger, the Viscount de Foix and his fiancée Isabella Morgan.

Yvette opened her large almond shaped eyes; the blood rushed to her crimson cheeks and remained stunned, openmouthed for a long minute. She recovered, however, soon. Enchanted to know you Mr. Viscount, she says with a stereotypical smile, I hope you become a client of the bistro of the Elm?

Why not, dear Madam, we are neighbor, aren't we?

You want a table for four that I see?

No! For five, corrected Isabella.

I heard you Madam, please follow me.

They crossed a large room where many outspoken tourists ate. The Bistrot de l'Orme, to what it seems was very busy. They were taken in the courtyard of the restaurant, surrounded by a tight row of Elm trees. These giant trees planned their oblique and crisscrossed shadows on the circular area reserved for the banquet of the customers.

The bowers decorated with multicolored balloons, ribbons of bright colors; draped flags and banners, embellishments of climbing plants; served as a decor for this unprecedented and rustic gastronomic experience.

The crystal tinkling and tintinnabulation of the bells brightened the atmosphere and made even more charming this beautiful decor. A vast and silent pond where a flock of white snow swans swimming majestically.

Peacocks doing the wheel, wandered among the tables, pecking crumbs with indifference.

Just sitting, a servant brought to each of them, a bowl of bouillabaisse with buttered rusks. Mister Lavignac, a bit offended by the presence of the driver on the table, unbent a little, with the first spoonful of soup swallowed. A white wine of the region was served to sharpen the full bodied taste of this Provence specialty.

Isabella and Carl, unaccustomed to this very spicy food, drank a sip of wine at each spoonful, to try to soothe the burning sensation in their palate.

A maid removed the bowls, another wiped the crumbs from the table, while a chubby cook brought in a large wooden tray, steaming plates of an omelette with herbs and a large dish of black apples pudding. The wine went from white to red.

Everyone ate with excellent appetite. The conversation was reduced to a few inexpressible onomatopoeias expressing satisfaction and pleasure.

The driver Rémy and the notary Auguste Lavignac were the only ones to enjoy the wild hare stew. Mister Lavignac literally licked his chops and declared: I have to visit the campaign a little more often; I stayed lock in my office too much. Princess Mireille compliments! You have the flair of a true gastronome.

We will not dwell further here. It is already four o'clock; we still have to visit the castle of Val d'Armor. Then get ready for this evening's reception; concluded princess Mireille who took in charge the itinerary of this hectic day.

The maid brought the addition directly to Dr. Sommers. It was already giving his credit card, when Mireille interposed:

Carl Roger you are my guest... don't you do that.

Dr. Sommers threw a furtive glance at his fiancée and promptly handed the note to his cousin.

Thanks, Carl Roger.

Dr. Sommers slipped fifty euros under his glass half filled with water. Isabella did as much, the notary left twenty euros and the driver Rémy put five euros under his.

Yvette accompanied them to the car and thanked the Viscount to have honored the Bistro of the Elm of his visit from his first tour in the region.

The castle of the Val d'Armor, former country residence of the counts de Foix, was bequeathed by Henri IV, King of France: (the last count de Foix), to his nephew Jacques d'Albret. He had distinguished himself in the battle of Paris) where the Henris' clashed with rage and determination. Henri III King of France; Henri IV King of Navarre and Henri 1ˢᵗ the Lorraine Duke de Guise. The coalition of Henri IV, won a decisive victory over the Catholic League, led by Henri de Lorraine Duke of Guise.

To reward his nephew for his bravery and especially to avoid eliminating completely the illustrious lineage of the counts de Foix, Henri IV made him Viscount de Foix, in 1489, Lord and master of a hereditary domain.

Royal decree creating the Viscounty stipulated, among other innovations, the right of succession by women. The Viscounty had pass intact to each heir apparent, (according to the mandatory clauses governing the succession, by order of primogeniture) i.e. by birthright.

In his prescience and for ensuring sustainability and prosperity of the area and its inhabitants, King Henri IV codified a series of regulations that are still underway so far.

Thus spoke Mireille Simonet, Princess de Foix, improvised historiographer; coming up to the castle of Val d'Armor.

The notary got out of the car, took a set of keys in his suitcase, choosing a square shaped key, he activated the electronic mechanism of the gate, and it opened as provided by sesame.

Mr. the Viscount said Mr. Auguste Lavignac emphatically: I am giving you the keys to your lovely domain, may the grace and the protection of the Lord be always with you.

The notary went back to the car and the Rolls Royce slowly crosses the barrier that closed after them. Rémy accelerated to climb a stiff slope of the hill leading to the doors of the castle of Val d'Armor.

Dr. Sommers was taken by a sudden dizziness at the sight of this imposing building with white walls, a blue slates roof, the last rays of the setting sun has put in perspective. That was his castle... The princely residence which he had long dreamed to offer to his beloved Isabella... This was a miracle... The sky had forgiven him his wrongdoing... He was grateful.

He took his courage in both hands, and smiled to his fiancée who hold him by the arm. It is even more beautiful than the Petit Palais, said Isabella, in her naive admiration. It was there, a familiar term of comparison to externalize her feelings towards this dream house which will be hers soon.

Princess Mireille joined and took the keys from the hands of her cousin. She climbed the seven steps of a granite porch and opened the massive door, iron studded to the old fashion way. The door slipped on its hinges without any resistance against the frele and delicate young girl.

Albert, the guardian, appeared at this time, his rifle in hand, a little out of breath. He stopped recognizing Mr. Lavignac:

It is you master? I wasn't informed of your visit. Ah! Princess Mireille! He said seeing the girl standing near the entrance. You have some dealing with the castle?

Yes Albert, said Mireille the Viscount Carl Roger is coming to visit his home.

Albert threw his rifle on the impeccable lawn of the park surrounding the castle, and felt to his knees before Dr. Sommers:

Welcome, my Lord, I am Albert Silvorac, faithful and devoted servant of the House since thirty years.

Dr. Sommers took the arm, I'm happy, Albert, to have you at my service.

It is mademoiselle Monique Thérèse who had employed me, may her soul rests in peace.

They entered a broad Flagstone lobby of marble. On each side, and back-to-back walls, were war armor complete with helmet visor and spearhead of battle. The wall was lined with many hunting trophies.

Viscount! I must leave, said Mr Lavignac. My car has arrived. I leave you with Princess Mireille who knows the nooks and crannies of the castle, for having lived here since childhood.

He took the Viscount aside, and handed him an envelope telling him: to open in the master bedroom; instruction of the Viscountess Simone. I am at your service; you've been more than generous to me and my people, I thank you once again.

Carl Roger called Mireille, when the notary was gone; she stood before a lithograph of the castle in the 17th century by Géricault.

As you can see in this drawing, the architecture is different from the archaic, massive and complicated structures of this time. The castle had not been built to support sieges or deal with an enemy, but as a secondary residence for the Counts of Foix, (hunting and racing enthusiasts) whose main abode was their huge feudal Castle at Foix.

The building has three floors, continued the young princess, and has a trapezoidal roof surrounded by a parapet with balusters, who toured the building. Three rows of windows with multicolored tiles embellish the rectilinear facade. Flanked on his left, is a polygonal tower topped by a dome. The entire construction takes the appearance of a home much more sophisticated than it is in reality.

From the top of the tower of Albret, people dominates the entire valley of the Côtes d'Armor and the Bay of Saint Brieux. More than the castle itself, the twenty acre park that surrounds it, is a breathtaking beauty; announced Mireille with pride; rejecting her hair back in an elegant gesture of feminine coquetry.

It was getting dark in the hallway. The sun sets early at the end of autumn. Mireille switch up the light, saying:

We could see the house better. They crossed, without really stopping, a suite of rooms, one more spacious than the other: lounges with antique furniture with a discreet and aristocratic luxury. They visited the immense ceremonial dining room and the formal every day one. They lingered in the spectacular kitchen, the weapons Gallery where are exposed, in addition to a wide range of weapons of all kinds, the portraits of all the Viscounts and Viscountesses of Foix, since Jacques d'Albret until Gaston XV and Simone Cassale de Foix.

Look! Isabella, you recognize this person? Asked Mireille in approaching an array of portraits.

But, it's Carl!

Don't talk nonsense beloved Isabella. How could I be already hanging on that wall?

Come take a look, yourself, she told her fiancée.

Dr. Sommers remained speechless; it was indeed his portrait, only a bit clearer obviously.

He is the Viscount Archibald d'Albret Grailly portrait .He was the Viscount from 1738 to 1821

When you entered the room this morning, at the notary studio, Hubert made everybody laugh. He said up loud: Viscount Archibald is mingling among the living. What a shame!

Isabella was taken by an irrepressible giggle. Her contagious good humor reached Carl Roger who laugh also at an hilarious pun.

We have no time to go down to the basement, said Mireille, still laughing out loud. There are two staircases leading to it, one at each end of the castle.

We will visit the rooms. There are seventeen bedrooms and three suites. Each of the suites has three bedrooms, a living room and a dining room. This amount to a total of twenty-six bedrooms. As said my father, we could house a full regiment of legionnaires here.

Dr. Sommers was unquestionably pleased to listen to his cousin: princess Mireille. She deployed her eloquent zeal to explain in detail the history of the castle. He lingered a bit too long at the panoply of ancestors hanging on the walls of his castle. In addition, there by a miracle unheard of heaven, he found his family that he believed was lost.

Isabella who was already preparing to climb the monumental staircase leading to the upper floors, returned on her steps. Let's go my darling! You'll have plenty of time to ruminate about everything, she said, giving him a stealth kiss.

What time it is? He asked to his fiancée.

Five forty five, she answered, it is still early.

Do you know where is Rémy?

I have no idea.

Mireille has also came back. I'll inquire is whereabouts Carl Roger don't worry.

She approached the wall, where there's an intercom and says:

Albert, do you know where is Rémy, our driver?

He is with me Princess, do you need him?

 Bring him on the first floor; the Viscount wants to talk to him.

Very well Princess, we are on our way.

The couple went up to the first floor, where Mireille introduced them in the intimacy of the Lords who had, at one time or another, lived happily with their families; in this house, now, abandoned and sad.

The Viscount wanted to see me, said Rémy when he was in his presence.

 How long from here is the Ker Moor hotel? Do you know very well the area? I guess so, replied Remy.

Mr. Viscount we are about one hour from the hotel. I just told

Albert, the guardian that I had to return with the car at seven o'clock at the latest, but, I don't know what the Viscount himself had decided.

That's annoying! What do you say Mireille?

What? She asked, because she was not paying attention to the conversation between her cousin and the driver. What do you want to know Carl Roger?

The driver has just told me that he has to leave. Therefore we will have to cut short the visit, so that we can go to the hotel and change, in order to arrive on time at the reception.

Rémy, come this way, I want to speak to you, ordered Mireille without consulting her cousin. Mireille led the driver in the hallway, handed him one hundred euro, telling him: on the part of the Viscount. You can go on we will call you tomorrow morning.

Thanks mademoiselle, you save my life.

Mireille came back in the room, we continue the visit I have everything arranged with Rémy.

The rooms were opened except one. My cousin gives me the keychain I handed to you ?

Here it is, said Isabella while rummaging through her handbag. It is the room of grandma; I do not know why it's been kept locked?

Oh! The beautiful room! Cried Isabella who was a connoisseur in that field.

. The bedchamber was furnished with a modern and sophisticated way. Curtains, rugs, four poster carved bed... If I had to choose, it is this one that I would choose?

I don't understand you at all, Carl and you my dear Isabella this is your house. All the rooms are yours. This is your house that you are visiting dear cousins; the rooms belong to you Cousin Isabella. I don't know why Carl Roger wants at any price to return at the Ker Moor?

But, Mireille, replied Dr. Sommers, this is where we staying; our luggage is there. We must go to change.

Mireille dropped herself full length on her grandmother's bed and burst out laughing as a hysterical lady. She beat the mattress simultaneously with her arms and her feet and seemed to have suddenly lost her mind.

What's going on , Mireille asked her cousin Carl Roger?

She said, sitting on the bed, I've sent Rémy home. I gave him one hundred euros on your behalf, my dear cousin. You are at home. I am telling you once for all. You have an army of maids and servants at your disposal, (just touch a word to Albert). Therefore you don't need the rental car, because you have a stable of luxury cars in the basement: Bentley, Rolls Royce, Mercedes, Citroen, you name it? I don't regret coming here with you...

What have you decided for the rest of the evening, cousin Mireille? Asked Isabella unflappable.

I am glad, at last, you become reasonable my cousin!

Firstly we complete the visit.

What remains to be seen? Asked Sommers submissive.

The tower answered Mireille. The library, the octagonal office, laboratory and Observatory.

You say that there is a laboratory in the tower?

Of course, said Mireille, who couldn't imagine someone could doubt her knowledge of the castle.

Let's see the tower! My darling cousin.

It was nearly six o'clock when they descended on the first floor.

It is now too late to get to the hotel. How will I go to aunt Joëlle?

Just wait cousin Isabella. Mireille entered a room and opened a cupboard which occupied a whole section. All of these dresses are your size. She took her in two other rooms, make your choice.

Let's take a bath? The maids are en route to help us dress up; we will be ready on time. Don't worry sweetheart; the Manor is only a half hour from here.

I will take care of the recruitment of a temporary staff; go tell your fiancé he can find a tuxedo in the adjacent room to grandmother.

Isabella went in search of Carl, who she found in the modern room reading something.

What are you doing here my love? Asked Isabella a little intrigued...

I am reading grandmother's instructions that will allow me access to the vault of the castle. The notary handed me this sealed envelope before leaving.

Dr. Sommers carefully, read the instructions twice and proceeded to the opening of the first hurdle. The wall cracked showing a narrow door that faded under the pressure of his hand applied to the right place. He then discovered a large safe recessed in the wall.

He wrote the code and pulled to himself the door who gave way. Isabella followed with interest the conduct of the operations. Carl first, took the two heavy solid gold crowns, set with precious stones, and passed them to his fiancée who put them on the bed. He pulled out then five gold bars, an ancient bag full of Dukes of florins, ecus. Piles of plates and medals, a gold diamond encrusted crucifix.

In a lower floor of the safe, he retrieved a heavy metal case; he brought it himself on the bed. It contained, (he didn't lingered to count them), adornment of diamonds, rubies, emeralds, Topaz, turquoise, sapphires, pearls; of all shapes and all sizes.

He chose a full adornment in Topaz, and another in diamond, he slipped surreptitiously into the pocket of his jacket, when Isabella moved back the crowns into the trunk. He closed the safe, put it back in its place, and made the same with other items.

He just closed the bulkhead when Mireille entered the room by saying:

I was looking for you Isabella, the maids have arrived, and they will help us get ready.

My cousin says Mireille, I leave you in the expert hands of Clemence, grandma's maid, I used the services of Laure; she worked for mother, when we lived in the castle.

Clemence welcomed Isabella with the usual astonishment of those who met the lady for the first time.

You are so beautiful? She said peering her from head to toe. The Viscount is a very lucky man. He had discovered the most beautiful lady.

Enough compliments, Clemence, you make me blush.

I have prepared a bath for you, Madam…I've poured a balm for you to relax your body after this tiring day. How should I call you Madame?

I am Isabella, replied the girl, a little embarrassed and on edge by the untimely familiarity of the maid.

Clemence wrapped Isabella in a robe of wool and wiped her body vigorously, to, (according to big Clemence) accelerate the circulation of the blood, everywhere.

I don't have underwear Clemence? What should I do?

You actually have plenty Madam Isabella; I took the freedom to prepare everything while you're in the bath. Pantyhose and black bra, yellow dress glitter gold, tight at the waist, flared skirt; color gold shoes and a small handbag. I understood at the first glance that madam favorite color was yellow!

You have noticed?

Of course, and anything else yet.

What do you mean Clemence? Put me in your confidence.

It's too intimate things, too personal, I don't know if I could dare?

No matter what it is, I won't be mad...

Since madam insists: I had observed with great surprise and much notable appreciation that Madam is still a virgin...

What! How can you know such a thing?

I had warned you that it was intimate things. Whispered "Clemence who was aware of having committed a blunder. Excuse me madam, I ask you to forgive my indiscretion.

I'm not mad at you, only surprised that, at first view, you can identify my virginity status. Are you a witch?

Everyone asks me the same question. No Madam I don't practice witchcraft. It's a natural gift, a gift of the providence.

CHAPTER XVI

While chatting, Clemence was busy with an iron, curling Isabella hair. In no time, she made her a beautiful hairstyle, curls and frizz, arranged in tiered cascade that fell on the shoulders and on the back of the girl.

She then helped Isabella dress, helped put on her shoes and make her a light makeup, just to emphasize the beauty, said Clemence, of your delicate velvet skin.

I do not know if Madame would like to wear gloves; anyway, I took the liberty to put in your handbag, a pair of gloves with the toilet kit and a lavender scented batiste handkerchief.

You think at everything Clemence?

It is the job that requires it, Madam. You are splendid. You look tonight like the marquise de Pompadour.

Flattering tongue too? Clemence! I think I'll keep you in my service.

Thank you Madam Isabella, I thank you a thousand times! Among other things, the dress you wear belonged to mademoiselle Monique Thérèse, when she was about your age. She was a nice lady. Only the princess Mireille has her resemblance.

They knocked on the door. Who there? Said Clemence who hastened to open the door.

Ha! The Viscount cried Clemence. Madam Isabella is ready.

You may enter.

Darling my love! You are beautiful. You'll overshadow everyone. You're even more beautiful than when I saw you on the beach for the first time. God! You were so lovely then!

Don't begin Carl! You put me upside down, when you speak to me like that.

I just came to ask you to fix my bow tie. I never knew how to use this thing.

If Mr. the Viscount allows me?

Go ahead

In a jiffy, Clémence fix, impeccably, the bow tie at the neck of Dr. Sommers.

Then speaking to his fiancée, he told her that something was missing in her outfit.

What is it Carl darling? You just tell me that I was perfect.

Of course, but. Turn and closes your eyes. She did so obediently. He took in his tuxedo pocket, the topaz necklace and passed it around her neck; closed the bracelet on her slender wrist, then hung the earrings at the sensitive lobes of his fiancée.

You can open your eyes now. Go look at yourself in the mirror!

You look great.

You shouldn't have... stated Isabella...

What do you say Clemence?

The Viscount is a man of taste. Ms. Isabella will be the most beautiful lady at the reception tonight.

Dr. Sommers discretely slipped a twenty euros bill in the of the apron pocket of the maid saying: go tell the princess that we are expecting her in grandmother's room.

Carl Roger! Said Isabella (as princess Mireille would say) you look like a true Viscount tonight! They burst into laughter. You're ruining my makeup.

Me! Are you kidding me Bella mia?...

What so funny? Asked the princess intrigued.

You are the prettiest girl in town, my cousin! You are incomparably chic and elegant. She was all dressed in white.

But, insisted Mireille, what did you do to make Carl Roger laugh like that?

Isabella said, imitating your musical accent: Carl Roger you look like a true Viscount tonight!

Mirielle burst into laughter. You said it well cousin Isabella, Carl Roger is definitely handsome, he has the princely look of a seasoned aristocrat.

Isabella you are wearing your topaz adornment? When I got home I will put my jewelry.

Come, nearer my cousin, we'll tackle the problem immediately.

He puts to his cousin's neck a river of diamonds, and handed over to Isabella, a bracelet to clasp on her wrist and earrings to hang at Mireille ears.

Carl Roger, said Mireille, as a thank you, you are an exceptional man in less than a day, you have won the hearts of all your subjects.

Mireille kissed her cousin telling him: thank you, it is a beautiful ornament; you're too generous Carl Roger....

Norbert the driver of late Viscountess Simone, resuming the service chooses the luxurious white Bentley, to drive the Viscount, his lovely fiancée and the Princess Mireille, to the reception in their honor. Norbert had glossy the body of the car, which shone in the spotlight that illuminated the Park of the castle of Val d'Armor. He was waiting at the wheel, the arrival of his new bosses. As soon as the front door opened, Norbert went down and came to pay his respects.

Norbert, said Mireille, I present to you my cousin, Carl Roger and his fiancée Isabella.

Glad to know you Viscount delighted to make your acquaintance Miss Isabella; said Norbert, by bowing deeply.

We are going to the Manor Du Vallon, said Mireille to the driver, in intercalating herself between Carl Roger and Isabella, who wanted to sit next to her fiancé, obviously.

You know, said Mireille, as soon as they had crossed the barrier: it is only since the death of grandmother and my uncle Gérome, we went live in the Manor. We lived all in the castle, but, father said that he couldn't maintain this mogul's life, because the money did not belong to him.

It will depend on him to return, said Carl Roger, this house is too big for the two of us anyway.

I'll try to persuade him. It is the most restive of the band.

If I understand well, intervened Isabella, you rule everybody with your magic wand? Isn't it my cousin?

Isabella, you are too insightful for me. In broad daylight, you have unveiled my little secrets. Your fiancé won't walk under my command. He is already in the column of the intransigent; is it true my cousin?

They burst out laughing. Norbert, who knew well the Princess, and her authoritarian, but conciliatory nature, smiled behind his large mustache. He understood that the new Viscountess won't be easy to handle or manipulate.

Isabella and Carl had spent a great day with Mireille. The contagious spontaneity of the girl, (even as a teenager) had conquered them. Instinctive affection she had shown them from the first moment; made them forget the dramatic change that had occurred in their life, and the inevitable anxiety, inherent to any sudden rehabilitation.

Joelle and Hugues Simonet received their guests, standing under the porch of the mansion, illuminated for the occasion. Joëlle had a glare, and grasp her husband arm to avoid falling; seeing Isabella descended from the Bentley.

She believed seeing her sister Monique, in a stealthy retrospective vision, in this sudden amazing appearance.

Her sister wore this same yellow gold flaked toilet. She sported with this majestic posture of a queen, this same topaz adornment. She was capped in the same way, with the same profusion of blond curls falling on her shoulders. She descended from the same car returning from a reception, holding her father's arm; thirty years ago...

What happened to you my love? Asked her husband, suddenly alarmed.

A slight dizziness... nothing serious, it is already gone.

She recovered soon, indeed. Hugues could guess the cause of her discomfort. All this had happened before she met him a few years later.

She welcomed her nephew with a boundless outpouring of tenderness and hugged Isabella and whispering, in the hollow of the ear: "I love you very much, my darling, you are beautiful".

I love you to, Aunt Joelle, you are to kind.

Joëlle loosened her hug to admire the beautiful creature coming to comfort her premature loss of her older sister that she so admired. She embraced Isabella on her heart, once again.

Mireille observed from a distance, but with a real satisfaction, develop this affinity between her mother and her cousin. She could already count on it, to persuade her father to return to the castle.

Hugues look your daughter, said Joëlle to her husband.

My pretty Princess is even more beautiful this evening. You are truly beautiful sweetie. I noted with pleasure that your cousin had spoiled you already, and how? Said Hugues Simonet, touching the river of diamonds at the neck of his daughter.

In the grand salon of the Manor were reunited, the family and some friends. Hugues presented the Viscount and his fiancée to the Mayor of Saint Brieux: Bruno Métoncourt and his charming wife Hélène.

The only other official in the room was the young and brilliant lawyer, Councillor: Jacques de Boucard accompanied by his lovely wife: Fabiola de Alcantar.

The Carcassonne had cornered the Viscount, bombarding him with questions. They presented him to the Advisor Boucard, a progressive, said Pierre de Carcassonne; a man of the future who will go very far.

The Viscount was overwhelm by the abundance of attention directed at him and did not know what to do. His aunt came and pulled him from this embarrassing situation by inviting everyone at the table.

Aunt Joëlle had killed the fatted calf to accommodate with pump and circumstances, the arrival of her prodigal nephew. It was a true feast of King.

The meal finished, Isabella gave an improvised recital. She played a few of Beethoven sonatas, a few waltzes of Chopin, and two pieces by Debussy. Then accompanied by Hubert on cello and Mireille at the violin, she played the trio in B major by Brahms.

The pathetic accents of this original and passionate work enchanted the audience. The artists were warmly complimented for their brilliant performance.

Then, the musical group «Les Trouvères» entertained the guests, until three in the morning. All the men wanted to dance with Isabella. The Viscount, him, requested by the ladies, danced without interruption and without interval.

The alluring Fabiola de Alcantar (wife of the Advisor: de Boicard) wanted to dance only with the Viscount. Isabella followed from a distance her subtle courtship, her languorous gazes, her sliding fingers on the shoulder of her fiancé and rubbing against him with lewd gestures.

Isabella was not worried unduly; her man had resisted much more dangerous attacks, but she knew. She trusted Carl, but, she would have to keep this Minx in tight leash, when she'd come to live in the region.

Isabella, much more than the Viscount, was the star of the evening. They admired her beauty, her talent, her kindness, her natural ways of being a lady, her contagious good humor.

They hardly took leave from the guests, who did not want to let them go; hailed their parents and went out stealthily in a hurry.

They remained silent during the ride back. Isabella cradled herself on the soft cushion of the Bentley, puts her head on the shoulder of her fiancé and felt asleep.

She drank too much, danced all night; on her feet for over eighteen hours; she couldn't bear no more.

The Viscount handed his keys to Norbert so he could open the door of the castle. Isabella was still asleep; her fiancé had not the courage to wake her up. He took her in his arms and carried her into the Viscountess Simone bedroom; the room Isabella preferred among them all.

Clemence came immediately; I am in charge of the rest, Mr. the Viscount.

Above all, don't undress her. She likes to sleep with her dress.

Good note is taken, Viscount I am going to fix her hair and take off her shoes, that's all.

How many people sleep at the castle? Can you tell me Clemence?

There are Laure the chores lady, Andrea the cook, and I who reside here. The other lodged in the outbuildings adjacent to guardian Albert's villa.

Thank you said the doctor going away...

I took the liberty to prepare the room vis-à-vis for Mr. the Viscount.

Great! Clemence, good night.

He found a grey blue Pajamas spread on the bed, a matching gown, suspended from a hook carved walnut and a black leather slippers.

He lay down, but could not sleep. The day's events greatly upset him. In an instant, he had become rich and successful, adored by a large family he had just meet miraculously.

He couldn't even believe it. It was an extraordinary reversal of fate. It was an incredible miracle, an unexpected favor from heaven to his humble servant.

A little drowsy, lost in his thoughts and flooded by fatigue, he didn't hear the door to his room open. Isabella still wearing her yellow dress in gold flakes climbed on the bed and lay down next to her fiancé saying:

Horrible boy! You have left me sleeping all alone in this big unknown house...

What are you doing here? Said Sommers suddenly awake. Dear Isabella, it is inappropriate. You cannot come sleep in my bed. What will think the servants?

Carl darling, since when we obey the ridiculous conventions of this hypocritical and corrupt society? Everyone hides behind social conventions to act badly. As had told my mother "it is inappropriate already to travel alone, without chaperone, with her fiancé. But "honni qui mal y pense" Let's call mother. She is certainly worried.

Isabella saying. She nestle her head in the shoulder notch of Carl.

It is ringing, he said handing the phone to Isabella.

Hello mother!

Isabella answered the questions of her mother: we were at a reception in honor of the Viscount de Foix. The Viscount de Foix: is Carl Roger Sommers. Let me just tell you dear Elsa, starting from the beginning.

Comfortably installed, Isabella made a detailed account of all the events that occurred during the last 24 hours.

She told (thread in needle) their arrival at the hotel Ker Moor in Saint Brieux. The suspect episode of their exchanged rooms against a suite; the meeting of the Carcassonne, whom were also invited at the opening of the wills at the notary of Mister Lavignac. Isabella didn't spare nothing to her mother. The largesse of Carl; the visit to the prefecture, to homologate the noble title of the Viscount de Foix. The visit to the real estate agency, (the administrative center of the Viscount); lunch at the bistro of Elm; the visit of the Val d'Armor; everything that has occured. The timely intervention of Carl's cousin, the beautiful Mireille Simonet, Princess of Foix, as guide and historian. The discovery of the secret vault, a true cave of Ali Baba that left them gaga. She took a particular pleasure to tell the highlight of the day, the reception at the Manor, the home of the aunt of Carl : Joëlle Simonet.

She talked during one hour to her mother, without interruption, and fell asleep in the arms of her fiancé, who had fallen into a deep sleep shortly after the beginning of the conversation between Isabella and her mother.

Isabella turned on her side, her right leg was now entangled inside her fiancé's legs; they slept entwined like two lovers.

Dr. Carl Roger Sommers, Viscount of Foix, awoke the first. He was really embarrassed to find himself in this compromising position. He felt the breath of the girl on his face and smelled the sweet and delicate fragrance that emanated from her languorous body.

He dared not make the slightest movement, fear of wake her up. Isabella slept like an angel, confident, and abandoning herself completely to the respectful affection of her companion.

Isabella woke up; finally, she smiled with real satisfaction. Dear Carl, she said with her proverbial naïveté: I never slept as well in my life. I warn you, dear Viscount, I will never sleep on a pillow again. Your shoulder is a thousand times better than the softest pillow.

I am going to my room, she said, before that nosy Clemence came snooping in what that is not her business.

Don't bother! No need to flee like Cinderella, darling, Clemence came twice already to see if I was awake. She certainly saw you in my arms.

So, no need to hide. Besides what do I care!

Carl got up from the bed, put his robe and called Clemence through the intercom.

Yes! Mr. the Viscount, answered the maid.

She entered the room, a smile on her thin lips saying:

Madam slept well? Hello Mr. the Viscount. Are you taken your breakfast here or near the poolside?

We don't have bathing suits?

Madam has everything in her house. I'll be back in a moment.

She returned very quickly, in fact, she brings three bathing suits: a blue, a black, a yellow. Madam may choose. She gave the Viscount a red bathing suit and a bathrobe of the same color.

Carl, I'm going to change, said Isabella leaving the bedroom. I'll be back momentarily.

The Viscount was waiting in the large hallway, dressed in his bathing suit and bathrobe. Isabella appeared, her hair collected in a silk scarf, imprisoned under a plastic cap. She wore a flat heel yellow sandal and the yellow swimsuit that sheathing her svelte and splendid body.

No comments please! Viscount, said Isabella who had read in the eyes of her fiancé, that same look of fire that had seduced her at their first meeting.

Where are we going? Asked the Viscount to Clemence?

Follow me please.

At the end of the corridor on the right, they borrowed a hiden stairway (common in the typical architecture of the time of the construction of the castle), which directly led to the small chapel richly decorated, furnished with upholstered armchairs and priedieux.

The pretty chapel cried Isabella!

At the time of the Viscountess Simone, taught them Clemence, a priest came to say mass every Sunday for madam and her guests.

They left the chapel through a side door open directly onto the pool area. It was a beautiful facility located inside a glass cage. It was heated automatically as soon as the water reached a certain temperature and throughout the winter.

A sliding door gave access to the discovery terrace, where was the chairs, lunch tables scattered here and there.

The terrace dominated a large part of the Park populated by all sort of trees. The Park stretched out of sight until the bottom of the hill.

Andrea, the cook, came to present her respects to the Viscount, she asked madam what she wanted to eat.

Prepare us one of your specialties. Andrea, said Isabella, bring us first very strong black coffee.

At once said Andrea.

The pool was heated during the winter, said Clemence. The water is very good now. Dr. Sommers plunged into the pool and invited Isabella to do the same.

They played like two children. It was the first time they bathed together. Matter of fact, it was the first time they fully enjoy their intimacy, participating in such enjoyable activity.

Andrea served, andouillettes grilled with buttered toasts, curdled milk with grenadine syrup, gruyère cheese corn cakes, baked in the oven.

If I don't watch myself, said Isabella, who ate with good appetite; the cuisine of your hometown will swell me like a cow.

You should have said rather, retorted her fiancé: the food is excellent in my castle of Val d'Armor. I should watch myself, orherwise, me, Isabella Morgan Viscountess de Foix going to swell like a cow.

But the castle belongs to you Carl?

Isabella I gave you my soul, my heart, my life; everything I got is yours. You are the only thing that matter to me. Without you Isabella Morgan, life is worthless for me. I love you more than you never could imagined.

Isabella her eyes watering like fountain, kissed her fiancé without a word.

After this hearty breakfast, Albert offered them a horse ride to visit the Park and the immediate vicinity of the vast domain.

Back from the tour, they deepened their exploration of the big house. Carl went to the tower, more specifically at the sophisticated and modern laboratory, which could emulate the installations of the same kind that he had visited.

Isabella retreated in the library, to be more acquainted with the ancestors, leafing through family photo albums, aligned on a long shelf.

Laura brought the mail to madam; as she used to do from the time of the Viscountess Simone. The Viscount French passport had arrived. Loads of people invited the Viscount to dinner, shows, others sought an interview, to expose their grievances or present their curriculum.

Isabella went to find her fiancé, perched at the top of the tower, with a powerful telescope, observing the strange maneuvers of a war ship, in the Bay of Saint Brieux.

Isabella admired the magnificent landscape spread before her, head resting as in the usual on the shoulder of her fiancé.

From distance to distance from the white hamlets aligned along, slope to slope of the hill, to the edge of the sea.

Honey! Said suddenly Isabella: why don't we pay a visit to the staff? If we must trust them, then at least we have to know them.

You are the mistress of the house; you know better than me in fact how to manage a home. Let's go sweetheart.

A narrow path paved with bricks led to guardian Albert's pavilion and dependencies where the other employees of the castle lived.

Arm in arm, they arrived at the small charming pavilion. Isabella rang at the entrance. A woman in her fifties came to open the door. Seeing them, she cried, turning inward: Albert, Mr. the Viscount.

Albert appeared immediately. Mr. the Viscount, Mrs. Isabella, enter please. They entered a small lounge, simply furnished where the last rays of the setting sun penetrated galore by a large glass window.

Emma just greets Mr. the Viscount. My wife told them Albert with a certain pride in his voice. But, sit please.

You have no children? Asked Isabella to Emma.

My son Julien is an infantry captain; my daughter Rose is married and lives in Rennes, Emma replied with a smile.

No grandchildren? Asked Isabella.

Yes! A pretty girl, her name is Louise.

Compliment Emma, said Isabella.

Albert, I would like to meet the staff of the castle, the people you have recalled yesterday. I would also like to know the amount of their salary.

I'll do what is necessary, Mr. the viscount.

Can I offer you something? Asked Emma.

Tea, if it is possible said Isabella.

Hum! Says Isabella, this tea is superb. Where do you buy it Emma? I would like to bring some to my mother.

We cultivate the aromatic leaves that fall into the composition of this mixture. I still have some left, not much, but I think I can pass you two dozen teabags.

Thank you very much.

Albert gathered all the staff under the porch of the pavilion. Viscount! Says Albert, everyone is gathered outside.

The Viscount and his fiancée shake their hands. There were: Clemence, Laure and Andrea and Norbert, they had already met. JeanLuc the mechanic, Pedro the head gardener and his wife Conchita who had the burden of the laundry and Grégoire dealing with the maintenance.

I am very pleased to know you, the Viscount tells them. I give each of you a fifty euro wage raise, effective immediately.

I'll be away for a few days, I will return in a month, continued the Viscount; I note with pleasure that the castle is well kept. Continue to do your best.

The Viscount took leave of his servants, they were happy with the way he welcomed them.

Isabella telephoned aunt Joëlle, when Andrea came to ask her what she would like to eat for dinner. We are going to dinner in the city, tonight. Prepare us something for tomorrow morning preferably.

Very well Madam, may I bring you a drink?

Thanks Andrea, we just drank tea at Emma's.

I am expecting you, therefore, at six o'clock, explained aunt Joëlle to Isabella. The representation of Cyrano de Bergerac (by the itinerant troupe of the Comédie Française) begins at eight o'clock. Be punctual, so we can have time to go to dinner at the Authentic Restaurant, near the train station; before going to the Modern Theatre, located in the old quarter of the ancient city.

Have you already bought the tickets, aunt Joëlle?

Not necessary; the Viscount has a private lodge at the Modern Theater.

During the aperitif at the Authentic Restaurant, Hugues Simonet asked Carl Roger if he could come tomorrow morning, so he could give him the record of his management of the Viscounty since the death of the Viscountess Simone and uncle Gérôme.

It is not possible uncle Hugues, explained Carl Roger, I am expected in Paris tomorrow evening, invited to a symposium at the Sorbonne by Professor Saurel Chaussonnet.

I formally promised to be there, I can't default on my commitment at the last moment. Advise me uncle! Continued the Viscount, I do not know if I have to travel by train or fly.

Paris is only three hours from Saint Brieux; asked Norbert to drive you. He can guide you through the city of light (he is a former taxi driver in the capital) you will keep his services through the duration of your stay in Paris.

I am not coming back here. I returned directly to the United States. I must attend the wedding of Isabella's brother.

How! Uttered loudly Mireille who followed with a discreet

attention the conversation, you are already leaving Isabella?

Carl must go to Paris for two days; then we fly to the United States; not only to attend the wedding of my brother Harry, but especially to fulfill his obligations to the hospital Sainte Cécile where he has been in charge for a year.

There are no other doctors in this hospital? Asked the Princess.

Precisely, Carl has been replaced by a friend and two other doctors from a nearby town. He needs to go relieve them. They had given him eight days.

And, when your brother's wedding? Asked Mireille in a sorrowful voice.

On 21st November. Soon after, we will return to Saint Brieux, as we decided, Carl and I, to get married here.

Have you already chosen a date, cousin? Said the princess whose somber mood disappeared at the prospect of a grandiose wedding at Val d'Armor.

On the 21st of December.

Ask mother to take care of the publication of the wedding. I believe that it spans over three Sundays. But, when are you coming back cousin Isabella? Inquired again, Mireille with a turnover of grief in her throat.

If all goes as planned, as soon as Carl finds a replacement at the hospital to help doctor Merville. You can except us by the first week of the coming month.

Only Isabella took a delectable pleasure attending the performance of the incomparable masterpiece of Edmond Rostand. The others: the Viscount and Hugues Simonet in business discussion, paid little attention; anxious, Joëlle, fearing drastic changes in her train of usual life, with the arrival of her nephew, Hubert who was thinking of his transfer to the Sorbonne and Mireille visibly upset by the precipitated departure of her cousin Isabella; gave only sporadic attention to the play.

During the trip back, the Viscount explained to Norber his travel plans. Norbert concluded that it was an excellent idea and that he would ask JeanLuc, the mechanic to designate a suitable vehicle for the journey.

Dr. Sommers took the opportunity to go down to the parking garage that was in the basement, just below the chapel.

They were about 20 cars, a landau and two golden carriages. The Viscount chooses a Mercedes, the most recent car in the stable; for the trip to Paris.

Darling, said Isabella entering the modern room, should we bring some small souvenirs to your volunteers: Dr. Morton, but especially doctors Ashley Martin and Christina Henry, who stand at the Petit Palais, do you think Carl?

We will delve into the cave of Ali Baba, said Carl.

Take this gold watch for Simon; this emeralds adornment for Mona Lisa, as a wedding gift; Elsa doesn't need jewel, trust me my darling, we will buy a few trinkets for her in Paris.

Look, at those two small pretty money boxes! Let's put this pearls adornment and one ecu, and, this rubies bracelet in the other with a guilder. This is for the ladies!

We will buy two costumes for Dr. Morton, shirts and ties. Your friend is always wrong dowdy; this is not to criticize him...

I'll give this ring to my girlfriend, Lisa Troy. She is a dedicated and discreet girl, I like her. Harry loves perfume himself we will provide the means. Amelie asked for French lingerie and a bottle of perfume Anaïs by Cacharel. I have a whole list, Isabella told him, a long list of things to buy; that I will fill doing my shopping at the Champs Elysées.

Hubert and Mireille came early morning at the castle, to wish a good trip to their cousins. The entire staff of theVal d'Armor, was aligned on each side of the porch to honor, to greet the departure of the Viscount and his fiancée.

They went first to the Ker Moor hotel, collected their luggage and settle their account. The director of the hotel: Master Thibauld didn't want to hear anything. The suite was, for free, at the disposal of the viscount de Foix and his lovely fiancée.

The noise has spread around. The son of Monique Thérèse, (the undignified and ostracized daughter) who married a black American; came to inherit the fortune and the title of Viscount of Foix. According to Adele de Carcassonne, born de Foix, who sang the praises of the new Viscount. Indeed, he showed extreme generosity toward his family.

Isabella had booked a suite at the luxury hotel: Elysees Regencia, located in the center of the Golden Triangle, i.e., between the avenue of the Champs Elysées, avenue Montaigne and the Georges V avenue.

It was two o'clock in the afternoon when Norbert entered the courtyard of the Regencia. The travelers stopped in Brest to take lunch and refueled.

Norbert ensured that the Viscount and his fiancée were comfortably installed to go looking for a hotel room, somewhere in Paris.

He would return at six o'clock to drive them to the professor Chaussonnet symposium. He welcomed with a sigh of relief, the call from Dr. Sommers announcing that he was in Paris and will be timely present.

Isabella lay on the bed as soon as she was in her suite at the Regencia. She had awake throughout the previous night, partly to choose gifts for her parents and her friends in the treasure island that was the secret safe in the modern room; but above all, because Carl had refused to let her sleep in his room next to him.

Do you know what you're doing here, Isabella? He affectionately admonished her mildly. It is not right, thus, to languish. The anxiety of waiting and the throes of desire can no longer torture your heart. Dear love, we have met with courage and confidence this terrible ordeal; we have overcome our legitimate concerns and swept away like straw in the wind, the malefic forces which opposed our love. I thought you'd be happy to live those irreplaceable moments, in the euphoria of a pure, innocent and ineffable happiness.

Carl darling, you have interpreted very badly, the visceral and irresistible, this huge attraction that you are for me. This bewildered feeling that makes me search for your presence and your warm contact, constantly. I am sorry that you're obliged to reproach me, my reckless naiveté and my excessive affection; replied tearfully Isabella.

Don't cry darling my love, trying to comfort his fiancée. He took her on his lap while tightening her over his heart. I don't blame your behavior at all, you are sure about yourself, such, that you can act with unwavering confidence. Me, I don't know the extent of my weakness. I already made considerable efforts to remain calm and resist temptation. You don't know how much I love you my love! A month! In a month will end for you and me, this torment of Tantalus which makes me suffer in waiting and happiness.

She remained a long time, her head resting on the shoulder of her fiancé, sitting on his lap, enjoying this wonderful and tender moment of intimacy. Isabella was touched, moved by Carl's confession. Carl who, for the first time, poured his soul and revealed to his beloved Isabella his unsuspected vulnerability.

Isabella kissed her fiancé and went to bed in the modern room, but didn't sleep the whole night.

Carl woke her up at five thirty. He demonstrated since the incident much tenderness and affection.

I won't have time myself to get ready Carl? If you need to leave at six o'clock.

Take your time my darling; we will go only when you are ready.

The reception of the Regencia announced to Dr. Sommers that his driver was waiting at the lobby. Isabella, despite her apprehension, was ready in time. She wore a blue suit with white velvet facings: collar, sleeves and at the bottom of the jacket. Carl, wore his steel gray suit bought in New York the day of his departure.

He locked all the jewelry that his fiancée had chosen, in a safe box at the reception of the hotel. They worth a small fortune.

Norbert led them through the illuminated streets of the capital to the buildings of the Faculty of sciences where the Conference was being held.

Professor Chaussonnet welcomed them warmly and presented them to the other participants: Anton Levine an astrophysicist of Kiev; Andrés de Costa Luna de Barcelona: a speleologist from renon; Georg Schawz of Nuremberg: doctor in geology and Oceanography; Albert Crowley of Sydney Australia: a Professor of Geodesy, expert in Geodynamics.

Dr. Sommers, who believed that the Symposium would be held in strict privacy, was surprised to find himself in a room full of journalists, scientists and others of the same ilk: the curious and idlers.

Professor Chaussonnet presented to the assistance, blasé and skeptical, the seated speakers along a table.

Professor Anton Levine opened the hostilities by declaring all at once, as the Copernican theory, although factually and indisputably proven, is not consistent with the scientific reality of our times. The assumption introduced by the discovery of quanta and the photon (called grain of light by Einstein) is different from the conventional standards that govern the mechanics of the attraction of the universe.

On one point, Ptolemy was right. The Earth although it is not the center of the Galaxy, however exercises greater influence on the evolution of the cosmogony, than the sun itself.

The fate of the universe is closely related to the inevitable vicissitudes of the planet. The poet William Blake said: the universe could be, entirely contained in a grain of sand. This visionary already compared the cosmos with a single atom in active expansion up to the threshold of the infinite.

The Earth is entering a critical phase of his ontological development. The loss of his vital energy, i.e., systematic depletion of the volume of oxygen in the atmosphere (reduced by half according to experts) created the ideal conditions to galactic disorders.

As the atom, Earth cannot exist without the volatile, indispensable and invisible core energy.

My work on quantum energy corroborate the theory of the young American scientist. He has been struck by the ineffable illumination, exclusive prerogative of men of genius.

Andrés de Costa Luna then took the floor to ring the alarm at the approach of this impending disaster: the formation of underground and underwater faults, made possible by the indiscriminate exploitation of the oil slicks seekers.

These artificial rifts that go deep in the bowels of the Earth, had made unstable the drift of tectonic plates that forcing their underground movement, cause of terrible earthquakes followed by devastating tsunamis.

Georg Schawz, developed the controversial theory of accelerated global warming. He pointed out emphatically, worrying phenomena that underline the beginning of an irreversible and aberrant mutation structural and ecological that unbalanced the earth.

All, they put the emphasis on the dangers posed to the biosphere: the race to nuclear armament, the reckless pollution of the elements, atomic and chemical waste, and the stupid destruction of the environment by this generation of hungry predators of immediate enjoyment.

Dr. Sommers stated his theory in clear and concise terms. The volatilization of petroleum by the repeated actions of refineries and combustion engines is and remains the primary cause of the apocalyptic scourges that threaten to destroy the world.

In perforating the ozone layer that protects the Earth against cosmic rays from elsewhere, carbon monoxide and other toxic gases have paved the way for space dispersed energy.

This irreplaceable loss reducing the planet creates a chain reaction which considerably decreases the chances of survival of the planet.

It is clear, continued Dr. Sommers, that recorded atmospheric disturbances lately, would not be enough alone to explain these aberrant weather change: el Niño, la Niña, the accelerated melting of the glaciers of the two poles, the increased violent weather in regions spared so far. Without introducing into the equation, the concept of the virtual axis of the Earth relief.

More the Earth feels lighter, more will widen the unusual phenomena and the dangers they pose to life on Earth.

In addition, this axial correction eliminating some points of contact with other heavenly bodies, also decrease the maximum pull of the planet at its peak, and cause a significant deviation from its gravitational curve.

This orbital gap, almost imperceptible on a human scale, has the terrifying potential of placing Earth on the unpredictable ellipse of a froleur (Apollo, Amor or Aten) asteroid approaching dangerously Earth orbit, at regular intervals, with the consequences that can be guessed.

One of this day (if we are unable to convince the skeptics and unbelievers), the urgent need for a dramatic change in how we operate and use the planet's resources; the Earth would start to drift and go, simply returning to the initial stage of its fantastic odyssey. The planet will go astray in the terrible inferno of the Kuiper belt, located beyond the orbit of Neptune. In transit before returning, emptied of its human cargo, to the elliptical orbit of Aldebaran where it will die.

The systematic exploratory probes and space telescopes, authoritatively had confirmed the exclusive originality of the Earth compared to the other planets in the milky way. Equipped with all the apparatus necessary for the maintenance of life, it is unique in its kind, next to sterile, barren and inhospitable rocks and masses of harmful gases that make up the other planets in the galaxy.

The Earth also came and placed under the protection of this decadent galaxy devastated by exterminating wars of the demiurgic and jealous Titans who destroyed themselves reciprocally.

The Earth is much older than the life it contains, but selfishness and stupidity of human are destroying the biosphere.

It is a fairy tale you have narrated here, Dr. Sommers, said one of the representatives of the oil industries in attendance. You have concocted this ridiculous fable, it seems, during one of your sleepless nights, in this town infested by the black curse, isn't it?

There are lot of fabulists, countered Dr. Sommers, who changed the course of history. I am in very good company, indeed. Einstein, with his theory of relativity; Charles Darwin, for his theory of evolution; Galilee, advocacy of heliocentric theory of Copernicus.

Robert Oppenheimer for his theory of the black hole, Christopher Colombus to have imagined the whimsical fable of a continent beyond the horizon; all were ridiculed and treated like crazy.

Did I mention Heinrich Schliemann and the mounted cabal against this simpleton, this wacky, (by all the European press) who sold the dowry of his wife to go looking for the city of Troy.

During more than a year, the newspapers and magazines of all major European cities: Paris, London, Berlin, Madrid, Rome, Moscow, and so forth, ridiculed Schlieman without mercy.

That fool of Schliemann, the illiterate, the prankster, dared to give the fable, to the fantastic story of Homer, a historic and lively reality?

When Schliemann returned with King Priam's treasure, the press plunged into consternation, had swallowing its taunts and retract its invectives.

"I rest my case".

They bombarded Costa Luna with questions about artificial faulting. Many earthquakes in depth were recorded at an accelerated pace, replied Costa Luna; have provoked devastating tsunamis impacts.

A Russian journalist asked Professor Anton Levine, what empowered you to give the title of scientist to Dr. Sommers? What have he did so remarkable in the field of science? He refused to answer the question and passed it to the person concerned.

I don't believe I have added this prestigious title of scientist in my thin curriculum, said Dr. Sommers, because I did nothing to deserve this honor. The assistance burst out laughing.

Dr. Sommers is too modest, took the floor, Professor Chaussonnet. Though he is young and fresh out of the University, Dr. Sommers has developed a revolutionary method to retrieve brain tumors without damaging the neurons. In addition, he has manufactured a nuclear serum which destroys the cancerous tumor inside the growth cells that he sprays using an instrument of his own invention. This method and this serum can revolutionize the treatment of brain cancer and embolism.

In addition, he composed a miracle ointment that has already proved its worth. This ointment erases scars, blemishes, congenital stains and all other marks on the skin, in two or three days. Many had entered the history book with less baggage.

Professor Chaussonnet concluded the meeting by inviting the participants to continue their research in their field of expertise to coordinate a smart response to this apocalyptic drama that threatens the world.

After the Symposium, Norbert led Isabella and Carl to Le Printemp for shopping. Isabella bought some gifts for her servants. Then she went to the Galeries Lafayette to complete her purchases.

Norbert took his bosses to express transport agency to ship the packages to Elsa Morgan at the Petit Palais address in Montjolly; so they could have everything at hand at their arrival.

About ten o'clock, the Viscount gave leave to Nobert, after he had driven them to the restaurant: Le Fouquet, at the Champs Elysees, close to the Regencia hotel.

Isabella and Carl returned to the hotel, walking slowly, arm in arm, along the illuminated avenue, the elegant and cosmopolitan crowd who walked with reckless carelessness at this late hour.

When she was at her boarding school in Switzerland, Isabella had visited Paris several times. She proposed to Carl to visit some monuments of the city of light.

Carl darling! I am proud of you. My instinct inspired by a striking premonition and intuition has recognized from the first glance, this extraordinary and noble man that all the girls in Montjolly wanted to steal from me.

My love! I've been struck down literally at your sight. In an introspective vision, I saw the angel who would heal my panting, wounded heart. You have transformed my life and giving meaning to my absurd existence.

For me, said Isabella clinging heavier to the arm of her fiancé; this was a profound metamorphosis. I lived since then, the ineffable ecstasy of a dream's love. I lived by you and only for you. The world would disappear without me knowing; as long as you're with me. I am exaggerating, you would say? But, believe me if you want, so I can explain this strange fascination which attaches my soul irresistibly to your soul. Fate has delivered me, body and soul to you. I thank God for it.

Bella mia! Not only you are exaggerated, but you are rambling ... This is you, on the contrary, that locks me in the jealous enchantment of your exclusive passion... It is through you that I receive haven's largesse... All this would have escaped me, if I hadn't met my goddess on the Montjolly beach.

Carl Roger! said Isabella imitating princess Mireille slightly tangy accent: nobody never told you, that you're an incorrigible flatter?

Who would dare disrespect a personality as important as me?

Carl, supporting Isabella tipsy by wine and compliments, painfully walked to the Regencia hotel. Isabella fell immediately asleep in her room; all dressed, naturally.

Isabella served as a guide to her fiancé, drive by the former taxi driver Nobert Lenfant. She stopped first at the Arc de Triomphe and visited the Place de l'Etoile.

Then she made him climb to the top of the

Eiffel tower, where he was able to admire the incomparable beauty of the city, restored by the Baron Haussmann under Napoléon III. From there, she went to the Moulin Rouge for a brief overview of the famous cabaret, because she had no time to linger to watch the show. She passed in front of the Invalides without stopping. They visited The Cathedral Notre Dame. Then, the Louvre where she stopped only for an hour. Since they now will live in France reminded him Isabella, you'll have plenty of time to visit the monuments and museums of Paris. Isabella ended the day at Versailles.

They ate, all three, in the Garden of the Roy, (a very busy restaurant) in the Général Leclerc street, in Versailles, before returning at night to their hotel.

Norbert led them very early at Orly the next morning. Their flight was leaving at six o'clock. Dr. Sommers gave the driver an envelope containing five hundred euro. He asked the Viscount when would he be back.

I will let you know in advance, because I think I would have other people with me. We will take the necessary steps in time? Nobert? Yes sir at your service.

CHAPTER XVII

The Airbus of Air France arrives at two o'clock sharp at Kennedy airport in New York. Carl and Isabella passed customs without difficulty and showed up at the Jet Blue Counter, where they had booked two tickets to Jackson Mississippi.

They arrived at Thompson Field, Jackson Airport at five o'clock in the afternoon. Carl my love, said Isabella, you are too tired to drive to Montjolly, we will rent the services of a driver at the Agency.

Let's do better, suggested Isabella to her fiancée. We rent a small car, but travel in the Cadillac; the two drivers will be able to return together, this will spare us unnecessary charges.

Isabella nestled her head on the shoulder notch of her fiancé, and fell asleep as soon as the car had left the downtown area to engage on the highway.

Dr. Sommers dozed, rather daydreamed, ruminating in his mind the events of these last days, compared to the painful memories of his childhood.

Isabella changed her position; laid her head on the lap of Carl, cradle on the seat she resumed her interrupted sleep peacefully.

Dr. Sommers rehashing the dramatic changes that occurred in his life during the past week. Besides this girl who was sleeping confidently on his knees, (the apple of his eye, his reason for living) he found his family that he believed forever lost. In addition he had inherited a prestigious noble title that brought him a respectable and unexpected fortune.

He couldn't believe it even now. This was a miracle! He remembered his mother Monique recommendations, when he left for the Jesuits boarding school:

Whatever happens, remember that you are the heir of a illustrious family whose lineage goes back to the time of the Crusades. Always conduct yourself as a man, worthy, respectful, and proud.

These recommendations had guided him and strengthened his determination to become someone to honor the memory and the wishes of his mother.

During the reception given in his honor, his aunt Joëlle had spoken at length to him. She explained to him why the Viscountess Simone had waited the death of her husband Gaston of Foix, to try to find you.

Monique was the favorite of her father. He passed her all his whims. All the squires of Brittany, local princes and rich bourgeois, had sought the hand of the most beautiful heiress in the area. She had refused to marry, wanting to continue her journalistic career and see the world.

Besides her heart had not yet spoken. Also what was the amazement of her father when she wrote to him from Lebanon, that she had fallen in love with a handsome American, a nigger. The Viscount Gaston de Foix became terribly angry. He shut the door in the nose of his favorite daughter and threatened to disown her if she persisted in her outrageous madness. The Viscount interdicted all communication with the renegade. Mother suffered much, added his aunt Joëlle, but she couldn't do otherwise. My father sworn to expulsing from the castle, anyone in contact with Monique.

Mother almost die when she learned, coincidentally, three months after the tragedy, that Monique had perished in a fire. Father became unbearable and short tempered. He made everyone miserable around him, and retreated, until his death in the Tower of his castle which became sad and silent.

After the Viscount's death, mother began research to know the circumstances of the death of her daughter; it is at this moment only, that she learned that you haven't perished with your parents.

His aunt told him, how she had almost fainted when she saw Isabella descend from the Bentley. Your bride is exceptionally beautiful, but your mother was beautiful. She had the same golden blond hair, the same port of head princely majestic, the same size of wasp, even graceful and elegant silhouette, the same angelic smile that enchants and seduces. I understand why you love her so mush; she reminds you Monique.

The driver pulled him out of his nostalgic reverie. Dr. Sommers, he says, I must stop to fill up the car. It is okay! answered Dr. Sommers.

Isabella awoke when the car stopped at the gasoline station. Where are we darling? She asked, straightening her legs. At the Rest area 20, answered Carl, we will be home soon. On the other hand, my love are you hungry? Amélie is cooking us something, said Isabella, I wouldn't ruin my appetite for anything in the world.

The façade of the Petit Palais was illuminated like a cathedral chandelier all the family members were gathered to wait for the travellers and share the welcome meal, prepared with care of the devoted Amélie.

Laura who watched at the window, opened the front door as soon as the Cadillac stopped in front of the porch. Here they are cried Laura who rushed outside to help Miss Isabella.

Dr. Sommers handed an envelope containing two hundred fifty dollars to each of the drivers, as tip and thanked them for their services.

We are at your disposal doctor; let us know, regardless the hour, day or night. They both got in the rental car and went away happily.

Carl and Isabella entered the vestibule, it was then, embraces, hugs to no end. Simon was the first to congratulate Dr. Sommers: "happy who like Odysseus did an excellent journey" he said, tapping him on the shoulder as a sign of affection.

Elsa hugged her future son-in-law on her heart, muttering to the hose of the ear: I'm proud of you, thanks for everything, Carl darling.

Mona Lisa, Michelle, Joyce, Joan and Cathy Morgan, everyone surrounding Dr. Sommers and asked him a lot of questions.

Doctor Ashley Martin and Christina Henry who stayed at the Petit Palais, returning from work at the hospital joined the crowd. Amélie invited the guests to pass at the table.

Isabella was in verve, she was in charge of the conversation. She described with force details, the castle of Val d'Armor and the beautiful park surrounding it.

She narrated the portrait's episode of Archibald of Albret Grailly, who looked surprisingly like Carl Roger, as his cousin princess Mireille de Foix called him.

She spared them nothing; not even Mister Auguste Lavignac's meeting with Isabella. She brushes a description of each of the characters gathered for the opening of the Viscountess Simone de Foix will, Carl grandmother.

The meal finished, Isabella proceeded to the distribution of gifts. Mona Lisa received her emeralds adornment, Joyce received a antique broach, a ruby cut as a rose, with a golden stem and two emeralds as leaves.

Dr. Ashley Martin received the box containing the adornment of pearls and Dr. Christina Henry, the money box and bracelet of rubies. Harry thanked her sister for the colognes; Simon, connoisseur, admired the gold watch, an ancient piece of rare beauty. Aunts Joan and Cathy, whom Isabella had forgotten received the gift she bought for Elsa: a collection of Paris Match, since the first issue released in 1946 and a valid subscription for five years.

These ladies wept with joy and gratitude. I see that you have thought about us beloved Isabella. Nothing could make us as much fun as this wonderful gift.

Michelle got the bite of the King: a river of diamonds of exceptional beauty, dated from 1743, a jewel like no other's.

I will come to your wedding, she told her cousin, you have not forgotten me. Can I ask you an intrusive question my dear cousin?

In the mess where I am, I have nothing to hide to you my dear Michelle.

Michelle remembering the answer she had given to her cousin in the hospital; burst out laughing. Touchée! replied Michelle.

All these gems have cost you a fortune my cousin? Did you splurge?

I haven't bought any jewelry in France. All of this comes from the family collection jewels, a part of the legacy to the Viscount de Foix.

Isabella spoke these words with a certain pride and a bit of contentment.

Tell me frankly Isabella; you knew these things before embarking yourself on this adventure that everyone considered a folly?

I was not aware of anything, to assume that the man who had fascinated me on the beach, the man chosen by my heart at first sight, was this prince charming, heir to a large breed and rich as Croesus. It is a gift of the Providence.

You can tell, my dear, it is rather, a fairy tale, a wonderful fairy tale.

The party guests gone, Isabella brings together the staff in the small dining room for the distribution of the gifts. The driver, Teddy Jules dealing with maintenance and Barry the gardener were first served. Pants, shirts, ties, shoes, colognes, not forgetting the hat of Jules, the only demand he had made to mademoiselle.

It is even more generous than the Christmas distribution of last year, said Barry taking away its gifts.

Elsa leaving these gentlemen: Simon, Harry and Carl, great conversation, joined her daughter, sitting on the floor with the maids, who unwrapped their gifts.

Amélie received, her bottle of Anaïs, her lace lingerie, two nightshirts and two matching bathrobes, a gold chain with a medal bearing the effigy of our Lady of Lourdes.

Laura, preferred Charade by Guerlain, a very sophisticated fragrance; Isabella brought for her, in addition, underwear from Coco Chanel, a blue suit by Cardin and a cultured pearls necklace, purchased at La boutique Le Printemps.

Brenda the housekeeper and Cloe the cook, were also satisfied and thanked Miss Isabella generosity.

Elsa had made available a room at the Petit Palais for Dr. Sommers, but he refused the hospitality of his future mother-in-law, thanking her, all the same, for this thoughtful offer.

Isabella, got upset, she did not succeed this time. Don't waste your time said Carl to his fiancée, don't spoiled this wonderful getaway by this useless quarrel.

Carl darling, you can no longer continue to live in this den. The Vaudreuil's villa is no longer suitable for you.

You're greatly wrong sweetheart; I don't see any problem at all. A few more days to spend at the villa. Incidentally, I'll be here most of the time. Don't you actually agreed?

At two o'clock in the morning, mortified and despaired, she let him go. Don't go to the villa insisted Isabella, until the last moment. I wouldn't like you to sleep there.

During his way to the villa, Dr. Sommers moved by the tears of his fiancée, changed his itinerary and went to the hospital. Premonitory intuition of a woman in love, he thought, often results in disastrous omen. Many people were killed for not having the wisdom to take account of their lover's intuition.

Dr. Sommers took refuge; therefore, in his office via the service lift, he didn't want to be seen. He fell asleep, once lying on the poorly padded sofa that served him as a bed.

The next morning Dr. Morton took leave of his friend who gave him a suitcase prepared by Isabella, this suitcase contained piles of clothes: suits, shirts, ties, shoes, gold cufflinks.

Ashley Martin and Christina Henry thanked him once more Dr. Sommers and Dr. Merville for their gracious hospitality by promising to return if the opportunity is renewed.

Dr. Merville has wonderfully recovered. Bernice had followed to the letter the recommendations of Dr. Sommers and imposed a drastic plan to her husband who, sometimes reluctant, but resigned himself to swallow the pill to please his wife.

During the absence of Dr. Sommers, Dr. Merville had interviewed and hired two physicians that the sudden fame of the city had attracted in this lost village.

Dr. Merville sensed that his invaluable collaborator (viewed rumors already circulating in Montjolly) would not linger too long in his current job.

The news propagated in tow,, that Dr. Sommers had inherited a colossal fortune; that he could now afford the luxury of marrying the most beautiful and richest heiress in the city.

Dr. Merville presented to Dr. Sommers the recruits: the surgeon and cardiologist Georges Weston and Robert Smith, general practitioner. Sommers gave them a tour to the hospital and assigned them their field of duties.

The Petit Palais was buzzing. Mona Lisa who had expressed the desire to dwell in the residence of her dreams; the current occupants of the house were forced to carry out a painful commotion.

The servants of the house: Teddy, Jules and Barry, were relocating the bridal bedchamber Elsa had occupied since her marriage, in favor of the furniture that Harry had ordered for his future wife.

Simon Morgan was not quite agreeing with this untimely change. But his wife made him understand that now; she is not incline to remain year-round in Montjolly. He had to think to live, to travel; which she was deprived to conform to this outdated ideology the black curse had swept effortlessly on its passage.

Isabella on her side, with the help of Laura, packed her belongings: clothes, jewelry, photo albums, and irreplaceable souvenirs, for shipment to the Val d'Armor.

It was agreed that Elsa would accompany her daughter in Saint Brieux, so she can ensure preparations of her marriage. Amelie and Laura travel with their employers to help them in their task. They were, absolutely excited by the unexpected project, which would allow them not only to see the country, but also to attend Ms. Isabella wedding.

Guests of the Hollemberg arrived already. The Villarossa hosted people coming from South Africa and Australia, Joyce parents and Max relatives. The Petit Palais hosted also a few guests; the house was boiling. The maids and servants worked hard so that everything should be ready to welcome the guests of the Hollemberg family.

The priest Ted Vogel deployed an extraordinary pomp in the decoration of the Church. The nave was decked streamers and banners; the choir was decorated with flowers: roses, carnations and orchids.

The wedding procession from the Villarossa including an impressive number of white limousines, run slowly through the city saluted by the applause of the curious gathered at every street corner.

The groom had already travelled to the Church from the Petit Palais, accompanied by a caravan of luxury cars, which caused a sensation in the city.

Mona Lisa was beautiful in her wedding dress. She marched down the central aisle, on her father's arm, followed and preceded by a plethora of girls and groomsmen.

After the Gospel, the priest pronounced the traditional sermon on the incredible miracle of Cana, the first miracle of Christ; to emphasize the importance of the religious consecration and solemn union of two human beings who love each other and becoming one.

The priest then proceeded to the exchange of the rings. It was a moving ceremony.

Michelle Morgan led the parish choir. She sang the Ave Maria by Franz Schubert during communion and the Magnificat by Scarlatti at the end of the mass. The Wedding March by Mendelssohn accompanied the release of the couple, the applauded by the guests.

More than five hundred people took part in the reception held in the flowering Villarossa's illuminated gardens galore for the occasion.

Max Hollemberg offered to his guests a gargantuan feast. Champagne, wine, cognac sank galore until five in the morning.

The traditional ceremonial, the speech of the first witness, toasts of some parents, catching the wave sheaf of the bride (the sheaf of happiness). Which took place in the grand salon, was broadcast by CCTV on giant screens, so the people feasting in the garden to participate more intimately, in all the festivities of the evening.

Around midnight, the newlyweds went up in a helicopter that they had chartered to transport them to the Thompson Field Airport to Jackson, where they were to fly with Air Italia for Venice, first stop in their honeymoon journey.

Carl and Isabella danced all night. Contrary to his habit of sobriety, Dr. Sommers ate unreasonably, drank too much alcohol. The couple wildly enjoyrd themselves.

. Dr. Sommers drunkenness was apparent, as Joyce Hollemberg, (attentive to everything that happened in the party) gave her own driver the responsibility to drive them home.

Nothing more restrained the Viscount de Foix in Montjolly, after the wedding of Mona Lisa. Dr. Carl Sommers, said a parting farewell to all those who had testified him their friendship or affection; for the population affected by the terrible scourge of the black curse, with unparalleled dedication.

The Dr. Merville, (fully restored) assisted by his new colleagues, took in charge the administration of the hospital Sainte Cécile.

Carl, Isabella, Elsa, Amélie and Laura landed at Orly airport (a week after the wedding) where awaited them: Albert his guardian and Norbert the driver.

They loaded the large suitcases on the roof of the Peugeot, stuffed to capacity with luggage: suitcases, handbags, various packages of all kinds. They sat Laura in the Peugeot next to Albert; the other passengers traveled in the Citroen, Amélie in the front seat, Isabella between her mother and her fiancé in the back.

Elsa was very impressed by the breathtaking beauty of the castle of Val d'Armor, fallen tree leaves, yellow and crimson, the dazzling and traditional adornment of nature during the fall season.

Aunt Joëlle and uncle Hugues welcomed the travellers under the porch. Carl Roger presented his stepmother to his parents. Come! told them aunt Joëlle, Andrea had prepared a small snack for us. I think you should be hungry.

At table, Joëlle made Elsa aware of the initiatives already taken to begin, the preparations for the wedding.

She had printed different copies of invitations cards which she submitted to the appreciation of Elsa and the choice of Isabella.

She had drawn up a provisional list of guests. She had limited the number to give to the parents of the bride most possible latitude.

How many people are you going to invite? Asked aunt Joëlle Isabella and her mother.

I have twenty-two guests who will come from the US, Professor Salih Chaussonnet, the notary Auguste Lavignac and Master Thibault, director of the Ker Moor Hotel.

When Isabella made her choice, she presented the card to her fiancé who approved with enthusiasm, relying on the excellent taste of his beloved fiancée.

Meanwhile, Hugues Simonet initiating the Viscount on the customs and traditions of the Viscounty and his responsibilities towards his subjects.

Besides, he said, you must visit the twelve lifetime concession farms, six forest concessions, the real estate agency, to introduce the future Viscountess of Foix. You must also grant them a sum of money equivalent to a reduction of six months of lease. And above all, inviting the staff at the wedding.

We should double our effort to get through all this in time. The farms are far from each other and we party after the symbolic visit of each property.

In connection, continued uncle Hugues, old Moussignac can no longer take care of his farm and his daughters don't want to inherit his lease. You'll need to replace him before the winter. There are four suitors interested in the succession. I will give you their folder so you can choose one of them.

Tomorrow, definitely, I will give you account for my management, and submit to you in detail, the financial state of the Viscounty.

My uncle, why this ritual? You do not consider me as your nephew? No ceremony between us.

You're right Carl Roger, I formalize myself too often, Mireille blame me for that, who, in my opinion, is too familiar. Anyway, I did that outline the subtle code of conduct inherent in this function, but, you have to initiate yourself to the archaic mysteries of the craft of Viscount de Foix.

The ladies had a lot to do. Elsa sent the cards to her husband who would distribute them. There were, in addition, require an immediate response, so that we can make reservations and buy tickets.

Isabella was in a quandary. She had to choose between the wedding dress from her mother, her grandmother and the Viscountess Simone. Her choice stopped (after many fittings) on the spectacular dress of the Viscountess whose trolling was twenty meters long.

Build the reception menu, constituted a real challenge; having regard to different tastes of guests expected and the desire of pleasing equally everyone.

They had fixed and furnished the basement garage, due to the weather, it was impossible to have the reception in the Park as planned.

Elsa and Joelle agreed perfectly. They coordinated their efforts and talents to the realization of a wedding worthy of the illustrious scion of a so high lineage.

Mireille came back from Rennes where she was studying medicine. She wanted to lead Isabella in the city to help her make her shopping. But she argued the fatigue of travelling to avoid the excessive petulance of her beloved cousin (at least, temporarily).

The days passed quickly. Every morning, very early, Hugues Simonet, (that the Viscount had confirmed in the position of Comptroller general of the Viscounty) sometimes accompanied by his wife, embarked Carl, Isabella and Elsa in an endless adventure among the farmers.

Everywhere it was Isabella they receive with this same enthusiastic devotion. She is beautiful the Viscountess! Constantly repeated the peasants dazzled by her beauty, charm, simplicity, the natural kindness of their suzerain.

People ignored the Viscount, their attention was focused on Isabella, who impressed them and had won, by her presence alone, the heart of her subjects.

The Mayor, Bruno Métoncourt and his wife Hélène, gave a reception in honor of the viscount, to present to the authorities and influential personalities of the city, the new residents of Val d'Armor.

The Viscount Carl Roger, his fiancée and Elsa Morgan went to Paris, on Thursday morning, to receive the coming U.S. delegation attending Isabella's wedding.

Simon Morgan had met the other guests in New York for the crossing of the Atlantic aboard Air France. The delegation included: the Morgan sisters, Joan and Cathy, Michelle and her fiancé Charles Lewis, Dr. Merville, his wife and his children, Max Hollemberg and his wife, j. Crampfort, Dr. Ricardo Ponce, Professor Peter Grant, the sheriff Al Linden and his wife Lucy, Admiral John Dexter and daughters Paula and Amy, Nancy Morice, director of the high school, Lisa Troy, Isabella's friend, Matt Potter, two musicians from the Roms: Manolo and Renalto.

The Viscount chartered a caravel to transport his guests to the Tremuson airport, located seven kilometers from Saint Brieux.

Customs formalities completed, the Viscount brought the troupe to the Caravel of Air Inter which was waiting on the runway, ready to takeoff.

The caravel landed at Tremuson Armor airport, after an hour of an uneventful flight. The passengers embarked, soon arrived, in two rental minibus which led them to the castle of the Val d'Armor.

The travellers have been gathered in the grand living room for an aperitif before moving to the dining room.

Harry and Mona Lisa made their appearance a few moments later. They returned directly from Greece. Norbert picked them up at the Rennes airport, located an hour and a half of Saint Brieux.

Meanwhile, Amélie equipped with a list and aided by Albert and Gregory, was struggling to classify the luggage of the guests in their respective room.

The Hollemberg, Harry and his wife found themselves in the master suite. Dr. Merville and his family occupied another one. Admiral Dexter, his daughters and Nancy Morice, were assigned the third. Everyone was lodged to the hostess satisfaction.

Isabella sent two cars get the guests who were staying at the Ker Moor: the Carcassonne, the Cassale, Professor Chaussonnet and his wife Anna, and many others.

As soon as the Simonet had arrived the party begun. The festivities lasted late into the night. Michelle Morgan sang some lieders of Franz Schubert accompanied at the piano by Mona Lisa fulfilled and sensual.

The Trouvères of Armor hosted the ball until four o'clock in the morning. People ate, drank, and served by an army of attentive and dedicated servants. The young people played madly. Isabella, whose penetrating insight, never missed a thing; perceived already the drafting of a romance between

Rachel Merville, vivacious, flirtatious, full of enthusiasm and Hubert Simonet who danced with her throughout the evening.

The castle of Val d'Armor was reborn to life. It got rid of the veil of sadness and melancholy that cast a shadow period of mourning, since the death of Monique Thérèse. The silent corridors, once again, awakened with the echoes of loud conversations and laughter of tipsy and happy guests.

The parents of Gaston Viscount and Viscountess Simone were ostracized by the Viscount who had banned from his castle, all fun and all joy.

Around midnight, Joelle, Elsa warned their respective spouse, that they are taking Isabella to rest at the Manor. Mireille joined the party, as Amélie whose presence was requested by Isabella herself.

During the trip to the Manor, Joëlle instructed Isabella about some customs and ceremonial tinged with superstition, observed in the matrimonial rite of the Brittany region.

The bride had to cut all contact with her future husband, at least, twenty four hours before the ceremony. She had to withdraw, without eating or drinking, all day, from six o'clock in the morning to six o'clock in the evening; to meditate and pray. She had to attend church after him, and so many other absurd taboos which bring luck or the Jinx to a newly wed; according to local legend.

Isabella spent the day, Friday, in complete isolation. In the silence of the closed room, she surrendered herself in a deep introspection. She analyzed her feelings, her thoughts, her incomprehensible love, designed within a blink, love that had brought her the joy of living by making her experiencing the madness of love with all her heart, in her soul, in her whole being.

Mireille pouted and mumbled all day against these old outdated customs which deprived her of the presence of her beloved cousin. She was the first to visit Isabella, when she completed her retreat. She brought Isabella a bowl of consommé, prepared with care by Amélie.

How are you Isabella? I bring you something to appease your hunger.

I feel rested. I am very well. But I'm really not hungry. Replied Isabella.

No question, countered Mireille, you must regain strength, you're going to need it. Tomorrow will be very tiresome for you in particular.

I know replied Isabella, everyone trumpeted that to me, you are the last to date.

Touchée! Did you sleep at least?

No honey, I thought about this extraordinary adventure I'm living since a year.

Tell me about it my cousin.

Not now darling. Later, I'll tell you everything, thread to needle.

Someone knocked on the door of the room.

Enter! Cried Mireille a little upset at this inopportune visitor.

Elsa came to see her daughter to make her final recommendations.

You have not tasted your food? This is unreasonable on your part. Then turning to Mireille she tells her with gentleness and authority: do you mind leaving us dear Mireille? I have chatting to do with Isabella.

Mireille retreated, but as a Parthian, by sending a snide arrow shot at the intruder.

It's the time of the confession, what it seems?

This girl is very sticky, said Elsa, when Mireille had left the room.

She has adopted me from the moment she saw me. She is a very nice girl, a little nosy however.

Are you ready for the big day? Asked Elsa with a kind of concern in her voice.

Of course, I am ready mother! Replied Isabella.

We already have vaguely addressed the topic; the first time is sometimes a bit painful and well girls do not experience any pleasure. Arm you with patience, moreover, Carl is a doctor, he knows surely and will teach you...

Hearing those words, Isabella burst out laughing. She was shaking so convulsively, she overthrew the rest of the consommé in the tray on her lap.

Stop Isabella! What does this mean? Asked Elsa a little taken back by the uncontrollable hilarity of her daughter. Did I say a no brainer?

Mother, began Isabella, seriously, do you remember the day when I wanted to confide a secret? The day when you had this long conversation in the garden with Carl?

I remember. I answered you better keep your secrets; so what?

This evening, sitting on the square with Carl, he asked me to be patient, saying that things had changed in our favor in a providential way. He added, to persuade me of the need to wait; we had already gone through the most difficult steps and that soon we will be together for time and eternity.

That's your big secret? Asked Elsa.

Isabella didn't even notice the scathing persiflage of her question and continued:

I have told him, then, that the wait for a girl was really frightening, traumatic and much more problematic than for a young man.

And why? had he asked me.

You asked me to be patient, I replied, because you already, probably, have experimented?

Speak for yourself, he replied. You are the first and the only girl that I embraced in my life.

Do I understand correctly what you just say Carl?

I've never slept with a woman. You know Isabella, calling my name with deep emotion in his voice: you are and you'll always be the only love of my life, the only woman in my life, the only woman I will always worship.

Then, I jumped on his neck, sat on his knees telling him: I love you. I love you, I love you... I was ecstatic. These words had upset me. Me who was counting on you to teach me the secrets of lovemaking, I told him in a whisper full of gratitude? We will learn together, my dear, he replied.

Mireille was right when she said it's the confession time! I've fallen from the clouds, continued Elsa. It is indeed, a strange revelation, an unusual confession for a doctor, evidence of exceptional trust from your fiancé. There is nothing that seals the intimacy and reinforces the mutual affection of a couple; nothing that would consolidate their union, continued Elsa, than the mutual offering, the pledge of love and loyalty: his innocence and your virginity. I envy you my daughter, you are born with luck. I give you my blessing and wish you happiness through your whole life. Heaven has filled your existence with priceless gifts, Isabella honey, be grateful for that, make people happy around you.

Elsa took her daughter in her arms; they remained silent, entwined, their heart throbbing with emotion and tenderness.

Rest! Said Elsa pulling away from the embrace; everything is ready, your wedding will be grandiose! I promised.

The castle of Val d'Armor was bubbling. It was only in the early morning that the hosts, already tired by the journey to Saint Brieux, withdraw in their room. Those dwelling at the Ker Moor Hotel left last, despite themselves. Because the ladies could no longer stand on their feet; they were fallen asleep; the men reluctantly went along.

Laura, Clemence and Emma (the guardian Albert's wife), guided the women to their respective rooms, giving them everything they needed to settle comfortably. Albert, Norbert and Gregory were busy doing the same for these gentlemen.

The Viscount had taken refuge on a couch he found in the laboratory of the tower. He had transferred his room to uncle Hugues completely drunk and Hubert who didn't want to lose a dance with his philandering; had decided to stay at the castle where the beautiful Rachel Merville was staying.

The castle woke up very late Friday, the eve of the wedding. They served breakfast in the suites and in some rooms, those whose occupants were sleeping.

Joan and Cathy, Michelle, Lisa Troy, Charles Lewis and Matt Potter, went down a little earlier, and ate by the pool.

A little later, when everyone was on foot, the Viscount brought

The troupe to the stables to admire the thoroughbred horses trained for the parade, mares of Ardennaise race, to the superb chest, the powerful native black stallions of Brittany, and a few horses, from the bastards Pyrenean Ariège race.

About three o'clock everybody embarked on the rental minibus for a city tour. Hubert volunteered as guide.

The beautiful Rachel Merville was in attendance.

They took lunch in the garden of the Manoire des Quatre Saisons; a very upscale restaurant, frequented by the gourmets, lovers of the good Breton cuisine.

Hubert deployed all its verve and his talent as a consumed comedian, to impress his flirt. After much fervent prayer, Rachel consented to walk with her flirt, as groom and maid of honor at Isabella's wedding.

Hugues Simonet retreated in the octagonal tower with the Viscount Carl Roger desktop, to develop the latest details of the ceremony.

The Viscount approved all the suggestions and recommendations of his uncle. In addition, he appreciated the special care that he took to the details to make his marriage a classic event. The elaborate and traditional, ceremonial imposed to him by his uncle, included a few extravagances that seemed unnecessary; but, the Viscount didn't objected, knowing already, that he couldn't change nothing to the rigid tradition.

His uncle then took him in a small refrigerated room at low temperature where has been stored luxurious clothing. Priceless clothes, fine lingerie, otter coats, ermine, mink, you name it.

Hugues Simonet opened a cabinet and said to his nephew:

You can choose the uniform you're going to wear tomorrow.

I won't wear those ridiculous getups, for anything in the world. I have never endorsed a uniform in my life; this is not tomorrow that I will begin.

Listen to me Carl Roger, told his uncle; by inheriting the title of Viscount of Foix, you inhérited, ipso facto, the rank of colonel in the French army. You are entitled to that rank conferred at perpetuity by the Emperor Napoleon Bonaparte to Viscount Albert Roger and his heir, for his heroic charge against superior numbers of Cossacks. This memorable action defeated, Mikhail Kutuzov (the Russian general leader of the coalition) at the battle of Austerlitz on December 2nd 1805.

That's very nice! But, its ancient history, my uncle, replied the Viscount. I will not do, believe me my uncle, no hitch in the legendary bravery of this ancestor, if I don't wear this uniform tomorrow.

Hugues Simonet sensing a stubborn resistance on the part of the Viscount, bowed to the firm resolve of his nephew and offered him an outfit less flashy: a frock coat of pageantry.

The American delegation, (as Hubert called the guests from America), dined very early on their return from the trip. Dr. Sommers, saddened by the absence of his fiancée, touched his food with his fingertips. His spirits, his soul, were elsewhere.

The castle of Val d'Armor wake up very early this Saturday morning. The house rustled like a smoky beehive. The ladies were rushing, because they had to go to the Manor to accompany the bride to church.

It was very cold. It was the shortest day of the year: December 21st, the winter solstice, a day that brings happiness. When these ladies were ready, the minibus drove them at the Manor.

Twenty four horsemen of the company of the Hussars of the Viscount (parade uniformed, red and white) had already led the carriage drawn by a team of six beautiful alezans Thoroughbred; in the courtyard of the Manor Du Vallon.

The ceremony began at eleven o'clock. Then at ten o'clock, the Viscount in redingote took place aboard an antique Rolls Royce. His uncle, Hugues Simonet, his first witness, accompanied him.

The Viscount in ceremonial costume wore around his neck a gold necklace and the great cross of the order of Saint Louis. He had, pinned on his chest the insignia of the coat of arms of the house of Albret.

The escort consisted of more than twenty five cars. They drove slowly in the direction of the medieval cathedral of Saint Brieux.

A platoon of soldiers lined up in front of the church saluted military and granting honors to the Viscount descending from his car.

The soldiers began to salute and hailed by a rumbling of drums.

Accompanied by his uncle, witness of the marriage, he went to sit in the choir of the Basilica, on the chair which was booked. The rest of the procession remained at the church vestibule to await the arrival of the bride.

A large crowd posted on the course that would borrow the carriage, to see and applaud the young Viscountess, adorned with an extraordinary beauty, whose fame was spread throughout the region.

Twelve riders in gala uniform preceded, twelve others followed the gleaming carriage that sported the colors, red and white, of the Viscounty. On the glass doors were painted in gold, the arms of the Viscounty of Albret, officially adopted by the House of Foix, from the year of 1509.

Isabella, molded into her taffeta silk and lace dress, smiled shyly and saluted waving her hands gloved of white.

With the approach of the parade, SaintBrieuc Cathedral people heard the melodic chime of its sound bells.

Isabella got out of the carriage with the help of her godmother, Cathy Morgan, who was also the witness to her marriage. The military platoon paid her honors playing the trumpet.

The bride entered the vestibule of the Basilica where the procession is organized nimbly. A Herald bearing the colors red and white, was placed at the head of the procession with a banner with the emblems of the House of Foix.

Ludmilla Gauthignac and JeanLuc Freiburg: holders of rings, walked in front of the bride. Isabella, on the arm of her father, her face covered with a veil, stepped slowly down the main aisle of the spacious nave of the old church; under the majestic accents of the bridal march of Wagner, (from his opera Lohengrin), punctuated by the enthusiastic applause of the amazed guests.

Twelve girls and groomsmen supported the long tail of Alençon lace, (point de Fée) made by the distinguished craftsmen of Burkina, for the wedding of the Viscountess Simone.

The two witnesses of the nuptial followed with imposing solemnity. Cathy Morgan, moved to tears, in the arms of Hugues Simonet; felt in her heart, proud to have been chosen by Isabella.

Cathy should rather thank Joëlle who had suggested to her niece that the Breton legend promised happiness and prosperity, to the bride who chose for her wedding an authentic bridesmaid.

Carl Roger and all the guests of honor seated in the choir, stood up to welcome the bride. She went to sit down in front of her fiancé, next to Hugues Simonet her witness. Cathy Morgan took place near the Viscount.

The Bishop Paul Delattre officiated. Michelle Morgan, sang the Latin liturgy of the mass accompanied by the choir of the Basilica.

Monseigneur de Guzman, in his homily, praised the remarkable qualities of heart and spirit of the new Viscountess who has been spontaneously adopted by the entire population of Saint Brieux for her beauty, her simplicity and her generous prodigality.

Before continuing with the Eucharistic prayer, the Bishop asked the couple to approach the altar, for the actual wedding ceremony.

Dr. Carl Roger Sommers, Viscount of Foix, do you want to take Miss Isabella Thérèse Morgan for your legitimate wife, promising to love her, cherish, during the good and the bad days, all the time of your life?

Yes, I promise, replied the Viscount firmly.

Isabella Thérèse Morgan, would you take for your lawful husband, Carl Roger Sommers, Viscount of Foix, promising to love him, to cherish him, whatever happens all the time in your life?

Yes, I promise.

The Bishop took off his shawl, and in a symbolic gesture, knotted both hands of the spouses together and spraying them with holy water.

Monseigneur de Guzman motioned with a nod to the assistant priest to bring the rings. But the box was empty. Mademoiselle Ludmilla Gauthignac (four years old) had found the way to lose the rings, during the journey from the vestibule to the choir of the Cathedral.

Elsa and Simon who closely followed the scene, took off their wedding rings. Elsa brought them to the crestfallen Bishop, who didn't know to what saint to devote himself.

Isabella! I give you this ring as a token of my love and my loyalty. Before God and his Church, I swear that you are and will always be the only love of my life.

Carl! Replied Isabella, I give you this ring to pledge my love, my loyalty and my affection to you. Before God and his Church, I swear that you are and will always be the only love of my life.

I declare you: husband and wife. Viscount you may kiss your wife, said the Bishop.

Carl lifted the veil that hid the face of his beloved and placed a tender kiss on her lips.

The servants brought then two massive gold crowns. The deacons purified the newly weeds with Frankenstein. The Bishop blesses them. Then addressing the Viscount, he said:

Descendant from an illustrious lineage, heir to a noble and revered family, Carl Roger, Viscount of Foix, be the protector of your subjects. Always act with honesty and fairness in all your dealings, conduct yourself always with honor and dignity.

Monseigneur Delatre placed the crown on the Viscount's head. Carl took, then, the other crown and put it gently on his wife's head, saying:

My darling accepts this crown, symbol of our responsibilities towards the subjects who have been entrusted to us by the Providence. But it adds nothing to your nobility of heart and spirit, the purity of your soul, to the strength and the sweetness of your incomparable character.

A round of applause greeted the spouses descending the steps of the altar returning to their seats. Isabella smiled shyly, dazzling with beauty and grace.

Spotlights of local television who retransmitted the ceremony lit the diamonds and emeralds of her crown. The cameraman flashes from time to time, her river of diamonds (her husband's wedding gift). Her face shone with intense joy; her large blue eyes sparkled as two candles under the crudity of light. Isabella inspired admiration, wearing an aureole of purity and virtue, draped in a mysterious aura of ineffable love.

During communion, Michelle accompanied by Mona Lisa at the piano and Manolo (violinist of the Roms), performed back-to-back the Ave Maria by Schubert, and Gounod.

At the end of the mass, before giving his final blessing, Monsignor Delatre signed the register of marriage, the spouses, the witnesses, the personalities: the Prefect and the Mayor, relatives and friends sitting in the choir.

The Wedding March by Mendelssohn accompanied the exit of Viscount and Viscountess of Foix, under a thunder of applause and a shower of rice which, according to legend brings luck to the newlywed couple.

The bells were unleashed. A large crowd had invaded the esplanade of the Basilica of Saint Brieux to pay tribute to the newlyweds. The carriage waited for the Viscount and the Viscountess at the front of porch of the Cathedral.

The Hussar riders, banners unfolded, took the lead of the procession. The carriage was slowly pulled by six beautiful thoroughbred horses from the castle's stables.

The crowd cheering acclaimed them: Vive Isabella! Long live the Viscountess! Long live the bride! Hooray for the Viscount! The crowd ranged throughout the route of the procession, from the Cathedral to the castle of Val d'Armor.

At the level of the Bistro of the Elm, where there was a popular dance (commissioned by the organizers of the wedding); overexcited fanatics wanted to see up close the Viscountess and touch her dress.

The Hussars surround the carriage and shoving a few individuals too enterprising, to allow the parade to continue its route. The Coachman accelerated the pace to avoid the repetition of such incident.

The general controller of the domain, in this case, Hugues Simonet; had distributed (to honor centuries old tradition) over 1,000 coupons to the inhabitants of the Viscounty. These coupons allowed them to drink, eat, to participate in the festivities organized in several restaurants of Saint Brieux and the surrounding area.

Approaching the castle, Isabella attracted the attention of her husband:

Carl darling, you hear?

What is it? My love.

You don't hear the bells? Insisted Isabella.

It doesn't surprise me the least.

Why? Asked his wife, a little intrigued.

Your father has had a long interview with the Sexton and the Bell ringer of the Cathedral, according to Hubert.

That's nice, you don't find?

Your father is proud of you; who wouldn't be with such a wonder?

Don't start Carl?

What I have said is the exact truth?

Today Carl darling, I don't want to hear your impart, your comparatives nor your superlatives.

Madam, it seems, is very ticklish today?

Ha! Suddenly shouted the Viscount. Who had just received an elbow shot on his ribs?

That will teach you to avoid making fun of me Carl Roger.

Isabella, always smiling, greeted the crowd agglutinated at the gate of the castle. The Coachman had to forge a passage in the middle of this crowd.

Joelle and Elsa who had left the parade to throw a last glance at the preparations before the arrival of the guests; welcomed the newlyweds with embraces and congratulations.

In the middle of a wide clearing in the Park, the organizers had drawn up three adjoining tents; they were decorated in red and white stripes as the flag of the Viscounty.

Around the tents and alternating distance, the flags and coat of arms of the Viscounty mixed a note of solemnity to this garden party atmosphere that reigned in the Park of the castle.

The chairs of the spouses have been placed on a dais covered with a Persian carpet. The married couple tent located between the other two; was fitted in a most luxurious manner. His disposal allowed everyone to see and participate in all phases of the traditional ritual of the wedding festivities.

A circular wooden floor, placed on the ground, in front of the dais, was used as a dance floor. The tables of the guests of honor were placed all around.

The Trouvères of Armor, entertained the guests during the endless parade of people who came to greet the newlyweds.

Meanwhile, an army of servers and waitresses doled out champagne for the guests. A few impatient guests shouted aloud to attract the attention of the servers by raising their still empty glasses.

Hugues Simonet (witness of the groom) made an academic speech; with sobriety he put emphasis on the dual role of the Viscount: his responsibilities to his family and his obligations toward his subjects.

Hugues Simonet sang the praises of the Viscountess Isabella who, the population of Saint Brieux had already adopted her for beauty and for her unquestionable generosity of heart and spirit.

People offered toast for the couple health and happiness. The Prefect of Côtes d'Armor, the Honorable Marcel Guycamp, toasted to the beauty of the Viscountess and the maintenance of the traditional relationship between the prefecture and the Viscounty administration.

The Mayor of Saint Brieux, Bruno Métoncourt, made similarly; and Simon Morgan: the bride's father, Dr. Merville, Max Hollemberg, Matt Potter and Professor Peter Grant.

It was already dark outside. Night falls early in the winter in these northern regions of France. The Viscount and the Viscountess excuses themselves for a moment and went to the castle, accompanied by the maids of honor. The Viscountess Isabella went in her room to get rid of her crown and the paraphernalia of her clothing of Viscountess bride.

Elsa ran up with a cup of nobody knew what and says:

Drink it my daughter! You haven't taken anything since this morning.

Without arguing, Isabella swallowed the cup on a stroke. She was literally starving. Carl stored the crowns and jewelry in the safe and went down to the small living room with his wife.

It was a haven of peace next to the tumult that reigned in the left wing of the castle. The stunning noise which amounted in growing every moment louder in the overheated, full to overflowing tents.

Isabella sat on the lap of her husband, threw both arms around his neck and posing her head on his shoulder, whispered in one breath:

I am so happy that I want to cry.

They remained entwined, silent, savoring this moment of intense joy, this ineffable happiness, this coveted moment that ushered in the reality of their love. This wonderful dream, more beautiful than a fairy tale.

Carl was drunk with joy and happiness, which slid along the cheeks of his wife as nectar of love. A subtle drunkenness invaded his failing heart and mind in a trance.

Hey! Hey! The lovebirds, cried Mireille opening the door of the sitting room, you could at least waited the departure of the guests before the mating season?

Let's Mireille! Said Isabella outraged.

People are looking everywhere, since a long time, declared the girl relentlessly, they are expected you to eat.

She announced to them that it was snowing in profusion and needed to cross all the left wing of the castle to avoid the rigors of the cold.

The untimely intrusion of Mireille in the first instant of their secret intimacy, had broken the bewitching charm of this ineffable sensuous moment.

During their absence, they have arranged a table on the dais, for them, their witnesses, the boys and girls of honor.

Carl begged Isabella to please eat something. You will not be able to hold up any longer my love, he said.

I can't swallow anything. My throat is tight and my stomach would not to take anything. I feel good, however, and full of energy.

The party went on until the early morning. Isabella sought everywhere, danced all night without interruption. The Viscount himself, demonstrated to these too eager French women, the measure of his talent as a dancer.

Hubert Simonet danced with his partner all night. Bernice, attentive to the sudden changes in her daughter mood, discovered with stupor that Rachel was fallen in love with this handsome French gentelman. She feared, with good reason, she could be lost for Monjolly and the hospital Sainte Cécile, of this future doctor which promised so much.

About five o'clock in the morning, exhausted, Isabella apologized to the guests and asked her husband to take her to their room. Supported by her husband, her legs wobbling, she made it to the the left wing of the castle, where their suite was located. They arrived at the monumental staircase leading to the second floor. Isabella looked her husband and told him that she couldn't make it. Carl took her in his arms, and carried her up into the modern room that once belonged to the Viscountess Simone. Isabella was asleep. He laid her gently on the bed, still dressed. He took off her shoes and covered her up to her shoulders. The Viscount undressed himself, put on his pajamas and slipped under the blanket next to his wife. Exhausted, he fell asleep almost immediately. Isabella, feeling the presence of her husband next to her, turned and laid her head on her husband's heart.